Bridges to Burn

A native of Dundee, Marion studied music with the Open University and worked for many years as a piano teacher and jobbing accompanist. A spell as a hotel lounge pianist provided rich fodder for her writing and she began experimenting with a variety of genres. Early success saw her winning first prize in the *Family Circle* Magazine short story for children national competition and she followed this up by writing short stories and articles for her local newspaper.

Life (and children) intervened and, for a few years, Marion's writing was put on hold. During this time, she worked as a college lecturer, plantswoman and candle-maker. But, as a keen reader of crime fiction, the lure of the genre was strong, and she began writing her debut crime novel. Now a full-time writer, Marion lives in North-east Fife, overlooking the River Tay. She can often be found working out plots for her novels while tussling with her jungle-like garden and walking her daughter's unruly but lovable dog.

Also by Marion Todd

Detective Clare Mackay

MARION TODD
Bridges to burn

CANELO CRIME

First published in the United Kingdom in 2024 by

Canelo
Unit 9, 5th Floor
Cargo Works, 1–2 Hatfields
London SE1 9PG
United Kingdom

A CIP catalogue record for this book is available from the British Library.

Print ISBN 978 1 80436 215 0
Ebook ISBN 978 1 80436 214 3

This book is a work of fiction. Names, characters, businesses, organizations, places and events are either the product of the author's imagination or are used fictitiously. Any resemblance to actual persons, living or dead, events or locales is entirely coincidental.

Cover design by Black Sheep

Cover images © Getty

Look for more great books at www.canelo.co

Printed and bound in Great Britain by Clays Ltd, Elcograf S.p.A.

2

MIX
Paper | Supporting responsible forestry
FSC® C018072
www.fsc.org

For my Canelo Crime buddies, Sheila Bugler, Jeanette Hewitt, Rachel Lynch and Sarah Ward. Thank you all for keeping me sane and for making me laugh out loud especially when the book just won't work!

Saturday night

Chapter 1

The bar was jumping when Clare drew into a space outside. A group of smokers stood leaning against the stone walls, chatting as they puffed. The door was propped open, and even from inside the car she could hear the hubbub. Detective Chief Inspector Alastair Gibson (or the DCI, as she still referred to him) leaned over and kissed her softly on the lips. She smelled his cologne, felt the warmth of his body as briefly it pressed against hers. Then she drew back and gave him a smile.

'Have fun,' she said. 'And for the love of God don't let them tie him to a lamppost.'

He grinned. 'Do my best.' He reached for the door handle. 'Don't wait up. I'll book a taxi.'

She watched him walk towards the bar, tall and lean, her eyes lingering as he moved. A couple of the smokers turned, following his progress until he was swallowed up by the bar crowd now spilling onto the pavement. Clare found she was smiling. She hoped he'd have a good time. Chris, her detective sergeant, about to marry her PC Sara, was still a bit wary of the DCI but hopefully he'd relax after a few drinks. A burst of laughter reached her ears and she threw the car into reverse, turning to back out of the space.

Benjy, her English Bull Terrier, was breathing hard behind the door as she put her key in the lock. She pushed the door open and he barrelled out, then raced back in, sniffing at the takeaway bag in her hand.

Sometimes – and this was one of those times – she forgot the DCI had sold his own house six weeks earlier and moved the entire contents into Daisy Cottage, the home they'd shared for the past couple of years. Clare had always thought his house was quite sparsely furnished. But that was before the furniture van had turned up with two burly men disgorging its contents, their faces scarlet by the end of the day.

She stopped for a moment, taking in the extra furniture, wondering what they would do with it all. Her eyes came to rest on the piano. *Ah yes.* The piano.

She carried her takeaway bag through to the kitchen and took a plate from the dishrack. Benjy sniffed hopefully as she spooned the curry out and she remembered he hadn't been fed. She put down the spoon and bent to retrieve a bag of dog food from a cupboard. He began to drool as she quickly filled his bowl, setting it down on the floor. He shot her a glance, looked back at the bowl, then up at her again.

'Good boy,' she said, nodding towards the bowl. 'On you go.'

He didn't need a second telling and fell on the food, gobbling it noisily.

Benjy dealt with, she loaded a tray and carried it through to the sitting room, wondering idly how the stag was going. She hoped Chris wouldn't drink too much. The last thing she wanted was to have her own DS arrested for being drunk and disorderly!

As she ate, her eye kept going to the piano. She hadn't even known he played, let alone had his own instrument. He'd put it in storage while his house had been rented out.

'Didn't want the tenants wrecking it,' he'd explained, sitting down on the stool, running his fingers over the keys. 'Can you play?'

Clare had shaken her head. 'Jude does. But she was always good at stuff like that. Probably because she practised.'

'And you didn't?'

'Nope. Wasn't interested.'

'I could teach you.'

'I doubt it.' She'd eyed the instrument. 'I suppose you want to keep it?'

But he hadn't heard her as he'd crashed his way through something that sounded to Clare as if the music book was upside down.

Yes. There was the piano.

It was just after eleven thirty when her phone buzzed and she wondered if he needed a lift home after all.

> Taxis ordered for 1.30.
> No need to wait up
>
> Love you
> A xxx
>
> PS your sergeant is now sporting a gold lamé minidress
> Photos to follow!

She smiled at the idea of Chris, her burly sergeant, in a minidress. No doubt there'd be some sore heads in the morning. She forced herself up and off the sofa. Whistling to Benjy, she opened the back door to let him out for a last pee. He scampered round the garden for a minute then trotted back inside, settling himself in his basket. She locked the door, switched off the lights and headed upstairs to bed.

It was past two when Benjy's barking heralded the sound of voices and a car door slamming outside. The front door opened and closed, the DCI whispering to the little dog. She waited for the creak of the stairs but instead heard the squeak as he opened the

3

sitting room door. Maybe he was fetching a glass of water. And then her heart sank as the sound of the piano being played by a very drunk DCI drifted up the stairs…

Monday

Chapter 2

'Good night, then?'

DS Chris West rubbed his eyes. 'Yeah. It really was. I'm still recovering.'

'And the gold minidress?' Clare raised an eyebrow.

'Dunno. Someone produced it. Said they'd buy me a pint if I put it on. Seemed like a sweet deal.'

Clare regarded him. 'I've seen worse, to be honest.' She hesitated. 'Thanks for inviting Al. You didn't have to but he really enjoyed it.'

'No probs. He's a cool guy – when he's not being a boss.'

She smiled. 'Yeah, he is.'

'Said he'd sold his house.'

'He has.'

'Moved all his stuff in.'

'Yep.'

'Must be a bit crowded. Daisy Cottage's not that big.'

They were in the station kitchen, waiting for the kettle to boil. Clare glanced over her shoulder and moved to close the door. Chris raised an eyebrow.

'Don't tell me he has a sex machine…'

'Worse.'

He waited.

'A piano.'

'What, a real piano? One of those big jobs?'

'Nah. Digital. Quite compact, really.'

'How quaint. Does he play?'

Her face fell. 'Jazz, Chris. He plays jazz.'

He considered this. 'D'ye mean big band stuff? Or the *when-does-the-tune-start* stuff?'

Clare sighed. 'The latter. If he'd even play something… well, something I'd recognise.'

'He'll have you nodding away in smoky clubs while the drummer goes off on a five-minute solo before you know where you are.'

'It's all right for you.'

'Tell you what, Inspector: I'll swap your DCI's jazz piano for Sara's mum's incessant to-do lists. And the table plan has to be done again because no one told us two of the guests at table six haven't spoken for years.'

The kitchen door opened and Sara looked in. Chris's face fell, no doubt wondering if he'd been overheard. She eyed him then turned back to Clare. 'Suspicious death over at Albany High. Looks like one of the pupils.'

–

A tall woman with short dark hair was standing just inside the main glass door, her hands clasped in front. Clare and Chris drove into one of the visitors' spaces and stepped out of the car. Seeing them, the woman pressed a button on the wall and the glass door swung open. She was simply dressed in dark trousers and a bolero jacket, a lanyard with an ID badge round her neck. Clare thought she might be in her early forties and, on any other day, the model of efficiency. But today her expression was one of anguish.

'Alison Greig,' she said, moving forward to greet them. 'Headteacher.'

Clare introduced herself and Chris. 'If you could show us…'

Alison nodded and stepped back to let them in. They passed into the cool interior of the school and followed the headteacher towards a set of double doors. 'We can cut through to the back of the school this way,' she explained. 'Less conspicuous.' She led them past the reception desk, nodding at a young man who'd been tapping at a keyboard. His fingers were still now as he watched their progress, his face grave.

He knows, Clare thought, and she wondered how many more of the staff and pupils had heard about the morning's events.

Two girls in short black skirts and white school shirts were having a whispered conversation beside a row of coat hooks when they spotted the headteacher. They gathered up their belongings and hurried off, clearly fearful of a rebuke, but Alison Greig hardly seemed to notice them. She took Clare and Chris down a flight of stairs, towards a set of fire doors at the bottom. The smell of chlorine reached Clare's nostrils and she was instantly transported back to her school swimming lessons and the humiliation of having to appear in a costume in front of the boys.

A gust of air rushed in as the headteacher opened a door to the school grounds. She indicated an athletics track.

'Just beyond there,' she said. 'In the trees.'

Clare looked around as they walked, taking in the facilities. To the left she could see a chain-link fence surrounding three tennis courts, while a long rectangle of grass to the side was marked out in what she guessed was a football pitch. Next to this was a tarmacked court, for netball or basketball, maybe. She wasn't sure. The facilities looked great but none of it excited Clare. She hadn't much enjoyed sports at school – except for running. Pretty much the only sport she could do. Had PE classes improved since her time? Didn't they do things like street dance and aerobics these days? That sounded so much better than touch-rugby in the bucketing rain.

'I've cancelled outdoor games,' the head said, stopping for a moment. 'It seemed...'

Clare nodded and they began walking again. As they moved further from the school building she glanced back, aware their progress was being watched from classroom windows. They were nearing a wooded area and Clare could see some figures through the trees.

'Two of your officers are with – well, they're waiting – where it happened,' the head said, appearing to struggle for the right words. 'And Alfie, our caretaker. He's the one who found her.'

Clare could see Gary and Gillian, two of the uniformed officers, standing at the edge of the trees talking to an older man in dark overalls. An aluminium stepladder stood against a tree and a few feet beyond this a cream honeycomb blanket was spread on the ground, the shape of a body beneath it. They were hidden now from the school building and she wondered how long the girl – whoever she was – had been there.

She approached the trio, holding out her ID badge for the caretaker. 'DI Clare Mackay and DS Chris West.' The caretaker gave a nod acknowledging this. He was in his fifties, Clare thought. Not tall, but stockily built with weather-beaten hands that spoke of a life spent outdoors. He held himself erect, his eyes meeting Clare's unflinchingly, and she had the sense he was making an effort to remain in control. 'I gather you were first on the scene,' she said.

He nodded again but said nothing.

'Can you tell us what you found please?'

His eyes rested on the blanket for a moment then he indicated a substantial tree, beyond. 'The oak,' he said. 'She was... she was hanging from there. It's my sash cord,' he added.

Clare raised an eyebrow.

'For the windows. There's an old building in the grounds. Predates the school. Has the older kind of windows. One of the cords had frayed so I'd bought a hank to fix it. I'd left it on a low wall outside my office. I was going to do this morning...'

Clare studied the tree. The branches were thick, certainly sturdy enough to bear the weight of a teenage girl – if that's what she was. High enough as well. 'How would she get up there?'

'Sophie was a keen climber,' Alison Greig said, her voice quavering.

'That was her name?' Clare asked. 'Sophie?'

Alison looked pained. 'Sophie Bakewell. She'd represented the school in competitions. Bouldering.'

'No ropes,' Chris said, his voice low, and Clare nodded. She smiled at the caretaker. 'I know this must be distressing but can you take me through everything that happened please? Let's start with why you were in this part of the grounds this morning.'

Alfie shot a glance at the headteacher but she waved her hand in dismissal.

'If you were out here having a fly cigarette, Alfie, I honestly couldn't care less. Please – just tell the officers what happened.'

He glanced at her again then turned back to Clare. 'Like Mrs Greig says, I was out here for a fly puff. Out of sight of the school, you know? Anyway, I caught a glimpse of something through the trees. Thought maybe some of the kids were skipping classes. So I went further in and… I saw her. Just hanging there.'

'Was there any movement?' Clare asked. 'Any swinging at all?'

Alfie shook his head. 'Dead still, she was.' He looked back at the oak tree. 'That long branch there.' He pointed. 'That's the one.'

Clare put up a hand to shield her eyes from the sun. What seemed to be part of a thin cord was wrapped round a sturdy tree limb. 'She was hanging from that branch?'

'Aye. If you look at the trunk you can see where she's dug her shoes into the bark – where it's fissured, yeah? I reckon she climbed up there, went along the branch, lashed the cord to it and tied the other end round her neck. Then she must have dropped…'

Clare followed where he indicated, a sick feeling developing in her stomach as she imagined this young girl's last moments. What on earth had been so bad it had driven her to this? Her gazed moved down to the honeycomb blanket then back at the branch. Sophie had chosen well. It was a sturdy one. No sign it had given at all. 'How did she come to be on the ground?'

Alfie reached into his pocket and took out a Stanley knife, the blade retracted. 'This,' he said. 'I ran back to my tool shed – fetched this and the ladder. Cut her down as fast as I could. I was pretty sure she was gone but I couldn't leave her up there.'

'Did you touch her at all?' Clare asked.

He shook his head. 'Thought I'd better not. But I did touch the cord. Didn't want her falling in a heap. So I grabbed it as I cut and took the weight. But I couldn't hold her. Cord slipped through my hands. Broke her fall, though,' he said, his hand rubbing at his face. 'It was so tight, you know? Round her neck. Really tight. I tried to cut it off in case there was a chance... but I didn't want to nick her neck so it took a minute or two.' He broke off and swallowed. They waited while he composed himself. 'I did nick her neck in the end. Just a bit. But there was no blood so I knew she was gone. I called reception from my mobile and got hold of Mrs Greig. She brought a blanket and we called you lads.' He waved a hand towards the blanket. 'The bits of cord are there. On her chest.' His shoulders sagged. 'If I hadn't left that cord lying around...'

Alison put a hand out and patted him gently on the shoulder. 'You're not to blame,' she said. 'Please don't think that.'

Chris felt in his pocket, retrieving a clear plastic bag. 'Need to take that,' he said, indicating the knife.

Alfie nodded and dropped it into the bag.

Clare turned to Gary, noting a used CPR faceguard in his hand. 'You tried reviving her?'

'Tried for five minutes, boss. But it was no good. She was away.'

She stood thinking for a moment. 'Did Sophie attend any classes this morning?'

Alison ran a hand through her hair. 'I've not had time to check. I can find out though...'

The sound of a mobile cut through the stillness. Alison reached into her pocket and put the phone to her ear. She spoke a few words then the colour drained from her face. 'It seems one of the girls in Sophie's class texted her mother, who phoned Sophie's parents. They're on their way here. I'm not sure what...'

Clare put a hand on her arm. 'We'll see them,' she said. 'But we do need to be as sure as we can it is Sophie.'

Alfie indicated a black Nike backpack at the foot of the tree. 'I did look in there,' he admitted. 'Couple of jotters with her name. Bus pass as well.'

Clare considered this. It seemed likely this poor girl was Sophie Bakewell; and it did look like a tragic suicide. But she didn't want to risk compromising SOCO's work. They certainly couldn't have a formal identification until the body had been moved to the mortuary. 'I'll speak to the parents when they arrive,' she said. 'Let them know we're investigating the death of a young girl.' She glanced at Chris. 'But no more details for now,' and he nodded.

'Gary, get onto SOCO,' Clare went on, 'and Gill, give the pathologist a call. Then ask Jim to send someone over to tape off this part of the grounds. I don't want anyone near the trees. Ask Sara to come over as well, please. We might need someone to go home with the parents.' She turned back to Alison. 'Is there a room we can use?'

Chapter 3

Brian and Laura Bakewell were perched on the edge of two plastic bucket chairs when Clare and Chris entered a small room. Judging by the narrow bed and green first aid box it doubled as the school medical room. The Bakewells were in their late thirties or early forties. Brian, his dark hair threaded with the odd silver strand, was casually dressed in black jeans and a pale grey sweatshirt. Laura was slim with corn-coloured hair scraped back in a ponytail. Clare's eye was drawn to her lilac tunic and she tried to make out the logo. Not one she recognised – *Riverton* or something.

A small round tray with two mugs of tea – or perhaps coffee – sat on a table between the chairs but it didn't look as if the drinks had been touched. The couple rose as the headteacher led Clare and Chris in, Laura taking hold of her husband's hand.

'Is it true?' she blurted out. 'Has something happened to Sophie?'

The headteacher closed the door softly and pulled three more chairs across the room. 'Perhaps we could all sit,' she said, indicating the chairs.

Laura ignored this, turning instead to Clare. 'Please,' she said again. 'Tell us…' Her face was twisted in despair, eyes full of fear. Her husband's face was a mask, the skin stretched tight over the skull, his jaw rigid with tension.

Clare felt her mouth dry as she prepared to deliver the worst news any parent could hear. She looked from one to the other, took a deep breath and began. 'I am Detective Inspector Clare Mackay and this is my colleague Detective Sergeant Chris West. We were called here about half an hour ago because the body of a young girl believed to be a pupil at this school was found in the grounds.'

A sob escaped Laura's mouth and her husband put his arm round her.

'Is it our Sophie?' he asked, his voice husky. 'Is it her?'

'We haven't made a formal identification,' Clare said. 'But there was a backpack found nearby and the contents indicate it belongs to Sophie.'

'I want to see her,' Laura said, her voice shrill. She rose from her seat and started towards the door, bumping the small table. The mugs wobbled, slopping hot liquid across the tray. The headteacher steadied it then she took a handful of paper towels from a shelf and placed them on the tray to soak up the spill.

Laura was shaking and Brian rose to stand beside his wife. 'I think we would like to see her,' he said.

Clare nodded. 'We'll arrange that as soon as possible. But I'm afraid it won't be for a few hours yet.' She indicated the mugs. 'Maybe a hot drink? I think Mrs Bakewell should have something.'

'I don't want a bloody drink,' Laura snapped. 'I want to see my daughter,' and she began to sob loudly. Brian took his wife in his arms and held her for a minute, one hand stroking her hair. Then he eased her back down on the chair and sat beside her, moving his own chair closer.

'I assure you,' Clare said when Laura's sobs began to subside, 'we'll let you see your daughter as soon as possible, assuming of course it is Sophie. In the meantime, if you feel up to it, maybe I could ask a few questions? Find out a bit about Sophie.'

They made no response to this and Clare pressed on. 'How was she this morning? Before she left for school?'

The couple looked at each other. 'I – er, same as usual,' Laura said. 'Bit quiet I suppose. But she's not a morning person.'

'Anything she might have been worried about?' Clare asked.

Brian's brow furrowed. 'Why are you asking that? Is there something – you mean it's not, like, a heart attack?' He glanced at his wife. 'Has someone *done* something to Sophie?' His voice rose as he spoke, his eyes searching Clare's face.

'Oh please, no,' Laura said, her voice quavering. 'Please don't say someone's hurt her.'

Clare felt Chris shift on his seat, his discomfort evident. It was the absolute worst part of the job but it had to be done. She took a deep breath. 'The girl found near to Sophie's backpack – the girl we think could be your daughter – we think she may deliberately have ended her life.'

There was silence for a few moments as they took this in, Laura's eyes flicking from Clare to Chris and back to the headteacher. Alison met Laura's gaze and she gave her a slight nod. And then Laura began to scream.

–

Sara and Gillian were despatched to go home with the Bakewells.

'I want you with them until a family liaison officer arrives,' Clare said. 'I've not spoken to them properly yet. They weren't in a fit state to help us. But I don't want them left alone. Once I'm done here I'll head over. Meantime, see if you can get their GP to call round. The mum looks like she's in shock.'

Clare watched the Bakewells leave with Sara and Gillian then she sought out the headteacher.

'It looks like Sophie was at registration this morning,' Alison Greig said, tapping her computer screen.

'What time was that?'

'Eight fifty to nine o'clock.'

'And after that?'

Alison shook her head. 'She should have been in French at nine then Chemistry at nine forty-five but she didn't appear in either class.'

'Any problems in these classes? Or any of the others?'

'Quite the reverse. Sophie was doing well. Staff were very happy with her progress. She was popular with her classmates too. No problems were brought to my attention.'

'Is that usual?' Clare asked. 'Or might staff have dealt with problems without informing you?'

'No. We have a weekly welfare meeting where staff can flag up anything that might develop into an issue. We try to be proactive, you see? Not always easy but we do our best.'

Clare considered this. 'What about registration this morning – anything happen? Anyone kick off?'

Alison reached across her desk and picked up a telephone, clicking a button. After a moment Clare heard a voice answering.

'Would you ask Sue Perry to pop into my office please?' Alison said into the phone. 'Quick as she can,' then she put the phone down. 'Better you speak to the registration teacher yourselves.'

A minute or two later there was a tap on the door and a young woman in her late twenties entered. She was slim, casually dressed in wide-legged linen trousers and a pale blue shirt. Clare thought she had a face that smiled easily, her mouth wide, eyes kind. But her expression today was serious, her frame full of tension.

Alison ushered her in and explained the officers were asking about registration that morning.

'I'm not sure what I can tell you,' she said. 'It's such a busy ten minutes, barely five if you allow for stragglers.'

'But Sophie was there?' Clare asked.

'Oh yes. She was sitting near the back I think. But she was definitely there.'

'Did she seem different at all?' Clare went on.

Sue Perry spread her hands in a gesture of apology. 'I'm sorry. I had a couple of girls with notes asking to leave for appointments, three off, two came in late. I hardly had a minute to notice anything.'

Clare tried again. 'Maybe she was talking to someone?'

Sue sighed. 'Honestly, I couldn't say. Sorry,' she added.

'What about friends,' Chris said. 'Was she friendly with anyone special?'

Sue thought for a moment. 'Well, there's Maria DiAngelo. She and Sophie seem pretty close. But she's away just now.'

The headteacher nodded. 'She's visiting family in Italy.' She tapped her keyboard and peered at the screen. 'Back next week, I think.'

'No one else?' Chris went on.

'Best ask the parents,' Alison said. 'They'll know her friends.'

Clare wasn't so sure about that. Some of the teenagers she'd come across would move heaven and earth to keep their friends away from their parents. But maybe Sophie was different. She glanced at Chris. Was there anything else to be learned here?

'We could speak to her registration class?' he suggested.

Alison made a few clicks with her mouse then turned back to Sue. 'They're at music.'

Sue nodded. 'Would you like me to take you to the music department? You could speak to them there.'

'Yes please,' Clare said. She rose from her seat. 'I'll keep in touch. Meantime, if you could ensure everyone stays away from where Sophie was found.'

'Of course. And… I'll have to speak to the school. Make some kind of announcement. Is there anything I should or shouldn't say?'

'Just let them know a pupil has died but the identity hasn't been confirmed. Maybe warn them not to gossip.'

A wry smile crossed the headteacher's face. 'I can try,' she said. 'It won't work, mind you. But I'll do my best.'

-

As they approached the music department Clare could hear the sound of a wind band playing something vaguely familiar.

'I recognise that,' she whispered to Chris, but he shrugged.

'Don't ask me.'

'I think it's Dave Brubeck,' Sue Perry said. 'It's a bit slow but I'm pretty sure that's what it is.' She smiled at Clare. 'Do you like jazz?'

Chris emitted a noise that might have been a snort and he hurriedly turned it into a cough. Sue Perry glanced at him then held open a door to another corridor. The wind band noise grew louder then suddenly it stopped and a teacher's voice could be heard, giving instructions.

'I'll nip in before they start again,' Sue said, stopping at a door marked *Band Room*. 'If you could wait here…'

They stood outside the room for a few minutes then Sue emerged and ushered them in. A group of pupils was sitting in a semi-circle, backs to Clare and Chris, necks craned looking round at them. They were holding a variety of instruments, some of which Clare recognised, others she vaguely recalled from a school visit to a professional orchestra – a long afternoon when at least two of her classmates had nodded off.

The music teacher was standing at the front next to a shiny black grand piano, a baton in his hand, and he waved them forward. Clare and Chris weaved their way between the metal music stands and took up position facing the class. She appraised them and saw one or two were dabbing their eyes. Clearly they'd heard about Sophie.

She decided there was no point in wasting time. 'Sorry to interrupt your practice,' she began. 'We'll keep you as short a time as possible.' Across the room a red-haired boy with a saxophone was looking down and she guessed he was checking his mobile phone – maybe even texting friends to let them know the police were in the school. She stopped speaking, her eyes on him until he became aware and looked up. His hand hurriedly disappeared into a pocket and Clare carried on.

'You may be aware the body of a pupil was found in the school grounds earlier today.' She watched them carefully for any reaction. 'While a formal identification has not yet taken place, we have reason to believe it may be that of your classmate, Sophie Bakewell.'

A girl in the front row began to cry quietly. Clare's eyes rested on her for a moment, wondering if she was a special friend to Sophie. 'Until we have a positive identification,' she went on, 'I would ask you to keep speculation to a minimum. Please do not post publicly on social media. That kind of thing can only hurt Sophie's family. What I would like you to do, however, is to tell us if Sophie had any problems recently – anyone she'd fallen out with, anything she was worried about – anything at all. It might seem a small thing but the more information we have the sooner we can work out what happened.' She scanned the room. 'Anyone?'

It was as if they had all suddenly developed a fixation with their instruments. Valves were pressed, mouthpieces adjusted, music fiddled with – their eyes were anywhere but on Clare.

'Were any of you friendly with Sophie?' she said, trying again.

A few heads nodded but no one seemed keen to speak. 'She was nice,' a small voice said, eventually.

Clare looked to see who had spoken and her eyes, along with those of everyone in the room, fell on a boy of about sixteen. His blond hair was closely cropped and he held what Clare thought was a clarinet between his hands. He glanced around him and his face flushed at the attention he had drawn. Then he shrugged. 'That's all, really. She was nice.'

They waited to hear if anyone else would add to this. When no one spoke Chris scanned the room again. 'Any boyfriends?' he asked. 'Or girlfriends? Anyone she was close to?'

In spite of the seriousness of the situation a few of the girls eyed Chris speculatively and he smiled back. 'Come on, guys. Surely someone has something to say?'

Sue Perry stepped forward. 'I'll be in the guidance base for the rest of the day, so I can pass anything on to the officers.' She turned back to Clare. 'I hope that's okay?'

The teacher had a point. If any of the pupils did know something they might not want to say so in front of the rest of the class. 'That's fine,' Clare said. 'I'll give Miss Perry my contact details in case any of you would like to speak to me – or Chris, here. He might look a bit rough but I promise he doesn't bite.'

A ripple of laughter spread through the room and Clare smiled round at them. 'Remember what I said about social media,' she said. 'Please think of Sophie's family and don't gossip about this.' She nodded her thanks to the teacher and threaded her way back through the music stands towards the door, Chris at her back. Reaching into her pocket she gave Sue Perry one of her cards, then they followed her along the maze of corridors to the front entrance.

Chapter 4

'SOCO's arrived,' Chris said, indicating a white tent visible through the trees.

They walked smartly towards the tent, cutting across the running track. Robbie, one of the uniformed officers, was standing at the edge of the cordon now marked by blue and white police tape. A white van, one of the SOCO vehicles, was parked to the side, the back doors open wide. A figure in a white protective oversuit was retrieving equipment from the van, moving between it and the tent which screened what they now believed was the body of Sophie Bakewell.

Clare nodded to Robbie, who was not long back from an extended period of sick leave. In spite of the tragic circumstances she was pleased to see him looking more like his old self. She stepped under the tape, holding it up for Chris to follow. Another white-suited figure stood just inside the tent directing a photographer who was moving round the body, capturing it from every angle. They waited until the photographer had finished and, as he moved away towards the tree to take more shots, the white-suited SOCO spotted Clare and Chris.

'We're not suited up,' Clare called from just inside the cordon. 'But I'm guessing it's not suspicious.'

The officer came closer and pulled down his mask. Clare recognised him as Raymond, the SOCO she'd worked most closely with. 'I doubt it,' he said. 'But we'll know more in a bit. Doc's been,' he added. 'Life definitely extinct.'

'One of the officers tried CPR,' she said, and Raymond acknowledged this. 'Did the doc say when the post-mortem might be?' she asked.

Raymond shook his head. 'Sorry. I was busy setting up this lot.'

'Fair enough.' Clare hesitated. 'I need to speak to the parents again. They were pretty distraught when they heard but I'm hoping to get some background from them. Is there anything I can tell them?'

'Too early to say. For what it's worth, it appears to be a straight suicide. But you'll need the PM to confirm that. I certainly can't see any sign she was forced up there.' He glanced over at the body. 'How did she get down?'

Chris indicated the bag the caretaker had dropped the knife into. 'Stanley knife. Caretaker cut her down.'

'We'll check that as well,' Raymond said. 'If you give it to Gerry,' and he nodded at the figure bent once more over the back of the van.

'There's a backpack,' Clare said. 'Can we check if there's a mobile in it? Or it might be in her pocket.'

'Will do. I presume you'll want it to go to your techy folk?'

'Please. Might be something that'll explain why she did it.'

'No problem. We'll prioritise that.' A shout from the photographer interrupted them. 'I'd better get back,' he said, and Clare nodded her thanks.

They stepped carefully under the tape and made their way back towards the school. A bell began ringing in the distance and a minute later they heard the sound of voices as pupils poured out, breaking off into groups, some heading purposefully for a burger van parked just outside the school drive. 'Lunchtime?' Chris said.

'Not for you, Sergeant. You and I are going to call on the Bakewells. See if they're calm enough to tell us anything.'

–

Brian and Laura Bakewell lived in a compact semi-detached house in Kinnessburn Road opposite the narrow Kinness Burn that gave the road its name. It was an attractive house, dating from the 1930s, with a steep gable roof and an overhang sheltering the front entrance. A wooden garage with a brown up-and-over door stood at the end of a narrow drive, a neat square of garden to the front of the house. A police car was parked outside and Clare drew up behind it, shutting off the engine.

'Ready?' she said, and Chris exhaled heavily.

'As I'll ever be.' He snapped off his seat belt. 'Come on, then.'

'Gently, mind,' she said, following him towards the house. 'Remember they've just lost their daughter.'

'We think.'

'Well, yeah.'

Sara opened the door to them. She gave Chris a furtive smile and moved back to let them in. 'Doc's been,' she said, closing the door softly. 'Gave Mrs B a mild sedative.'

'How's the husband?' Clare asked.

Sara frowned. 'Hard to say. He's not said much. But he seems calm enough.'

'Okay. We'd better see them.' She glanced towards a door off the hall. 'Gill in with them?'

Sara shook her head. 'I said I'd manage so she's gone back to the school.'

Clare nodded at this. 'Can you hang on please? I'll need you to stay until the FLO gets here. Who is it, by the way – Wendy?' she added, hopefully.

'Some bloke from Glenrothes. Paul someone. Apparently Wendy's on another job.'

Clare tried not to let her disappointment show. She'd worked with Wendy Briggs on many cases and always asked for her when an FLO was needed. But it couldn't be helped. The important thing was having one. 'Come on, then,' she said. 'Let's see what they can tell us.'

The couple looked up when Clare and Chris entered the room. Laura seemed to have shrunk into herself, a tiny figure enveloped by the chair she was curled up in. Her eyes were pink with crying, her cheeks blotchy. Brian sat opposite her, his face set in an expression Clare found hard to read, his eyes dark and empty. He rose stiffly, as though the very act of getting out of his chair was almost too much. She waved him down but he remained standing.

'Can't sit here any longer,' he said. 'I should be out there, doing something.'

'I do understand,' Clare said. 'But you're needed here.' She nodded towards Laura. He followed her gaze then he moved over to his wife, easing himself down on the arm of her chair. He stroked her hair and leaned in to kiss the top of her head. Then he glanced back at Clare, his eyes searching her face. 'So?'

Clare smiled at Sara. 'Maybe you could make us all some tea?'

Laura waved this away. 'I can't drink it.'

'Have you had anything since you came home?' Clare asked, and Laura shook her head.

'I think we'll have tea anyway. You might manage half a cup.'

Laura turned away and Clare motioned Sara towards the door. A moment later they heard the sound of a kettle coming to the boil.

While they waited Clare explained the SOCO team would go over the area where Sophie was found, checking for anything that might explain what had happened.

Laura's eyes were swimming, as she hung on Clare's every word. 'They won't leave her out there all night, will they?' she said, brushing away a tear. 'She'll be so cold.'

Clare felt an unexpected lump in her throat and she swallowed before answering. 'She'll be moved as soon as possible and I promise they'll be gentle.'

Brian put his arm round Laura and she leaned into him, sobbing audibly. The door opened and Sara came in bearing a tray of mugs. Chris rose and pulled a small table across for the tray. Clare guessed he was glad to have something practical to do.

'Perhaps we should drink these,' Clare went on. 'Then we can have a proper chat.' She softened her voice. 'I'd like to learn a bit more about Sophie.' She handed out the mugs and after a few moments Laura took one, her movements mechanical. They sat in silence sipping the tea, Clare taking in the room. Her eye fell on a photo of a smiling girl, a small trophy in both hands.

'That's a lovely photo,' she said, and the couple followed her gaze.

'Fife Schools Climbing Competition,' Brian said, his voice flat. 'She won first prize for bouldering.'

Clare smiled at this and Brian went on. 'She does speed climbing as well but she's better at bouldering.'

He spoke of his daughter as though she was still alive and Clare's heart went out to them. Reality would kick in soon enough.

'She was glued to the Olympics,' Laura went on. 'And her bedroom's covered in posters of that Shauna Coxsey.'

Clare raised an eyebrow.

'British climber,' Chris said. 'You remember – from the Olympics? It was the first time climbing had been included.'

Clare had a vague memory of this and she looked back at the photo.

'She was determined to be selected for the next Olympics,' Laura said, a watery smile crossing her face. 'Spent all her spare time practising. Out practically every night, wasn't she?'

Brian nodded, his face clouded. 'That's what she said, anyway.'

Clare saw her way in. 'Did you think she might be doing something else?'

His expression hardened. 'You tell me, Inspector. Until this morning I thought she was perfectly happy. So you tell me why she's lying there in the school grounds with your forensic people picking over every blade of grass.'

Clare sat forward in her seat and put down her mug. 'It's important we get a full picture of Sophie's life, particularly over the last few weeks. So,' she hesitated, making sure she had their attention, 'if there is anything that was different lately – no matter how small – you must tell us. We want to find out what happened to Sophie but we'll need your help.'

Gradually, the couple began to unbend and they talked about Sophie at school.

'Good grades,' Brian said. 'Sporty too.'

'Bit of an all-rounder?' Clare said, smiling.

Laura nodded. 'She was in the school hockey team but she gave it up to focus on climbing.'

'What about friends?' Chris asked. 'Anyone special?'

Brian and Laura exchanged glances. 'She gets on with everyone,' Laura said. 'Not that she brings many of them back here.'

'She's more friendly with Maria,' Brian said. 'Maria DiAngelo.' His brow creased. 'She's not been around lately, has she?'

Laura shook her head. 'She's in Italy. Something to do with her grandmother.'

'Do you have an address for Maria?' Clare asked. 'We can get it from the school, if not.'

Laura thought for a moment then she reeled off an address, adding, 'It's just a few streets away but I think they're all in Italy just now.'

They chatted on, Clare and Chris attempting to draw the Bakewells out. Sophie was their only child, seemed happy enough, didn't have a boyfriend.

'As far as we know,' Brian added. His expression darkened. 'If some lad's upset her...'

'We'll do all we can to find out what happened,' Clare said. Brian glanced at her but made no reply. Clare caught Chris's eye and rose from her seat. 'I wonder if we might have a look at Sophie's room now?'

Laura stood with some effort, putting a hand out to steady herself. Clare moved to help her but she waved this away. 'It's that damn stuff the doctor gave me. Just a bit dizzy for a moment.' She began walking to the door, her gait awkward as though her legs were heavy. She led them to a narrow flight of stairs and paused at the bottom.

Clare moved forward. 'I think you should stay down here,' she said. 'We'll find our way.'

Laura nodded, tiredly. 'Second door on the left,' and she turned, leaving them to climb the stairs.

'She wasn't joking about the posters,' Chris said, taking in the bedroom walls. A blonde woman dominated one wall, hanging from a variety of improbably small climbing holds, her face twisted in concentration. In other photos she was smiling widely, holding up medals. Clearly this was Shauna Coxsey, Sophie's climbing idol. But the most striking thing about the room was the décor and how starkly it contrasted with the rest of the house. While the rooms downstairs had been muted in soft greys and beige, Sophie's room was a riot of colour. Behind the posters they could see one wall had been painted a bright salmon pink, the others a vibrant turquoise. The same colours were picked out in a knitted bedspread with a scattering of cushions in mustard and lilac. A white-topped desk was neatly arranged with school textbooks at one side, an Anglepoise lamp at the other; and, in the centre next to a games console, sat a laptop, its cable trailing to a socket in the wall.

Chris pulled on a pair of gloves and bent to unplug this while Clare continued scanning the room. It was pretty typical for a teenager. The usual clothes, books, birthday cards, jewellery and computer games. A pinboard was covered in party invitations, nail bar flyers and photos of Sophie, one with a group of three girls but mostly just Sophie and a dark-haired girl. Maria DiAngelo, Clare guessed. She stood, looking at the photos for a moment. 'Odd that, at the school.'

'What about it?'

'That music class – none of them had anything to say about Sophie.' She indicated the photo. 'Even if this Maria's on holiday, you'd think one of the others might have said something.'

Chris shrugged. 'Not really. Kids that age don't much like the police.'

'Suppose.'

Chris was going through a chest of drawers now and she turned her attention to Sophie's wardrobe, trying to put her classmates' reticence to the back of her mind.

They worked on mostly in silence, exchanging the odd remark until a distant ring sounded downstairs. Clare moved to the window, drawing the curtain back. Another police car had pulled up close to her bumper and an officer stood at the front door.

'Looks like the FLO's here,' she said.

Chris stood, brushing carpet fluff off his knees. 'We done?'

She looked round the room then indicated the door. 'Come on. Let's see what he's like.'

He was standing in the hall speaking to Sara as Clare and Chris came down the stairs.

'They've not long had a cup,' Sara was saying, and something in her tone made Clare quicken her step.

'And you are?' she said as she reached the foot of the stairs.

He turned and Clare realised he'd a hand on Sara's arm. Had he been attempting to steer her into the kitchen to make tea? She hoped Chris hadn't seen this.

'Detective Sergeant Paul Henry,' he said, his tone smooth. 'I was saying to Sara here a cup of tea would be a good idea.'

Clare studied him. He certainly was good looking, his beard neatly trimmed, his smile warm. He was slim, tanned and he wore his blue/grey checked suit well, a pair of silver cufflinks poking out from the sleeves. Yes, he was attractive, and didn't he know it. She smiled at Sara, ignoring Paul Henry. 'Best get back to the station. Thanks for all you've done here.'

Sara threw her a grateful smile and headed for the door. Chris watched her go then he spun round to Paul, his face stony.

Paul glanced at him then turned to Clare. 'So, Clare,' he said, 'what's the situation?'

She studied him for a few moments before replying. She'd never been one to demand respect for her rank. *Call me Clare,* she'd say to even the newest recruit. She couldn't be doing with all that *Ma'am* malarkey. But usually they waited until they were invited to use her first name. There was something almost proprietorial about the way he'd said *Clare* – like the way he'd had a hand on Sara's elbow. She felt Chris stiffen beside her and she tapped his foot with hers. Maybe it was just youthful confidence. Best not get off to a bad start. The last thing the Bakewells needed was a squabble between officers. She explained quickly about Sophie, her voice low. 'We don't have a positive ID yet,' she said. 'I'm guessing that'll be tomorrow, by the time she's taken off to the mortuary.'

'Suspicious?'

Clare shook her head. 'SOCO are still there but so far there's nothing to indicate anyone else is involved.'

'So, my role…'

She looked at him. Why was he asking this? 'Is this your first FLO job?'

This seemed to wrong-foot him for a moment then he recovered. 'No, no. I meant was there anything specific you're looking for.'

Again, Clare decided to give him the benefit of the doubt. 'Just support them, keep them informed and if there's anything unusual let me know.' She indicated the door to the sitting room. 'Come on. I'll introduce you. Then we'll leave you to it.'

Ten minutes later Clare and Chris emerged onto Kinnessburn Road and headed for the car.

'I don't like him,' Chris said, trudging behind her.

'Nor do I. But we're stuck with him.'

'He's an arse.'

She stopped at the car and mentally measured the distance between her bumper and Paul Henry's.

'He's done that deliberately,' Chris said. 'Good job Sara moved away or you'd never have got out of this space.'

'Maybe you wouldn't have, Detective Sergeant. But some of us can drive properly.'

'You're a dreadful liar.'

'We'll never know, will we?' She threw him the car keys. 'Here you go, sonny. I'll let you drive for a treat.'

Chapter 5

It was almost five o'clock when Clare heard from Raymond.

'We're done at the school,' he said, the sound of wind buffeting his phone. 'The body's gone off to the mortuary. You'll have my report in a day or so but I can't see anything to suggest it's not a suicide. There's some damage to the tree bark that fits with someone climbing up. No indication of force being used.'

'What about the knot?'

'The cord? Consistent with a right-handed person tying it round her own neck. Pretty strong knot, too. Was she a girl guide or something like that?'

'Climber.'

'Ah, okay. That makes sense.'

'What about the caretaker's story that he cut her down?'

'Yes, I'd agree with that. The cord's slightly discoloured below the knot, as if he was gripping it while he cut. We could take his DNA to compare with the cord but it'll cost you. To be honest, I doubt it's worth it.'

Clare thanked Raymond and clicked to access her address book. She found the number for Neil Grant, the pathologist.

'Hi, Clare,' he said, his voice brisk as ever. 'Got your youngster here. Terrible thing.'

'I know. Look, Neil, I'd like to bring the parents over to ID her as soon as possible. I don't suppose...'

There was a sigh. 'You want them over tonight?'

'Is it possible?'

'Not really. But, as it's you...'

'Thanks Neil. Erm, sevenish?'

'Make it eight.'

She sent a message to Paul Henry, letting him know she'd be round to collect the Bakewells at seven twenty. Then she sent another message to Al to say she'd be home late. As she put down her phone the office door opened and Chris came in.

'Laptop and phone are off to Tech Support,' he said, sinking down in a chair opposite. 'There's not much more we can do,' he said, hopefully.

'Sorry,' Clare said. 'We're taking the parents over to the mortuary for eight.'

'Eight tonight?'

'Yep. Sooner the better.'

He yawned and rubbed his head. Clare reached into her bag and took out a twenty-pound note. 'Go and get us a couple of fish suppers. We can chat about it while we eat.'

His face lit up and he pocketed the note. But as he rose to leave, Jim the desk sergeant put his head round the door. Clare saw his expression and raised a hand to forestall Chris. 'Hold that fish supper a minute.' She turned back to Jim. 'Something up?'

He came into the room. 'A couple of uniforms brought in a shoplifter two hours ago.'

'And?'

'Schoolkid. Went into Temby's…'

'Where?'

'I know it,' Chris said. 'Deals in high-end second-hand electricals. Got an Apple watch for my wee cousin a while back. Really good nick. Decent price.'

'That's the one,' Jim said. 'Anyway, this lad went in, said he wanted to buy one of the iPads in the display case. When the assistant took it out he snatched it and ran for the door. He made it into the street where he ran into Mandy, out on patrol. She marched him back to the shop and called for a car to bring him in. Shop's given a statement and he's admitted it.'

Clare frowned. 'Any previous?'

Jim shook his head. 'Nope. I reckon it was out of character.'

'How old?'

'Sixteen.'

'I'm thinking a caution, Jim. Doesn't sound like he's a hardened criminal.'

'It's not that…' He rubbed his chin. 'The parents are here. Seem like a decent family.'

'Doesn't mean he's not a thief,' Chris said.

'But it's what he stole,' Jim persisted. 'The iPad. A second-hand iPad. According to the parents he had a new one last Christmas. He admits he still has it, it's not broken. But he won't say why he tried to steal this one.'

'Bullying?' Clare said. 'Someone forced him to do it?'

'Has to be,' Jim said. 'But he won't say anything.'

Clare sighed. 'You want me to have a go?'

'I know you're busy…'

She rose from her chair. 'Go on, then. But he'd better fess up quickly. There's a fish supper with my name on it.'

Josh McNeil's face was the picture of misery. He was tall but had the gangly look of a teenage boy yet to grow into his height. His hair, tousled on top, was shaved up the sides and there was a downy moustache on his top lip. He was flanked by a couple Clare guessed were his parents, the mother seemingly on the point of tears. Josh glanced at Clare as she entered the room then away again.

'It's Josh, isn't it?' she said, settling herself on a chair opposite. 'I'm Clare, the DI at the station.' She smiled at Josh's parents and his mother attempted a smile in return.

His father nudged him. 'The inspector's talking to you.'

Josh flashed Clare a look. 'Yes,' he mumbled. 'I'm Josh.'

Clare studied the trio. They seemed to be what her mother would have called a respectable family. Well dressed and clearly uncomfortable at their surroundings. She ran an eye over the details Jim had given her. 'Josh McNeil?'

'Yes.'

'And you are Mr and Mrs McNeil?'

The couple nodded. 'What's going to happen to Josh?' Mrs McNeil said.

Clare hesitated. 'Perhaps Josh could tell us about this afternoon.' She tried to catch his eye. 'I gather you took an iPad without paying for it. Is that correct?'

A flush spread up Josh's neck and he raised his gaze to meet Clare's. 'Yes.' His voice was little more than a whisper.

'Sergeant Douglas tells me you have your own iPad at home.'

'Yes.'

'Is it damaged? Something happen to it? Maybe you didn't want to tell your mum and dad? If that's the reason it's better to say so now.'

Josh shook his head. 'No. It's fine.'

'It's a good one,' Mrs McNeil said. 'He got it new, last year.'

Clare watched Josh as his mother spoke but his head was down, eyes on the floor. 'This was a second-hand iPad,' Clare went on. 'I'm wondering why you tried to take it.'

Josh shrugged but said nothing.

'The inspector's asking you a question,' his father said in a tone that suggested he was struggling to contain his temper.

For a moment Josh was silent. 'Dunno,' he said, eventually.

Clare studied the three of them and came to a decision. 'I'd like to speak to Josh alone,' she said.

The McNeils exchanged glances. 'Can you do that?' Mrs McNeil said after a moment. 'I mean, is it allowed?'

Clare rose and moved to hold open the door. 'It is, and I think it might be helpful.' She looked down at the lad. 'Is that all right, Josh?'

He raised his gaze. 'Yeah,' he said. 'It's cool.'

The parents trooped out and Clare closed the door, resuming her seat opposite Josh. She said nothing for a moment and was rewarded when he lifted his face to meet hers. She decided to get straight to the point.

'Did you steal that laptop for someone else?'

He seemed surprised by the directness of her question.

'Because it can't be for you, can it? Unless you plan to sell it; and people who steal things to sell are usually doing it for one reason. So, let's have the truth, Josh. Are you using drugs?'

His eyes widened. 'What? No! Why would you think that?'

She was taken aback by the forcefulness of his reply.

'Quite simply because you attempted to steal a valuable item which would be pretty easy to turn into cash.'

'Definitely not. I wouldn't touch that stuff.'

She sat back and studied his face. You never could tell with drug users but she was inclined to believe him. 'In that case, there must be another reason you took the iPad. Did someone ask you to steal it?'

He said nothing, his eyes back on the floor again.

'I'll take that as a yes,' Clare said. 'So now I want to know who – and why.' There was no response to this and Clare checked her watch. Almost seven. She had to pick up the Bakewells at twenty past. 'Are you being bullied?' she persisted. 'Someone making you steal things?'

Still he said nothing.

'Okay, Josh. Let's agree someone asked you to steal it,' Clare said. 'Do you know this person?'

He shook his head.

'Is it someone at school?'

He sat silent for a moment. 'I don't know who it was. I just… just got a message telling me to do it.'

'A text?'

'Yeah.'

'And you didn't recognise the number?'

'No.'

'So this person – the one who texted – did they threaten you?'

Josh shrugged again.

Clare sighed. 'Josh, I need you to work with me, here. No one steals an iPad without a good reason.'

He flashed her a look then away again. 'Kind of a threat.'

'Physical?'

33

'Yeah.' He shifted on his seat. 'Said they'd beat me up.'

'Did you report this?'

'Like you could do anything.'

'Well we certainly can't if we don't know about it.' Josh didn't seem inclined to say any more so she went on. 'What were you told to do with the iPad?'

There was another silence then, 'Botanics.'

'The Botanic Gardens?'

'Yeah. There's like some bushes, outside the gate. I was to take it there tonight. Hide it.'

'The person who threatened you said you should steal an iPad and leave it in the bushes outside the Botanic Gardens?'

'Yeah. In a Tesco bag.'

Clare studied him. Was this the truth? He didn't look like a typical drug user but he was only a schoolboy. Maybe he was new to the drug scene. Maybe he saw stealing the iPad as an easy way to keep his dealer sweet. She checked her watch again and rose from her seat. 'Okay,' she said. She opened the door and beckoned to the McNeils. They came into the room, their faces creased with concern.

'Josh will receive a caution for the attempted theft. We will look further into this and I may come back to you. But, in the meantime,' she said, her voice as stern as she could manage, 'I would like your mobile phone, Josh.'

'My phone?' His face had fallen a mile. 'But I need it.'

'So do we,' Clare said. 'I need to check what you've told me is the truth. And I'll send someone round for your iPad as well.'

'He needs that for his schoolwork,' Mrs McNeil said.

'We'll have it back to you as soon as possible,' Clare said. 'But we do need to have a look.' Josh's mother didn't look convinced but Clare ignored this, steering the trio towards Jim. She explained about the caution and Josh's mobile phone and was about to head for her office when an image of Sophie's body lying on the grass came into her head. She glanced at Josh and drew his father to one side. 'Keep an eye on him over the next few days,' she said. 'Whatever made him try to steal that iPad, he's had quite a shock.'

He stared at her for a moment as though unsure what she meant, then worry flashed across his face.

'I'll do that,' he said. 'And… thanks.'

She left them with Jim and escaped to her office. As soon as she opened the door the smell of fish and chips wound its way round her heart. Chris was sitting demolishing the remains of a fish supper, a cardboard box at Clare's place.

'I nearly ate yours as well.'

She looked at it with something approaching regret and picked up a couple of chips. Then she took a tissue from a box on the desk and wiped her hands. 'Come on,' she said. 'Mortuary time.'

Chapter 6

Paul Henry opened the door and stood barring the way. 'They're all ready,' he said. 'I'll drive, shall I?'

Clare pushed past him. 'No, you get off home. Chris and I can manage.'

He shrugged. 'You're the boss.' Then he stepped out and down the path without a backward glance. Clare moved up the hall and tapped on the sitting room door. The Bakewells were wearing coats and, on seeing Clare, Laura looked round for her handbag.

'It's here,' Brian said, handing the bag to his wife. He glanced at Clare. 'Are we going now?'

'When you feel ready.'

Laura reached out and took her husband's hand and they moved towards the door. Clare and Chris stepped out to let Brian lock the front door. Out of the corner of her eye she could see Paul Henry edging his car back and forth as he tried to manoeuvre out of the parking space. Chris had driven there and Clare hadn't noticed how closely he'd backed up to Paul's bumper.

'Extra chips for you,' she whispered, giving him a wink.

'I don't like wankers,' he said, walking down the path, clicking to unlock the car. He threw Paul a smile then held open the door to let Brian and Laura climb in. Once they were safely belted he went round to the driver's door. Clare watched as he took his time checking his mirrors, moving the car into neutral until eventually he started the engine and pulled away. She glanced back to see Paul performing a hurried three-point-turn and heading off in the other direction.

As Chris drove Clare explained they would view Sophie through a glass screen. 'I'm afraid, for now, you won't be any closer. But hopefully in a few days that will be possible.'

They said nothing to this and she turned back to face the front, the odd sniff from Laura the only sound punctuating the silence. The roads were quiet and they were soon across the Tay Road Bridge, heading for the police mortuary. The barrier was raised when they arrived and Chris nosed into a parking space close to the entrance. Clare clicked off her seat belt and stepped out, opening the door for the Bakewells. Brian was out first, offering a hand to his wife. As they walked towards the entrance two fire engines screamed past heading for Lochee Road, blue lights flashing, sirens wailing, but the couple barely seemed to notice. They were buzzed into the mortuary reception and Clare signed them in. It was strangely quiet, the day staff having finished hours earlier. Brian's eyes flitted round, taking it all in, but Laura kept hers on the floor. After a few minutes the attendant indicated they were ready and Clare took them through to the viewing room. She moved back initially to allow the couple space to look at their daughter but when Laura's legs buckled she rushed forward to help Brian support his wife. Laura fell into his arms and he held her tightly, whispering softly to her. She sobbed loudly into his chest and Clare watched as tears spilled down Brian's face. She indicated the seats then motioned to Chris and they stepped out of the viewing room.

'Think I'll get Jim to stick someone near the Botanics in an unmarked car,' she said, her voice low, anxious not to be overheard by the Bakewells.

'You believe his story – that lad?' Chris said.

'I'm not sure. The threat to beat him up doesn't ring true. But I reckon someone's got a hold on him.' She tapped out a message to Jim who replied with a thumbs up then she put her phone away.

'Shall we?' She headed back to the viewing room, Chris following behind.

She thought Laura seemed calmer and she went through the motions of asking them to confirm the identity. It took a few minutes for Laura to speak but eventually she stammered that, yes, that was her daughter, Sophie Elaine Bakewell. Brian confirmed this and Clare led them gently from the room to a slightly larger one with chairs arranged round a wooden coffee table.

'There is a drinks machine. The tea's usually not too bad,' she said.

'I think we'd like to go home,' Brian said, but Laura shook her head.

'I don't want to leave her. Not here. Not on her own.'

'Someone will be here,' Clare said. 'There's always someone on duty.'

Laura didn't seem convinced by this but, gradually, they persuaded her out to the car. A fine drizzle was falling now and Chris pulled out of the car park, flicking on the windscreen wipers.

It was almost dark by the time they drew up outside the house in Kinnessburn Road.

'We should have left a light on,' Laura said, her voice wooden.

'We'll come in with you,' Clare said. 'Make sure it's all secure.'

'Will that other one be there?' Brian asked. 'That Paul lad?'

Clare shook her head. 'He's gone for the day. But he'll be back in the morning. Meantime,' she fished in her pocket and withdrew a card, 'you can call me any time – day or night.'

They saw the Bakewells in, Chris checking the house was secure then they made to leave. Clare glanced at Laura, huddled on the sofa. 'Don't hesitate to phone NHS 24 if you're concerned,' she said to Brian and he nodded.

'I'll look after her. Don't worry.' He saw them to the door but before Clare could open it he said, 'What happened to her? Our Sophie?'

Clare hesitated. She couldn't see any reason not to tell them. Chances are it would be all round the school by now anyway. 'I'm so sorry, Mr Bakewell. It seems Sophie hanged herself in the school grounds.'

He stood for a minute, his face a mask, then he gave a slight nod. 'Thank you.' His voice was husky, his face grey. 'Thanks,' he repeated. Then he opened the door and stood, waiting for them to leave.

–

The station was quiet when Clare returned, Chris dashing straight for his car through what was now pretty steady rain. A note on Clare's desk next to the cold congealed fish supper told her Josh's iPad had been collected from his home and was on its way to Tech Support, along with his mobile phone. She carried the fish supper through to the kitchen and tipped it into the swing bin. Then she grabbed her coat, tapped out a message to let the DCI know she was on her way home and headed to her beloved Mercedes.

Tuesday

Chapter 7

'No luck at the Botanics,' Jim said as Clare shrugged off her jacket. 'To be fair it was a pretty foul night. That rain. Wouldn't have made sense to leave an iPad out in that weather. Mind you,' he went on, 'could be the lad warned off whoever was collecting it.'

'Yeah, maybe,' Clare said. 'Don't suppose we can justify another night watching it.'

'Leave it with me. Not that there's anywhere to hide, unless the house opposite…'

'Thanks, Jim. Tell Chris and Max to give me a shout when they get in,' and she headed for the kitchen to put her lunch in the fridge.

Her office still reeked of fish and chips and she reached up to open the window. Then she sat down to think about Sophie Bakewell. Her closest friend was in Italy. What had the headteacher said, Maria would be back next week? They couldn't afford to wait that long. She wondered again about Sophie's classmates. Just that one lad who'd said she was nice. Usually, when one starts, the others join in. Was there a reason they were keeping quiet? She'd have to send some officers to speak to them, one-to-one. See if they were less reticent without an audience. Unless of course that class tutor – Sue something – unless some of the kids had spoken to her. She wrote a note on her pad to call the school later. Or maybe she'd send Chris and Max.

The door opened and Chris ambled in. 'Max is on his way.' He sank down on the chair opposite, his tie already loosened at the neck, shirt coming adrift from his trousers 'So, what's on the agenda for today?'

'Today, Sergeant, I'd like you and Max to go back to the school and do a bit more digging. Speak to the staff first. Find out who else Sophie was friendly with and take it from there. Her friends might be more willing to speak if it's one-to-one.'

'Okie doke. Oh, any luck with the iPad last night? At the Botanics?'

'No. But it was a foul night. Jim's going to see if he can spare someone for tonight.' She sat thinking for a moment. 'Who was it brought the lad in?'

'Mandy stopped him in the street. I think she radioed for a car and one of the other cops went along.'

'Ask Mandy to pop in,' she said. 'Soon as she arrives.'

Chris went off to find Max and Mandy. A few minutes later there was a tap on the door and Mandy, a uniformed officer in her thirties, stood uncertainly in the doorway. Clare motioned her in.

'I'd like to know about the lad yesterday – the iPad theft.'

'Not much to tell,' Mandy said. 'I was heading up Market Street and he came tearing towards me, clutching the iPad. I saw one of Temby's staff waving from the shop doorway so I grabbed him.'

'And how was he? When you stopped him, I mean? Was he violent? Try to get away?'

Mandy shook her head. 'Quite the opposite. It was like the fight had gone out of him. Let me walk him back up to the shop, meek as a lamb.' She thought for a moment. 'I think he was near to tears, to be honest.'

Clare sat back, twiddling a pen in her fingers. 'You reckon it was a dare?'

'I mean, could have been. Pretty high value item for a dare, though.'

'It was second hand…'

'Even so.'

'What do you reckon, then? What's your best guess?'

Mandy considered this. 'I don't know what made him do it but he's not your usual light-fingered merchant. I'd say this was out of character.'

Clare nodded. 'My thoughts as well. I think someone put pressure on him to steal that iPad and he's too scared to say who.'

She let Mandy go then wandered through to the incident room where Chris and Max were chatting.

'I called the school,' Chris said, 'but no one there yet. I'll try again at half eight then we'll wander over. See what we can find out.'

Max saw her expression. 'Something else you want done?'

'Never volunteer,' Chris hissed, making Max laugh.

'Yes, actually,' Clare said. 'Can you check crime reports for the last month or two. Say this area and a ten-mile radius. Any similar thefts to our young lad yesterday. High value items snatched from shops, stolen from cars – that kind of thing.'

Max frowned. 'You're thinking there's more to it?'

'I don't know. But there's something about Josh that doesn't add up. He's definitely not the typical shoplifter.'

She left them to their research and headed back to her office, taking out her phone as she went. She found the number for Paul Henry and clicked to dial.

'On my way now,' he said. 'Should be with them in twenty minutes. Anything I should know?'

There was something in his tone that irked her; something she couldn't put a finger on. But he wasn't asking anything out of the ordinary and she put this to the back of her mind. 'They ID'd the body, last night,' she said. 'Definitely Sophie.'

'So,' he drawled. 'I'm guessing you won't be needing me much longer.'

'Probably not. But let's wait until after the PM's been done. In case there are any surprises.'

'You're the boss,' he said, his tone flippant.

She put down her phone. Why the hell was the police still recruiting folk like Paul Henry, and what was he doing as an FLO? It would be hard to think of anyone less sympathetic, unless it was for his baby-faced good looks. Maybe whoever appointed him thought families would relax around him. She couldn't help contrasting him with Wendy's measured approach – calm but sharp-eyed. The only thing Paul Henry would be looking out for was how his hair was sitting. But maybe she was being unfair. And Sophie's death was straightforward enough. It wasn't as if there was anything suspicious at home. Or was there…

A tap at the door interrupted her thoughts and Jim came in. 'Sorry, Clare,' he said. 'I know you're up to your eyes but I've a gent out front who insists on seeing the inspector.'

She raised an eyebrow. 'Isn't it something one of the lads could deal with?'

He put a hand to his chin. 'It's an odd one…'

Rory Craven was standing in the front office, a laptop case slung over his shoulder, fingers drumming at his legs. He was tall, dressed in a business suit, his grey hair receding at the temples. He turned as Clare and Jim approached and raised an eyebrow. Clare introduced herself and asked him to follow her to an interview room. She waited until he had taken a seat, allowing the laptop bag to slip off his shoulder, then she sat down opposite.

'I understand you have some concerns about – your father, is it?'

'Damn right I do,' he said, 'and I want you to put a stop to it.'

Jesus. Was it suddenly the season for alpha males? She fought back a growing irritation and began jotting down details. 'Your father's name?'

'Craven. Cliff Craven.'

'Address?'

He reeled off an address in Strathkinness High Road, a street Clare knew was one of the more expensive in the town.

She asked a few more questions then put down her pen, appraising him. His frame was less rigid now and, not for the first time, she thought how useful the calm routine of eliciting basic information was. She gave him a smile, a cool professional smile that didn't quite reach her eyes. 'Perhaps you could explain your concerns.'

'He's being taken advantage of,' he said. 'Plain and simple.'

'In what way?'

'It's that – what do you call it – cuckooing?'

Clare was suddenly alert. 'Has someone moved into his house?'

'Not moved in, exactly.'

'But you think his house is being used for some criminal activity?'

'As to that, I've no idea. But I do know he's being taken advantage of.'

'Who's taking advantage of him?'

'Her name is Hazel Sullivan.'

Clare noted this down. 'And what is it she's doing?'

He ran a hand through his hair, as if suddenly at a loss. 'I think she's taking stuff from the house. Valuable stuff,' he added.

'Is she a friend of your father's?'

'She wasn't until recently. He was in hospital a few weeks back. From what I can gather she was visiting someone in the next bed and they struck up a conversation. Soon as he was discharged she was there – visiting him and goodness knows what else.'

'And you think she's taking stuff from the house?'

'I know she is.'

'Are there particular items missing?'

He nodded. 'Two Dresden lace figurines – my mother's,' he added. 'A painting and a DSO medal that was my grandfather's. That's only the stuff I know about. Goodness knows what else she's had.'

'DSO?'

'Distinguished Service Order. Pretty rare these days.'

Clare noted this down. 'Have you asked your father about them?'

Rory's face softened and he shook his head. 'He's not well, you see. Only a few months left. I don't want to distress him.'

Clare put down her pen. 'How can you be sure he hasn't moved the items himself? Sold them, even?'

'Not possible. He's not so mobile these days. Gets about the house okay – downstairs, mostly – but he doesn't go out and he certainly wouldn't have managed to go up a stepladder and take down a heavy painting.'

'Where was the painting?'

'In his bedroom. Upstairs,' he added. 'Dad sleeps downstairs now. I doubt he's been upstairs since he left the hospital.'

'And the figurines?'

'Display cabinet in the dining room. Whoever took them moved the rest so there wasn't a gap. But I saw it straight away.'

'When was this?'

He sat thinking for a moment. 'The first time was a couple of weeks ago.'

Clare noted this down. 'And you are sure the figurines had been in the cabinet?'

Rory exhaled heavily. 'Yessss! I grew up in that house, Inspector. These ornaments were my mother's pride and joy. They were in that cabinet for years. You soon spot when something like that's changed.'

'I take it your mother…'

'Died three years ago. Dad's been on his own in the house ever since.'

'And you're sure he hasn't sold them?'

'No need. His pension's pretty decent and he has plenty in the bank.'

Clare glanced down at her notes. 'What about the medal?'

'In his study. He kept it on his desk.'

She hesitated, choosing her words carefully. 'Is your father still mentally sharp?'

'As much as anyone in their late eighties.'

'And he's not noticed these items missing?'

'No, thank God. And I don't want him to. So you'd better stop her before it goes any further.' The edge to his voice was back again.

46

'Hazel Sullivan, you said.' Clare ignored his tone. 'Perhaps you could tell me what you know about her.'

Rory checked his watch. 'I have a meeting in an hour. It'll have to be quick.'

Clare was tempted to say she had a teenage suicide to deal with but she bit her tongue and waited for Rory to explain.

'As I said, Dad was in hospital. This Hazel woman was visiting someone in the next bed. For some reason she starts chatting to Dad, passing the time of day. Next thing I know, Dad's discharged and she's popping into the house for tea and cake. That's when the stuff started disappearing,' he added.

'Have you asked your father about her visits?'

He nodded. 'Bit my head off. Said he was helping her with some research.'

'Oh?'

'Yep. Something about the history of local politics.'

'And your father would know about this?'

'He would. He was a councillor for years. Chaired several committees in his time.'

Clare frowned. 'And she's researching this?'

'So she says. Claims she's writing an article.'

'It's possible,' Clare said.

Rory snorted. 'Seriously? I doubt it, Inspector. I reckon she saw him in hospital. Maybe recognised he'd a bit of money about him and fluttered her eyelashes. Pound to a penny she turns up with a couple of doughnuts, tells him she'll put the kettle on and takes the chance to have a good snoop around. And I'll tell you something else,' he went on. 'I think she's been lifting cash as well.'

'Oh?'

'I keep his bank card. He's not able to get out to cash machines so when he needs some money he tells me and I take it out for him. But lately he's been asking for more and more. If you ask me she's found out where he keeps it and she's helping herself.'

'Do you have an address for this lady?'

He shook his head. 'I know she stays in the town but no idea where.'

Clare smiled. 'Not to worry. We'll look into it.'

'And you'll warn her off?'

Clare rose from her seat. 'As I said, we'll investigate and see what we can find.'

Rory took a card from his pocket. 'Call me any time. I want this woman out of my father's life.'

She saw him to the front door then wandered back to her office, mulling it over. Was this Hazel woman taking advantage of Rory's father? Or was it an innocent friendship? Often the lines between the two were blurred and it was impossible to tell. Maybe there was a bit of self-interest on the woman's part. But the same could be said for Rory Craven. Was he afraid his father would fall in love again? Change his will in Hazel's favour? Surely not. But he'd come in to report it so they'd have to check it out. She jotted a note on her pad and went in search of Jim.

He was tapping away at his computer in his usual two-fingered fashion and he looked up as she approached.

'Can you find me a Hazel Sullivan?' she asked. 'Lives somewhere in the town.'

Jim noted the name down. 'Problem?'

'Rory Craven thinks she's taking advantage of his father.'

'Leave it with me,' he said. 'Anything other than rejigging the holiday rota.'

She laughed and made her way back to the office, quickening her step when she heard her phone ring. A withheld number. She clicked to take the call and it took her a moment to recognise the voice; and then it came to her. Sue Perry – Sophie Bakewell's class tutor. She glanced at her watch and realised Chris and Max must be at the school already. So why was Sue Perry calling her? Why wasn't she dealing with the two sergeants?

'I wonder if you could spare me half an hour,' Sue said. 'There's something I think you should see.'

Chapter 8

The same young man was at the school reception desk, tapping at his computer and he smiled as Clare approached.

'Sue said to expect you,' he said lifting the phone. 'I'll let her know you're here.'

Clare wandered across to a display case filled with cups and shields. She wondered if Sophie's climbing awards were in the case and was peering at the inscriptions when she heard the sound of feet tapping along the corridor. She turned to see Sue approaching, a red-haired girl in school uniform at her side. The girl eyed Clare but when Clare met her gaze she looked away, her face flushed.

'Thank you for coming,' Sue said. 'If you could follow me...' She led Clare along a corridor, through a set of fire doors, the red-haired girl trailing in their wake. Then she opened a door to the left, flicking on a switch as she entered. The girl hesitated then followed Sue in, twisting a mobile phone in her hands.

Stepping further into the room Clare indicated the door. 'Should I...' and Sue nodded.

She waited until Clare had sat then she introduced the girl. 'This is Melanie. One of Sophie's classmates.'

Clare studied the girl, wondering why she was here. Was she the nervous type? Too shy to speak to male officers? Her face was spotted with acne and Clare thought briefly of her own teenage years and the crushing embarrassment of acne breakouts. It had done nothing for her self-confidence or her love life. She tried to remember the pupils in the band room, the day before. Had Melanie been one of the girls dabbing their eyes? Or the girl in the front row who'd been crying quietly? She couldn't remember but she gave Melanie an encouraging smile. 'Is there something you wanted to say? About Sophie?'

Melanie's gaze dropped and Sue sat forward.

'Your officers have been chatting to the class again today, asking some of them about Sophie. But Melanie – she didn't want to speak to them, maybe with them being men.' She glanced at the girl. 'Melanie received a message on her phone yesterday morning, on her way to school. The message had a link to a website which Melanie clicked on and – well – you'd better see for yourself.' She nodded to the girl who tapped a passcode into her phone and handed it to Clare.

'It's on Messenger,' she said. 'Fourth one down.'

Clare took the phone, clicked the Messenger app then scrolled down. The sender was someone called Bex. She opened the message and read,

OMG Mel! You gotta see this.

There was a hyperlink below, a web address ending in .ro, and she racked her brains. Was it Romania? She clicked to open the link and it buffered for a few seconds then took her to what seemed to be a video on a porn website. The content was behind a paywall but she was able to view the first thirty seconds free of charge. She watched in horror as Sophie's face came into view. And she wasn't alone. A boy of about the same age was straddling Sophie, both of them naked. Sophie's arms were thrown back, one hand wrapped round a brass bedstead, the other out to the side. And then, as the preview came to an end, the boy looked into the camera and grinned. His face remained frozen on screen and a banner appeared, inviting viewers to upgrade for the full video.

Clare suddenly felt sick. Had Sophie seen this? Was that what had driven her to take her own life – the shame of her friends finding it? What on earth had she been thinking, allowing herself to be filmed? Or had she not even known?

'Did you show this to Sophie?' she asked Melanie.

The girl shook her head. 'We weren't really friends. But maybe someone else did. That girl who sent it to me...'

'Bex?'

'Yeah, her. She probably sent it round the whole class. Someone would have told Sophie.'

It made sense now, the class staying silent. If Bex − or any of the others − had sent the video on to Sophie they'd be wracked with guilt by now. Clare looked back at the phone, studying the boy's face, then she held it out to Melanie. 'Do you know him?'

'No,' she said. 'Don't think so. He's not in our year, anyway.'

Clare turned to Sue. 'Is he a pupil here?'

Sue stared at the image. 'I don't recognise him either.'

Clare sat thinking for a minute. Then she took out her phone and copied the web address. 'Are my colleagues still with the class?'

'Yes,' Sue said. 'I gave them a room and they're working through the class list. Would you like to join them?'

Clare rose from her seat. 'I think I'd better. Erm, Melanie, I realise this may be all round the school but I'd appreciate you keeping it to yourself. For now, at least. This is going to be painful for Sophie's family and I'd like them to hear it from me, first.'

Melanie said *of course* and escaped with visible relief. Sue watched her go then shook her head. 'Poor Sophie.'

'Yes.' Clare agreed. 'Poor thing.' She gave Sue a thin smile. 'If you could take me to my colleagues...' They walked through the corridors without speaking and Clare was grateful for the absence of small talk. Her mind was racing with this revelation.

Sue stopped outside another door and tapped lightly on it. Then she opened it a little and peered round. 'Okay to come in?' Clare heard her say then she opened the door wide enough for Clare to enter. 'I'll leave you to it. But there's a phone in the corner. If you dial 21 you'll get Richard at reception. He'll find me.'

Clare thanked her and closed the door softly. Chris and Max were seated at a table, a frightened-looking boy opposite. 'Hello,' she said. 'I'm Clare, the DI here in St Andrews.' She took a chair from against the wall and pulled it up opposite the boy.

'Ben,' the boy said, his eyes going between Clare and the two sergeants.

'Ben here's been showing us a weblink,' Chris said, indicating the boy's phone. 'Might have a bearing on Sophie's death.'

A glance at Ben's phone told Clare it was the same website. 'Can I ask how you came by this link?'

Ben flushed and looked away. 'Another lad in the class sent it.'

'And did you tell Sophie?'

He was near to tears and she hastened to reassure him. 'It's fine if you did, Ben. We just need to know.'

He swallowed a couple of times. 'I didn't know it would make her...' then the tears began to flow. 'I'm sorry,' he stuttered. 'I'd never have sent it if I thought...'

Clare sat forward. 'Ben, you've done nothing wrong here. Sophie would have found out sooner or later. And there's no way you could have predicted what she would do. So please don't worry. What we do need to know is how you found out about the video.'

Ben's face was scarlet now, misery written all over it. 'One of the lads, he watches this stuff. You have to pay,' he went on. 'And, like, we all chip in a few quid...'

'You and your friends club together so you can watch some of these films?' Clare said and Ben nodded.

'When do you do this?'

'Lunchtimes, mostly. Sometimes after school.'

'And who was it spotted Sophie?'

Ben said nothing.

'He won't be in any trouble,' Clare said. 'But we do need to know.'

He eyed them. 'You won't say it was me who told.'

'No, don't worry,' Chris said. 'We'll just do like we did with your phone and ask for a look.'

He was quiet for a moment. 'Darren,' he said eventually. 'Darren Spencer.'

Clare noted this down. 'Is this the only time you've recognised someone in one of the films?'

'Yeah. I mean, I don't even watch, sometimes…'

Clare glanced at Chris and Max to see if they had any more questions but they indicated they were finished and she let Ben escape. When he'd left she closed the door behind him.

'So now we know.'

'Yup,' Chris said. 'We've spoken to eight of her classmates so far. All of them knew about it and four admit to forwarding the link to Sophie herself. A couple of the girls said she was devastated. Apparently she ran off after registration. They assumed she'd headed away from school.'

'Poor thing,' Max said.

'Anyone recognise the boy in the video?' Clare asked.

Chris shook his head. 'No one admitting to it, at least.'

'Then we'd better have young Darren in next.'

Darren Spencer was stockily built, with a round face and a shock of strawberry blond hair. He came slowly into the room, dragging his feet, one hand on a backpack slung over his shoulder. Clare was struck by his apparent lack of distress, compared with Ben and Melanie. Was there even a hint of hostility in his manner? Ben's unwillingness to name Darren made sense now. Clare reckoned he would make a bad enemy. She introduced the three of them and smiled, hoping to put him at his ease.

'I gather a video of Sophie was circulating yesterday morning,' she began.

Darren nodded but didn't speak.

'I'd like permission to look at your phone,' she went on. 'You have the right to refuse but it would help us greatly if we could check whether you've viewed the video we're concerned about.'

He looked at them for a moment then he dug in a trouser pocket and took out his phone. 'Suppose.'

'If you could unlock it please and open up the link to the video – if you did view it,' she added.

He tapped the keypad and handed the phone to Clare. She glanced at the screen to check it was the same video. Then she muted the volume and pressed play. She watched long enough to be sure Darren had paid to view the full clip then she stopped it.

'You recognised Sophie, yes?'

'Yeah.' Darren's voice was quiet now.

'And the boy?'

He avoided her eye. 'Don't know him.'

'Might you have seen him here, at the school?'

'Definitely not.'

Clare watched him for a moment but she didn't think he was lying. 'Darren, from what I've seen,' she went on, 'this video is pornographic. And while Sophie was old enough to consent to be filmed she was still under eighteen. That makes it illegal for anyone other than consenting participants to view these images.'

Darren's eyes widened.

'I'm not suggesting any charges would be brought this time,' Clare said. 'But I have to tell you this is risky behaviour and you could end up in serious trouble. I'm guessing you sent this on to your classmates, yes?'

He said nothing for a moment then, 'Yeah.'

'I appreciate your honesty.' She handed back his phone. 'That too is illegal. So, in future, please remember viewing and sharing this kind of content could be against the law.'

He flicked a glance at Clare then away again. 'Sure. Can I go now?'

She watched him lumber towards the door, hefting the backpack onto his shoulder again. But she thought some of the bravado had gone. She hoped so.

'I'd like you two to carry on speaking to the classmates,' she said, rising from her chair. 'See if anyone knows the boy in the video. From the way he turned round to the camera I'd say he's the one who set it up.'

'Could be they both agreed to it,' Max said.

'I know. But that video didn't get onto the porn site by accident. It's a pay-to-view site so whoever uploaded it exploited Sophie and I'd say that contributed directly to her death.'

She left them and, by some miracle, found her way through the corridors back to reception where she signed herself out. She emerged into the morning sun and stopped for a moment to take in a few deep lungfuls, as though cleansing herself of the grubby video. 'Poor wee Sophie,' she said, her voice soft. 'All that potential.'

In the car she tapped at her phone until she found the number for her friend Diane Wallace at the Tech Support Department, twenty miles away in Glenrothes.

'Clare,' Diane said, 'great to hear from you. How's things?'

'Oh, you know.'

'Yeah, I heard about your teenager. Awful. I think we have her phone and laptop somewhere. Craig logged it yesterday.'

'That's why I'm calling. Any chance you could look at her phone? Particularly Messenger.'

'Sure. Anything special you're after?'

She explained about the video. 'I'd like to know if it was filmed on Sophie's phone. We'll have to try and get it taken down. She's under age, never mind what's happened.'

'Of course. That it?'

Clare thought for a moment. 'Can you get me a headshot of the lad please? Sooner we find him the sooner we'll know how that video ended up on a Romanian porn site.'

'Leave it with me,' Diane said. 'I'll see what I can do. How are the parents coping? I'm guessing they'll be shattered, poor things.'

Clare exhaled heavily. 'Even more so when I explain about the video. They don't know yet but I'll have to tell them before someone else does.'

She thanked Diane and tapped out a message to Paul Henry, warning him she was on her way with some news for the Bakewells. Then she put down her phone and started the car.

Chapter 9

She was greeted at the front door by Laura Bakewell, her eyes pink with crying. Why had Paul Henry allowed her to answer the door? It could have been a reporter, for goodness sake.

'Paul says you have some news,' she said, her voice rising. 'Have you found something? What's happened?'

Clare guided Laura back inside, trying not to let her annoyance show. What the hell was Paul thinking, telling them this? He was hovering in the hall, behind Laura.

'Pop the kettle on,' she said to him, her tone business-like.

'We've not long...'

'Kettle,' she hissed, her voice low. She put a hand on Laura's arm, guiding her into the sitting room. Brian was standing near the window and he turned to greet Clare.

'Some news, the lad said?'

'If we could sit down...'

The couple exchanged glances then Brian moved beside his wife and they sat together on the sofa. Clare sat down opposite them and took a deep breath.

'I believe a video of Sophie was circulating at school yesterday morning, before she left the building.'

Laura glanced at her husband. His face had darkened. 'What sort of video?' There was an edge to his voice.

'It showed Sophie with a boy of about the same age.'

'Boy?' Laura said. 'What boy?'

'We haven't been able to identify him,' Clare said. 'Not so far. But I have to tell you,' she paused, as though delaying the news would somehow soften it, 'they were both undressed and engaging in sexual activity.'

Laura's hand went to her face and she let out a cry so anguished it brought a lump to Clare's throat. Brian's eyes were on the floor but Clare could see the rise and fall of his chest as his breathing quickened. Laura was crying now. 'Oh Sophie…' she sobbed, her voice cracking.

Brian moved to pull her into his arms and he eyed Clare over his wife's shoulder. 'Can I see his photo – the lad? Please?' he added.

Clare nodded. 'Our technical team will capture a few face shots. We'll find him.'

The door opened and Paul came in bearing a tray of mugs and a plate of biscuits. Clare shot him a warning look and, thankfully, he seemed to read this. He set the tray down on a table and began handing out mugs.

Laura took hers mechanically but said nothing.

'So what now?' Brian asked. 'Surely you have to find whoever was responsible for this? They as good as killed our Sophie.'

'We will,' Clare said. 'Our technical team will find where the video originated and we'll work out how it found its way to the website.'

'Website?' Brian growled. 'You mean it's – *online*?'

Laura's eyes widened and she began to cry again.

'I'm afraid so,' Clare said. 'But it'll be taken down as soon as possible.'

'Can't you do it now?' Brian's voice was tight.

'It's not a UK site,' Clare explained. 'But we have a team working on it.'

There was a pause then Brian said, 'I want to see it.'

Clare glanced at Paul, who raised an eyebrow. 'I really don't advise it,' she said. 'This is not how you want to remember Sophie.'

Brian took a deep breath in and out, as though trying to keep his temper in check. 'You don't understand,' he said, emphasising every word. 'If this is what drove Sophie to – to do what she did then I have to know.' He let his head droop into his hands. 'I should have been there to protect her,' he said, his voice muffled. 'I should have been there for her.'

Clare let this hang in the air for a moment. 'Brian, we can't be with our children every minute of the day. They have to learn to navigate the world by themselves. And sadly – tragically – sometimes they make the most dreadful mistakes. But you couldn't predict this. No one could.' She was babbling. She knew it, but she had to steer the Bakewells away from viewing that video. It could only add to their pain in the most dreadful way.

'I wonder,' she said, 'if you could help us.'

Brian raised his head.

'I know Sophie's friend Maria's in Italy but are you in touch with her parents at all?'

Laura drew a hand across her eyes. 'I have her mother's number,' and she looked round for her mobile phone. Brian rose and picked the mobile up from a side table. He handed it to his wife then resumed his seat. Laura tapped at her phone for a minute and held it out for Clare to see.

'She's called Pippa,' Laura said. 'Pippa DiAngelo. Why do you want her number?'

'She might be able to help us identify the boy Sophie was with.'

'I'd like to do more than identify him,' Brian said, and Clare nodded.

'I do understand, but you must leave this to us. I assure we'll find out who's to blame here.' She sipped at her tea then said, 'There is one more thing.'

The couple stared at her.

'We'll have to put out a press release,' Clare said. 'Someone's bound to contact the papers. If it goes out today you may have reporters in the street, or they might phone, asking for a comment. I suggest you leave Paul here to answer the door and let him screen your calls as well. Or don't answer the phone.'

Laura shook her head. 'It's like a bad dream. Only, I can't seem to wake up.'

Clare rose and moved to squeeze Laura's shoulder then she caught Paul's eye. 'I'll leave you for now. Paul will see me out. But I'll keep in touch. You have my number so don't hesitate to call if you have any concerns.'

In the hall she explained to Paul about the video and he gave a low whistle.

'Poor bastards,' he said. Clare wasn't sure if he meant Sophie and her boyfriend or her parents, but she pressed on. 'You'll have to keep the press at bay. Soon as they get a sniff of this they'll be outside. I'll put an officer on the gate overnight. Don't head home until they've arrived, okay?'

'Sure thing,' he said and, again, she wondered at his tone. Admittedly an FLO had to have an air of detachment, not become too absorbed with the family's emotions, but there was something almost flippant about Paul.

She walked down the path towards her car, conscious he was watching her go, and she turned back, hoping to shame him into closing the door. But he stood on, as though making sure she was leaving.

In the car she took out her phone and dialled the number for Pippa DiAngelo and was slightly surprised when the voice that answered sounded Scottish.

'I'd like to speak to Mrs Pippa DiAngelo.'

'That's me,' the voice said. 'Who's this?'

Clare explained who she was and told Pippa that, sadly, Sophie had died.

'Oh how dreadful,' Pippa said. 'Laura must be in bits. Those poor things. What happened?'

Clare said the cause of death hadn't yet been confirmed. 'But we are keen to find out as much as we can about Sophie and I think she and your daughter were friendly.'

'They were,' Pippa said, lowering her voice. 'Maria will be devastated.'

'I wondered if Maria could help us,' Clare said.

'I'm sure she'd be happy to – if she can.'

'Laura and Brian seem to think Sophie didn't have a boyfriend. But we have reason to believe she did. Would Maria know?'

'I'd have thought so,' Pippa said. 'She hasn't mentioned it to me. But I'll ask her.'

'I can hold on,' Clare said, 'if you want to ask her now.'

'Sorry – she's gone to the beach with her cousins. But she'll be back later on. I'll phone you then.'

Clare thanked Pippa and put down her phone.

Chapter 10

The station was quiet when she returned, Chris and Max still up at the school. There was a message from Neil Grant to confirm the post-mortem would begin about two that afternoon, but she found she hadn't the heart for it. Another message from Raymond confirmed fibres from the sash cord had been found on the Stanley knife and the manner of the cut confirmed the caretaker's story. There didn't seem any doubt Sophie had died by her own hand, almost certainly from the shame of finding herself in an online porn video. Clare decided she could sit this post-mortem out and began typing a reply to Neil.

As she clicked *Send* Jim appeared at the door, a piece of paper in his hand. 'I've found your Hazel Sullivan.'

Clare's head was full of Sophie's tragic death and she had to think for a minute who Hazel Sullivan was. And then she remembered. That man who'd come in – was it only this morning? It felt like days ago, now. He'd claimed a woman called Hazel Sullivan was taking advantage of his father. It seemed so trivial compared to Sophie's death. But perhaps there was a problem. Maybe if this Hazel woman was warned off it would save a lot of upset in the future.

'The lads still up at the school?'

'Aye,' Jim said. 'Max phoned a wee while ago. Thinks they'll be done by the end of the day.'

Privately, Clare thought they could have been done a lot sooner, particularly now they knew what had driven Sophie to her death. But maybe they were digging deeper – trying to find out how the video had ended up online. She was finding it hard to shake the image of Sophie's body out of her head. Perhaps it would do her good to think of something else for a bit. 'I'll take it,' she said holding her hand out for the paper.

The address was Irvine Crescent, a quiet residential street that looped round the south end of town. The house was bordered at the front by a row of dwarf conifers, the rest of the front garden laid in pink Balmullo chips. It was a long bungalow with a white front door in the centre, windows to the left and right. Clare's eye was caught by a woman standing on a two-step ladder, washing the windows with a bucket and sponge. Who did that these days? Clare certainly paid a window cleaner to do hers. This woman was putting her to shame.

As if sensing her gaze the woman turned. Her eyes rested on Clare for a few seconds then she stepped down and put the sponge in the bucket, wiping her hands on her jeans. 'Are you lost?' she said.

Clare took her in and decided there was a warmth about her. She looked like she was in her forties, with short sandy hair and an athletic build. Her face was free of make-up but she had a healthy glow that spoke of an enthusiasm for life.

'I'm looking for Hazel Sullivan,' Clare said, walking towards her. As she rounded the conifers she saw a cocker spaniel, sunning itself on the front doorstep.

'That's me,' she said. Her brow creased. 'Do I know you?'

Clare shook her head and took out her badge. 'Could you spare me a few minutes?'

'Of course. I could do with a break anyway.' The dog rose stiffly to its feet and wandered slowly over to Clare, its brown eyes melting her heart. She bent to stroke it and was rewarded with a lick to her hand.

'You've made a friend there,' Hazel said.

'Probably smelling my dog.' She checked the tag round the dog's neck. 'Cassie,' she read. 'Lovely name. And she's so well-behaved.'

'Oh, she's an old lady now,' Hazel said. 'A bit arthritic but not too bad for her age. Shall we?' She led Clare up a short hall bathed in sunlight and into a cheerful sitting room. Cassie padded in after her. 'I'll just deal with these,' she said, indicating the bucket and sponge, and carried them through to the kitchen.

'Cup of tea?' she called, 'or coffee?'

'No thanks. But don't let me stop you.'

Hazel popped her head round the door. 'Think I will if you don't mind. It's thirsty work.'

While she waited Clare took in the room. The easy chairs were brick-red with curtains to match, the walls a buttermilk cream. There were posters in click-frames, photos propped up with ornaments and a small bookcase filled with paperbacks. At the other end of the room a gateleg table stood with a chair at either end. A vase of chrysanthemums sat in the centre of the table, an unopened pile of post next to it. Hazel clearly didn't have a lot of money but there was a warmth and homeliness in the room and Clare began to feel the pain of Sophie's death fade into the background.

Her thoughts were interrupted as Hazel returned, bearing a tray. 'I brought an extra mug in case you changed your mind,' she said.

Clare smiled. 'Why not. It feels like a long day already.'

Hazel poured out two mugs. 'Milk and sugar?'

'Just milk please.'

She added milk and handed Clare a mug. 'Please,' she said, indicating one of the easy chairs, 'have a seat.'

Clare put her mug down on a side table and sank back into the chair. Cassie wandered over and sniffed at Clare's knee. 'Is she allowed up?'

'I mean she is, but just ignore her. She'll soon settle.'

Clare leaned forward, picked Cassie up and settled the dog on her knee. 'Sorry – it's those eyes.'

Hazel laughed. 'Tell me about it.' She sipped from her mug then put it down. 'So, how can I help?'

Suddenly Clare didn't want to tell Hazel why she'd come. The summer sun was streaming in the front window and Cassie was warm on her lap. All she wanted was to sink back in her chair and drink a mug of tea with this cheerful woman. And then she recalled herself. 'We've had a complaint.'

Hazel's eyebrows shot up but her expression didn't change. 'About me?'

'I'm afraid so.'

'Am I allowed to ask who's complained?'

'A man called Rory Craven.'

Her lips tightened. 'Let me guess. He thinks I'm going to seduce his elderly father into marrying me so I can do him out of his inheritance, yes?'

'Not quite.' Clare watched Hazel carefully. 'He thinks you might be stealing from his father.'

Hazel's expression darkened. 'How dare he,' she said, an edge to her voice. 'I may not have much, Inspector, but what I have I've come by through honest hard graft.'

Clare considered this. Hazel seemed genuinely offended by the accusation but it wouldn't be the first time a guilty person had put on an act and fooled them all. 'But you do visit Mr Craven?'

She shrugged. 'Yes.'

'How often?'

'Depends on my shifts. Maybe two or three times a week.'

'Where do you work?' Clare asked.

'At the leisure centre. I'm a swimming coach; and a personal trainer,' she added. 'Demand for trainers varies. Some weeks I'm busy, others less so.' She appraised Clare. 'I have an introductory offer,' she said. 'If you ever fancy it.'

'I'll bear it in mind,' Clare said, and Hazel nodded. 'How do you know Mr Craven?'

'I didn't, until recently. I met him at the hospital. Ninewells.'

Clare knew the large teaching hospital in nearby Dundee. 'How did that come about?'

'Visiting. I was in seeing an old colleague who was recovering from an operation. I'd been in a couple of times and said hello to Cliff. He was in the next bed, you see? Anyway, one day I went in and Tam who I was visiting wasn't there. Cliff told me he'd gone for a scan and would probably be about half an hour. I thought I'd wait and Cliff didn't have any visitors so we got talking. It kind of went from there.'

'Tam?' Clare said. She fished in her pocket for a notebook, disturbing Cassie, who eased herself off the chair and wandered over to Hazel. She scooped the dog up, cradling her in both arms, a defensive gesture that wasn't lost on Clare. She sensed the atmosphere in the room was changing and she smiled pleasantly at Hazel, hoping to defuse the tension.

'Thomas Jury,' Hazel said, fondling Cassie's ears.

'And when was this?'

'About six weeks ago. You can ask the hospital. They'll confirm it.'

Clare noted this down then she took a moment to frame her next question. 'Can I ask the nature of your friendship?'

'Well I'm not after his money,' Hazel said. 'If you really must know, he's helping me with some research.'

'Oh?'

'I'm interested in local history; and in how politics has worked in this area over the years.' She flushed. 'It probably sounds stupid but I'd like to write about it. Maybe an article, or a book, even.' She picked up her mug and sipped from it. 'Not that anyone would read it. I know that. But it's something I'd like to do.' She put her mug down again. 'I don't want to be one of those people who goes to their grave wishing they'd done this or that.'

Clare couldn't imagine Hazel leaving anything undone. 'And Mr Craven – he knows about this stuff – the politics?'

'He does. He was on the council for years. Knows a lot about how it works, how it's changed over time. He likes talking about it and it's a huge help hearing it from someone who was there. I don't think he gets many visitors,' she finished. 'His family sometimes, the odd old friend or colleague. But he's always glad to see me.' She looked Clare squarely in the eye. 'I can assure you, Inspector, that's all there is to it; and I'm certainly not stealing anything from that house. Have a look round here if you like.'

'Have *you* noticed anything missing from Mr Craven's house? Maybe something you saw that's no longer there?'

She shook her head. 'It's not like I go wandering round. I make us a cup of tea. Cliff usually comes through to chat while I brew up. Then I carry a tray back to the sitting room. And occasionally I use the downstairs loo. But that's it.' Cassie, disturbed by Hazel's tone, began licking her hand and she shushed the dog, stroking her head. 'Whoever's stealing from Cliff,' she said, softening her voice, 'it certainly isn't me.'

Chapter 11

Clare drove back to the station, Hazel's words running through her head. Her story certainly matched what Rory had said. But was anyone actually stealing from Cliff? Maybe he was becoming forgetful and putting things in the wrong place. And then she remembered there was a painting missing; one he'd had to have used a stepladder to move. According to Rory he was too frail to manage that. So who had taken that painting? Or was there another reason Rory wanted Hazel out of his father's life? Did he really suspect her of trying to inveigle her way into his affections? And, if so, was he right? It was maybe worth paying the father a visit. See how he was for herself. Mind you, it was hardly a priority. Hazel, if she did have ulterior motives, had been warned off now. Maybe Clare's visit would put an end to it.

Chris and Max were in the kitchen. She'd heard voices outside the door but the talking had stopped as soon as they saw her. Chris flushed and put a piece of paper in his pocket. Max flicked a glance at Clare. 'We're just making coffee,' he said unnecessarily.

She looked from one to the other. 'No you weren't. What's going on?'

'I'm not telling you,' Chris said, and he pushed past her out of the door.

Clare eyed Max and he lowered his voice.

'He's practising his wedding speech. I was trying to give him a few tips.'

She laughed. 'Oh Max. All he has to do is say "On behalf of my wife and myself" and no one will care about the rest. Anyway – how did it go at the school?'

'More of the same,' he said. 'Pretty much the whole class saw the video, most of them shared the link with friends. Sophie realised everyone knew and rushed off in a dreadful state. A couple of the girls said if Maria had been there she might have calmed Sophie down. But we'll never know about that.' He indicated the kettle. 'Actually we were going to have a cup. Fancy one?'

Clare shook her head. 'I've done nothing but drink tea this afternoon.' She checked her watch. 'I might head home soon. Not much more we can do today.' Her phone began to ring and she glanced at it. 'That'll teach me to tempt fate.' It was a mobile number she didn't recognise and she clicked to take the call.

'It's Pippa DiAngelo,' the voice said. 'You wanted me to ask Maria if Sophie had a boyfriend?'

'Oh yes,' Clare said. 'Any luck?'

'I think so. Maria says she did have a boyfriend. He was called Ethan.'

Clare began walking smartly towards her office, as she spoke. 'Surname?'

'Sorry. Maria doesn't know. Only that he was called Ethan and he wasn't at the same school.'

Clare was in her office now and she picked up a pen to jot the name down. 'I'd like to send over a photo,' she said. 'I don't have it yet but when I do I'd like to know if it's Ethan.'

'Oh…' Pippa broke off and Clare heard a murmur of conversation. 'Sorry,' she said, after a minute. 'Maria never met him.'

Clare clicked her tongue in irritation. 'Might Sophie have shown Maria a photo? Maybe a selfie of her and Ethan?'

There was another pause, another murmur of chat. 'No,' Pippa said. 'Apparently Sophie was a bit cagey about him.'

'Was that usual? Had this happened with previous boyfriends?'

'I think Ethan was Sophie's first serious boyfriend.' Clare heard a *yeah* in the background and took it Maria was agreeing with this.

She asked a few more questions but learned nothing more about the mysterious Ethan so she thanked Pippa and put down her phone.

Max had followed her through and she explained about Pippa's call. 'His name's Ethan, apparently. But we don't know any more than that.'

'I'll get onto Sophie's socials,' he said. 'See if he's a friend or a follower.'

Clare lifted her phone again. 'I'll try Diane. She might have something.'

The phone was answered by Craig, Diane's assistant. 'She's at a meeting,' he explained. 'Is it the young girl's phone you're after?'

'Yes. You got anything for us?'

'Hold on...' Clare heard him tapping at a keyboard. 'Okay,' he said after a few minutes. 'We've downloaded her data. I'll pop it up on the network for you. Loads of videos but it doesn't look like the porn one is on her phone.' He was quiet again for a minute. 'Lots of messages sent on Monday morning, all forwarding the link to Sophie's phone.'

'Any replies?'

'Nope. But she did access the link herself. Probably had no idea what it was until the preview opened up. Poor kid,' he added.

Clare thought for a moment. 'Any luck having it taken down?'

'Not yet,' Craig said. 'I can see Diane's contacted a liaison officer in Romania. No reply yet.'

'Can you tell who uploaded it?'

'Nah. VPN,' he said. 'In theory the website owner could try and resolve the IP address...'

'Can you give me that in English?'

'Sorry – they could try to find out who uploaded the video, but they probably won't be able to trace the source. Best plan is to try and have it removed.' Clare heard him tapping at the keyboard again. 'I have a couple of good headshots of the boy's face. I'll send them over now.'

A minute later it popped into her Inbox and she clicked to open the images. As the face filled the screen she was taken back to the moment she viewed the video preview. She stared at him. He couldn't have been much older than Sophie and she wondered who he was. More importantly, did he know what had happened to Sophie?

'Max,' she said, turning her monitor so he could see the image. 'I'm going to upload this to the network. Could you do a reverse image search please? And go through Sophie's contacts list as well. If there's an Ethan, or anyone who might be him, I want to speak to him.'

'No problem.'

Left alone in her office Clare wondered if there was anything else she could do that day. Chris and Max were more than capable of tracking down Sophie's boyfriend and they could phone if there was any problem. And if they did manage to find Ethan there would be plenty to do tomorrow. She shut down her computer and went through to the front office.

'That iPad…' Jim said, as she stopped by his desk.

For a moment she wondered what he meant and then she remembered Josh McNeil. 'Oh yes?'

'The householder opposite the Botanics has agreed to let an officer sit just inside the front window tonight. If someone turns up to look for the iPad we'll nab them.'

She smiled, thanked Jim and made her way out to the car. It was warm, clammy even, the previous night's rain having done nothing to clear the air. She switched on the car aircon and drew out of the car park.

The DCI was already home and unpacking food in the kitchen. Benjy was sitting at his feet, face upturned for any morsel he might drop. 'Fancy a chicken salad?' he said, rinsing tomatoes under the tap.

What Clare really fancied was an enormous pizza she could eat with her fingers. But he was right. It was a sticky night to have the oven going full blast. 'What can I do?' she said. 'Give me something to chop.'

He handed her a bottle. 'This is your strong suit, Mackay. Decork that and pour us both a glass.'

She fetched the corkscrew from the drawer and heaved herself up onto a tall stool, twisting the cork. It came out with a satisfying *pop* and she poured two glasses.

'Good day?' he asked, running a sharp knife round an avocado.

'Not really.' She took a glug of wine and began telling him about Sophie.

He shook his head. 'Poor kid. And they're all at it, too. You should hear what the guys at vice turn up. These kids are so easily exploited.'

'I've a watch on the Botanics, as well,' she went on. 'Jim set it up.'

'Drugs?'

'No. We'd a kid in yesterday. Tried to steal an iPad.'

'I thought the shops had those things chained to the wall.'

'Second hand. Temby's?'

'Oh yeah.'

'He asked to see it out of the display case then he grabbed it from the assistant and ran for the door. Didn't get too far.' She took another glug of wine. 'Claims he was bullied into stealing it. Told to leave it in the bushes at the Botanics gate. But of course…'

'…it rained last night,' he finished.

'Yeah. They're trying again tonight.'

He began cubing the avocado. 'Is it worth the manpower? For a second-hand iPad?'

She frowned. He had a point. 'Maybe not. But there was something about the lad – I spoke to him on his own. Thought maybe he didn't want his parents to know why he took it.'

'And?'

'Nothing. Said he was sent a message, threatening him. But he wouldn't say much more than that.'

'You believe him?'

She considered this, sipping her wine. 'I'm not sure. I think he was afraid of something but his story didn't ring true.'

He scraped the avocado into a bowl and began making a dressing. 'Let's hope you catch someone tonight, then.'

'Amen to that.'

Over dinner they chatted about the project the DCI was working on. 'We're developing a security toolkit for online dating. Trying to make it safer for those who use it.'

Clare thought back to a case she'd worked on a few years ago when online dating had been used to lure women to their death. 'Maybe we could run some workshops – once you've rolled it out? Or take it into workplaces.'

'What we'd really like to do,' he said, 'is to have a standard app pre-installed in mobile phones. iPads too.' He seemed about to go on then he stopped, his glass held in the air.

'Al?'

'Just thinking,' he said. 'Your iPad thief – how old is he?'

'Sixteen, I think. I'd have to check but old enough for me to speak to him without his parents.'

'And your suicide?'

'Same.'

'You don't think that's a coincidence? Two of them on the same day?'

'I mean…' Clare stopped, considering this. 'It's not like he killed himself – I hope! I did tell the parents to keep an eye on him.'

'He was pretty upset, then?'

She nodded. 'Miserable. I got the impression he hadn't done anything remotely like that before.'

He put down his glass. 'Clare, I could be wrong here, but you've got one girl, most likely her boyfriend persuades her to make a sex tape and it ends up online. She's devastated enough to take her own life. Then you've a boy, apparently bullied into stealing a high value item, probably out of character.'

She looked at him. 'What are you saying, Al?'

'For a lad like that to do something as stupid as trying to grab an iPad in a busy shop, he must have been desperate. What kind of hold might someone have over him to make him do that?'

Suddenly Clare's mouth was dry. 'Oh, Al. You're saying maybe this lad was in a sex tape as well?'

'I don't know. But two kids of the same age, both doing something pretty extreme on the same day – I'd want to look further into that. If I were you I'd have that Josh lad back in and ask him if he's done any sex tapes lately.'

Wednesday

Chapter 12

'Think we've got the boyfriend,' Chris said as Clare waited for her computer to come to life.

'Oh yeah?'

'Ethan Robertson. Found his photo on Facebook.'

'Any of him and Sophie?'

'Nope.'

'Bit unusual, isn't it?' Clare said. 'Usually teenagers are all over that stuff.'

'Remember the parents didn't know about him. She probably said to keep photos off social media.'

'Good point. Address?'

'Winram Place. Near the hospital.'

Clare nodded. She knew it.

'But he'll likely have left for school by the time we get there,' Chris said.

'Albany High?'

He shook his head. 'Some private school south of the town. Kinaldy College.'

Clare noted this down. 'We'll head over there after nine. Only…'

'What?'

'If he hasn't heard about Sophie it'll be a hell of a shock. We'd better have an adult present. How old is he?'

'Seventeen.'

'Don't need to involve the parents, then,' Clare said. 'Not at this stage anyway.'

'I'll call the school. See if they can spare a guidance teacher.' He was about to leave when Clare stopped him.

'That lad Josh...'

'The iPad?'

'Yes, him. Do you think it's a coincidence, him and Sophie – you know – on the same day?'

He considered this. 'I can't see a connection. What's on your mind?'

'I'm thinking they both did pretty desperate things.'

'There's quite a difference.'

'Yeah, I know. But I reckon, for Josh, the iPad thing was right out of character. He more or less admitted he was bullied into stealing it. Something like that could wreck his future, stop him getting into uni. It must have been something pretty serious for him to try and steal an iPad.'

'So?'

'So, I'm going to have Josh back in. Ask him outright if it was anything to do with a sex tape.' She drummed a pen on the desk. 'Can we find out which school he's at without asking the parents?'

He shrugged. 'Shouldn't be too hard. There's only four or five in the area. I'll call round.'

She studied him. 'You're being uncharacteristically helpful. What are you after?'

'Nothing. Only...'

'Un huh?'

'We've got the wedding rehearsal tonight,' he said. 'Don't suppose...'

'What time do you need to be away?'

'Six, latest. Sara too.'

'Obviously Sara, too! Unless you've tricked some other poor soul into marrying you.' She smiled at him. 'Just remind me if it's getting late.'

76

Chris went off to call round schools and Clare looked down at her notepad. Thomas Jury. She stared at it for a moment. Of course – the patient Hazel Sullivan claimed to have visited when she'd struck up a friendship with Cliff Craven. She lifted the phone and dialled the number for Ninewells Hospital in Dundee.

'We'll have to verify you are calling from the police,' the call handler told her. Clare gave the station number and her extension, then ended the call. She sat staring at her phone for a few minutes as if willing it to ring. The door opened and Max came in. 'Chris has tracked down our porn star,' he said, and Clare nodded.

'I'd like to see him myself,' she said, 'but I'm waiting on a call.'

'Funny thing,' Max went on. 'That other lad – Josh – he's at the same school as Ethan.'

Clare stared at him. 'Is he now? That is interesting.' She thought for a moment. 'Let Chris know we'll head over there as soon as my call's done.'

As if on cue her phone began to ring and she snatched it up. 'DI Mackay?'

'Elma Stewart,' the voice said. 'I'm a charge nurse at Ninewells. I understand you were asking about a patient.'

'Yes, that's right. Thomas Jury. I don't need any details of his condition. Only how long he was there and, if possible, who else was in at the same time.'

'One moment…'

Clare waited then Elma spoke again. 'He was admitted seven weeks ago and discharged ten days later. Erm, there were quite a few other patients while he was with us. Do you want all their names?'

'Actually, no. I'm only interested in whether a Cliff Craven was in at the same time.'

'Oh Cliff! We all remember him. Quite the ladies' man. Eighty if he was a day but still had a twinkle in his eye.'

'And he was there at the same time as Mr Jury?'

Again there was a pause. 'That's right,' Elma said. 'They were in the same bay.' There was a noise of shouting in the background.

'Look, I really need to go. It's pretty busy here. Is that all you need?'

Clare tried quickly to recall her conversation with Hazel Sullivan. 'Just one more thing. Mr Craven – can I ask if he was suffering from any form of dementia? Memory loss? Any strange behaviour?'

'No,' Elma said. 'Nothing like that. Sadly he has an inoperable tumour. But mentally he's as sharp as a tack. So, if that's everything…'

Clare thanked Elma and put down her phone.

Max was hovering.

'Something and nothing.' She rose from her seat. 'It's nearly nine. Chris and I will head to that school. Give me a buzz if anything comes up.'

Chapter 13

Kinaldy College was five miles south of the town, surrounded on all sides by rich farmland. A board at the road end announced proudly it was a co-educational secondary school founded in 1956. A long tree-lined drive gave onto a gravel area in front of a modest sixteenth-century castle, typical of those found in this part of Scotland. The castle itself was well maintained, the exterior little altered from the original. To the rear a newer building appeared to provide the main school accommodation and they made their way towards this, following signs for visitors.

A young woman in a tartan pinafore sat behind a long reception desk and she moved to greet them as they entered. Chris introduced himself and Clare and the woman smiled.

'Who would you like to see first?' she asked.

'Ethan Robertson,' Clare said, and the woman picked up a phone.

'I forgot to ask,' Chris said, as they waited for Ethan, 'any luck at the Botanics?'

'No. Waste of time. I'd say whoever put Josh up to it was either watching when he was arrested or somehow got wind we'd lifted him.'

'I reckon...' Chris broke off as a tall man in a dark suit came along the corridor, a boy they now knew to be Ethan at his side. But the face that had grinned at the camera, frozen as the video preview had come to an end, was different now. This Ethan looked distinctly unsure of himself. She wondered what he'd been told or even if he'd heard about Sophie.

'Gregor Donald,' the man said, holding out his hand. 'I'm Ethan's class tutor.' Clare shook his hand and turned to the boy.

'Ethan?' and he nodded. 'I'm DI Clare Mackay from the police station in St Andrews and this is DS Chris West. Is there somewhere we can talk?'

Gregor Donald led them to a small room off the main corridor. It was more welcoming than the interview room they'd used at Albany High, with comfortable chairs arranged round a coffee table. A bookcase behind a mahogany desk was filled with books on French and German while the desk itself bore family photos and a neat pile of papers, a slender fountain pen to the side. 'This is the dep head's office,' he explained. 'He's at a conference today so he won't mind us using it.' He indicated the chairs. 'Please, make yourselves comfortable.'

Clare waited until Gregor and Ethan had sat, taking a moment to study the boy. He perched on the edge of the chair, clearly ill at ease. Perhaps he too had been made aware of the video. But did he know Sophie had died? Had he seen the news online? It must be everywhere by now. Surely someone would have told him, unless, like Sophie, he'd kept their relationship a secret. Had she called him when she'd learned about the video? They hadn't been through her call history yet but it was possible. It was time to find out.

'Ethan, am I correct in thinking you're in a relationship with Sophie Bakewell?'

He flicked a glance at Gregor, then back at Clare.

'Is that correct?' Clare repeated.

Ethan cleared his throat. 'Erm, yes. I suppose.'

'Sophie is your girlfriend?'

'Yeah. Like I said.' He eyed them as though wondering why he was there.

He doesn't know, Clare thought. *He can't, unless he's a bloody good actor.* 'Then I'm very sorry to have to tell you Sophie died on Monday morning.'

'No! What? Sophie? You're not serious?' He broke off, running a hand through his hair. Gregor Donald moved his chair so he was side-on to Ethan. He glanced at Clare then back at Ethan.

80

'I'm afraid so,' Clare said.

'How?' Ethan said. 'What happened?'

Clare ignored the question. 'Can you tell me when you last heard from Sophie?'

He looked at her for a moment. 'Erm, Saturday,' he said eventually. 'We went out. Pizza,' he added.

'Did she phone after that? Or text?'

He seemed to be struggling for the right words.

'I'll get us some water,' Gregor said. He left the room and they heard him cross the corridor and speak to the woman on reception. He returned a minute later. 'Joanne will bring us some drinks. It might be best if we waited…'

A minute later there was a tap on the door. Gregor rose and opened it, backing into the room with a tray which he set down on the coffee table. He picked up a jug and poured a glass of water which he handed to Ethan. The boy took it, his hands shaking.

'Have a drink,' Gregor said, and Ethan put the glass to his lips. Then he set it down on the table.

'Ethan,' Clare went on, 'we do need to ask you some questions. But if you want a break at any time please just say.'

Ethan nodded and Clare pressed on. 'Did Sophie and you text at all after Saturday night?'

'Couple of WhatsApps on Sunday,' he said. 'But Soph had some coursework so I said I'd message her through the week.' He met Clare's eye. 'What happened to her?'

She hesitated. He'd have to know. Was there anything to be gained by keeping it from him? 'I'm afraid Sophie took her own life,' she said, watching him carefully.

The choking sob that came from Ethan told Clare he had no idea of Sophie's distress and she wondered about that. Could he really have thought she wouldn't find out about the video? Maybe with it being a Romanian site he thought no one here would see it. Admittedly, the amount of porn there was online these days…

His eyes were brimming, lips trembling and she waited, giving him a moment to compose himself. He reached into his pocket and took out a crumpled tissue, dabbing at his nose. Then he blew it and replaced the tissue. Gregor nudged the glass towards Ethan and he took another drink, longer this time. Then he drew a hand across his eyes.

It was time to tell him.

'Ethan,' Clare said, 'I have something to share with you and it may come as a shock.'

He stared at her, his eyes wide, lips parted as if about to speak. When he said nothing she took out her phone.

'On Monday morning several of Sophie's classmates sent her a link to a website.' She tapped at her phone. 'I'm now about to show you the website.' She navigated to where she'd stored it and tapped to play the video, handing the phone to Ethan. She watched him carefully as the video loaded. It took him a moment to react, then he slammed the phone face down on the table, making Clare thankful for the screen protector. The sound from the video played on, a tinny and incongruous presence in this rather lovely room. Clare retrieved her phone and stopped the video, and for a few moments an awkward silence hung in the air.

Gregor glanced at them but Clare was watching Ethan, his head in his hands.

'I don't understand,' he said eventually, his voice muffled.

'What is it you don't understand?' Clare asked.

'That – that video. How is it online? It was meant to be private. Just Sophie and me.' His face was scarlet now, tear-streaked, far from the grinning lad in the video.

'You admit you recorded it?'

He was silent for a moment, then he nodded. 'Yes,' his voice a whisper. 'But Sophie – she was all for it. We thought it would be… well, you know?'

'You recorded it on your phone?' Clare said. 'And Sophie agreed to the recording?'

'Yeah. I mean, obviously if I'd known…'

Clare looked intently at him and when he met her glance she said, 'This is very important, Ethan.' She paused for a moment. 'I want you to tell me how the video found its way to that website.'

'But that's what I'm telling you,' he said. 'I don't know. I would never do that!' His voice was becoming shrill and Gregor put a hand on his arm.

'Did you share it with anyone?' Clare persisted. 'A friend? Brother? Anyone at school?'

He shook his head vehemently. 'Definitely not. It was private.'

Clare glanced at Chris, who took the hint.

'You strike me as a pretty switched-on guy,' Chris said. 'What's your best guess? How do you think it happened?'

Ethan was sobbing again, wiping furiously at his eyes. 'I don't know! I don't know what else to say. I have no idea.'

They tried a few more questions but either Ethan knew nothing else or was sticking firmly to his story.

'Okay,' Clare said. 'And now I'll have to ask you for your mobile phone.'

'Eh?' he said. 'You can't do that.'

'Ethan, whoever uploaded this film has broken the law. So I am within my rights to take your phone. If you don't agree we'll be forced to arrest you which will give us the power to seize your phone anyway. So…'

He met her eye, his face contorted with misery, and he held out his phone.

'Passcode please?'

He reeled it off and Chris noted it down. Clare thanked him and nodded to Gregor. He rose and followed them out the door, leaving Ethan in the room.

'I'll have to run him home,' Gregor said. 'He's in no fit state to go back to class.' He hesitated. 'You wanted to see another lad?'

'Josh McNeil,' Clare said. 'Is he one of yours as well?'

'He is.' He looked at his watch. 'It'll take me twenty minutes to get Ethan home then get back here. If you could wait…'

'We can see Josh by himself,' she said. 'He's old enough.'

Gregor frowned at this. 'We are in loco parentis, here. Let me ask Josh and see what he says.'

She was about to say she didn't need Gregor's permission but she didn't want to cause any more upset so she nodded and watched as he walked back to the reception desk.

Minutes later he reappeared with Josh in tow. Josh eyed Clare and Chris over Gregor's shoulder and, after a brief conversation, Gregor walked back across.

'Josh is happy to speak to you alone,' he said. 'I'll just fetch Ethan and be out of your way.' He disappeared into the deputy head's office, returning with Ethan. Josh eyed Ethan's tear-streaked face with something approaching alarm but he said nothing and followed Clare and Chris into the room. Chris closed the door and Clare indicated the seats.

'We won't keep you long,' she said.

Josh lowered himself slowly down, his eyes never leaving Clare's. 'Am I going to be charged?'

Clare's face softened. 'No,' she said. 'We're satisfied a formal caution is the best course of action. But I do want to ask you a question, and this time I'd like a straight answer. Okay?'

He eyed her for a moment. 'Suppose.'

'Good. So it's this: you admit you stole the iPad because someone made you do it, yes?'

Josh mumbled something Clare didn't catch.

'Sorry, Josh. I didn't hear that.'

'Yes,' he said.

'Were they blackmailing you? By that I mean threatening to do something if you didn't steal the iPad?'

'Yes.' His voice was little more than a whisper.

'Okay, Josh. Would you like to tell me what hold this person has over you?'

His head drooped and he said nothing.

'Then I'll tell you,' Clare said. 'I believe this person had a video of you in a compromising position and they threatened to put this video online if you didn't do what they asked.'

He stared at her as if not believing what he was hearing. 'How...'

'Am I right?'

Josh seemed to be working things out in his head before trusting himself to speak. Eventually he said, 'Not a video.'

'Then what?'

'Photos.'

'Photos of you?'

He nodded.

'Were you undressed in these photos?'

He nodded again, his face scarlet now.

'Was there anyone else in the photos?'

'No. Just me.'

'Did the photographs show your genitals, Josh?' Clare said, her voice as gentle as she could make it.

A single tear escaped from Josh's eye and began running down his cheek. For a moment he didn't speak.

'Josh?' Clare prompted again.

'Yes,' he said, his voice cracking.

She waited a minute. 'This next question is very important, so think carefully before you answer. Did you share these photos with anyone?'

'No,' he said. 'I mean I thought about it. Loads of folk in my class do it. Boys and girls. So I took a few and thought I might. But I was too scared to do anything.' He shook his head. 'I don't understand how they got hold of them.'

Clare's heart went out to him. Poor lad, trying to navigate the transition to adulthood. Whoever had his photos, however they'd done it, it clearly wasn't this lad's fault. 'Josh,' she said, leaning forward, 'that means you are a victim of crime. The person who accessed these photos and used them to blackmail you is guilty of a very serious crime. With your help we can find and charge them.'

He was shaking his head violently now. 'I can't,' he said. 'What will they say?'

'Who?'

'Everyone! My parents, the rest of the school? They'll think it's hilarious. I'll never be able to face them again.'

He was right, Clare thought. And that was how these people got away with it, knowing these vulnerable teenagers would be too ashamed to report it. But they had to try. 'We'll do everything possible to keep your name out of any prosecution,' she said. 'But we do need your help to find out who's responsible.'

'But that's just it,' he said. 'I don't know. I don't know how they got these photos. I don't even know who they are.'

'How did they contact you?'

'Text message. The first message had one of the photos.' He broke off for a moment. 'I couldn't believe it when I opened the attachment. Then the next message said it would be sent to all my contacts unless I did what they wanted.'

'Was the iPad the first time you'd stolen for this person?'

'Yeah.'

'Okay,' Clare said. 'We'll leave it there for now.' She rose from her seat. 'Do you want me to tell the receptionist you need to go home?'

He shook his head. 'No. It's fine. I'll go back to class.'

Clare smiled at him. 'You were very brave to tell us. Take a few minutes for yourself.' She fished a card out of her pocket. 'If you do remember anything else about this person – no matter how small – give me a call.'

They watched him head back along the corridor then made their way to reception and signed out. As they emerged into the morning sun, strolling towards the car, Chris exhaled audibly.

'I'll tell you this much,' he said, 'I'm bloody glad I'm not growing up these days.'

'I wouldn't worry, Sergeant. I can't see *Fifty Shades of Chris* taking the porn world by storm. Not unless you gave up the Wagon Wheels...'

Chapter 14

Sara was despatched to deliver Ethan's phone to Tech Support.

'If Diane's not there give it to Craig,' Clare said. 'I'll let him know it's on the way.'

Sara left and Clare tapped out a message to Craig. Then she sought out Chris and Max. 'Can we talk this over?' she said. 'I need to get my head round it.'

They followed her through to her office.

'Any biscuits?' Chris said, sinking down on a chair.

'Nope. And, even if I had, you could do with shifting a few pounds before the big day.'

He assumed an injured look. 'None taken, Inspector.'

'Let's start with Sophie,' Clare said, ignoring him. 'She's in a relationship with Ethan Robertson. He makes a sex tape...'

'Did Sophie consent?' Max asked.

'He says she did,' Clare said, 'and we've no way of proving otherwise. Let's assume they both consented.'

'No crime so far,' Chris said.

'Correct. But somehow that video found its way to a Romanian porn site. Whoever did that has committed an offence. Chris and I interviewed Ethan this morning,' she said to Max, 'and I'd say he knew nothing about it being on that website.'

Chris nodded. 'Agreed. But it doesn't mean he didn't share it with someone.'

'And if he did,' Max said, 'even if it was a friend, he's as guilty as the person who uploaded it.'

'He is,' Clare agreed.

'Will you charge him?' Max asked.

She shook her head. 'Too early for that. His phone's on its way to Tech Support. Let's see what they can tell us and take it from there. Meantime, any thoughts on our iPad thief?'

Max looked from Clare to Chris and she realised she hadn't relayed their conversation with Josh.

'He took some naked selfies on his phone,' she explained. 'He claims he didn't share them with anyone but he started getting text messages threatening to send the photos to all his contacts, tag him on social media – that sort of thing.'

'And you think it could be connected to Ethan's video?'

'It's a hell of a coincidence if it's not,' Clare said. 'Both boys are at the same school, remember.'

'So it's someone at school,' Chris said, and Clare nodded.

'Has to be.'

Max frowned. 'That's pretty serious stuff for a schoolkid.'

'They're not kids in the eyes of the law,' Chris said. 'And most teenagers are pretty clued up when it comes to tech stuff.'

They fell silent for a moment.

'I'm not sure where that gets us,' Clare said eventually. 'Unless Tech Support come up with something.' She checked her watch. 'Sara should be there by now. Depending on how busy they are we might get something back by the end of the day.'

Chris rose from his seat. 'I feel an early lunch coming on. Want a coffee?'

Clare shook her head. 'Think I'll nip out for a bit. There's something I want to check.'

–

Clare always enjoyed the drive along Strathkinness High Road, particularly in the summer months when the trees and hedges were in full leaf. The Fife Park building was missing its student population and, while the flats were no doubt occupied by tourists or those attending summer schools, the road was much quieter when the students were away. As she drove along, the houses became more widely spaced and much grander, and she thought it wouldn't be surprising if an elderly resident was a target for the unscrupulous.

Cliff Craven's was one of the last before the houses gave way to farmland on both sides of the road. A wide gate bordered on either side by neatly trimmed privet hedges was closed and latched and the road was busy with parked cars so she reversed back along until she saw a space. She climbed out of the car and walked towards the house. A garden gate stood open and Clare went through to find the house set back from an immaculately tidy garden. A curved drive in pristine pea gravel came to an end in front of the house and she took it in with something approaching envy. She did love her own Daisy Cottage but this house, a substantial early twentieth century building with its white-harled walls and protruding gables – it was quite something. She approached the covered porch which sheltered a door painted in a soft sage green, six small glass panels at the top, and she rang the bell.

For a few minutes she thought there must be no one at home. And then a sound came from within and she stood back to wait. The door was opened and an elderly man peered out. Cliff Craven, she guessed. His white hair was swept back, revealing a face lined with age and weathered with the sun. His blue eyes were alert, the hint of a sparkle but the whites were yellowed and Clare remembered this was a man who hadn't long to live. She held out her ID badge and introduced herself.

'Well I don't know what you want, officer,' he said, 'but I definitely didn't do it.'

She laughed at the joke and asked if she could come in. He moved back gingerly and Clare stepped into an impressive entrance hall. The polished floorboards either side of an Axminster runner were mahogany, matching the other woodwork. Several doors led off to the right, a wide staircase to the left. As he led Clare along the hall to a door which stood open she took him in. He'd been tall at one time, but he was hunched over now, his slippered feet shuffling along the carpet, his breath wheezing in his chest. His trousers, elasticated at the waist, hung loosely round his legs and his checked shirt gaped at the neck. *What a way to go,* – the inexorable decline that comes with a terminal illness. She thought of her own parents, still hale and hearty, as far as she knew. Would the day come when they too would be shuffling around, a bony hand with paper-thin skin feeling along the wall, for fear of falling? She didn't like to think of it.

She followed Cliff Craven into a small sitting room with windows to the rear of the house. A wave of heat hit her as she entered the room. In spite of the summer sun outside, he'd lit the gas fire. It was a north-facing room with heavy curtains partly obscuring the window and she had the feeling almost of stepping back in time – back to when Cliff Craven had been a younger, fitter man. He eased himself down in a chair next to the fire, stifling a groan, and indicated the chair opposite. Clare thanked him and sat down. She gave him a moment to catch his breath then she looked round at the room.

'You're nice and cosy here,' she said, and he nodded.

'I feel the cold these days.' And then he smiled back. 'So, Inspector, what can I do for you?'

She hesitated. It was a delicate situation. Rory Craven had said he didn't want his father to notice things were missing. But Hazel Sullivan had flatly denied taking anything. Might it be possible to raise this with Cliff without mentioning the missing items? She didn't want to upset an elderly man with a short time to live. But Rory had made a complaint and she had a duty to investigate.

'I had a visit from your son,' she said.

His eyes narrowed. 'Rory?'

'Yes. He was concerned for you.'

'Concerned for my money, more like,' Cliff said. 'He showed precious little interest before he knew I was on my last legs.' He broke off as a spasm of coughing overtook him. Clare rose from her seat.

'Can I fetch you some water?' The coughing eased and he took a crumpled handkerchief from his pocket and dabbed at the corners of his mouth. Then he replaced the hankie and nodded at Clare.

'Go on then,' he said. 'Let's hear it. What exactly is he concerned about?'

She took a moment, choosing her words. 'He noticed some – some items weren't where they usually were.'

'Items?'

'Items of value, I gather,' Clare said.

He studied her for a minute then a light came into his eyes. 'I don't suppose he told you I'd been entertaining a young lady, did he?'

'Have you?' she said, avoiding the question.

'Well if I have, it's bugger all to do with him.'

Clare softened her face. 'I think he is genuinely concerned for you.'

Cliff opened his mouth to speak but he seemed to be struggling for the right words. 'Young Hazel, well she's a breath of fresh air, you know? She's writing a book or some such thing and she comes here to find out about the old days.' A smile had crept over his face. 'I like her company,' he said. 'It's as simple as that.'

'What about money?' Clare said. 'Have you missed any lately?'

He inclined his head. 'What if I have? I've enough to do me.'

'So you have missed some money?'

'I honestly don't know. Rory, he takes money out with my bank card and he leaves it in one of the kitchen drawers. I pay the cleaning lady in cash and she gets me bits of shopping as well. But she always leaves a receipt.' He shook his head. 'I don't check it. I trust her. Mind you, she doesn't know that.'

Clare took out her notebook. 'Can I have her details please?'

'Her card's on the kitchen notice board.' He made to rise but she motioned for him to stay seated.

'I can check that,' she said, 'if you don't mind?'

He waved this away and she went on. 'Anyone else come to the house?'

He thought for a moment. 'Sometimes an old friend drops in. Not that often, though.'

'Any friend in particular?'

'No. It's mostly Hazel who visits. I very much doubt she's coming here to steal things but, frankly, if she is then she's welcome to them. She's brightening my days and I don't have many of them left.'

He began to cough again and Clare rose. 'I'll fetch your cleaner's details. Then I'll be out of your way.'

'Don't pay any attention to my son,' he said, between coughs. 'His concern for me has come a few years too late.'

Clare left him and made her way to the kitchen, at the end of the hall. Pushing open the door she found herself in a large square room with sun streaming in a west-facing window. The light oak units were dated but in good condition, the work surfaces clean and tidy. A ready meal from a local farm shop sat defrosting by the microwave, a tray set with a plate and cutlery next to it. She scanned the kitchen and her eye fell on a notice board next to another door and walking across she saw the door led to a utility room. The cleaner's business card was pinned neatly on the board and Clare took a photograph with her phone. Then she turned to survey the rest of the room. There were drawers below the work surface on two sides and she walked across to the first and drew it open quietly, moving along until she found what she was looking for: a bulldog clip securing a bundle of ten and twenty-pound notes. Anyone visiting Cliff and offering to make a cup of tea could easily slip the odd note out of the clip. She closed the drawer silently and made her way back out to the hall. Glancing in at Cliff she saw he'd fallen asleep, his head resting against the chair wing. She watched him for a moment then went softly down the hall and let herself out of the front door, drawing in a deep breath of fresh air. Then she walked smartly to her car, trying to shake an unaccountable feeling of sadness.

As she signalled to pull out she saw an elderly man emerge from a dark blue car and she watched him for a few moments as he clicked to lock the car then began making his way along the pavement, his progress slow but steady. He glanced up as he passed her car, his expression wary, and she wondered if there was more they could be doing to safeguard the increasingly elderly population. And then he was past and she started the engine. It was time to get back to work.

Chapter 15

Clare decided it was better to warn Rory Craven she'd visited his father. She checked her notepad and found his number.

'Craven,' he barked into the phone.

'Clare Mackay,' she said, 'Inspector at St Andrews station. We spoke yesterday – about your father?'

'Ah yes. You've spoken to the Sullivan woman.' It was more a statement than a question.

'I have, yes,' Clare said. 'And I've also spoken to your father.'

'You've what?'

'It wasn't possible for me to investigate properly without chatting to your father. I didn't mention any of the missing items, only that you had some general concerns.'

He was silent for a moment. 'And?'

'He admitted Miss Sullivan visits, he's quite confident she isn't stealing from him and, generally, he seemed quite relaxed about it. However, I plan to speak to his cleaning lady. If I have any concerns after that I'll let you know. Otherwise, I suggest you keep a careful eye on your father. He doesn't seem a well man.' A thought struck her as she was about to end the call. 'The items you think are missing…'

'I *know* they're missing.'

'Do you have photos?'

'Erm… I'll have a think. I might have something.'

Clare gave him her number. 'If you could forward them to me we'll log them as potentially stolen.'

Rory said he'd check through his photos and Clare ended the call. She swiped to find the photo she'd taken of the cleaner's business card. There was no address, just the name, Alma Hayder, and a mobile number. She dialled the number and when it went to voicemail left a message asking Alma to call.

As she put down her phone an email from Neil Grant popped into her Inbox. Sophie's post-mortem. She read quickly through the main points. Death was due to cerebral hypoxia, consistent with hanging. 'No real surprise,' she murmured. She considered if there was any need to delay releasing the body to the family. Admittedly it looked as if a crime had been committed and she was determined to go after whoever had uploaded that video. But, while that may have driven Sophie to hang herself, she didn't think they could bring any charges relating to the hanging. No, they'd have to go after the sexual harm element. Probably the best they could do for Sophie and her family.

She stared at her Inbox, willing it to display a message from Tech Support, and then she gave up and went to make a cup of tea.

'You're remembering I'm leaving early?' Chris said as she poured water onto a teabag.

'Yes, no problem.' She set down the kettle. 'How's the speech coming along?'

He rolled his eyes. 'That's the last time I tell Max anything.' He paused for a moment. 'I keep forgetting it.'

'Practice is your friend,' Clare said, slapping him on the back. 'Out loud,' she added. 'It's the only way.'

'You've been a best man, have you?'

'No. But I had a six-month secondment to Tulliallan,' she said, 'back in the day.' She shook her head. 'Teaching new recruits. Bored me stiff. But one of the other tutors told me to practise out loud before I went anywhere near the students. Give it a go,' she said. 'It works.'

He considered this. 'Can I use your office? To practise in?'

'Not a chance, Sergeant.'

'Harsh, Inspector. Harsh.'

By the time Chris and Sara left for their wedding rehearsal, chatting excitedly as they went, Clare decided she'd also had enough for one day. She'd called Tech Support on the off chance they'd been able to look at the mobile phones but Craig had said they'd been swamped.

'First thing tomorrow,' he promised and, with that, Clare had to be content. She called good night to Jim and went out to her car, throwing her bag in the passenger seat. For some reason she felt vaguely discontented with her day's work. Even if Tech Support managed to get something from Josh and Ethan's mobiles she felt sure whoever had uploaded the footage would have covered their tracks; probably used a burner phone and a VPN to disguise their location. It was likely they'd never know who was responsible. Cold comfort for Sophie's parents.

And then there was Cliff Craven. She'd liked him. In spite of his poor health there was still a spark of something in those eyes. He'd looked like a man who'd enjoyed his life. And now his son was sniffing round, fearful of losing his inheritance to Hazel Sullivan. Clare thought Hazel had seemed straightforward and honest. But was there something more to her interest in Cliff? A woman who worked as a personal trainer writing a book about local political history? It sounded unlikely.

A volley of barks cut across her thoughts as she stepped out of her car. Benjy cannoned into her, the DCI behind, dog lead in hand. He stooped to kiss her and took her bag from the car. 'I was thinking,' he said.

Clare locked the car and followed him into the house.

'Fancy eating out tonight?'

'Definitely! I've had a...' she stopped, about to say she'd had a rotten day, but she found she didn't want to explain. What had happened to Sophie, to Ethan and Josh – it was somehow so sordid and exploitative and she wanted to wash her mind clean of it.

He watched her, waiting for her to finish. 'You've had a what?' he asked, eventually.

She shook her head. 'The kind of day I don't want to remember.' She gave him a smile. 'Eating out sounds perfect. Only…'

'Only?'

'Nowhere that plays jazz.'

He raised an eyebrow. 'You telling me you don't like my piano playing?'

She smiled. 'You can have too much of a good thing, Al.'

Half an hour later they were both changed and ready to go. Benjy had been fed and was settled in the window enjoying the evening sun.

'I'll drive,' the DCI said, jingling his car keys. 'You can have a glass of something soothing.'

They climbed into the car and were soon cruising the streets, looking for a parking space. They found one in North Street near the cathedral and made their way to The Heron's Nest, a restaurant in South Street. Clare remembered interviewing the owner in connection with a fraud but now it was under new management and she put the case out of her mind.

The restaurant was busy and it was a few minutes before they were shown to their table. As they sat and menus were placed before them she recognised a voice and looked across to see Chris and Sara at a large table.

'Want to say hello?' the DCI said but she shook her head.

'I'm guessing that's the wedding party. I recognise the parents from the engagement do. I suppose the others are the best man and bridesmaids.' She watched them for a few minutes. Sara's eyes were shining with excitement, Chris watching her as she recounted some story that made them all laugh. Then he pulled her towards him and kissed the side of her face. Clare was glad to see them out enjoying themselves, so happy with each other.

'It's going to be a good wedding,' she said, watching them for a moment longer. And then her eye was caught by a man at a table further down the restaurant. It took her a moment to realise it was Rory Craven. He must have come from work, judging by his business suit. But his shirt was open at the neck, no sign of a tie. Perhaps he too had come home, too tired to cook or change his clothes. Pulled off his tie and discarded it on the back of the sofa. She held her menu up partly screening her face and took the opportunity to observe him. He had a glass of red wine in his hand and, as she watched, he took a long drink then put it down, lifting a bottle from the table to top it up. Opposite him sat two young people, their attention focused entirely on their mobile phones. She thought they were in their late teens or maybe early twenties. It was so hard to tell these days. The girl was small, petite with long curly hair framing her face, the lad taller. He was slim too, almost rangy in the way teenage boys often are, as they take time to grow into their frame. She watched for a few minutes and in all that time not one of them spoke. Was this Rory's family? His children? There was little sign of interaction or interest between the three and suddenly she understood why Cliff Craven might enjoy the attentions of a woman like Hazel Sullivan.

The young woman lifted her eyes from her phone and looked idly round the restaurant. Then she yawned without covering her mouth.

'Ready to order?' a voice said. Clare smiled politely and turned her attention back to the menu.

Thursday

Chapter 16

'Right,' Diane said into Clare's phone, 'there's quite a lot to unpick here.'

Clare drew a notepad across the desk and picked up a pen. 'Go on.'

'First of all, the lad Ethan's number is in Sophie's phone. It's stored as Evie but it's definitely him.'

'Okay.'

'Both boys – Ethan and Josh – have had messages from another number which we suspect is a burner phone.'

'Can you give me the number?'

Diane reeled it off and Clare jotted it down.

'But the really big news is both phones have been jailbroken.'

Clare knew the term but she wasn't sure what it implied in this case. 'Can you explain?'

'It's an app you download from a website. Once installed it removes software restrictions allowing the user to modify the phone. So, with iPhones, for example, you can only install Apple-approved apps and sometimes kids want to install something a mate's got on Android. Jailbreaking lets them do that. It's not recommended by the phone companies and usually voids the warranty. Plus it can leave the phones vulnerable to hacks. But lots of them do it anyway.'

'Including Ethan and Josh.'

'Yep. And, unsurprisingly, there was malware on both – the same malware.'

Clare was silent for a moment. 'Is that unusual?'

'Hmm, it is a bit. There are lots of malicious apps out there. But the same malware – lads at the same school? That does make me suspicious.'

'Me too,' Clare said. 'Is that it?'

'No. Josh forwarded his naked selfies to that other number.'

'The burner phone?'

'Yep.'

Again Clare thought for a moment. 'Can we be certain he forwarded them?'

'You're ahead of me, there. The malware installed would allow another person to take control of Josh's phone and forward these photos. If it was done during the night he'd likely not have noticed. Then whoever it was would delete it from the Sent folder.'

'So a hacker could send the photos to a burner phone and Josh would be none the wiser?'

'Exactly.'

'And I'm guessing Ethan…'

'Afraid so. There's an app called WeTransfer on his phone. It's hidden away but it's there. That video of him with his girlfriend was a pretty big file so he couldn't send it using a normal message.'

'He used WeTransfer?'

'He did. Or someone did.'

'Just so I'm clear,' Clare said, 'you think both boys' phones have been hacked in order to send the photos and video to another phone?'

'Yes, that's it.'

'And Sophie's phone?'

'Nothing there,' Diane said. 'Also, I've still had no reply from the liaison officer in Romania. I'll keep trying but I'm afraid the video's still up there.'

Clare asked a few more questions then went in search of Chris and Max. She relayed the conversation with Diane. 'If I'm right,' she went on, 'someone persuaded both boys to jailbreak their phones so they could be hacked.'

'Then we've got them,' Chris said, scraping back his chair. 'We just ask the lads who did it and pick them up.'

'It might come to that,' Clare said. 'But I'd rather whoever did it wasn't forewarned. Let's see what we can find out first. Start with social media. See if either of the lads have friends in common.'

'Bound to,' Chris said. 'They're at the same school.'

'So maybe our jailbreaker's at Kinaldy College as well. Have a look at their Facebook and Instagram.'

Chris shook his head. 'You are so old, Inspector. It's all TikTok and Snapchat these days.'

'Aye, whatever.' Clare's phone began to ring and she tipped her head towards the door. 'Go on, vamoose.'

'Rory Craven,' the voice said when she answered the call. Clare immediately thought back to the restaurant the previous night and wondered if he'd caught her staring at him.

'Just to say I've a few photos,' he said. 'Stuff missing from Dad's house. It's maybe better if I email them.'

She gave him an email address and he said he'd send them over. A minute later the message arrived. She clicked to open it and watched as the images began to appear. The first two were of the Dresden lace figurines. They looked quite old fashioned to Clare, the kind of thing her grandmother might have had. But there was no mistaking the delicate lacework. She recalled something about real lace being dipped in porcelain clay, the lace burning off as the clay was fired. Quite a process. But were these things still valuable? She opened up eBay and typed *Dresden lace figurines* in the search box. There were some for as little as ten pounds, others for hundreds. She couldn't see any like the photos Rory had sent. They'd need an expert to place a value on them and the budget wouldn't run to that. The next photo was of a cross-shaped medal with a red and blue ribbon. This must be Cliff's DSO. eBay was flooded with cheap replicas but, on further searching, she found the genuine medals could be worth a few thousand pounds. 'Definitely worth nicking,' she murmured, waiting for the last photo to load.

The screen filled with a splash of colour, a painting so vibrant she had to wheel her chair back to take it in properly. It showed dancers on a background that reminded her of stained glass windows. Scrolling down the email she saw the artist was Jamie O'Dea, not a name she recognised. A bit more googling told her he was from her home town of Glasgow and his paintings sold for a few hundred pounds each. 'Not a fortune,' she said, 'but worth it to someone.' But was that person Hazel Sullivan? Or was someone else stealing from Cliff Craven?

As if on cue her phone began to ring again; it was the number for Alma Hayder, Cliff's cleaning lady. She wanted to interview her face to face. See how she reacted.

'I'll be in town this morning,' Alma said. 'I can pop into the station in half an hour. Erm, what's it for?'

'Nothing to worry about,' Clare said. 'But I'd rather not discuss it over the phone.'

–

Alma appeared half an hour later, a neat pin of a woman, aged about sixty and pencil-thin. She wore dark trousers and a navy tabard over a T-shirt and she was carrying a canvas bag. Clearly on her way to a cleaning job. Clare led her to an interview room and she followed, her head down as though embarrassed by her surroundings.

'Please,' Clare said, smiling. 'Take a seat. I just need to ask a few questions.'

Alma sat, perching on the edge of the chair and Clare sat down opposite.

'I understand you do some work for a Mr Cliff Craven,' Clare began.

Her expression clouded. 'Yes,' she said, carefully. 'I clean for Cliff.'

'How often?'

'Mondays and Thursdays. I'll be over there this afternoon.'

'He seems a nice man,' Clare said, and Alma nodded.

'Lovely,' she said. 'Wish they were all like that. I think he fancies himself as a bit of a ladies' man,' she added. 'And he's eighty, if he's a day.'

Clare was glad to see Alma relaxing. 'I gather Mr Craven's in poor health,' she said. 'But I wondered how his mind was.'

Alma's face softened. 'Poor thing. I don't think he has very long left.'

'And his mind?' Clare persisted. 'Do you think that's affected?'

She shook her head. 'Not Cliff. There's nothing wrong with his head.'

'He's not forgetful? Putting things back in the wrong place – that sort of thing?'

Alma appeared genuinely puzzled by this. 'No,' she said. 'Sometimes I'll arrive and he's not washed his breakfast dishes but that's fine. I'm happy to do it.' She looked at Clare. 'What makes you think he's losing his mind?'

Clare watched her carefully. 'It seems there may be some items missing from the house.'

Alma stiffened in her chair. 'I hope you're not suggesting…'

'Oh not at all,' Clare said quickly. 'Mr Craven's son was looking for some items. I'm trying to establish if they might have been mislaid.'

This seemed to mollify Alma and she shrugged. 'Not that I've seen. He can't get upstairs, Cliff, and the downstairs is pretty tidy. I haven't noticed anything. Only…' she broke off.

'Yes?'

'There was a painting in his bedroom, upstairs – the room he used before he went into hospital. It was on the wall over the mantelpiece. Soon as I went in I saw it wasn't there.'

'Can you say when that was?'

'Not exactly. I don't do upstairs very often. Maybe once a month. The rooms are pretty much shut up, blinds drawn. It only needs an occasional dust.'

'When was the last time you were up there?'

She thought for a moment. 'Actually, I did go up last week. Cliff wanted something from his wardrobe and I had a quick look through the rooms, just to see everything was all right.'

'And that's when you noticed the painting was gone?'

'Yes. It stood out, you know? There was a mark on the wall where it had been.'

'Did you ask him about it?'

She shook her head. 'I assumed Rory had taken it. Maybe he thought he'd try and sell it. I don't know.'

Clare took out her phone and opened the email icon. She found the message from Rory and clicked to open the attachments. A minute later she held out her phone. 'Was this the painting?'

Alma's face cleared. 'That's the one. Have you found it?'

'Unfortunately not. I just wondered if you'd seen it anywhere else in the house?'

'No. Sorry.'

Clare thought for a moment. 'Who else visits Mr Craven?'

Alma's eyes widened. 'I've no idea. A couple of times I've seen another older man, maybe a friend; and there's that woman who's writing the book. I've seen her up at the swimming pool a few times. Think she works there.'

'The older man,' Clare said, 'do you know him?'

'Sorry, no. I'm not even sure he visits that often. But, like I say, I just do Mondays and Thursdays.'

'And you've never had any suspicions someone might be taking or moving things in the house?'

'No. But, if you ask me, it's probably Rory. Maybe he's realised his dad doesn't have long left and he's trying to deal with some of his stuff. Spread it out, you know? I remember clearing my mum and dad's house,' she said. 'Council gave us two weeks and it wasn't nearly long enough. Maybe Rory's trying to make things easier – for when the time comes.'

Clare decided there was nothing more to be learned from Alma and she thanked her for coming in. Alma escaped with obvious relief. Clare watched her go then wandered into the incident room. Sara and Robbie were poring over a laptop and they looked up when she entered.

'Boss?' Sara said.

'You guys know the town pretty well,' she said, and they nodded. 'Where would you go if you wanted to sell something?'

'What sort of stuff?' Robbie asked.

'Say, antiques – paintings – a medal?'

'Valuable?' Sara asked.

'A few hundreds' worth.'

They exchanged glances. 'There's a couple of junk shops,' Robbie said. 'But for more valuable stuff I'd say Retworth's.'

'Yeah,' Sara agreed. 'That's your best bet. You want us to go round there?'

'Yes please. I'll send you some photos. I need a description of anyone who might have sold the items or anything similar in the past few weeks.'

'We might be lucky with the CCTV,' Robbie said. 'Most shops keep it for a month.'

Clare took out her phone and tapped at it. 'That's the photos sent. Let me know how you get on.' She left them to it and went to make a much-needed mug of tea.

Chapter 17

'They've fifty-odd Facebook friends in common,' Chris said. 'Thirty of them are definitely at the same school.'

Clare lifted her head from a pile of paperwork. 'And the other twenty?'

'Most of them look about the same age. Might be they haven't added the school name to their profile.'

She sighed. 'It's too many. We'll have to ask them.'

'I did suggest that.'

'Yes you did.' She glanced at her watch. 'Probably lunchtime just now. Could you and Max head over there for just after?'

'Yeah, okay.'

Clare turned back to her paperwork then looked up again when he didn't leave. 'Yes?'

'I was thinking...'

She put down her pen. 'Spit it out, for God's sake. I've a mountain of work to do.'

He put a hand to his face and rubbed his chin. 'Do you – do you think I should open with a joke?'

She stared at him. 'At the school?'

'No! In my wedding speech?'

His face was full of concern and it took all Clare's self-control not to laugh. 'Oh, I don't know, Chris. It can sometimes sound a bit wooden – if you're not used to it.' She thought for a moment. 'What about a funny story from when you and Sara met?'

His brow creased as he considered this. 'There was the time she was called to help an old woman who was stuck in the bath...'

'No! For the love of God not the bath story.'

'The man who put his—'

'Nope.'

He thought for a moment. 'What about the woman who reported a man watching her from the garden across the road?'

Clare began to smile. 'I remember that. Wasn't it a life-sized dummy?'

'Yeah. Bought for Hallowe'en. Pretty realistic too. It was dark by the time Sara went to check it out. Scared the bejesus out of her.' He smiled. 'Thanks, Clare. That'll do nicely.' He took a piece of paper from his pocket and began jotting down notes.

'The school?'

'On my way.'

She returned to her paperwork and was lost in the station budget when the door opened and Jim came in. Before she could ask if it was urgent he cut across her.

'Triple nine call,' he said. 'Looks like assault and robbery. Householder's unresponsive.'

Clare pushed back her chair. 'Who's available?'

'Sara and Robbie are on their way now.'

She reached down and grabbed her bag. 'I'll follow on. Address?'

He passed a scrap of paper across the desk. She glanced at it: Strathkinness High Road. An anxious feeling was growing in the pit of her stomach. 'Who called it in?'

'Cleaning woman,' Jim said. 'An Alma Hayder.'

Clare headed for the side door, calling to Jim to get Chris and Max on the radio. 'Tell them to meet me there.'

It took her a little over five minutes to reach Cliff Craven's house. She pulled in behind Sara's car and jumped out, taking a forensic suit from the boot of her car. She stepped into it, pulling it up and over her head. Then she donned a face mask, gloves and headed up the drive to the house.

The front door stood open, Robbie stationed outside. A white-faced Alma Hayder stood beside him, her arms clutched across her chest. Clare approached, pulling her hood and face mask back.

'Are you all right?' she asked and Alma nodded.

'Bit of a shock,' she said. Her eyes were teary but she seemed calm enough.

'If you could bear with me for a minute,' Clare said, and she drew Robbie over to the side, out of Alma's earshot.

'Did she say anything?' she asked, her voice low.

'Only that the door was open when she arrived. She went in and found him. Then she called us.'

'Okay,' Clare said. 'I'll speak to her myself in a minute.' She turned back to the house. 'Had a look round?'

'Just a quick look. Didn't want to contaminate the scene. Sara's checking round the back but there's no one else in the house. Front door's been forced,' he added.

'What about the householder? Did you try to revive him?'

He shook his head. 'Too late. He's starting to stiffen up.' Clare checked the time. Half past two but that room had been warm when she'd visited Cliff the day before. That would certainly hasten rigor.

'Any sign of assault?'

'Not that I could see. But I didn't want to disturb the scene.' He glanced across to where Alma was standing. 'Cleaning lady says he lives alone.'

Clare nodded. 'He does.'

Robbie looked surprised. 'You know him?'

'I met him yesterday for the first time.'

She left Robbie pondering this and walked across to Alma, drawing her over to a garden bench.

The woman eyed Clare, but finally was persuaded to sit, one hand twisting a wedding ring on the other. 'He's dead, isn't he?' she said.

'I believe so. I'm so sorry. It must have been a shock. Maybe you could tell me what happened?'

Alma swallowed. 'I – er – I arrived just before two as usual.'

'How did you travel here?'

'Walked. It's a nice day so I walked up from the town. Mr Craven, he always says – he said to take a taxi – that he'd pay. But I wouldn't do that.'

Clare smiled. 'So you walked here. When did you notice something was wrong?'

'The door,' Alma said. 'It was open. Not wide but ajar, you know? I think someone forced the lock. It was like they'd taken a chisel to it. I thought Cliff must have been burgled and I was worried because he doesn't go out. Like I said earlier, he's not well.'

She broke off for a minute as though fighting back tears. 'So I went in and called out. I always say hello when I arrive. Anyway, I went into the room where he usually sits and…' The tears began to course down Alma's cheeks. Clare reached into her pocket and withdrew a packet of tissues but Alma took a hankie from her pocket. She wiped her eyes and blew her nose. 'Sorry,' she said after a bit. 'It's just seeing him there…'

Clare waited then Alma went on.

'I touched him, on the cheek you know, and that's when I knew. He was cold.'

'That must have been a dreadful shock,' Clare said, and Alma nodded.

'I've seen all these programmes,' she said. 'Knew I'd better not touch anything so I came out and dialled 999.'

'Very sensible,' Clare said. 'Can you think back to when you went into the house. Did you notice anything unusual?'

Alma's brow furrowed. 'Like what?'

'Anything out of place – something knocked over – things missing – that sort of thing.'

'No,' she said. 'I mean I could go back in and have a look,' but Clare waved this away. Out of the corner of her eye she saw Sara appear round the side of the house. 'I'm going to ask one of my officers to drive you home,' she said. 'We'll need a proper statement but, unless there's anything else just now, it can wait until you're feeling a bit calmer.'

She rose from the bench, leaving Alma seated and moved to speak to Sara.

'Anything round the back?'

The PC shook her head. 'Back door's secure. Shed and garage are locked. No windows broken.'

'Okay,' Clare said. 'Could you drive the cleaning lady home please? Then straight back here to start house-to-house. See if anyone saw anything earlier today or even last night.'

As Sara left with Alma, Chris and Max arrived and Clare explained what had happened.

'Been in for a look?' Chris asked.

'No. Robbie and Sara checked the house. I'll wait till SOCO get here.'

'No luck at the school,' Max said.

'Oh?'

'Yeah. Josh's class are away on a geography field trip and Ethan was off sick.'

'Tried his house?'

'We were on our way round there when Jim phoned,' Max said, 'so we diverted over here.'

A crunching of tyres on gravel announced the arrival of the SOCO van. Clare went to greet Raymond.

'That was quick,' she said as he jumped down from the van.

'Just luck. We were heading to another job but this sounded more urgent. What's the situation?'

'Front door forced, elderly man dead inside.'

'You been in?'

'Thought I'd better not. A couple of my officers have, though. Checked the victim and round the house.'

'Okay,' he said. 'I suppose you'll want a look?'

She indicated her forensic suit. 'Please?'

'Fair enough. Let me get suited up and we'll go in together.'

The house was eerily quiet when Clare stepped into the hall, moving carefully on the plates one of the SOCOs had put down to stop them disturbing any evidence. It was only twenty-four hours since she'd last been in this hall but somehow it felt different. It would shortly be crawling with SOCOs gathering evidence, a photographer recording the scene but, at that moment, the absence of life was almost palpable.

'Just in here,' she said to Raymond, indicating the room where she'd left Cliff sleeping the previous afternoon.

He was in the same chair, his head slumped to the side, the colour drained from his face. She took him in as Raymond moved closer. There were no obvious signs of injury, as far as she could tell. Maybe he'd heard the burglar and the stress had caused his heart to give out. Hopefully the post-mortem would help. As Raymond bent over Cliff's body she stood looking round the room. This time – the so-called Golden Hour before the forensic team moved in – it was so important. She stood behind his chair and tried to imagine what he would have seen. And then she looked back towards the door. If he'd heard a burglar he'd have turned towards it. Perhaps tried to get out of his chair. He'd have used his hands to lever himself up. But his hands were folded across his lap, almost as though he was only sleeping. Could he have died before the burglary? Slept away in his chair? It was possible.

She switched her gaze from Cliff and moved back to the door, her eyes sweeping the room. She was the burglar now – standing, looking into the room. What had he – or she – seen? What could they easily convert to cash? The TV was too big. They'd have needed a van to make off with that. Maybe Cliff had an iPad or laptop. Much easier to slip one of those inside a jacket. She tried to recall if she'd seen one on her previous visit but she wasn't sure. Her eye was drawn to a cable plugged into the wall. It seemed to disappear over the arm of Cliff's chair but she couldn't see the end of it. Most likely his mobile. There was something niggling at her. Something was wrong but she couldn't work out what it was. Raymond was muttering but, between his mask and her hood, she hadn't heard what he said.

'Sorry?'

'Petechiae,' he repeated, stepping back from Cliff's body.

'He was strangled?'

'More likely smothered,' Raymond said, and then she knew what was wrong in the room.

'That cushion.' She indicated a chair with a small cushion propped against the back. The cover was plain calico but the day before it had been a bright needlepoint pattern, different from the others which matched the curtains. She hadn't realised the back had a plain cover at the time but now she could see it was the same cushion turned round. 'Can you bag that please,' she said, 'whoever did this may have used it to suffocate him.'

Raymond nodded and continued his assessment. Clare was keen to see if anything else in the house had been disturbed but she didn't want to risk contaminating the scene. She retraced her steps, emerging into the afternoon sunlight. Chris and Max were waiting.

'Well?' Chris said.

'Looks like he was murdered,' Clare said. 'Smothered with a cushion, unless I'm wrong. But we'll have to wait for the PM to have it confirmed.'

'So what now?' Max asked.

She glanced towards the gate. 'Max, I'd like you to find any houses in the street with CCTV or video doorbells. Could be whoever it was tried a few front doors or even car doors. See if the householders have any video footage you can check; and get onto the press office too. No details yet but we want dashcam footage from anyone who drove along this road from…' she stood thinking for a minute. They didn't have a time of death. Might not have one for a few hours; and even then it wouldn't be a precise time. Cliff was dressed and she thought he was wearing the same shirt from the day before, but was that significant? Maybe he didn't put a fresh one on each day. Rigor had set in so it must have been at least a few hours earlier. He might even have been killed the night before. She wished she'd checked in the kitchen for any sign he'd made breakfast. But it couldn't be helped now. Better to play it safe. 'Let's say between three yesterday afternoon and ten this morning.'

Max took out his phone to call the press office and Clare turned to Chris. 'Come on,' she said. 'Let's break the news to his son.'

Chapter 18

Rory Craven had not sounded encouraging when Clare phoned, asking to come over.

'I'm at work,' he said. 'We're very busy.' But he'd relented and given them the address of his premises.

Craven Gelateria was a square flat-roofed building just outside Guardbridge, five miles west of St Andrews. Clare pulled into the car park and they walked towards a sign marked Visitors.

A thin-faced woman looked up from behind a desk as they entered, a professional smile fixed in place. Clare showed her badge and said Mr Craven was expecting them. The woman made no response but picked up a phone and tapped at it.

'Two policemen to see you,' she said.

Clare raised an eyebrow at this but said nothing. A minute later a door next to the reception desk opened and Rory Craven came out. His tie was loosened at the neck, his shirt straining at the waist and his expression was not encouraging. He stared at them.

'Well?'

'Is there somewhere we can talk please?' Clare said, conscious of the receptionist's eyes on them.

He turned without a word, tapped at a keypad next to the door which had swung shut behind him and pushed it open again, holding it for them to follow. He led them down a short corridor stopping at another door bearing his name with *Managing Director* underneath. He closed the door behind them and nodded at a couple of chairs pushed against the wall. Then he moved round the back of his desk and sat in a leather chair, swivelling left and right while they took their seats. The room was unpleasantly stuffy, a hint of sweaty armpits mixed with a foody smell Clare couldn't quite place. She glanced towards the window but saw it was shut. An empty plastic tub was on a tray next to the desk, a fork balanced on the edge, remnants of his lunch, she guessed. Something fishy – tuna, maybe.

'You caught the thief?' he said.

She took a deep breath. 'Mr Craven, I'm afraid I have some bad news.' She broke off for a moment to let this sink in. 'Your father was found dead at home this afternoon. I'm very sorry.'

He stared at her as if trying to take this in, then his hand went to his chin and he blinked a couple of times. 'I knew,' he said, eventually, 'I knew he didn't have long but I didn't think it would be so soon.'

Clare glanced at Chris, then back at Rory. 'It seems your father's house was broken into.'

He said nothing for a moment as if trying to take in what he was hearing then he sat forward, making the leather on his chair squeak. 'You what?'

'We're not sure what happened yet but there's a forensic team at the house now. It looks as if the front door was forced.'

The colour drained from Rory's face. 'Someone *did* this? Someone hurt Dad?'

'At the moment it's too early to be sure. But it is possible, yes.'

His eyes flicked left and right as though processing this. 'Did she do this? That Hazel woman? Is this her doing?' The skin on his face tightened. 'I'll bloody have her,' he said. 'You mark my words.'

Clare shook her head. 'It really is too early to say but I would doubt that's the case. This type of robbery – it's usually young men after whatever they can sell. iPads, jewellery – that kind of thing.'

He rose from his chair. 'I'd better get over there. See what's missing.'

Clare moved between Rory and the door. 'I'm so sorry,' she said. 'That won't be possible for a day or two. We have a team working at the house just now. It's important we don't do anything to disturb any evidence there might be – fingerprints, DNA – things like that.'

He stood for a moment, his eyes on Clare, then his face crumpled and he sank back down in his chair again. 'Was he – was he badly injured?'

'Not that we could see. But we'll have a fuller picture once the forensic folk have finished. In the meantime,' she hesitated, 'perhaps you could tell me when you last saw your father.'

He looked at her for a moment as though not understanding. 'Erm, the weekend. Sunday, I think.'

'And did you notice anything unusual? Anyone in the street who stood out?'

'No.'

'Did your father mention any other visitors? Anyone different?'

Rory spread his hands. 'No one comes to mind. That woman, obviously, and his friends sometimes. From his council days, you know?'

'Any friend in particular?'

'I can't recall their names,' he said. 'There is one who used to visit. Johnny... someone. Can't remember his surname. Not sure if Dad still sees him. And there's Alma of course,' he added, 'but she's been going to Dad for years. Anyway, she has her own key and you said the lock...'

Clare asked a few more questions but Rory didn't seem to know a great deal about his father's life. 'Is there anyone we can call for you?' she said. 'Other family members?'

He shook his head. 'I'm divorced. Ex-wife's in Spain with her new toy boy.' There was an edge to his voice and Clare wondered about that.

'Are you in touch with her?'

He reached for his phone. 'I've a number somewhere.' He pulled a notepad across the desk and, one eye on his phone, jotted the number down. 'Shirley,' he added. 'Mitchell – unless she's taken Pedro's name.'

'Pedro?'

He shrugged. 'I don't actually know his real name. That's what the kids and I call him.'

'It's fine,' Clare said. 'I'll take the number, but we shouldn't need to call her.' The mention of his kids took Clare back to seeing him in the restaurant the previous night. 'You have children?' she asked, keeping her tone light.

'Boy and a girl. Almost grown up. Marcus is in sixth year, Lauren – she's on a gap year. Couple of years, to be honest.' He rolled his eyes. 'When I was their age I couldn't wait to get a job. Trouble with those two is they've had it too easy. Handed it on a plate. Dad,' he explained, 'he gave them an allowance. They've never had a job between them. Not even a paper round.' He broke off for a moment then seemed to recover himself. 'They're good kids, though. They'll find their way.'

'Would you like us to let them know – about your father?'

'No, it's fine,' Rory said. 'I'll head home shortly. Marcus'll be home from school soon. I'll sort it.' He smiled at them. 'Thanks for coming to tell me. Sorry if I was a bit...'

Clare rose. 'Not at all.' She took a card from her pocket. 'I will be in touch,' she said. 'I'd like to speak to your children and,' she hesitated, 'we will need to take DNA from you all.' He raised an eyebrow and she hastened to reassure him. 'It's for elimination purposes – at the house,' she said and he nodded. 'In the meantime, if anything occurs to you, please give me a call. Anytime at all.'

Rory took the card and stood looking at it.

'We'll see ourselves out,' Clare said.

They crossed the car park slowly, Clare relieved to be out in the fresh air again. A cool breeze was blowing and the trees screening the building from the prevailing wind were swaying back and forth. She stood for a moment watching them, enjoying the rhythmical swishing sound.

'Believe him?' Chris said.

She forced her thoughts back to Rory and his reaction. 'Too early to say. You?'

'Seemed sound enough to me.' He glanced back at the building, one hand on the car roof. 'Might be worth checking his finances, though. See if he has any money troubles. That house in Strathkinness High Road…'

'I know what you mean,' Clare said. 'If the house is anything to go by he's about to become a very wealthy man.' She opened the car door. 'Let's see what Neil and Raymond say and take it from there.'

Chris climbed in beside her. 'Tell you what?'

'Yeah?' She started the engine.

'You drive and I'll practise my speech then you can tell me what you think.'

'Oh God…'

Chapter 19

'Right,' Clare said as Chris and Max carried coffees into her office. 'Where are we?'

'Press office put a shout out for dashcam footage,' Max said.

'No details?'

'No. Just wanted in connection with an incident on Strathkinness High Road earlier today.'

'Good,' Clare said, ticking this on her notepad. 'House-to-house?'

'Nothing yet,' Chris said. 'A few folk in the street have sent footage from video doorbells. Sara and Robbie will go through it as soon as they're back.'

Clare glanced at her watch. It was past four now. 'Might have to hand it over to the late shift.' She checked her notepad again. 'Raymond says the body's off to the mortuary now. Anything from Neil?'

'He's scheduled the PM for tomorrow,' Chris said, 'but it might be later on. Oh, one bit of good news.'

'Yeah?'

'Diane called. She's managed to get that video taken down.'

Clare smiled. 'That is good news. Any luck tracing the source?'

'Not a chance. Burner phone, VPN. She says we'll never find them. Better to track those two lads down and find out who jailbroke their phones.'

'Fair enough.' She sat thinking for a moment. 'I think we'll release Sophie's body to the family. And that lazy arsed FLO can leave them in peace.'

'If Cliff Craven was murdered,' Max said, 'you'll be needing an FLO for that.'

He was right. And what's more they would need a DCI as well. They were still pretty thin on the ground. She could only hope someone decent was available. 'I'd better call this in,' she said. 'See if they can find us a DCI. Meantime, could you two look into Craven's ice cream business? Get onto Companies House. See if the last few years' accounts throw up anything.' She glanced at her notepad again. 'Why have I written antique shops down here?'

'Cliff Craven,' Max said. 'Didn't his son think someone was pinching Cliff's valuables?'

Clare nodded. 'That's right. I sent Sara and Robbie off to look into it then they were diverted to Cliff's house.' She put down her pencil. 'Could it be connected?'

Chris shrugged. 'I can't see how. If Rory Craven's right these items were taken by someone visiting Cliff. But that, today – well the lock was forced for a start.'

'And Raymond noted petechiae,' Clare said. 'He thinks Cliff was suffocated. Would one of his visitors really force the lock if he didn't answer the door?'

'Maybe thought he'd died,' Max said.

Clare frowned. 'Then why break in? Why not call us? Or an ambulance?'

'Unless one of his visitors is the light-fingered thief,' Max persisted. 'Let's face it: if Cliff had died of natural causes this would be the visitor's last chance to lift whatever he fancied.'

'Or she,' Chris added.

They fell silent, considering this. 'Pretty farfetched,' Clare said eventually. 'The visitor wouldn't have had anything to force the door – not if they were just visiting.'

'Wasn't there a garden shed?' Max asked.

'Locked,' Chris said.

Clare put down her pen. 'It's immaterial until we hear from Raymond and Neil. So be a good pair of sergeants and see what you can find out about Rory Craven.'

'What are you going to do?' Chris said, earning him a look from Clare.

'I, Sergeant, am going to relieve that so-called FLO of his duties. Then I'm going to phone Hazel Sullivan to tell her about Cliff.'

—

Paul Henry could scarcely conceal his delight. 'Great,' he said. 'A nice early finish.'

'Don't make any arrangements for the next few days,' Clare said. 'I might need you for another job.'

'I'll check my diary. See how I'm fixed.'

She was about to retort when she thought better of it. To be honest, if she could get a different FLO for the Craven family she'd do it; and if she never saw Paul Henry again it would be ten years too soon. 'Don't forget to take the family through what happens regarding Sophie's body,' she reminded him. 'And Paul…'

'Yes?'

'Take a bit of time with them. Their world has just collapsed. So don't be rushing off, okay?'

'Anything you say, Inspector.'

She navigated to Hazel Sullivan's number and then thought she'd rather see Hazel's reaction face to face. Maybe even catch her at work – in a different environment. She put her phone away, logged off her computer and headed back out to her car.

Five minutes took her to the leisure centre. A woman in a pink sports top sitting at the reception desk looked up as Clare approached. Clare asked for Hazel and the woman tapped at her keyboard.

'She has a client. But she'll be free in ten minutes, if you can wait?'

There was a low *wuff* from behind the desk and Clare leaned forward to see Cassie curled up in a basket, a bright blue triceratops toy beside her. Her tail thumped against the side of the basket when she saw Clare but she made no effort to move.

The receptionist followed Clare's gaze. 'That's Cassie,' she said. 'She comes to work with Hazel sometimes.'

Clare smiled at the little dog. 'We've met.'

Cassie went back to chewing the toy and Clare elected to wait outside. She wandered across to a bench overlooking the East Sands. A few swimmers were braving the sea as the waves rushed in towards the sandy bay. A couple of lads were trying and failing to body-board. To the south-east the Fife Coastal Path led to Kinkell Ness, past the popular caravan site, perched on the higher ground. Somewhere distant a dog barked making Clare think of Benjy and she could hear children's voices carried on the wind, whether from the beach or the caravan park, she couldn't tell.

'Hello again,' a voice said behind her and she turned to see Hazel, wearing the same pink sports top as the woman at reception. Clare had to admit she looked the picture of health, her cheeks glowing with exercise.

'Are you taking me up on my offer?' she said, indicating the leisure centre. 'I've another client in fifteen minutes but I can pencil you in for an orientation session.'

Clare smiled. 'Maybe. But not today.' She let the smile fade. 'I'm afraid I have some bad news.'

In spite of her healthy glow Clare saw the colour drain from Hazel's face. 'Cliff?'

'Yes. I'm sorry, Hazel. He was found dead this afternoon.'

She sank down beside Clare and gazed out to sea. 'I suppose it had to happen.'

Clare took a moment, forming her words. 'We are treating his death as suspicious.'

Hazel's eyes widened, the surprise evident on her face. 'Seriously?'

'I'm afraid so.'

She stared at Clare. 'What happened?'

'It's too early to say. We'll know more in a day or two. But I thought you'd want to know.'

Clare watched her carefully as she took in this news. Was there more here than the normal shock and sadness that came with a sudden death? It was as if she was trying to work something out. 'Can I ask when you last saw him?'

Hazel stared at her. 'Am I under suspicion?'

Clare smiled. 'I'm just trying to establish Mr Craven's last movements. Who he saw, visitors to the house. That sort of thing.'

'Erm, Monday,' she said.

'Monday this week?'

'Yes.'

'Did you notice anyone hanging about? Or anything unusual? Anything different about Cliff?'

'No,' she said. 'He was the same as usual. A bit tired maybe but he often was.'

'No one watching the house?'

She shook her head. 'I honestly didn't notice.'

Clare nodded at this. 'That's fine,' she said. 'But if anything does come back to you please get in touch. And, as you were a visitor to the house, I'd like your permission to take a DNA sample.'

Hazel eyed her for a moment, then turned to look back out to sea again. 'Sure,' she said. 'Whatever you need.'

'Thanks, Hazel. I'll have someone call you to arrange it.'

Hazel said nothing, her face a mask. Had there been more to her relationship with Cliff than the book she claimed to be writing?

'I suppose that'll put an end to your research,' Clare said.

There was a pause then Hazel spoke again, her gaze still on the horizon. 'Oh no,' she said. 'Quite the contrary. My research is only just beginning.'

–

Clare pondered this as she drove home, via the supermarket. She had planned to pick up pizzas but remembering Hazel's offer of a personal trainer session she thought better of it and selected two ready-made salads. As she queued to pay for her shopping she wondered how Hazel would carry on with her research now

Cliff was dead. More to the point, why was she researching what seemed to Clare to be the most tedious subject on earth?

'Nine pounds, please,' a voice said and Clare reached for her purse. Walking back to the car she found herself thinking about Chris and Sara. It wasn't long now until the big day. She'd have to get them a gift – or maybe just a contribution towards the honeymoon. They were so different from each other, Sara so precise and careful in everything she did and Chris who bumbled along but got there in the end. Yet somehow it worked. They were going to be so happy. She just knew it.

For the first time in days she found she was smiling and she gunned the engine, turning the car towards home.

Friday

Chapter 20

'You'll need a DCI,' Al said over breakfast and Clare nodded, a slice of toast in her teeth.

'Already called it in,' she said. 'But I suspect they'll wait until we have the cause of death confirmed.' She eyed him.

'Don't even ask,' he said. 'I've my own job to do. Anyway, it wouldn't work, me supervising you. You're a bloody nightmare when you're on a case. My job's to point you towards the food and wine when you come home too tired to think straight. Speaking of which,' he went on, 'what on earth possessed you to bring home salad last night? Not that I'm complaining,' he added.

She wiped the toast crumbs from her mouth. 'Dunno. Thought I might book a personal trainer. Maybe for a few sessions.'

'They'll ask how much you drink,' he said.

Her eyes widened. 'Do they? Do they actually ask that?'

He rose from the table and carried his plate across to the dishwasher. 'Only one way to find out.'

-

'Right,' Clare said to the officers assembled in the incident room. 'Anything from house-to-house?'

'Nothing from speaking to householders,' Chris said. 'We have some door camera footage, though. Sara and Gillian are going through it now.'

'Any luck?'

He shook his head. 'Lots of folk coming and going but nothing significant so far.'

'Okay. Dashcam footage?'

'Nothing yet,' Max said. 'I'll ask the press office to put it out again on social media.'

Clare nodded at this and glanced down at her notepad. 'Max, I'd like you to arrange DNA tests for Hazel Sullivan and Alma Hayder, the cleaner. Both were regular visitors to the house so we'll need samples for elimination purposes.'

'Assuming they can be eliminated,' Max said.

It was a good point. 'Absolutely. There's nothing to suggest either of them's our killer but let's not rule anything out.'

'I reckon that Hazel woman's well dodgy,' Chris said. 'We can't ignore stuff going missing as soon as she starts visiting. And as for her writing a book about local political history, I don't buy it.'

Clare considered this. 'You could be right. But I've spoken to her twice now and she does seem nice. Not the kind of person to smother someone for a couple of ornaments.'

'Ted Bundy was apparently a sweetheart,' Chris said.

'Yeah, fair point. Okay. Let's see how she is when we take her DNA. See if it rattles her.'

'What about the Cravens?' Janey, an officer on loan from Dundee, said.

'I plan to see them this morning and I'll take DNA from them while I'm there.' She turned back to Chris. 'Anything on Rory Craven's business?'

'Maybe. His profits are down, from what I can see on the Companies House website. They were climbing steadily for the past five years but last year they dipped about 30 per cent.'

'Could be inflation,' Bill another Dundee officer said. 'Cost of everything's shot up.'

'Or capital expenditure,' Max suggested.

Clare acknowledged this. 'I think we'll get a warrant. Take a closer look at his finances. If the business is in trouble, and he thought his dad was suffering, he might have decided to help him on his way.' There was no response to this and she went on. 'Rory has two almost grown-up children. A son Marcus in sixth year and a daughter Lauren who's a year or two older. Both had been receiving an allowance from Cliff.'

'That rules them out, then,' Chris said. 'They lose out by his death.'

'Unless they're beneficiaries,' Max said. 'Maybe they knew Cliff had left them something in his will.'

'Let's find out. Chris, can you check who the family solicitor is please? We need to know who benefits by Cliff's death, and I'd rather not ask the Cravens if I can avoid it.'

Chris acknowledged this and Janey raised a hand.

'Could the cleaner have been stealing from Cliff?'

Clare scanned her notepad again. 'Who was checking with that shop – Retworth's?'

'Sara and Robbie,' Chris said. 'But you pulled them off for house-to-house.'

'Okay,' Clare said. 'Ask them to phone ahead to Retworth's and say we need their CCTV for – let's say the past three weeks. If they still have it,' she added. 'And we'll need photos of Hazel, Alma and the Cravens to compare with the footage.'

She scanned the room. 'One last thing: check on known offenders, especially any released from prison in the last few weeks, anyone bailed for housebreaking. Bill and Janey, can you take that please?'

The pair nodded and Clare was about to end the briefing when the incident room door opened and a tall figure in a sharp suit ambled in, kicking the door shut behind him.

Their DCI.

Clare's heart sank to her boots. Tony McAvettie.

–

'I really can't run an investigation without the use of my office,' she said, determined not to let Tony take ownership of it.

A smile spread over his face, languid, a hint of disinterest. He leaned back on his chair and crossed one long leg over the other. 'Relax, Clare. If it means that much to you I'll find another room to use.' His eye fell on her coffee mug. 'And, as I'm being so obliging...' he tapped the mug with his fingers, '...if you're making...'

Clare bit her tongue and rose from her seat. 'Want me to ask Zoe if she has any cake?' she said, referencing the time Zoe, her admin assistant, had baked Tony a cake laced with dog food after he'd toyed with her affections.

He laughed. 'Touché. Maybe not. I'll have one of your nice sergeant's Wagon Wheels instead.'

She sighed deeply, recalling yet another of Tony's indiscretions, when he'd slept with Chris's then girlfriend, resulting in Chris bursting Tony's nose. Honest to God, he was such a liability. Would they get through this investigation without him upsetting someone else in the station? 'Even if I knew where he kept them,' she said, 'you're the last person in the world he'd let have one of his biscuits.'

'Just a coffee, then,' he said, taking out his phone and swiping to unlock it. 'Two sugars.'

Clare found Chris and Sara in the kitchen, Chris's face like thunder.

'I've told him to ignore the DCI,' Sara said, 'but he won't have it.'

'Stay out of his way,' Clare advised. 'And keep your Wagon Wheels out of sight.'

Sara raised an eyebrow. 'What Wagon Wheels?'

He shrugged. 'Haven't had any for ages.'

'You're a shocking liar,' she said.

Clare took pity on her DS and changed the subject. 'Any luck with the doorbell CCTV?'

Sara shook her head. 'No one remotely suspicious. Just posties, DPD vans – that kind of thing.'

'Okay,' Clare said. 'Can you and Robbie get back onto looking for Cliff's missing items please? Start with the second-hand shop.

And you,' she turned to Chris, 'find me the Cravens solicitor!' She poured water into mugs and stirred two sugars into Tony's. 'I'm going to bring Tony up to speed then you and I will call on the Cravens.'

She carried the mugs back to her office to find Tony on the phone. From his side of the conversation and his self-satisfied smirk she guessed it was his latest love interest. She banged the mugs down on the desk, slopping Tony's over the side, and sat opposite, looking pointedly at him.

'Better go,' he said into the phone, one eye on Clare. 'Duty calls.' He put his phone down and nodded at it. 'Women, eh?'

Clare ignored this. 'Let me fill you in,' and she related the events of the past few days.

'And you've not found the porn king?' he asked.

'Or queen. Doesn't necessarily mean it's a man who shared the footage. But no,' she added. 'Whoever did it used a VPN and a burner phone.'

'Best forget that one,' he said. 'Needle in a bloody big haystack.'

Clare made no reply to this but went on to explain about Cliff Craven. 'I've a couple of cops going round the second-hand shops,' she said. 'We might get lucky there.'

'Any dashcam footage for the day he died?'

'Not so far but the appeal's going out again this morning.'

Tony drew Clare's box of tissues across the desk and mopped the coffee spill. Then he picked up the mug and slurped from it. 'Any warrants needed?'

'Yes, I think so. I'd like to look into the victim's family.'

He raised an eyebrow. 'Reason?'

'Just being thorough. I reckon the victim was worth a bob or two. Big house on the edge of town – gave the grandkids an allowance.'

Clare's phone began to ring. Raymond. 'I have to take this,' she said, swiping to answer the call.

'Your cushion victim,' Raymond began.

'Hold on,' she said, clicking to put the phone on speaker. 'Okay, go on.'

'First of all, positive match for saliva on the cushion.'

'So he was smothered?'

'It's highly likely. We'll check it for DNA from whoever held it over the victim's face. Might get something off it. But there's a complication.'

'Oh?'

'The front door.'

'What about it?'

'It was forced from the inside.'

'Eh?'

'The lock was damaged from the inside.'

'How can you tell?'

'Direction of the marks. That and the fact the door was open when it was forced. I say *forced* but it wasn't really.'

'Someone damaged the door while it was open?'

'I'd say so.'

'To make it look as if it had been forced?'

'You're the detective,' Raymond said. 'But, on balance, it's consistent with that theory.'

Clare thanked Raymond and put down her phone.

'So it's an inside job,' Tony said.

'Looks that way.' She was quiet for a moment, turning this over in her mind.

'You're not convinced?'

She leaned back in her seat. 'I dunno, Tony. Something about it doesn't feel right.'

'Murder generally isn't. You got an FLO with the family?'

'Not yet. We had one for our suicide victim's family but he's gone now.'

'Easy enough to get him back,' Tony said. 'Who was it?'

She hesitated. 'Paul Henry.' She was about to explain the issues she'd had with him when Tony's face broke into a smile. 'Paulie! He's a good lad. Trained him myself,' he added.

Clare sighed inwardly. That explained a lot. 'I might see if someone else is available.'

'I'll give him a bell. Have him up by lunchtime.'

There didn't seem any point in arguing and she forced her thoughts back to the case. 'As I said, I'd like a warrant to invest-igate the Cravens. All of them, including the victim.'

He nodded. 'Makes sense. You draw it up and I'll authorise it. Better find out who benefits by his death,' he added.

'Chris is on it,' Clare said, drawing her computer keyboard across the desk. 'So the sooner we get that warrant the better.'

Chapter 21

'I've moved my Wagon Wheels,' Chris said as Clare bounced her way along the speed bumps on Lamond Road. 'They're in the boot of my car now.'

She glanced at him, signalling to turn right. 'Bit risky, isn't it?'

'Up here,' Chris said, pointing towards the Grange Road that led south, out of town.

'Sara's bound to find them.'

'Doesn't matter. I'd rather risk Sara's wrath than have that prick finding them.'

'You mistake him,' Clare said. 'That would require effort. When did our Tony ever do anything that took work?'

He shrugged. 'I'll take my chances, all the same. Just here,' he said. 'Or a bit further along. I think it's that modern one on the end.'

Clare pulled up outside a modern detached house finished in a blend of white render and dark grey cladding. A glass-fronted balcony on the upper level looked north towards St Andrews, with two patio chairs and a small table. 'Nice spot to have a drink,' she said.

'Nah. North facing.'

'Suppose.' She looked towards the drive where a black Audi sat next to a pink VW Beetle convertible. 'Looks like they're at home.'

'You going to mention the lock being forced from inside?'

'Not yet. Let's see whàt they can tell us.'

They walked across the monobloc drive towards the front entrance, Clare taking it all in. The house was different in character from the neighbouring properties – clearly a newer build.

She'd heard about kit houses and she wondered if this was one. Max would know, she thought, recalling her DS's obsession with house renovations. The grass was neatly trimmed, two narrow borders planted out with red geraniums alternating with silver-grey cinerarias. It was all very neat and tidy – like the house – but somehow it lacked personality.

'They're not short of a bob or two,' Chris said, indicating the cars, and Clare nodded. She pressed the bell and stood back to wait. After a minute the door opened and Clare came face to face with the girl she'd seen sitting with Rory in the restaurant the other night. The light had been dim in The Heron's Nest but now, with the benefit of daylight, she saw the resemblance to Rory. This must be Lauren Craven.

She was shoeless, with scarlet toenails, part of a tattoo visible on her ankle. Her hair was swept over one shoulder and, while she wore no make-up, she was striking, with olive skin and dark eyes. Without shoes she seemed even smaller than she had in the restaurant. She raised one foot and tucked it behind the other leg, a self-conscious gesture Clare thought, perhaps in response to them being so much taller. She stared up at them. 'Yeah?'

Clare held out her badge and introduced herself and Chris. 'I'm guessing you must be Lauren,' she said.

The girl stood back to let them in. 'Dad's in the kitchen.'

She led them through to a large room with a kitchen at one end and a sofa at the other. There were patio doors out to a garden which, from what Clare could see, was laid mainly in grass, a high fence beyond; and in front of the doors Rory Craven sat at an oak dining table, tapping at a silver MacBook.

He was casually dressed in salmon pink shorts and a white polo shirt. He rose to greet them and Clare saw he wore brown leather sliders on his feet.

'Coffee?'

She smiled. 'Only if you're having one.'

'Lauren'll do it,' he said looking round. But his daughter had vanished and he wandered across to the coffee machine.

'How are they?' Clare asked, as he took mugs from a cupboard. 'Your children, I mean.'

'Okay, I suppose. A bit quiet. But they knew he was dying. So it wasn't a complete shock.'

'You told them about the forced entry?' Clare said.

'Kind of.' He turned back to face her. 'I didn't want them upset. Didn't want them thinking their grandad had – you know – suffered. Erm, milk? Sugar?'

'Just milk in both,' Clare said. She indicated the MacBook. 'Working from home?'

'Supposed to be. Hard to concentrate, though. There's so much to do; and it doesn't help not being able to get into Dad's house.'

'We shouldn't be too much longer,' Clare said.

Rory carried the mugs over and put them on the table. Then he closed the MacBook and moved it to the end. 'Please,' he said. 'Take a seat.' He waited until they had sat then he resumed his own seat. 'So, any news? You arrested that Hazel woman yet?'

'We do have some news,' Clare said, dodging the question. 'About your father's death.'

He stared at her. 'Go on, then. Let's have it.'

'The post-mortem is being done today so we don't have an official cause of death yet. But traces of your father's saliva were identified on a cushion found near to his body.'

Rory's eyes narrowed. 'Cushion? What cushion? You mean…'

'It's possible the cushion was used to suffocate your father.'

The colour drained from Rory's face and he swallowed a couple of times. 'Dad was – smothered?' His voice was hoarse.

'We think so,' Clare said. 'But for a man in your father's condition, I think he would have lost consciousness quite quickly. He wouldn't have suffered for long.'

Rory sat back in his seat. His mouth opened and closed as though he was struggling for the right words. 'Could a woman have done this?' he said eventually.

'Mr Craven…'

'I'm asking you,' he said, his voice level, 'if a woman could have done it.'

Clare watched him for a moment. 'It's possible,' she said at last. 'But...'

'Then why are you here and not out arresting her? It's not enough she was robbing him blind. She has to kill him as well. What happened, eh? Was she helping herself to something when he saw her? You know she's some kind of keep fit coach? More than a match for an old man, wouldn't you say, Inspector?'

Clare let him talk on for a bit and when he seemed to have run out of steam she said, 'We are looking carefully into everyone who had access to your father's house. If there is anyone else, you need to tell us.'

He nodded but made no reply and she pressed on.

'As I said yesterday, we'd like to take DNA samples from you and your children.'

He eyed her for a moment but still said nothing.

'We expect to find different DNA profiles in your father's house,' Clare went on. 'Every time someone visits they leave some sort of trace. If we know a particular profile belongs to a family member we can ignore that. It saves us time,' she added, hoping this would persuade him.

He was silent for a moment. 'And you'll test her? Hazel?' he added, his lip curling as he said her name.

Clare nodded. 'And Mrs Hayder, the cleaning lady. So, if there is anyone else who visits your father it would be helpful to know.'

'Makes sense,' Rory said. 'I'll have a think. You want to do it now?'

'If you don't mind.'

He scraped back his chair. 'Sooner the better. I'll fetch the kids.' He stopped for a moment then turned back to Clare. 'Just give me a minute to tell them – about Dad.'

He returned a few minutes later with Lauren and the tall lad Clare had seen in the restaurant, Marcus, presumably. They hung back, behind their father as if unsure how to deal with this new development. Lauren's hands were driven deep into her pockets and despite her tear-stained cheeks, her head was raised, chin stuck out. A show of defiance, Clare thought. The lad's face was stony and he eyed them, looking from Clare to Chris.

'Dad says you want our DNA,' he said, his voice flat.

'It really would help,' Clare said. 'We'll be isolating lots of DNA profiles at your grandad's house. If we know some of them belong to the three of you we can disregard them.'

Marcus glanced at his sister and she gave a shrug.

'If it helps find out who did it,' she said. 'You want to do it now?'

Clare indicated the chairs. 'Why not sit down first. Tell us about your grandad.'

Lauren stood for a moment then she nodded to her brother and the pair sat. Did he always take direction from his sister? Clare couldn't help contrasting their body language, Marcus perched on the edge of his chair, Lauren leaning forward, her arms on the table.

'What do you want to know?' Lauren asked.

'How often did you see him?'

'Not that often. Weekends sometimes.'

'And when was the last time?'

Lauren brushed a speck of something off her top. 'Not last Sunday but the one before. Marcus was with me,' she added.

Clare eyed the lad. 'And was that the last time you saw your grandad?'

He flicked a glance at his sister then back at Clare. 'I was there again two days later.'

Something flashed across Lauren's eyes. It was brief, but not brief enough for Clare to miss. Was it annoyance? And, if so, was she annoyed because he'd gone without her or because he hadn't told her? She was starting to think Marcus didn't do anything without his sister's say-so.

'I didn't know that,' she said.

'Don't tell you everything.'

'I don't get it,' she persisted. 'Why did you go?'

'He asked me.' He glanced at Rory, who was watching him as well. 'He wanted some painting taken off the wall.'

Rory straightened in his seat. 'What painting?'

'That thing in the black frame. In his old bedroom,' he added. 'The Jamie O'Dea?'

Marcus shrugged. 'Yeah. The one with the dancers. Loads of colour.'

Rory stared at him. 'So you took it down?'

'Yeah.'

'Did he say why he wanted it?'

Marcus shrugged. 'Said he missed seeing it – since he couldn't get upstairs. I offered to hang it downstairs but he said just to leave it down for now.'

'Was it a particular favourite?' Clare asked.

Rory nodded. 'Anniversary present a few years ago. From the kids and me. Dad chose it.' He turned back to his son. 'Where did you leave it?'

'Propped it up on a chair – so he could look at it.'

'Which chair?' Clare asked.

'The one on the other side of the fireplace. I thought he'd see it better there.'

'Well it's not there now,' Rory snapped. 'Why the hell didn't you tell me?'

Marcus looked blankly at him. 'You didn't ask.'

Clare cleared her throat and they turned to look at her. 'Could your father have moved it again? Would he have been strong enough?'

Rory ran a hand through his hair. 'I mean, maybe.' He glanced at Marcus. 'Was it heavy?'

'Not really. I reckon he could have put it somewhere else – if he'd wanted to.'

Clare smiled at Marcus. 'Did he ask you to move anything else? That day or maybe on another visit?'

'No. Just the painting.'

'Are we gonna do this DNA thing?' Lauren asked. 'Only, I need to go out.'

Rory raised an eyebrow.

'Just seeing some people,' she said, an edge to her voice.

He watched her for a moment then he gave a flick of his hand. 'Course. Let me know when you'll be back.'

Clare reached down for her bag. 'We'll do the tests now,' she said, 'then we'll get out of your way.'

–

'What do you reckon?' Chris said as they drove back to the station.

'The Cravens? Not sure. Rory Craven certainly seemed shocked when we told him about the cushion.'

'Agreed,' Chris said. 'I think that was genuine. But the kids…'

'I know what you mean,' Clare said. 'Mind you, we call them kids – they're both adults, really. And they'd had a day to get used to it. But Lauren – she was more bothered her brother had visited Cliff without telling her.'

'Yeah. I reckon she wears the trousers. Odd about that painting, though.'

'Not really. Strikes me Rory Craven's looking for an excuse to have a go at Hazel Sullivan.'

'You like her, don't you?'

Clare signalled to turn right into Tom Morris Drive and slowed to let a stream of cars pass the junction. 'She's all right.'

'Don't let it cloud your judgement,' Chris advised.

'Okay, Dad.' A gap appeared in the traffic and Clare took her chance. 'Check my phone, would you? I messaged Jim to see if that painting's still in the house.'

Chris picked up her phone and tapped in the passcode. Then he squinted at the screen. 'What the hell are all these apps? Can you even play chess?'

'Just check my messages.'

He was quiet for a minute, scrolling through messages. 'No sign of the painting,' he read.

Clare turned into the station car park and backed into her usual space. 'You reckon Marcus is telling the truth?'

'About the painting?' Chris considered this. 'Yeah, I'd say so. I doubt he'd know if it was valuable or not.'

Clare clicked off her seat belt. 'Agreed. But if Cliff did like that painting so much he asked Marcus to bring it downstairs, where is it now?'

Chapter 22

'Got DNA from the two women,' Max said, as Clare and Chris entered the station. 'Hazel and Alma,' he added.

Clare nodded her thanks and he went on.

'Sara and Robbie are at Retworth's now. Hopefully they'll be back soon with some footage.'

'They have photos of the missing items?'

'They do.'

'Thanks, Max. We have the Cravens' DNA here, as well. Could you arrange for someone to take all the samples over to the lab in Dundee?'

'Will do.' He hesitated.

'Something up?'

'The DCI…'

Clare groaned. 'What about him?'

'Neil phoned, wanting to start Cliff Craven's PM. Tony – he said…'

'Let me guess – he'd try to make it but was tied up and Neil should start without him, yes?'

'Pretty much.'

Clare shook her head. 'When was this?'

'Not long after you'd left for the Cravens.'

Clare checked her watch. By the time she headed over to the mortuary she'd have missed most of it. 'Thanks, Max. I'll catch up with Neil once it's over. Is that it?'

'Cliff's solicitor. We've tracked her down. It's Valerie Grimmond.'

Clare raised an eyebrow at Chris. 'Weren't you meant to do that?'

He shrugged. 'I was with you. At the Cravens,' he added helpfully.

She turned back to Max. 'Name rings a bell.'

'Jim says you dealt with her on another case. Those hit and run deaths?'

'Ah yes. Got her. Has she said anything?'

'Not yet. But she's going to call back once she's checked Cliff's will.'

Clare thanked Max and was making for her office when Jim stopped her. 'Got some dashcam footage coming in. A couple of drivers went along the street, different times of the morning.'

Clare smiled. 'It's a long shot, Jim, but you never know. Might spot someone.'

'Aye. The DCI's still in your office, by the way. Want me to sort him out a room?'

'Please.' She made her way to her office and stopped outside the door at the sound of voices. At first she thought Tony was on the phone again, chatting up his latest conquest. And then she heard another voice. She pushed open the door to find Tony sitting behind her desk with Paul Henry sprawled opposite, his feet up on another chair. He made to sit up when he saw her but she was too quick for him and kicked the chair away, knocking it over.

'Temper temper,' Tony said, a grin spreading over his face. 'Young Paul here was just relaxing before heading over to the Cravens.'

Clare glared at Paul and held open the door. 'Out,' she said. 'I'll call you back in when I want you.'

His eyes widened and he glanced across at Tony who gave a noncommittal shrug. Paul stood and very deliberately set the chair back up then he strolled out of the office. Clare resisted the temptation to slam the door. She stood, waiting for Tony to vacate her seat. 'Jim's sorting you out an office,' she said as he got to his feet.

He studied her for a moment. 'You want to relax, Clare. It's not good for you, all this stress.'

She pressed her lips together, not trusting herself to speak. And then as he wandered to the door she said, 'One more thing.'

He turned, his hand on the door, 'Yeah?'

'You're the senior officer here. I do know that. But this is my office and if you ever let that little shit over the door again I will not be responsible for my actions.'

He laughed. 'Seriously, Clare. Chill out.' He opened the door then stopped. 'Pop into whatever cubby hole Jimbo puts me in, say, twenty minutes? Bring me up to speed.' And with that he ambled out of her office. She stood for a moment, breathing deeply, trying to get hold of her temper. Then she followed him out and nodded at Paul Henry, who was leaning against the wall, his arms folded.

'Incident room.' She marched off, leaving him to trail in her wake.

'This job,' she said, launching straight in to avoid the need for small talk. 'It's different from the last one. Cliff Craven was killed by someone who took a chisel to the front door lock to make it look as if it had been forced.'

'It was done from the inside?'

'Yep. But the family don't know that and, at this stage, I do not want them told. Got it?'

He shrugged 'Sure. They in the frame for it?'

'Too early to say. They seemed pretty shocked he was murdered. Well, the victim's son did at least. He's Rory Craven. Has an ice cream business but he's working from home just now – laptop at the kitchen table. His son Marcus is in his final year at school but obviously not in today. And there's a daughter, Lauren. Bit older than Marcus. She might not be there when you arrive.'

He nodded. 'Anything else I should know?'

'Rory thinks someone was stealing from his dad – ornaments, a painting and a medal, possibly valuable. He's convinced it's a woman called Hazel Sullivan who was calling on Cliff. But, so far, we've no evidence to support that.'

'Cool. So you want me hanging around? Ears open?'

'Mostly, yes. But bear in mind they have lost a father and grandfather. Clearly it's not as tragic as Sophie's death but it's still a big loss for them. So go easy, yeah?'

'You're the boss.'

She watched him go, wondering if she was being too hard on him. The family liaison role was such an important one. But was he up to the job?

–

'No real surprises,' Neil Grant said, when Clare phoned later that day. 'He was suffocated – something held over his airways, possibly Wednesday night or Thursday morning.'

'Would a cushion have done it?'

'I'd say so.'

'Any defensive wounds?'

'Nothing on his hands. But the chair he was found in was quite an upright one so it's possible whoever did this could have been standing in front. If so, you might find bruising on their shins.'

'Anything else?'

'No, pretty straightforward.'

Clare thanked him then called Paul Henry.

'Just arrived,' he said.

She relayed her conversation with Neil. 'If you get the chance, see if any of them have bruising to the shins. If so, try to find out how it happened. But subtle, mind.'

Her office door opened as she ended the call and Max looked in. 'Cliff's solicitor,' he said. 'The will.'

'Go on.'

'Ten thousand to each of the grandkids, a bequest to the National Trust and the rest to Rory.'

Clare considered this. 'No real surprises.'

'Nah. Mind you, the solicitor reckons the whole estate will be worth a fair bit. Apparently he was insured for a tidy sum as well. Definitely inheritance tax territory.'

'Hmm. Any sign of that warrant? I want to know if Rory Craven was in financial trouble.'

'Not yet. But if Cliff was dying, why would Rory risk a murder charge? He'd have had the money in a few weeks anyway.'

'Estates like Cliff's can take ages to sort out,' Clare said. 'And a few weeks can make a world of difference if a business has cash flow problems.'

'Suppose.' He turned to leave but Sara appeared in the doorway.

'Something you should see.'

Clare followed her to a laptop in the incident room. 'I've been going through Retworth's CCTV footage. Still hours to go but...' She clicked to play the footage. Clare sat down beside her and peered at the screen.

'Isn't that...' Sara said.

'Hazel Sullivan. Yes it is. Can you see what she's doing?'

'It's not that clear. The shop's really busy and there's a big man who keeps getting between Hazel and the camera. He's there when she enters the shop.'

'So you can't see if she brought anything in with her?'

'No. She did have a shopping bag, though.' Sara jabbed the screen. 'There,' she said. 'That's big enough for those figurines, isn't it?'

'Definitely. What about when she leaves?'

Sara moved the footage on a minute then let it play. The man was still standing between the camera and the counter but as Hazel neared the door she passed him, her face clearly visible.

'It's definitely her,' Clare said. 'Can you get over to the shop please? See if the owner remembers if she brought anything in to sell.' A thought occurred to her. 'I suppose you've checked the shop for Cliff's missing items?'

Sara's face coloured. 'I'll get onto that,' she said. 'Sorry. I didn't think.'

Clare waved this away. Sara was normally so diligent and it wasn't long until her wedding to Chris. She had a lot on her mind.

She found Tony in one of the interview rooms, engaged in seeing if he could stretch his arms out far enough to touch the front and back walls at the same time.

'Compact and bijou, I think we'll call it,' he said as Clare entered the room.

'Good to see you're busy.'

'Delegation, Inspector,' he said. 'It's the art of good management, you know.'

Clare ignored this. 'We've had a development.'

Tony listened as she explained about Hazel in Retworth's shop.

'Sara's heading back there now to see if the owner remembers her.'

'What was the date stamp?'

'Just over a week before Cliff was killed.'

'You bringing her in?'

'Probably. But I'll wait to see what Sara can find out first. I'd like to search the house,' Clare said, 'but simply being in that shop isn't enough. We need more.'

'Appeal to her better nature,' Tony said. 'She might let you search the house without a warrant.'

'And pigs might fly.'

'See what the fair Sara brings back first. Speaking of whom, when's the happy day?'

'You mean you've not had an invitation?' Clare said in mock astonishment. 'They must have missed you off the list.'

'Seriously,' he said, 'you've a murder and a suicide to deal with and those two are about to go off on leave.'

He had a point. She didn't fancy trying to carry on this investigation without Chris and Sara. 'We'd better get it wrapped up, then,' she said and left him pacing the room, trying to work out if it was bigger than a prison cell.

Back in her office she called up the staff rota, wondering how she could rejig it to cover Chris and Sara's leave. Maybe she could borrow some more cops from other stations. Dundee had been helpful, loaning her Bill and Janey. They might let her poach a few more.

Or maybe she could find Cliff's killer before the wedding. She'd have to hope so.

Chapter 23

It was after four by the time Sara returned from Retworth's.

'He has had some Dresden figurines,' she told Clare, stirring milk into her coffee. 'But he's sold them on and he's not sure who brought them in. He's going to check his records to see if the seller gave a name. But it could have been a false name.'

'What about Hazel?'

'He thinks he remembers her but he doesn't think he served her. Said it might have been his Saturday girl.'

Clare stood, weighing this. 'I'd say she was more likely to be buying than selling, then.'

Sara frowned. 'Why?'

'Well, if someone came in and wanted to sell something, you wouldn't expect a Saturday girl to put a value on it.'

Sara's face cleared. 'Oh, I get it. The things he had for sale would already have been priced.'

'Yes, I think so. What about the painting?'

'Bit more luck there,' Sara said. 'He remembers someone phoning up about a painting.'

'Oh yes?'

'He didn't take the call himself – one of his assistants, but he can't remember which one.'

'He doesn't remember much,' Clare said.

'Apparently it was a Saturday and the shop was busy.'

'Saturday past?'

Sara shook her head. 'He thinks a couple of weeks ago. Anyway, he told his assistant to say they didn't buy paintings but to try this other man who's a bit of an expert.'

'Get his details?'

Sara nodded. 'I've written them down.' She handed Clare a piece of paper. 'It's a Giles Paterson. Apparently he lives at Radernie.'

'Ra-whatie?'

'Radernie. It's a tiny place near Peat Inn.'

Clare took out her phone and tapped Radernie into Google maps then she scrolled out to see how close it was to St Andrews.

'Five or six miles,' Sara said, looking over her shoulder.

'Higham Toll?' Clare said, reading the map. 'Never heard of it.' She glanced at her watch. 'I'll give him a call. See if he can see us.'

She wandered back to her office, keying in the number Sara gave her but it went to voicemail and she left a message asking Giles to call.

By five o'clock they were no further forward and she decided to call it a day. Tony had left an hour earlier, stating he'd be in a bit later the following day. Bill and Janey were still working through a list of known offenders and Chris had an appointment with the wedding caterers.

'I've no idea why I have to go,' he muttered, pulling on his jacket. 'I'm not even that keen on what we're having – all that fine dining crap. Tiny bits of stuff and it all seems to come with blackcurrant coulis. Even the soup,' he added.

Clare laughed. 'At least we're having soup.'

'Cold.'

'Eh?'

'The soup's served cold.'

'Hmm. Did I say I was coming?'

'You did, Inspector. And if you're not there I will hunt you down, wedding or no wedding.'

–

Clare and the DCI carried their pizzas out to the garden to eat in the evening sun. Benjy took up residence at her feet, ever hopeful.

'You making progress?' the DCI said, taking scissors to his pizza.

'We do have a pizza wheel,' Clare said.

'It's blunt. Belongs in the bin.'

She shrugged and tore off a bit of pizza in defiance of his neatly cut slices.

'And are you?' he said. 'Making progress I mean?'

'Not really.'

'Who's in the frame?'

She shook her head. 'Absolutely no one. I'm starting to think it was a random attack. Someone going along the street, trying door handles. Maybe he rang the bell, Cliff answered and he saw how infirm he was. He blags his way in and starts lifting stuff. Cliff tries to stop him and he goes for him. Shoves him back in his chair then he sees the cushion...'

'I don't know,' the DCI said. 'Wouldn't he just have punched Cliff? Knocked him down?'

'Maybe Cliff recognised him; or said he had a memory for faces − that kind of thing. So whoever it is has to silence Cliff, permanently.'

'I suppose. It's a very particular murder method, though.'

'Meaning?'

'The cushion. It strikes me almost as a kinder way of killing someone, particularly someone you might be fond of.'

'Because you don't see the victim's face?'

'Exactly. The sort of thing we associate with mercy killing. No real pain or mess. A few minutes gasping for breath. And the possibility it won't be picked up. Especially when the victim's terminally ill.'

'So...' Clare began slowly.

'If I were you, I'd be looking closer to home.'

They munched on in silence for a few minutes, Clare considering this. Did any of the Cravens really have a strong enough motive to hasten Cliff's death? Admittedly the two kids would net a tidy sum and Rory's business problems − if he had any

– would be over now. But they'd have inherited anyway, most likely in a few weeks. Would any of them really have risked a murder conviction for the sake of a few weeks' wait?

And then there was Hazel Sullivan. She seemed genuinely fond of Cliff and she didn't benefit by as much as a penny. No motive there, unless of course he'd caught her stealing from him. And, if so, would she really have reacted by smothering him? She was far too sensible for that.

'How you getting on with Tony?' the DCI said, cutting across her thoughts.

'Oh, you know. Same old same old.'

'Apparently he has a new woman.'

'No change there, then.'

The DCI reached forward and topped up their glasses. 'No, really. This time he's smitten.'

'Go on, then. Who is it?'

'You remember that DS who left the Force under a cloud last year? Something about fudging witness statements?'

Clare picked up her glass. 'No! Seriously?'

'Yep. Apparently she's split up from her husband. House is on the market, three kids and Tony's been taking the young lad to footie practice on a Saturday.'

'He did say he'd be in late tomorrow,' Clare said slowly. 'Can he really be that daft? Last I heard she was in a load of debt.'

'She is. She's also twenty years younger than him. I reckon she saw him coming and fancied a bit of his DCI's salary. As for him, he can't believe his luck – or so he thinks.'

'Look at the moon and fall in the midden, as my gran used to say.'

'A wise woman,' the DCI said. He held out his hand for a moment, palm upwards, then rose from his chair. 'I think it's going to rain. Let's take this inside.'

They carried the remains of their pizzas and wine into the house, Clare kicking the door closed as the first spots began drumming against the kitchen window. She looked out across the garden, her eye falling on a sturdy oak in the woods beyond and her thoughts went back to poor little Sophie Bakewell, her last moments on earth hanging from a tree in the school grounds. She'd taken her eye off the ball on that one and she made a mental note to chase up those two schoolboys in the morning.

The DCI was busying himself in the kitchen, humming as he cleaned up the pizza trays, and suddenly she thought how lucky she was to have found him. It had taken a while, a few false starts but here they were, happy together, even if was a bit too fond of playing jazz piano.

He turned, as though sensing she was watching him, and he smiled. She caught a whiff of his cologne and she let the fragrance linger in her nostrils.

'Fancy an early night?' she said.

He leaned across and kissed the top of her head. 'Always.'

He took hold of her hand and pressed it to his lips. 'You go on up,' he said. 'I'll take Benjy out for a quick run.'

She watched him clip on the little dog's lead and head out the front door into the rain, then she began climbing the stairs, all thoughts of Cliff Craven and Sophie Bakewell drifting further away with every step.

Saturday

Chapter 24

Clare heard the woman before she saw her and quickened her step, entering the station by the front door. Jim was standing at the public enquiry counter, a woman in her late forties gesticulating with her hands.

'I'm absolutely sick of it,' she said. 'You need to tell her to leave me alone.'

Clare was about to head for her office but Jim beckoned her over. She raised an eyebrow but moved across to greet the woman. 'Hello,' she said. 'I'm Clare, the DI here in the station. And you are?'

'Beth Gilmour.'

'Nice to meet you, Beth. I gather there's a problem.'

'Too right,' the woman said. She opened her mouth to continue and Clare steered her over to a row of seats in the waiting area. There was no one else in the station this early and she hoped this would be enough to placate the woman, whatever the problem was. She waited until Beth had sat, and smiled.

'How can I help?'

'You can tell that bloody woman to leave me alone,' she repeated.

'Woman?'

'Hazel Sullivan. If she calls me just once more I will not be responsible for my actions.'

Clare glanced across at Jim. 'Just excuse me for a minute,' she said to Beth and she went back to where Jim was standing. 'Is Chris in?'

He nodded. 'In the kitchen, making a coffee.'

'Ask him to join me,' she said. 'Interview room two.'

She led Beth to one of the small interview rooms, making small talk until Chris appeared, then she gave Beth a smile.

'Maybe you could start by telling us where you live.'

'Here in the town,' Beth said, and she reeled off her address and contact details. Clare took a note of these then she put down her pen. 'I understand you wish to make a complaint?'

Beth sighed. 'It's not that I want to get anyone into trouble. I just want this woman to stop calling me.'

'You said her name was...'

'Hazel Sullivan,' Beth confirmed. 'She's called me three times this week and twice last week. And if what she says is true then I'm not the only one she's calling. Chances are the others have blocked her. But she's got hold of my landline number and I don't know how to block callers on that.'

'Perhaps you could tell us why she's calling?' Clare said.

Beth eyed them for a moment. 'It's not me,' she said. 'It's my mum. I don't want her upset. She's old now and she's not well.'

Clare glanced at Chris and he took the hint.

'Let's start with the first time she phoned. Can you remember what she said?'

–

'Bring her in,' Tony said, when he finally arrived, sporting an Adidas track suit. 'We're not messing about with a murder case. She visited the victim, she was in that second-hand shop and now this. Get her in and make sure she has a solicitor.'

But it was another hour before they could track Hazel Sullivan down. 'Sara says she was out for a run,' Chris said. 'They're bringing her in now.'

Thanks to a delay in finding a duty solicitor it was almost lunchtime before Clare and Chris took their seats in the interview room. Hazel's solicitor, a middle-aged man with a combover, looked none too pleased to be there and Clare guessed they'd just ruined his Saturday.

'Why am I here?' Hazel said, her face still flushed from the exercise.

'I'm just going to set up the recording,' Clare said.

Hazel's eyes went to her solicitor who gave her a reassuring nod. A minute later, Clare cautioned Hazel formally and began the interview.

'You recall we spoke on Tuesday about your visits to Mr Cliff Craven.'

'Yes.'

'And I asked the reason for your visits.'

'Again, yes.'

Clare studied her, trying to work out what was going on in Hazel's head. Was there a note of impatience in her response? 'I'd like you to tell me again why you were visiting Mr Craven. For the tape,' she added.

Hazel met her eye, her gaze steady. 'As I said on Tuesday, I'm interested in local political history. I thought I could write about it. You only have to look at Facebook – loads of groups on local history.'

'Politics, though,' Clare persisted. 'Not always the most riveting of subjects.'

'Depends on the writing, I'd have thought.'

'Was Mr Craven able to help you with this?'

'He was.'

'What kind of information did he give you?'

Hazel shrugged. 'I can show you my notes, if you like.'

Clare smiled. 'Not at this stage. Just a rough idea.'

'Okay, then. Like I said, he was on the council for years. Chaired quite a few committees – planning and suchlike. He told me how the committees operated and how it had changed over the years.' She inclined her head. 'It's actually pretty interesting.'

She was starting to unbend and Clare asked a few random questions about Hazel's research to keep her talking. But when the solicitor began to shift in his seat she moved on. 'I'd like to go back to the items missing from Mr Craven's house,' she said.

Hazel's jaw tightened but she said nothing.

The solicitor leaned forward. 'Is Ms Sullivan under suspicion of theft?'

'At this stage we're simply trying to gather information,' Clare said smoothly. She reached into a folder and withdrew a screenshot Sara had printed. It showed Hazel at Retworth's counter speaking to an assistant. 'I am showing Ms Sullivan image 350/A, a still from CCTV at Retworth's second-hand shop.' She passed it across the desk to Hazel. 'Do you agree this is you?'

Hazel glanced at it. 'I suppose so. I've been to the shop a few times.'

'For what purpose?'

'It's a shop.'

'It's also a shop that buys second-hand items from customers so I'd like to ask if you were buying or selling.'

'Depends when it was taken.'

'Eleven days ago.'

'Then I was buying.'

'May I ask what you bought?'

'A cat ornament. Wemyss Ware,' she added. 'I have a receipt, somewhere – or I can show you the transaction on my banking app.'

'Anything else?'

'Nope.'

'And on other occasions,' Clare went on. 'Have you sold items to the shop?'

'A few.'

'Can you give me an example?'

Hazel thought for a moment. 'Some ornaments that belonged to my mother,' she said. 'After she died.'

'When was this?'

'Last year.'

'Were there any Dresden figurines among them?'

Hazel sat forward. 'No,' she said. 'They weren't to my mother's taste. And, for the avoidance of doubt,' she went on, 'I haven't so much as touched Cliff's ornaments, let alone stolen any of them.'

'Have you any evidence my client stole these items?' the solicitor asked.

Clare smiled. 'Just clearing up loose ends.'

The solicitor returned her smile. 'If there's nothing else…'

'One more thing: we had a complaint about Ms Sullivan this morning.'

Hazel's expression darkened. 'If it's that Rory—'

'It wasn't Rory Craven,' Clare said. 'The complaint was made by a Mrs Beth Gilmour.'

The colour drained from Hazel's face and she glanced at her solicitor.

'If we might have a moment?' he said.

'Of course.' Clare rose from her chair and paused the interview, nodding to Chris to follow her out of the room.

Chapter 25

It was a good twenty minutes before the solicitor indicated they were ready to continue. As they settled themselves down and Clare restarted the recording she thought Hazel was nervous, wary even, and she wondered what the solicitor had advised.

'I'd like to remind you you're still under caution,' Clare began and Hazel indicated she understood. 'Let's return to Beth Gilmour.'

'If I could explain,' Hazel said, and Clare nodded.

'My mother died last year,' she said. 'Long illness.' She paused for a moment. 'After the funeral I began clearing her things. And I found this notebook. Like a desk diary. I'd never seen it before and I realised it was a kind of journal.'

'Your mother kept a diary?'

Hazel shook her head. 'Not a diary as such – not like *Monday I did this then Tuesday it rained* – it wasn't that kind of thing. More like reflections on her life.' She smiled at the memory. 'I learned such a lot I never knew.' She broke off again.

'Go on,' Clare said, when it seemed Hazel had lost her train of thought.

'Sorry, yes. Well, I began reading and I learned she worked for the council – before I was born, you know? She was in the planning department and part of her job was to take minutes of committee meetings. Sounded like she was pretty good at it,' she said, her voice thick with emotion. 'Some of the meetings were at night and she was asked if she'd go along to take the minutes and she agreed. She'd married my dad by this stage but I think she still liked getting out by herself sometimes. And, from what I read, the councillors were a good bunch. Sometimes they'd go for a drink after.' She looked Clare straight in the eye. 'Cliff Craven was one of them,' she said. 'And he used to make a fuss of Mum, so her diary said. I think she quite liked it. Enjoyed the attention. But Cliff – he took it the wrong way. Long story short, he – he raped my mum.' Hazel's voice was husky now and she let her head droop.

'You're saying Cliff Craven raped your mother?' Clare said. 'He forced her to have sex with him, against her will?'

'Yes,' she said, after a moment. 'Yes he did.'

The solicitor had moved round in his seat and was facing Hazel, his face creased with concern. 'I think maybe Ms Sullivan needs a minute.'

'No,' she said, dabbing at her eyes. 'I want this out in the open. It's been hidden for too long. He got away with it for far too long.'

'Did your father know?' Clare asked.

'I don't think so. They divorced – about ten years ago. Then Dad died a few years after that. And I knew nothing about it until I found this book.'

'Did your mum have any sisters?' Chris asked. 'Or brothers?'

'No. She was an only one. Like me.'

'Friends?'

She nodded. 'Caroline. Her bridesmaid. Mum told her. It's in the book.'

'Surname?' Clare said, taking out her notepad.

'Wells.'

'Do you have an address?'

'She's in a care home, I think,' Hazel said. 'Not sure where but somewhere local. Mum visited a few times before she became ill herself.'

Clare smiled. 'We'll find it. And your mother's name, Hazel?'

'Isobel. Isobel Sullivan.'

Clare noted this down. 'And is that why you began visiting Cliff Craven?'

Hazel nodded. 'I knew his name from Mum's journal, obviously. But I'd no idea where he was. I hadn't even thought about contacting him until I was visiting Tam in hospital and I saw the name tag on his bed. Right next to Tam.' She smiled. 'It felt like fate, you know? Like God, or the universe or whatever is out there was telling me to pursue this. To go after Cliff Craven for what he'd done to my mum.'

Clare was silent for a moment, taking in what Hazel was saying. 'What did *going after Cliff Craven* mean to you?' she asked, at length.

Hazel shook her head. 'I honestly don't know. Maybe I wanted to understand a part of Mum's life I'd never known. I'm not sure.'

'Okay,' Clare said. 'How did you contrive to visit Cliff?'

She shrugged. 'It was easy enough. A few questions about his life, feigning an interest in what he'd done, a bit of flattery. When I mentioned writing a book he was sold. Appealed to his vanity, I expect. He gave me his mobile number and said to call him in a week or two when he was out of hospital.'

'And then?'

'I arranged to visit. Took him some cakes, made us tea and I asked him questions about his time at the council. Dead easy.' She eyed Chris. 'Like most men he loved to talk about himself.'

'Did you ask about your mum?'

'Not directly. And I don't think he made the connection. But he said all the ladies loved him. He called them his girls. I baited him,' she went on. 'Said I could see he had a twinkle in his eye, that I bet he'd been a bit of a lad in his day.' She looked at her solicitor. 'Am I allowed a cup of tea?'

Chris rose. 'I'll fetch some water.'

They waited until he had returned with two plastic cups of water which he placed in front of Hazel and her solicitor then Clare resumed the interview.

'Did Cliff Craven admit to assaulting your mother?' she asked.

'No, he was too sharp for that. But he did say a few of the girls had an eye for him and I pressed him. He barely remembered her name so I played along, suggesting a few names. When I said Isobel his eyes lit up. *That's it,* he said. *I remember her.'* She took a drink of water and set the cup down again. 'Made me sick to listen to him and then he started on about the other girls. I didn't want to put him on his guard so it took a few visits to get some of the names out of him. But there's another four, besides Mum. And goodness knows how many more he didn't tell me about.'

'How do you know he assaulted the other women?' Chris asked.

'I don't,' she said. 'Not for sure. But he spoke about the others in exactly the same way he spoke about Mum. I'm guessing he did it because he could.' She shook her head. 'I have no words for men like that.'

'And so you began to look for the other women?'

'I did. And I've found three of them so far. Beth's mum's still alive but she's in her eighties now. So I did a bit more digging and found she had Beth. I thought she'd be as angry as I was but she said her mum was ill and I wasn't to bother her again. I tried to explain we could all go after Cliff – if there were enough of us. Make him pay for what he'd done. But she said she'd enough to cope with, what with her mum being so ill.'

'And the others?'

'I don't think they believed me either. They said it was too long ago, they didn't want to ask their mothers, and how could we prove it anyway.' She shook her head. 'I just couldn't get through to them. In the end, one blocked my number, the other reported me to BT.' She sighed. 'They may not want justice for their mothers but I want it for mine.'

Clare glanced at Chris. Was it possible they were sitting across the table from Cliff Craven's killer? He gave her a noncommittal gesture and she turned back to Hazel.

'Think very carefully before you answer this next question.'

Hazel looked to her solicitor, who murmured it might be best to answer *no comment*. 'Go on,' she said to Clare. 'I've told you all I know so…'

Clare met her eye. 'Did you murder Cliff Craven in revenge for his assault on your mother?'

Hazel held her gaze for a moment before answering. When she spoke, her voice was steady, unwavering. 'No, Inspector. I did not murder Cliff Craven. I did not murder him for one very good reason. I wanted him to answer for what he'd done to my mother, and almost certainly to those other women. I wanted him sitting here in this chair being questioned, arrested, remanded and jailed. I wanted him to suffer the way he made those women suffer.' She took a deep breath in and out. 'But now? Now he goes to his grave, his reputation unsullied. So, I'm not glad he's dead. I'm *sorry*. Sorry because he has escaped justice.'

Chapter 26

'We've let her go,' Clare told Tony when Hazel had left the station.

'Bit of a risk.'

'I don't think so. I reckon she was telling the truth.'

'Checked her alibi?'

She shook her head. 'No point. All the PM can say is he died sometime between Wednesday afternoon and Thursday morning. She lives and works in the town. None of the CCTV we've examined places her in the street; but she could easily have nipped along, stuck a cushion over his face and been back home within half an hour.'

'You'll have to check the other women out,' he said.

'Yeah. That and the mother's friend. She's in a nursing home.'

'Not much use if she's gaga.'

'I'm going to pretend you didn't say that,' Clare said. 'If what you're trying to say is she might be suffering from a form of dementia then Hazel didn't think that was the case.'

'So what now?'

'Well, we interview the other women, the mother's friend and I've sent Sara over to pick up the mother's journal. See if it matches Hazel's story.'

'She could have written it herself,' Tony pointed out.

Clare frowned at this. 'What a bitter and twisted little man you are.'

'You can't ignore it. People are weird, Clare!'

She regarded him but didn't trust herself to reply. Instead, she said, 'I wonder if we can find someone who would remember Cliff Craven when he was a councillor.'

'Why not ask Jimbo,' Tony said, referring to the desk sergeant. 'He's as old as the hills.'

'Good point. Oh, any sign of that warrant?'

'Not that I've seen.'

'You did action it…'

'As if I'd forget.'

'As if.'

Clare sought out Chris and Max. 'See if Bill and Janey are around as well,' she said. 'We need a team talk.'

Five minutes later they gathered in the incident room.

'Right,' Clare began, settling herself on a desk. 'Known offenders. Any luck with that?'

Bill reached for his notepad. 'There's a few in this area but the smothering doesn't fit. The ones we know about would've taken a hammer to him, or a knife, even. And it's not your typical housebreaking. Too many small valuables they could have taken but didn't. Plus the door forced from the inside.'

'None of the prints SOCO picked up match with our database,' Janey added. 'I reckon we look closer to home.'

'The family, then,' Clare said.

'Any sign of the warrant for Rory's business affairs?' Chris asked.

'No. I reminded Tony.'

'Hah.'

'Never mind, hah. What about the Cravens?'

'That lad looked frightened to death,' Chris said. 'And that makes me suspicious. The sister's an odd one as well. Like you said, more bothered about her brother visiting Cliff than the actual murder.'

'What about the woman you've just interviewed?' Max asked.

Clare nodded. 'It's possible. Initially she said Cliff was helping her with research for a book. But we now know she was pumping him for information on the women who'd worked for him.' She hesitated. 'Hazel claims her mother was raped by Cliff while working for the council and she believes there were other victims.'

'There's your motive,' Bill said.

'Yeah, I know. But she said she wanted him alive to face justice.'

'She might have confronted him and lost control,' Max said.

'Could be. So we keep her in mind. She did give us a list of the other women she's been in touch with so we'll check them out as well.'

'We can take that if you like,' Bill said and Janey nodded in agreement.

'Thanks, both. I'd appreciate it.'

'Cleaning woman?' Janey went on.

'Again, I can't be sure,' Clare said. 'But I'd have said not. I can't see a motive.'

'Worth checking her out, though,' Max persisted. 'If she's a bit older she might even have been one of Cliff's victims.'

'I'm not sure she's quite that old,' Clare said, 'but there could be another connection. Check out her work history, Max, and see if she had any relatives in the council planning department. Oh, speaking of which,' she stopped and scribbled a note on her pad, 'I'm going to ask Jim if he remembers Cliff Craven as a councillor.'

'He's not as old as that, surely,' Bill said. 'Cliff Craven must have been retired for years.'

'Yeah, but Jim's lived here all his life. He might remember something.'

She was about to go on when her phone began to ring. Paul Henry. She swiped to take the call and put it on speaker for the others to hear.

'Just thought you'd want to know, I was comparing tats with the lad...'

'You were what?'

'Tats. Tattoos.'

Clare sighed heavily. 'Because?'

'Seemed like a good way to see his legs. Some blokes get tats on their legs.'

'And you have one?'

'Nah. Mine's on my shoulder.'

For a moment Clare considered asking what his tattoo was, then she decided she'd rather not know. 'And does he?' she asked. 'Does he have tattoos on his legs?'

'Yeah. He's got a kind of maple leaf on his calf. And that's not all he's got.'

'Bruises?'

'Yep.'

'Did you ask about them?'

'Course. I said what the fuck had he been doing to get his legs in that state and he said he played fives.'

'Fives?'

'Five a side footie. Jeez, Inspector, you need to up your game with the sports lingo.'

Janey let out a snort of laughter and even Max put a hand over his face in despair.

Clare took a breath in and out before going on. 'Where does he play?'

'I didn't ask.'

'Jeez, Sergeant,' she said before she could stop herself. 'You need to up your game with the family liaising. How do you know he wasn't making it up?'

'I'll ask him.'

'Try to do it subtly,' she said. 'Steer the conversation back to football, ask if he plays for the school, make up some wankery about you playing for the school when you were his age.'

'I played for Fife actually,' he said. 'I was their top scorer.'

'Just do it, Paul.'

She put down her phone.

'Where the hell do they find them?' Chris asked. 'Sports lingo?'

'He's Tony's protégé.'

Janey rolled her eyes. 'Then God help us all.'

'You reckon there's anything in it, though?' Max said. 'The bruises?'

'Dunno. Let's wait and see if he comes back to us.' She slid off the desk. 'Thanks everyone. Keep in touch.'

–

Jim agreed to do some digging into Cliff Craven's days as a councillor. 'I've an uncle used to work for the council,' he said. 'He's nearly eighty now but sharp as a tack. I'll see what he remembers.'

She thanked him and went to find Chris.

'I've found your nursing home,' he said, beaming with pride. 'All by yourself, too.'

'Count yourself lucky you're not partnered with Fife's Top Scorer.'

'Don't remind me. We have to get rid of him, Chris. He's driving me mad.'

Sara appeared with a large evidence bag. 'Got the mother's journal,' she said. 'And I saw the pottery cat she bought. I've taken a photo of it and the receipt so I'll check it with Retworth's.'

'Thanks Sara.' She nodded to Chris. 'Are we okay to visit… what's her name?'

'The mother's friend? Caroline Wells. And, yeah. We can go over anytime. They said to avoid mealtimes, though.'

She glanced at the clock. Two twenty. 'Come on, then. Let's see what she remembers about Hazel's mother.'

Chapter 27

Clare and Chris had visited the nursing home once before, seeking a suspect for an earlier investigation.

'Bad one, that,' Chris said and Clare nodded, her mind briefly back at what had turned out to be a complex case.

She drove on past fields dotted with bales of silage in their distinctive black plastic wrapping until they saw the red brick of the modern building warmed in the afternoon sun.

'Is that new?' Chris said as they neared the entrance. He indicated a play area where a dozen or more children were clambering over the wooden equipment.

'Think so. Good idea. Kids soon get bored, visiting a place like this.' She drew into the car park and nosed into a tight space at the end. 'I suppose weekends are when most families visit.' She clicked off her seat belt. 'Ready?'

'Yep. Can't say I'm expecting much, though. Old folk, you know.'

Clare locked the car. 'Don't you start. I've already had a go at Tony for suggesting old folk are all demented.' She walked smartly towards the entrance and pressed the buzzer. A man in a pale green polo shirt with the care home logo touched a button and the door swung open.

'We're here to see Caroline Wells,' Clare said.

'Family?'

'I called earlier,' Chris said. 'Spoke to Mrs Wilkins.'

'Just a moment.' The man disappeared into a door marked *Staff Only*, reappearing a minute later. 'That's fine. Mrs Wilkins is tied up at the moment but I think Caroline's in the quiet room.'

The sound of children's voices was carried on the summer breeze and Clare wondered if the quiet room was a child-free zone.

'Some of the residents don't cope so well when children come to visit,' the man explained. 'It's this way.' He led them along a broad corridor with handrails either side, stopping at a door. It was slightly ajar and he went in ahead of them. The windows faced the other side of the grounds from the play area and, as they followed him in, the sound of the playground merriment grew fainter. From the lack of sunlight Clare thought it must be north facing. Despite the heat coming from radiators the room was cooler than in the corridor and there was a stillness, almost a lack of life hanging in the air. On balance, Clare reckoned she'd rather have the children's noise.

There were only two residents in the room, a man slumped over in a high-backed chair, his eyes closed, an open mouth revealing a lack of teeth, and a silver-haired woman. She was long-limbed but spare, her clothes hanging on a bony frame and she sat erect, a Kindle in one hand, the other occasionally touching the screen. She looked up as they entered and smiled.

'Who's this you've brought, Cammy?' she said taking in Clare and Chris.

'A couple of police officers,' he said. 'Erm...' he turned to Clare. 'I didn't catch your names.'

'I'm Clare and this is Chris,' she said to the woman. 'Are you Caroline Wells?'

'I am, but I'm not sure how I can help you.'

Clare glanced round the room. The man in the chair appeared to be sleeping but this was a sensitive subject. 'Is there somewhere we could talk?'

Caroline eased herself up to her feet. 'Indoors or out?'

'Whatever you prefer,' Clare said.

She nodded and retrieved a walking stick that had been resting against her chair. 'There's a lovely spot in the garden,' she said. 'Away from the play area.'

They followed her to a side door which stood propped open, a welcome breeze drifting in. She reached for a handrail and walked slowly down a ramp and joined a path that wound its way round the side of the building. 'Will that do?' she asked, indicating a wooden garden bench with two chairs beside it.

'Perfect,' Clare said.

They followed her across a neatly trimmed patch of grass towards the bench, waiting while she sat slowly down. Clare put out a hand to help but she waved this away.

'Use it or lose it,' she said, grimacing as she sank into the bench. She indicated the other seats. 'Please make yourselves comfortable. Then perhaps you'll explain how I can help.'

They moved the other wooden seats to face Caroline and sat down. Clare took in the garden. A stone trough to the side of the bench was bursting with a gaudy array of summer bedding plants while climbing roses were spilling out from a wall in the same red brick as the building. She wondered again about her parents, getting older and a little less capable with every year. Might they have to move to a place like this? It was a lovely spot, surrounded by trees and shrubs, but did it feel like home for the residents? Hopefully she wouldn't have to think about it for a few years. She forced these thoughts to the back of her mind and smiled at Caroline.

'I understand you were a good friend of Isobel Sullivan.'

Caroline's eyes widened a little and it was a moment before she answered. 'Isobel, yes,' she said eventually. 'Friends since we were girls. I was her bridesmaid, you know?'

'Did you keep in touch after her wedding?' Clare asked. 'We're particularly interested in the time she spent working for the council.'

'We did,' she said. 'Maybe saw a bit less of each other when Hazel came along. But we never lost touch.'

Clare took a deep breath. 'I'm afraid I have to ask you about something rather unpleasant.'

Caroline shot a glance at her and Clare wondered if she knew what was coming.

'Did Isobel ever confide in you,' she said, 'about things that might have happened at work?'

She regarded Clare steadily. 'Things?'

Clare didn't want to put words in Caroline's mouth. 'Any… problems she had with colleagues, or other people she worked with?'

It was a moment before Caroline replied. 'Are you speaking of Councillor Craven?' she said, at last.

Clare felt Chris shift in his seat. 'Did Isobel have any problems with him?' she asked before Chris could interrupt.

'I wouldn't call it a problem,' Caroline said, an edge to her voice. 'I'd call it a crime.'

'Can you explain please?' Clare said.

'That man…' She broke off for a minute. 'He had a reputation, you know. I didn't work for the council and even I knew what he was like.'

'A reputation?'

'He was a sex pest, Inspector. There's no other word for it. He forced himself on poor Isobel and, from what I gathered, she wasn't the only one.'

'Just to be clear,' Clare said, 'you are saying Councillor Cliff Craven raped Isobel Sullivan.'

Caroline nodded. 'Isobel and a few others.'

'You knew about the others?'

'Not until after he'd assaulted Isobel,' she said. 'Or I'd have warned her. Actually I did try to warn her. But she couldn't see it. Couldn't see what a creep he was.'

'Did she complain?'

Caroline shook her head. 'She was so… ashamed! As if it was her fault. She thought no one would believe her. He was so influential, you know? And then there was her husband. She thought if she told him he'd leave her. Poor thing.' She broke off for a moment, her eyes full of sadness. 'So I helped her as best I could, you know? Let her talk. I did try to persuade her to go to the police but she wouldn't hear of it.'

'Did Isobel tell you the names of any other women he assaulted?' Chris asked but Caroline shook her head again.

'Sorry. I never knew their names. But you can take it from me – it happened.'

They left her soon after, walking slowly back to the car in silence, only distant laughter from the playground breaking the tension. They rounded a corner into the wind. Clare shivered and began buttoning up her jacket.

'What a bastard,' Chris said as they crossed the car park. 'It's just a pity whoever smothered him didn't do it thirty years ago.'

Clare stopped at the car, one hand on the roof. 'Does it change anything, though?'

'At least we know Hazel's telling the truth.'

'Looks like it. But does it make her more or less likely to have killed Cliff?'

'I still say she has a bloody good motive,' Chris said. 'I'm not sure you should have let her go.'

'Didn't have enough to hold her.' She looked up at the sky as the sun disappeared behind a bank of cloud. 'It's going to rain again. Let's get back for a cup of tea before it starts.'

Chapter 28

'I've been back to Retworth's,' Sara said as Clare flicked the switch on the kettle.

'And?'

'They confirm the Wemyss Ware cat came from their shop. Hazel's receipt matches their records.'

'She definitely bought it there?'

'Looks like it. Sorry, boss.'

'It's fine. I'm glad she's not our thief. Any luck with the Dresden figurines?'

'He's still looking.'

The kettle came to the boil with a rush of steam and Clare picked it up. 'Want one?'

Sara hesitated. 'Actually I was hoping to knock off on time tonight. It's all this wedding stuff...'

Clare checked her watch. It was after four. 'Get away now,' she said. 'Unless there's anything else?'

'There is one other thing.'

Clare poured boiling water into a mug and set the kettle down. 'Yeah?'

'Hazel Sullivan came back to the station while you were out.'

'Oh yes?'

'She printed a copy of the notes from her conversations with Cliff. It's on your desk.'

'Thanks Sara. Could you go to the property store and fetch me the mother's journal please? Might as well go through the two together.'

She left Sara to retrieve the journal from the secure store and carried her coffee through to her office. Tony had apparently left, pleading personal business, and she wondered vaguely if this was another outing with his new-found family. Who knows, it might just be the making of him.

A large manilla envelope lay on the desk addressed to DI Mackay. She put down her coffee and pulled it towards her. She withdrew a dozen or so printed pages and put these to one side. Sara tapped on the door a minute later and handed her Isobel Sullivan's journal.

'You get off home now,' she said. 'In sharp tomorrow, though.' She waited until the PC had closed the door then she checked her Inbox for urgent messages. 'Nothing that can't wait,' she murmured, and she opened the journal and began to read.

Judging by the early entries it looked as if Isobel had begun the diary in the weeks leading up to her wedding, the excitement of the young bride leaping off the page. Clare read on, scanning entries about the newlyweds' house and garden, clearly a source of great pride to Isobel. There were accounts of family outings and celebrations, and she thought this must have been an enthralling find for Hazel. A window into her mother's world before Hazel had been born, Isobel's hopes and wishes preserved in her neat hand. And then she came to the entry that stopped her in her tracks. It was simply headed,

Friday

Before she started reading, she knew somehow this was the entry. Something about the shakiness of the handwriting, the lack of neatness, the difference from the other entries. She drained her mug and began to read.

I don't know how to write this. But I can't tell anyone so this is all I have. I always thought the council men liked me because I did a good job. Now I know different. Last night Councillor Cliff

Craven raped me. The girls from work were going for a drink but he said he wanted to go over some notes from the meeting. I asked if he needed help and he said he'd love that. So I stayed. The caretaker was going round flicking off all the lights and Cliff said he'd be a bit longer but he'd lock up. So it was just us. I really loved it. I felt so important. Like we were running the council between us. It was warm, quiet, isolated from the world. Really special. We did the work and then he opened his drawer and took out a bottle of whisky. He had glasses too and he poured me a drink. I don't really like whisky. But I didn't want to say no. It burned on the way down. But then it was warm. Like central heating. He drank his and poured another. He tried to top mine up but I said no, that I'd better not go home stinking of drink. I didn't notice him moving his seat closer then he said something about my top, how it was pretty, that it suited me. He asked where I got it and I told him. Then he leaned forward and said it wasn't sitting right. He pulled at the shoulder then his hand slipped inside. I wanted to tell him to stop but I couldn't. There was this lump in my throat and the words wouldn't come out. I gasped trying to catch my breath and he said something about how I was enjoying it. But I wasn't. I didn't want it. And then he was up against me, his hands, grabbing at my clothes. Pulling at me – pawing me. I'm sure I said no. I think I did. But he didn't ask me so that's not right, is it? He didn't ask me. And he was so rough. I wanted to cry, scream, I wanted to push him away but he was too strong. And then he pulled back and zipped himself up and it was over. I just stood there, so ASHAMED. So embarrassed. I grabbed at my clothes, tried to tidy myself up then I ran. I saw the door to the Ladies and thought I'd be

safe there. I knew I was going to be sick so I wrapped
my arms round the seat. I don't know how long I was
in there but after a bit he knocked on the door. Said
he had to lock up and could I hurry. I flushed the
loo, straightened my clothes and went out. He was
standing there, smiling. He tried to put a hand out
to take mine but I just put my head down and left
as quickly as I could. When I got home I must have
looked a sight. I told Don I had a sick bug and would
he sleep in the spare room so I didn't pass it on. I
stayed in bed for the next two days then I went to
see Caroline. She's the only one I can tell. She wants
me to go to the police but I know what they'll say.
Staying after everyone had gone, drinking whisky
with him. Asking for it, they'll say. And everyone
would know and I couldn't bear that.

The entry finished and Clare found she was shaking. Whether
from emotion or rage she wasn't sure. Probably a bit of both.
That man – Cliff – that man who she'd thought was so kind, so
genial. He had ruined this poor woman's life. No wonder Hazel
had been visiting him, trying to piece together his inglorious past.
If it had happened to Clare's mother…

But she wouldn't go there. Couldn't. The bargain she'd made
with herself when she joined the Force was never to take her work
home with her. It wasn't always easy but she couldn't let the likes
of Cliff Craven into her head. Whatever he had done to Isobel
and the others, she had a job to do – bringing his killer to justice.

She returned to the journal reading the next entry.

Monday

So there it is. I went back to work today and the
bastard's had me reassigned. I've been moved to
Housing. I want to tell them all – tell all the women
he works with. Tell my replacement – Barbara. She

deserves to know – to be warned. But I can't. I haven't the courage.

Clare closed the journal and sat back in her chair. Those men. Those powerful men. How many more of them had abused their positions like this? How many more women had gone home, a smile painted on their faces, and got on with their lives while carrying this immense pain like a lead weight in their guts?

She sat for some minutes, ordering her thoughts. Yes, she had Cliff's killer to find and that was her priority. But she wanted justice for Isobel and the other women too. Didn't they deserve the same as the Craven family? Was there anything she could do for them?

She pushed the journal to one side and drew Hazel's research across the desk. Then she picked up a pen and began to write on her notepad.

Victims of Cliff Craven

–

'You're quiet,' the DCI said as she chased pasta around her plate.

'Just one of those days.'

He watched her for a moment, not speaking. Then he put a hand across the table and placed it on hers. 'Can I help?'

She looked at it. His hand on hers. Strong, capable, tanned from working in the garden that afternoon. She felt the callouses, rough and somehow comforting against her own hand, her skin so much softer. And then his hand tightened on hers as he seemed to absorb her distress. She squeezed his hand back and began quietly to cry.

Sunday

Chapter 29

'I'm concerned,' the DCI said over breakfast. 'I don't think Tony's the best person to oversee this case.'

'I *know* he isn't,' Clare said, spooning last night's uneaten pasta into a plastic tub for her lunch. 'But he's all we have so it can't be helped.'

'And you have Chris and Sara going off in a week's time.'

She stood, spoon in hand, gazing out of the kitchen window. Benjy had unearthed the remains of a basketball he'd spent the past few months ripping to shreds. She thought she'd put it in the bin but obviously not. He was worrying it as if it was some unfortunate rabbit or other creature and she allowed herself a smile. Then she turned back to the DCI. 'Don't worry. I'm fine. Last night – it was just, oh I don't know. Shock's the wrong word.' She put down the spoon. 'Al, I've taken a dozen statements from rape victims. More, maybe. Sat opposite them at possibly the lowest point of their life and I've done it. I've detached myself.'

'Because you had to,' he pointed out. 'You can't fall apart in front of a victim.'

'I know. But this felt so personal, so raw. The sheer helplessness of that poor woman. When we deal with rape victims we're there for them, ready to help. We help them identify the perp then we find and arrest them. Okay, most of the time we don't get a conviction, but at least we've put the rapist through hell in the meantime. But this – there was something so utterly hopeless about that journal. It got to me. That's all.' She forced a smile. 'I'll be fine. Now I've read it, it'll fade and I'll deal with it like any other crime.'

'Except this time your perp's dead.'

She nodded. 'I know. But it doesn't stop me wishing I could do something for those women.'

–

The station was filling up when she entered.

'Tony's called in some favours,' Jim explained. 'There should be a few more on the way.'

'Crikey. He does have his uses,' Clare said. 'Is he in yet?'

'Delayed.'

'No change there, then,' and she headed for her office.

Half an hour later she made her way to the front of the incident room, wondering where on earth to start. The case was growing more complicated by the day.

'Thanks everyone,' she said when the hubbub had died down. 'I'm particularly grateful to those of you from other stations. So let's get to it.' She paused for a moment. 'Cliff Craven, retired councillor in his eighties – smothered at home, probably with a cushion. He was elderly, hadn't long to live so would have been in a weakened condition. The front door lock had been damaged with a chisel but SOCO reckon it was done from the inside, possibly after Cliff had been killed.'

'To make it look like a break-in?' someone asked.

Clare recognised Erin, an officer from Glenrothes. 'Yes, we think so. Current theory is the killer either had a key, found the door unlocked or was let in by the victim. He or she then took their chance to kill Cliff and damaged the door to make it look like they'd broken in.'

'Someone he knew?'

'Could be.'

Benny, a DC from Dundee, raised his hand. 'What about the family?'

'One son, Rory. Businessman. Lives locally with his two kids, Marcus and Lauren. Marcus is in sixth year, Lauren a few years older. The FLO spotted bruises on Marcus's legs yesterday and SOCO reckon, from Cliff's position, he could have kicked out at his attacker. Marcus claims he got the bruises at football. The FLO's going to check that out.'

'Who is the FLO?' Benny asked.

'Paul Henry.'

From the glances exchanged around the room Clare guessed a few of them had come across Paul already. 'So we'll see what he comes up with,' she went on, her tone brisk.

'Any money worries for the family?' Erin asked.

'I've requested a warrant to look at the whole Craven family's finances. It does look as if Rory's business is struggling. Profits are down so hopefully the warrant will be through shortly. Rory Craven also complained some items have gone missing from his father's house.' She glanced at her notepad. 'Dresden figurines, a painting and a valuable medal. As yet we've not been able to confirm if the items have been stolen. The victim had asked his grandson to take the painting down from a bedroom wall so he may have been in the process of selling some things himself. We just don't know.'

She waited while they made notes then went on. 'Cleaning lady – who was looking into her?'

Max raised a hand. 'Council offices are shut until Monday. But no indication she'd any connection to Cliff or the council.'

'How did she end up cleaning for him?' Clare asked.

'Agency. She's been with them for the past twelve years. Does a few other jobs in the town.'

'And before that?'

'At home, bringing up two kids. Worked in a shop before the kids came along. No red flags.'

'Okay,' Clare said. 'Do check with the council in the morning, though.' Max indicated he would do this.

'A woman called Hazel Sullivan visited Cliff regularly over the past few months. She told him she was writing a history of local politics. Cliff's son doesn't believe that. He thinks she's responsible for the missing items. We don't think that's the case but we're still checking. He's also suggested she could have killed his father.'

'Alibi?' Erin asked.

'None. The window for when Cliff was killed is anytime from Wednesday afternoon to Thursday morning. She lives in the town so she definitely had the opportunity. But, having interviewed her, I'm inclined to say she wasn't involved. I'm bearing it in mind, though.' She looked round at them. 'There is a complication some of you are aware of already, but for those of you hearing it for the first time, it does not go outside this room. Not until we have more information, okay?'

Heads nodded and she carried on.

'Yesterday I learned Hazel's mother was raped by Cliff while she was a council employee; and Hazel believes her mother wasn't the only victim.'

'Dirty old bastard,' someone muttered.

'Quite. I have a list of other possible victims taken from a journal Hazel's mother kept. There are also notes of Hazel's conversations with Cliff so we may get some names from that as well; but most of the victims will either be dead or quite elderly. I interviewed the daughter of one and she's made it clear she doesn't want her mother questioned.'

'But if a crime's been committed,' Bill said.

'No go,' Clare said. 'Cliff's dead. There's no one to charge. But it still needs checked. It's not impossible one of his victims – or their relatives – went after him, looking for revenge. Unlikely, I know. But we can't overlook it. I'd like you and Janey to keep going with that.'

The pair nodded and Clare went on. 'Jim has an uncle who worked for the council. He may be able to give us some background information from when Cliff was there. Otherwise, it's back to basics. Checking the victim's finances, phone records, going over witness statements – you all know the drill.' She scanned the room. 'Any questions?'

Chris raised his hand. 'Just this: have we forgotten about the two lads with the jailbroken phones?'

–

The briefing over, Clare, Chris and Max sat round her desk, mugs of coffee and hunks of Zoe's latest traybake on paper towels.

'This is so good,' Clare said, breaking off another bit and popping it in her mouth. 'Tell her thanks, Max. Good of her to send it in.'

He beamed. 'She loves doing it. But I'll tell her.'

'Anyway...' Clare said, wiping her hands on the paper towel, 'I did let those two lads drop off the radar. Josh and Ethan.'

'The murder has to take priority,' Max said, but Clare shook her head.

'It needs looking into. If Ethan and Josh were exploited by the same person then who knows how many other victims there might be.' She sat thinking for a minute. 'I don't want whoever jailbroke those phones to know we're looking into it so let's stay away from the school. Go round to their houses after school tomorrow. Bring the two of them in at the same time. We'll see what an interview under caution does for their memories.'

Clare's phone began to ring, a number she didn't recognise, and she indicated to Chris and Max they were done. She waited until they'd closed the door then clicked to take the call.

'Giles Paterson,' the voice said. 'Returning your call.'

She racked her brains and then she remembered. The art expert, and she thanked him for calling back.

'Not at all. I've been away for a few days but picked your message up last night. How can I help?'

'Can you recall if you had an enquiry from someone selling a painting by,' she flicked back through her notebook, 'a Jamie O'Dea? It would have been within the past week.'

'Do you know which painting?' he asked.

'Sorry,' Clare said. 'I only know the artist's name. But I think it was dancers. Bright colours,' she added.

'I know his work,' Giles said. 'I did have a call about a painting, right before I went away. But I'd a train to catch so I'm afraid I was rather short. I suggested the caller contacted me again this coming week.'

'Did the caller mention the artist?'

'No. Only that he had a painting he was selling. But if it was an O'Dea I'd certainly be interested.'

'He?'

'Yes. It was a man.'

'Did he give a name?'

'I'm afraid not.'

'Is the number still in your record of calls?'

'One moment.'

She waited, the only sound Giles's breathing as he scrolled back through his calls.

'I'm afraid not,' he said after a few minutes. 'It was a withheld number.'

'What about his voice?' Clare said, grasping for anything that might help identify the caller. 'Did he sound young or old?'

He was quiet for a moment, as though considering this. 'Older, I think.'

'Mr Paterson, if he calls back would you ask him to make an appointment please? And let us know the date and time? We're most anxious to speak to him.'

'Of course,' he said. 'But should I be concerned? I live alone and work from home. The fact you're calling makes me...'

'I doubt you have anything to worry about. But perhaps you could suggest meeting in a café somewhere? If you let me know where and when we'll have some plain-clothes officers there.'

'I doubt the painting's that valuable,' Giles said. 'A few hundred certainly, but probably no more.'

Clare thanked him and ended the call. Her phone rang again immediately. Raymond.

'Not much for you,' he said, 'but we have found DNA on the cushion.'

'Does it match any of the samples we sent across?'

'Sorry. Not on the database, either. But I can tell you it's male.'

'But not Rory or Marcus Craven?'

'Nope.'

She thanked Raymond and put down her phone, tapping a pen on the desk as she ordered her thoughts. Male DNA on the cushion and a male possibly trying to sell the missing painting. That let Hazel Sullivan out. But if one of the other women Cliff assaulted had a son… She drew Hazel's research notes across her desk and began reading them through again.

Chapter 30

It was after four by the time Jim tapped on Clare's door. 'Finally got hold of my uncle,' he said. 'He'd been out on the golf course all day.'

Clare glanced out of the window. 'Lucky him. Was he able to help?'

'He remembers Cliff Craven, and one or two others. He's going to have a think and call me tomorrow.'

'Would he come in, do you think?'

'If we nab some of Zoe's traybakes I'm sure he would. He loves cake.' He hovered in the doorway for a moment.

'Something else?'

His face softened. 'It's a difficult case, this.' He nodded towards Hazel's research. 'Nasty stuff to read about.'

Clare nodded but said nothing.

'Maybe get yourself home. Sounds like tomorrow's going to be a busy one. Should have that warrant through as well. There'll be plenty to do. Why not knock off early while you can.'

She gave him a smile. 'Thanks. I might just do that.'

'See you do.' Then he left her, closing the door quietly.

She sat on after he'd gone, staring at Hazel's papers, reading what was there but taking none of it in. Jim was right. She logged off the computer, picked up her bag and headed out the side door. The sun was still warm and, as she crossed the car park, a car over the road disgorged a family, two small children still in swimming costumes and flip-flops. The parents were carrying armfuls of beach toys, colourful towels and a huge coolbox. One of the children, a girl of about three, her hair still wet, trailed after her mother, wailing. *Tired out,* Clare thought, smiling at the scene. No doubt a bath and a bedtime story would sort her out.

She reached her car and stood, tapping a message to the DCI to say she was on her way home. The reply came right back.

Fancy a BBQ?

She smiled and swiped to reply.

Definitely

Then she climbed into her car, started the engine and headed for home.

Benjy was beside himself with joy at her early return. He raced round the side of the house and jumped up, his paws muddy from the flower bed he'd been investigating.

'Benjy, down!' the DCI roared but Clare bent to ruffle the little dog behind the ears.

'I haven't the heart to scold him,' she said, clicking to lock the car.

'And that's why he's still such a thug.'

'Whatever.' She wandered into the house and out the kitchen door to the garden where the DCI had set up the BBQ.

'I've done some kebabs,' he said. 'Lamb and veggie.'

'I'll have the lamb,' she said, helping herself to a glass of wine.

'No. You'll have one lamb and one veggie,' he said. 'Unless you want to die at fifty.'

'Okay, Mum. Want me to do rice or something?'

'I've potatoes baking in the oven. I'll shove them on here for the last five minutes.'

She sank down on the garden bench and kicked off her shoes, flexing her feet. She turned her face up to the sun and closed her eyes. 'And don't ask about Cliff Craven or anything to do with him,' she said. 'Tonight is a night off. Jim's orders.'

He came over to her, the coals having ignited, and kissed her softly on the lips. 'Good for Jim,' he said. 'Good for Jim.'

Monday

Chapter 31

'Warrant's through,' Chris said, as Clare entered the incident room.

'Great. You and Max get onto that, please. Focus on Rory Craven first. See what you can find out before picking up the two schoolboys.' She glanced round the room. 'Bill and Janey?'

'They've found some more of the women Hazel thinks Cliff may have assaulted. Gone to take statements.'

She nodded at this and headed for her office. Flicking on the light she saw a note on her desk from Jim.

> *Paul Henry says there are photos of Marcus playing football on the school website.*
>
> *He reckons the bruises are legit.*

She put the note down. It was a long shot anyway, particularly with his DNA not being found on the cushion. Would Bill and Janey turn up something? If not, she'd absolutely no idea where to look next.

Jim opened her office door. 'My uncle,' he said. 'Is it okay if he comes in about eleven?'

'Perfect. If there's any of that traybake left can you grab it please, before the locusts out there get their hands on it.'

Jim went off to nab the traybake and Clare shook the mouse to bring her computer to life. Something was niggling away at her.

Something she thought they'd overlooked. But it wouldn't come so she turned to deal with her Inbox.

–

Larry Douglas arrived on the dot of eleven. Clare rose to greet him and was struck by the family resemblance. He was so like Jim across the eyes when he smiled and her gaze drifted between the two. He held himself well and she wondered if he'd been a military man. He approached Clare, his hand extended, and shook hers warmly. His grip was strong but the skin on his hands was papery thin.

'Milk and two sugars,' he boomed to Jim. 'And don't stint on the biscuits.'

Jim laughed and went to make tea. Clare indicated a seat and Larry settled himself, looking round the office.

'It's nice and bright,' he remarked.

Clare followed his gaze. 'Not as tidy as I'd like but…'

'I'm sure you're too busy for tidying,' he said. 'Jim tells me you never stop.'

She acknowledged the compliment. 'They all work hard,' she said, 'especially Jim.'

The door opened and Jim entered, bearing a tray. Clare wondered briefly where he'd found it and hoped it wasn't too dusty. He'd also managed to secrete the last of Zoe's traybake and she was amazed to see it was on a plate instead of the usual green paper towel. She thanked him and waited until he'd gone.

'Please,' she said, indicating the traybake. 'Our admin assistant Zoe makes the most wonderful cakes.'

He helped himself to a large piece of the traybake which he pronounced delicious. Then he wiped his hands on a white cotton handkerchief, tucking it back in his pocket. 'Jim tells me you want some information about Cliff Craven,' he said. 'Dreadful news.'

'When I was a young detective constable,' Clare said, 'there was a sergeant – probably one of the best police officers I've ever met. One of the things he told me, right back at the start, was if you want to know why someone died, find out how they lived.'

'Sounds like good advice. And you want to know how Cliff Craven lived?'

'Anything at all about him,' Clare said. 'Particularly back in his council days.'

Larry took a drink of tea and set down his cup. 'Are you interested in his personal or professional life?'

'Both, I suppose,' Clare said. 'We're trying to build up a picture of what he was like and…' she hesitated, keen not to put words into Larry's mouth, 'if there's anyone he might have upset.'

'Quite a few husbands, I'd have thought,' Larry said. 'He did have a bit of a reputation.'

'Anything particular come to mind?'

'There was one chap had a go at him – so I heard. Told him in no uncertain terms to stay away from his wife.'

Clare picked up a pen. 'Do you remember his name?'

Larry frowned. 'Lambert, I think. Gordon, maybe.' He shook his head. 'My memory's not what it was. But it was something like that.'

Clare noted this down. 'Do you recall anything else about it?'

'Not really. I think Mrs Lambert – I presume it was Mrs Lambert – worked in the planning department. I'm not sure what happened except the husband – Gordon – had a word with Cliff and that was the end of it. I think,' he went on, 'the lady in question was moved to another department. To keep her away from Cliff.'

The same as Isobel Sullivan, Clare thought.

'But there was that other thing,' Larry went on.

'Oh yes?'

His brow creased as he seemed to be trying to remember. 'Banarvale!' he said, his face breaking into a smile. 'That was it. Banarvale Estate.'

It wasn't a name Clare recognised. 'Where is it?'

'Oh it's gone now,' Larry said. 'But it was somewhere west of Kirkcaldy if I remember rightly.' He lapsed into silence, his head back, eyes to the ceiling, lost in thought again. Clare waited and her patience was rewarded.

'Holiday complex,' he said eventually. 'Lodges, restaurant, swimming pool – that kind of thing. There were… rumours at the time.'

'Involving Cliff?'

Larry nodded. 'He was an influential man. The Banarvale plans should have been turned down, from what I heard.'

'There was a problem?'

'Oh yes. I gather there were concerns about the land being a potential flood plain, but it was approved anyway. The builder who was awarded the contract had all sorts of schemes supposed to alleviate floods; but it was pretty clear to anyone with a brain there would be problems in the future.'

'And it's your view Cliff was instrumental in its being approved?'

'If I recall correctly,' he said slowly, 'Cliff recommended approval and the committee mostly followed his lead. Well him and that other chap…' He broke off, drumming his fingers on the desk.

Clare waited, sipping her tea.

'Meadows,' he said eventually. 'Johnny Meadows.' He leaned forward. 'I wouldn't like to be quoted on this but there was a strong rumour the two of them took a backhander.'

'They were bribed to approve the application?'

'So I believe. But I doubt you'd be able to prove it, especially after so long.'

Clare jotted Johnny Meadows' name down. 'What happened to the development?'

'Oh it was built in the end, on the cheap, so I heard. There were complaints from people who stayed there. Second-rate materials, shoddy workmanship. There were problems with the pool filtration – the usual, when things aren't done properly. And of course there was flooding. Eventually the company went into administration owing a lot of money. Half a million was mentioned at the time,' he added.

'Can you remember when that was?'

He leaned back in his chair. 'Oh, now you're asking.' He thought for a moment. 'I seem to recall something about millennium celebration bookings. I think the customers lost their deposits. So I'd say it went bust in 1999. The stuff about the bribes is all rumour, of course,' he added. 'But there's no doubt the development should never have gone ahead.' He popped the last of the traybake in his mouth and dabbed the edges with his handkerchief. 'That was delicious. I don't suppose your admin lady takes orders?'

Larry seemed keen to chat on but eventually Clare managed to extricate him from her office.

'Why not take Larry out for lunch,' she suggested to Jim and he smiled, doubtless aware it was a sure fire way of getting Larry out of the station. 'Take your time,' she added and Jim laughed.

She watched them leave, Larry walking as smartly as if he was on parade, and suddenly she remembered what had been niggling away at her. The DSO medal missing from Cliff's house. Of all the items Rory had reported missing, surely that had to be the most valuable. She already knew it could be worth several thousand pounds and she sat back in her chair to think Retworth's hadn't been offered the medal for sale so where was it? She was about to search for specialist dealers when Chris's head poked round the door.

'Rory Craven,' he said.

'You've found something?'

'Oh yeah.'

She rose from her seat and followed him to the incident room where Max was poring over a sheaf of printouts. He looked up as she approached.

'Got these from his accountant,' he said, tapping the papers.

'And?'

'He has pretty major cash flow problems,' Max said. 'HMRC are pursuing him for unpaid tax.'

'The accountant says they're threatening to have the business wound up,' Chris added.

Clare thought of the DSO medal worth maybe three or four thousand pounds. 'How much does he owe?'

Max scanned the printout. 'Just over forty grand.'

'There's your motive,' Chris said. 'I reckon he's gone to the old man, asked him for a loan and Cliff's refused. Maybe Cliff didn't have the readies or maybe he objected to bailing Rory out. Either way, Rory needs to inherit asap so he smothers the old man.'

Clare shook her head. 'No DNA on the cushion. Or not Rory's at least.'

'Could have worn gloves?' Chris said.

'In June? Don't you think his dad would get suspicious if his son turned up wearing gloves?'

'Maybe. Maybe not. He might have waited until Cliff had fallen asleep then found a pair of gloves and smothered him.'

Clare considered this. 'Suppose.'

'I don't know what you're waiting for,' Chris said. 'Let's get him in. See how he reacts to an interview under caution.'

'And if we're wrong? He's the victim's son. He could complain, go to the papers.'

'Sorry,' Chris said, 'but that's not a reason to be cautious. We've a job to do here.'

'I know that!' Clare struggled to keep the irritation out of her voice. 'But you're not the one who'll have to answer to Penny Meakin if he makes a fuss.'

Chris rolled his eyes at the mention of the superintendent's name. 'Suppose.'

Clare patted him on the back. 'It's good work, guys, and I'm not saying we won't have him in. But let's see what else turns up in the meantime.' She went back to her office, the conversation with Larry Douglas still running through her mind.

Chapter 32

'Banarvale Estate,' Clare said to a man from the council who'd introduced himself as Dave. 'It was a planning application maybe thirty years ago.'

'That would be archived,' Dave said. 'I'd have to put in a request. Might take a while...'

Clare held the phone away from her ear for a minute while she counted to ten. 'This is a murder enquiry, so I'm afraid I'll need the information as a matter of urgency.'

'Oh.'

'Quite. So...'

'If you let me know what you need, I'll see what I can do.'

She ended the call, having extracted a promise from Dave to call her back within twenty-four hours. Shaking the mouse to bring her computer to life she opened up Google and typed *Banarvale Estate* into it. The first result was a website but when she clicked the link it opened with a message that the page couldn't be reached. She filtered the search to show only news pages and one result was returned. It wasn't a newspaper she recognised but a website called The Scottish News Digest. The site loaded immediately, a maroon and blue banner across the top proclaiming the name. The front page showed the news stories of the day with photos credited to agencies and she wondered if it was some kind of independent news website. There was a search box so she typed Banarvale into this and pressed 'enter'. One article appeared, headed 'The Scandal of Banarvale'. An aerial photo showed a semi-circle of lodges dotted around larger buildings, the image credited to Terrow Media. She scrolled past the photo and began to read.

The Banarvale Estate opened in a blaze of glory on Easter Sunday, 1989.

Clare counted back. It was probably eight or nine years after Hazel was born but it still fitted with Cliff's time at the council. She read on.

But all that changed just ten years later. A succession of problems at the estate, coupled with floods which caused damage in the lower-lying lodges, resulted in complaints and claims for compensation. By the end of 1998 there were rumours the owner, Monique Taylor, was in financial difficulties. But the beleaguered company continued taking bookings, including one for a party of thirty who were tempted by the promise of 'A Millennium Celebration to Remember'. The package included champagne, fireworks and a chef from a top London restaurant.

The estate took deposits of 50 per cent from guests, citing upfront costs to secure the very best food, drink and entertainment. But the guests' excitement was short-lived when they opened the papers on the morning of 21 November 1999 to find the estate had gone into liquidation. So where did it all go wrong?

Where indeed, Clare thought. She skimmed the rest of the article, which referred to a surveyor's report, largely ignored by the planning committee. This confirmed Larry's account of things. But he'd admitted to being hazy on some of the details. She scrolled back to the start of the article to see when it was written. Just last year. Might it be possible to get in touch with whoever had written it? She scanned the sidebar menu and saw *About Us.* Following the link she watched as a photo loaded and she sat staring at it. She knew that face. To the side there was a short biography but she didn't need to read it to know the website belonged to Lyall McGill.

She'd met Lyall not long after arriving in St Andrews – only the second case she'd investigated. He'd been foisted upon her, thanks to an initiative between the police and press. To begin with she'd found him very hard work – he'd been like an enthusiastic dog, eager to please and desperate for approval. But by the end of the case they'd developed a mutual respect and they parted on the very best of terms. And here he was, now, with his own news website, a professional-looking one at that. There was a telephone number in the *Contact Us* section. Clare looked at it for a moment then reached for her mobile.

'Clare!'

Hearing Lyall's voice took her right back to the dreadful days of the missing baby case. It had been a race against time to find the tot who'd needed life-saving medication and it had almost cost Clare one of her officers' lives.

'How *are* you,' he went on. 'It's so lovely to hear from you.' He rattled on, Clare making several attempts to cut across him. Finally, when he drew breath she took her chance.

'I'm after a favour.'

'Anything for you,' Lyall said, sounding as if he'd won the lottery. 'I'm always happy to help.'

'How about lunch? My treat?'

–

The West Sands Inn was buzzing with holidaymakers enjoying lunch and a view over the beach when Clare arrived. Thankfully she'd phoned ahead and booked. As she approached the maître d' she saw a bespectacled figure in stonewashed jeans and a checked shirt rise from a table in the window. His face broke into a smile and he waved her across.

'My friend's over there,' she said, and the maître d' promised to bring them menus.

Lyall came to meet her, taking both her hands in his. 'It's so lovely to see you,' he said, his voice a little too loud. Clare noticed one or two diners looking round and she nodded at the table.

'Let's sit, shall we?'

'Oh yes, sorry!' He waited until she had sat then resumed his seat opposite. 'It's so lovely to see you,' he said again, his face all smiles. 'How is everyone? Is Jim still there? What about Chris?'

'It's great to see you too,' Clare said. 'Everyone's well. Chris and Sara get married in a couple of weeks.'

He beamed at that. 'Oh, how lovely. That's the best news ever! I must buy them a gift.'

Clare was keen to steer the conversation back to Lyall and his website. She indicated his clothes. 'You're a lot less formally dressed than the last time we met. Day off?'

He gave a small shrug. 'I'm freelance now. Mostly online stuff; and it's summer so…'

'Too hot for the tweed suit?'

'Just a bit.'

A waiter approached with a carafe of water and two glasses. Clare ordered a glass of ginger beer and Lyall said that sounded an excellent idea. The waiter arched an eyebrow and went off to fetch the drinks.

'I saw your website,' Clare said, when the waiter was out of earshot. 'Very impressive.'

He flushed and looked as if he was trying not to smile. 'I am quite proud of it.'

'Do you make a living from it?'

'More or less,' he said. 'I still write pieces for the broadsheets as well so I do better than a lot of journalists. So many have left for other jobs. I'm pretty lucky.'

Clare inclined her head. 'I think you make your own luck. You deserve to do well.'

He beamed again. 'Anyway, how can I help? I don't suppose you're offering me a scoop.'

'Afraid not. I would like some information, though.'

The waiter returned with their drinks and menus and, again, Clare waited until he was out of earshot. Then she leaned across the table. 'I saw your article on Banarvale Estate,' she said, her voice low.

Lyall's face assumed a serious expression. 'It's all true, you know. She walked away without paying a penny, that Monique. Had property in her husband's name. But the guests lost their deposits and there were other creditors too, not just the Revenue. Is that what you're interested in? Are you investigating her?'

Clare shook her head. 'Not at this stage. It's the early days that concern me – the planning application, how it came to be approved, that sort of thing.'

Lyall nodded. 'Definitely dodgy. A couple of councillors were friendly with Monique. I can't prove anything but there was a strong rumour she put them up at a fancy hotel for the weekend, all expenses paid. Wined and dined, and they waved her application through.'

'Did money change hands?' Clare asked.

Lyall hesitated. 'Again, I can prove none of this and it was well before my time. But I've spoken to journalists who were around then. Apparently it was an open secret these councillors could be bought. They reckon a whole load of applications were approved because they'd taken backhanders.'

'Do you know their names?'

'The councillors?' Lyall leaned forward. 'You can't quote me,' he said. 'I can't prove it and I don't want to be sued.'

'Strictly between us.'

He glanced over his shoulder then lowered his voice. 'Cliff Craven and Johnny Meadows.'

Chapter 33

Clare ordered the soup of the day and Lyall followed suit, pronouncing it delicious. They chatted over lunch then Clare held up her bank card and the waiter hurried over with the card machine. Lyall took a leather wallet from his pocket.

'My invitation, my treat,' she said, tapping her card against the machine. The waiter tore off a receipt and went off to take another payment. Clare pushed back her chair.

'I'd love to stay and chat more,' she said, 'but I'm in the middle of a murder investigation.'

'Any chance of a quote?' Lyall said. 'I'm guessing you're asking because of Cliff Craven's death.'

She smiled. 'There's not much I can say at this stage. But I will ask the press office to add you to their list.' They began walking to the door. 'What happened to Monique?' she asked. 'Is she still in business?'

'In Spain, last I heard,' Lyall said, holding the door open for Clare. 'Something to do with holiday lets.'

Clare shook her head. 'These people. They leave a trail of debt behind and move onto the next thing. It grinds my gears.'

They parted, Lyall full of smiles, Clare promising to stay in touch. She drove back to the office, her mind full of Banarvale. Maybe she could track down the builder if they were still in business. And then she remembered Reg, a local man who'd done some work at Daisy Cottage. He was in his sixties, she reckoned, so he might remember the development. She pulled into the station car park and took out her phone, scrolling until she found Reg's number.

'Reg Dunlop,' he said quickly, as if it was all one word.

'It's Clare,' she said. 'Clare Mackay from Daisy Cottage.'

'Ah yes, Clare. What can I do for you? I'm currently hanging off a chimney stack so I may need to call you back.'

'Crikey, Reg. Keep your hands on the chimney!'

He laughed. 'Ach, I'm used to it. And we've all gotta go somehow. So…'

'Would you have ten minutes for a chat? Maybe when you've finished today?'

'Aye, no problem. You want to come to the yard? I should be back about three thirty. Or I could pop round to the cottage tonight. Say, sixish?'

She thought for a moment. Chris and Max were due to pick up the two schoolboys around four. Could she guarantee to be home for six? Probably not. By the time they found solicitors for the pair she'd be lucky if the interviews had started by five. But if she was quick she could speak to Reg and hopefully be back at the station before the two lads arrived. 'I'll come to the yard, if that's okay,' she said. 'Three thirty.'

She entered the station by the side door and was heading for the kitchen when she heard Chris's voice.

'And what about the bridesmaids? Aren't they beautiful? I'd like to thank them for thanking Sara…'

'Supporting Sara,' Max's voice this time.

'Supporting Sara,' Chris repeated.

Clare coughed loudly and pushed open the door. Chris turned, his face flushed, and he put something quickly into his trouser pocket – his speech, she guessed.

'Speech sounds good,' she said, making for the kettle.

He shook his head. 'I can't get it right.'

'It's a lot better,' Max said, his smile encouraging.

'Look,' Clare said, 'speeches are not your forte, Chris. So to hell with it. Type it up neatly and read the damn thing. There's no rule says you have to do it by heart.'

His face lit up. 'Would that be okay?'

'It's your wedding – your big day. Do what the hell you like!'

He glanced at the door and lowered his voice. 'I don't want to let Sara down, though.'

Clare slapped him on the back. 'Sara loves you to bits. God knows why. I can't see it myself. But she'll be happy as long as you turn up and say *I do*. In the meantime...' she looked from Chris to Max, 'I've another job for the pair of you.'

'Why do I think we won't like it?' Chris said.

'Because you won't. I want you to look at Cliff Craven's finances now. Especially in the late 1980s.'

'The late Eighties?' Chris repeated. 'Could you be a bit more specific?'

'Not really. All I can tell you is it would predate the opening of the Banarvale Estate in 1989.'

'The Banarwhat?'

'It looks like Cliff Craven may have taken a backhander to put through a planning application for a Monique Taylor – a leisure development called the Banarvale Estate. From what I can gather it should have been refused but Cliff and another councillor called – hold on,' she reached in a pocket and took out her notebook, 'Johnny Meadows,' she said. 'It looks like both may have taken a backhander.'

'And you want us to look for cash deposits?' Max asked.

'Please. I've someone called Dave from the planning department calling me back when he digs it out so, at the moment, I've no idea when it would have been submitted.'

'Wouldn't it make sense to wait until we have a date?' Chris asked.

'Yes it would. But life's not like that so go to it, Sergeant!'

'Want us to look for Johnny Meadows as well?' Max asked.

'Yes, do that. I've no idea where he lives or if he's even still alive so it could be a needle in a haystack job.' She glanced at her watch. 'You've a couple of hours before you've to pick up Josh and Ethan. See what you can do.'

She left them before Chris could protest any further and went back to her office. There was a note on her desk from Bill to say the son of one of Cliff's possible victims was willing to make a statement. *He's away on business until tomorrow morning but happy to come in on Tuesday.*

She set the note aside and checked her watch. It was too early to head over to Reg's yard but she'd no appetite for the pile of paperwork on her desk, growing larger by the day. The DSO medal. She'd been about to search for a specialist dealer when Chris had interrupted her with the news about Rory Craven's money troubles. She pulled the keyboard towards her and began to type. A list of dealers appeared and she added Fife to the search terms. Scrolling down the results she saw there was a dealer that went by the curious name of Medalabilia near Dunfermline, about forty miles away. She picked up the phone and dialled the number. When it was answered she asked for the owner or manager. There was a soft murmur of conversation then a woman's voice said, 'Victoria Hartford. How can I help?'

Clare introduced herself and explained they were looking for someone who might have tried to sell a DSO medal.

'We did have an enquiry,' she said. 'About a week or ten days ago.'

'Was it by phone or in person?'

'Telephone. He didn't give a name.'

He. A male again. She was about to ask if Victoria had the caller's number then she remembered her conversation with Giles Paterson. No doubt whoever it was had withheld their number again. 'What was his voice like?'

There was silence for a moment. 'Scottish, not a strong accent, though. And an older voice, I'd say.'

'Can you remember anything else about the call?'

'Sorry. But I can take your number in case he gets in touch again.'

Clare left her number with Victoria and checked her watch. It was still quite early but if she headed for Reg's yard now she could be there when he arrived. And he might just be early. Calling to Jim to try and find solicitors for Josh and Ethan she went out into the summer sunshine and headed for her car.

Chapter 34

Reg was unloading his van when Clare arrived and she thought, not for the first time, he was exactly how she'd expect a builder to look. His T-shirt had probably been navy at one time but a thin film of dust seemed to be ingrained in the fabric, his cargo pants equally dusty. His face and arms were ruddy with working outdoors and there was a scab from a cut on the bridge of his nose. But his face broke into a smile when he saw her and she immediately felt her visit wasn't an unwelcome one.

'You're early,' he said, carrying a Stihl saw towards a steel storage unit, kicking the door open with the toe of his boot. 'Let me get the gear locked away then I'm all yours.'

She waited, enjoying the afternoon sun as she took in his yard. A flat-backed lorry was parked in front of a low sandstone building. It might have been a farm cottage at one time. Or a steading, maybe. He'd put a new roof on it and the windows were new as well. A nameplate on the door informed potential customers that he undertook all kinds of building and joinery work and a plaque on the wall next to this stated the opening hours. To the side he'd laid out samples of paving, to give customers ideas, she guessed.

'All done,' he called, clicking a substantial padlock on the door of the unit. 'Come into the office and tell me what you're after.'

She followed him in through the half glass door to a small room with a few chairs arranged round an old office desk. A Scots pictorial calendar was on the wall, the June photo showing Glamis Castle, its red sandstone walls bathed in summer sunshine. A telephone sat on the desk, a green light blinking, and she wondered if he had messages to answer. Reg moved round the back of his desk and indicated a seat. 'Please,' he said, running a hand through his hair. It was grey and wiry, and she watched as a cloud of dust escaped, some of it settling on his forehead, the rest on the desk.

'I won't keep you long,' Clare said, sinking into one of the chairs. 'But I'd like to pick your brains.'

He laughed, a throaty guttural laugh. 'You must be stuck, then. It's the cottage, is it? You got a problem?'

'Not this time,' she said. 'That work you did on the front porch was great.'

'Aye,' he said. 'Last you a lifetime, that will. Long as you keep it painted. So, if it's not the cottage...'

'I'm interested in a development built in the late 1980s.'

'Jeez, Clare. That's going back a bit.'

'I know. But you might remember this one.' She went on to explain about the Banarvale Estate and his expression changed.

'Oh I remember that one,' he said. 'A right mess they made of it, too.'

'You remember the builder?'

He nodded. 'I certainly do. Pete Willis. He's a yard out towards Newburgh. Just before you enter the town, on the Lindores road.'

'He's still trading?'

'Aye. God knows how. I wouldn't hire him to boil a kettle.'

'That bad?'

'Oh he gets the job done, right enough. But he cuts corners. That's how he gets all the business. He undercuts the competition.' He shook his head. 'You get what you pay for in this game. Anyway, Banarvale plans were approved and it went out to tender.'

'Did you bid for it?'

'Nah. Too big a job for me. I only had myself and a young lad at the time. Besides, when I heard Pete was putting in a bid I knew he'd get it – unless the landowner was fussy which, clearly, he wasn't.'

'She,' Clare corrected.

He laughed again. 'I could comment on that but I suppose I'd better not.'

Clare smiled. 'Maybe not. So you didn't know the landowner? It was a woman called Monique Taylor.'

'Nope. But I wasn't surprised when it closed a few years later. Matter of fact, I was surprised it lasted as long as it did. You hear things,' he went on, 'about how it was built. I went for a look around, after it was open. Cracked on I was thinking of renting one of the lodges. You could see how poor the finish was.'

They chatted on for a few more minutes then Clare checked her watch. 'I'd better go.'

Reg rose but she waved him back down. 'I'll see myself out but thanks for the info. It's really helpful.'

She backed out of the yard and turned towards the station, her head full of Banarvale. She arrived in time to see Max leading a white-faced Ethan into the station and she waited until they had gone inside. Then she climbed out of the car and headed for the side entrance. Time to see what the two lads had to say for themselves.

Chapter 35

Ethan Robertson eyed Clare warily as she and Chris entered the room. He was still in his school uniform, tie askew, shirt untucked. By contrast the middle-aged woman who sat next to him – his solicitor, Clare presumed – was neatly attired in a crimson bouclé jacket and wide-legged navy trousers. She smiled at Clare, a cool professional smile, and introduced herself.

Clare thanked them both for coming and said she would be taping the interview. The formalities over, she got straight to the point.

'Our technical support team have examined your mobile phone.' She waited a moment to see if Ethan would respond to this and when he didn't she went on. 'The first thing to say is your phone has been jailbroken.' She paused again to see if he would react. 'Would you like to tell us about that?'

Ethan shook his head. 'Dunno what you mean.'

'It means your phone has been altered allowing you to make further changes. Installing apps the phone company don't normally allow – that sort of thing.'

'I dunno,' Ethan said. 'I haven't done anything to it.'

'We also found an app had been installed and hidden. The shortcut isn't visible but it's there.' She glanced at the solicitor who had picked up her pen. 'It's called WeTransfer. I'd like to ask what you know about that.'

Ethan's eyes narrowed. 'I never installed any transfer thing.'

'I can tell you this app is not pre-installed on the type of phone you have.'

'What is this app used for?' the solicitor asked.

'It allows the transfer of large files from a phone to another device,' Clare said. 'Large files such as videos.' She watched Ethan carefully as she said this. There was a flicker of something in his eyes but he said nothing.

Clare softened her voice. 'Ethan, I'm aware what happened to Sophie must still be very raw for you and I'm sorry we have to keep going over this but I need to go back to the video of you and Sophie.'

The colour began to rise from Ethan's neck and he let his head droop, his eyes on the floor.

'As you know,' Clare went on, 'the video was made on your phone and we've been trying to find out how it came to be on that porn website. We now know it was sent to another phone using the WeTransfer app.'

He lifted his head and stared at her, his eyes wide, mouth partly open, as if he was about to speak. He swallowed a couple of times and cleared his throat. 'I didn't do that,' he said, his eyes beginning to fill with tears. He glanced at his solicitor. 'I didn't do it. I wouldn't do that to Sophie.' The tears began to spill down his face and the solicitor put down her pen.

'Is there much more you want to ask?' she said. 'As you can see this is very upsetting for Ethan, particularly as he's still coming to terms with losing Sophie in such tragic circumstances.'

Ethan drew a hand over his eyes and Clare pushed a box of tissues across the desk.

She smiled at the solicitor. 'I'm trying to find out how that video came to be sent from Ethan's phone. Installing a transfer app isn't illegal; nor is making a video with another person, providing all parties in the video consent. Sophie and Ethan are old enough to have consented but I don't believe Sophie did. In fact, it's possible she took her own life after discovering the video had been shared widely. So,' she turned back to Ethan, 'it's very important we know how that video came to be shared from your phone.'

He was shaking his head violently now. 'But that's what I'm telling you. I don't know how it got onto that site. I didn't share it,' he sobbed. 'I'd never do that.'

'Is it possible,' the solicitor said, 'that a jailbroken phone is vulnerable to hackers?'

Ethan's face cleared as he took in what the solicitor was saying. 'Yes,' he said, grabbing the proffered lifeline. 'That must be it. Someone got hold of my phone and jailbroke it. Then they put that app thing on. Probably some hacking thing as well.' He nodded at this. 'That would mean they could do stuff on my phone, wouldn't it? Like sending the video. That's it, isn't it?' He sat back, the relief evident.

'Has any such program been installed on Ethan's phone?' the solicitor asked.

'There is malware,' Clare admitted.

'And that would allow whoever downloaded it to Ethan's phone to access his videos? Perhaps use the transfer service?'

'It would.'

The solicitor picked up her pen and began to write. 'I think it's clear Ethan is the victim here. Whoever installed the malware is the guilty party.'

'Except,' Clare said, waiting for the solicitor to stop writing, 'phones do not jailbreak themselves.' She looked back at Ethan. 'Did you jailbreak your phone? You must tell us now if you did. It's not a crime, Ethan. It may invalidate your warranty but it's not something we could charge you with.'

'It's tempting,' Chris put in. 'Jailbreaking. Lets you put a lot more cool stuff on the phone.'

Ethan was shaking his head. 'I didn't. I wouldn't know how.'

'Did you give your phone to someone else?' Clare asked. 'Maybe a friend lost their phone. Asked if they could borrow yours?'

'No!'

'Is jailbreaking a quick process?' the solicitor asked. 'Could it be done, for example, with a few clicks? While someone pretended to be using Ethan's phone?'

Clare glanced at Chris.

'No,' he said. 'It would take a bit of time.'

'Then unless Ethan's phone was in someone else's hands for *a bit of time,* as you put it, Sergeant, I don't see how he can know who effected this change.'

'Unless he did it himself,' Clare said.

'But that's what I keep saying,' Ethan said, his voice rising. 'I don't know how to do it.'

Clare regarded him. Was he telling the truth? She found it impossible to know. 'Was your phone out of your possession for, say, ten minutes or more, over the past few weeks?'

'I don't...' he began, 'wait... yes it was!'

'When?'

'One day at school. Maybe a month ago. I lost it. Went to get it at break and it wasn't there. I'd had it at registration but by break it had gone.'

'How did you find it?'

'Lost property. A couple of first years found it in the boys' toilets. Lucky they handed it in.'

'How much later?'

'End of the day.'

Clare noted this down. 'We will check this with the school,' she said, and Ethan shrugged.

'I'm telling the truth.'

She watched him for a moment then pushed a sheet of paper across the desk. 'This is a printout from your phone company. It shows the transfer of the video to that number.' She tapped the paper. 'It's not saved in your contacts. Do you recognise it?'

Ethan studied the number and, for a moment, he said nothing, his eyes flitting back and forth as he took this in. 'Who is it?' he said, eventually. 'If you've got this, can't you trace it?' He whirled round to his solicitor, his expression pleading with her. 'They can do that, can't they?'

The solicitor glanced at him then back to Clare but Clare ignored the question.

'We were hoping you could tell us whose number it is,' she said.

Ethan's stared at her for a moment as though he still didn't understand. 'I thought you could trace phones. I thought you would know who did this. Can't the phone company tell you?'

'We've checked the number and it's unlisted,' Clare said. 'It's what we call a burner phone. Bought from a supermarket, pay-as-you-go so the user doesn't have to register their details.'

'Used by criminals,' Chris added.

The solicitor gave him a sharp look. 'I hope you're not suggesting Ethan is engaged in criminal activity.'

'Until we know who is responsible for sharing that video,' Clare said, 'we can't be sure.'

'For the avoidance of doubt,' the solicitor said, 'Ethan denies all knowledge of jailbreaking his phone, installing the transfer app and sending the video to the owner of the burner phone.'

Clare smiled at this. 'Thank you.' She scanned her notes then looked at Ethan, waiting until he met her eye. 'To recap then, Ethan, you believe your phone was stolen for the purpose of jailbreaking it, to allow malware to be installed. This then allowed the owner of the burner phone to take control of your phone, sending the video of you and Sophie to the burner phone, yes?'

Ethan glanced at his solicitor who gave a slight nod and he turned back to Clare. 'That's it,' he said. 'That's what must have happened.'

'In that case, I have one more question: who do you think stole your phone?'

–

Clare ended the interview shortly afterwards, leaving Ethan in conversation with the solicitor.

'Believe him?' Chris asked as they wandered through to the incident room.

She was quiet for a moment. 'I'm not sure. He did seem genuinely shocked the video had been sent from his phone. But that bit about the phone being stolen…'

'Bit convenient, isn't it?'

'It is.' She eased herself down on one of the desks. 'Oh I dunno, Chris. I could argue it either way.'

Chris glanced back towards the door where Max was signalling. 'Looks like the other lad's solicitor's arrived. Fancy a crack at him?'

If Ethan had looked wary, Josh looked downright terrified. The solicitor, a young man in a neat grey suit, smiled as they entered. He introduced himself and asked the purpose of the interview.

'I'll just set up the tape,' Clare said. Josh turned to his solicitor who put a reassuring hand on his arm. Clare cautioned Josh and explained she wanted to ask about his mobile phone.

'What about it?'

'Do you take it to school with you?'

'Yeah. Everybody does.'

'But presumably it has to be away while you're in classes?'

'Yeah. School rule. Usually keep mine in my pocket.'

'It's never off your person?' she asked. 'You always know where it is?'

'Well except at PE.'

'What happens then?'

'We have lockers,' Josh said. 'The keys are on wristbands.'

'So you put your valuables in a locker and keep the key on a wristband while you do PE, yes?'

He nodded.

'What about swimming?'

'Same. The keys are waterproof.'

'So, over the past few weeks, would you agree your phone has always been in your possession? You've not lost it or misplaced it?'

His eyes narrowed and he glanced at his solicitor who took the cue.

'Perhaps you could explain where you're going with this?' he said.

'Of course. Josh's phone has been jailbroken.' She watched him carefully as she said this. 'What that means is certain secure parts of the phone have been unlocked, allowing him to do things normally restricted by the phone company. So I'd like to ask if you did this, Josh?'

He turned to his solicitor. 'Do I have to answer this?'

'No,' the solicitor said. 'Don't say anything else until the inspector's explained why this is relevant.'

'Of course,' Clare said, forcing a smile. 'Josh's phone was carefully examined by our technical team and they found two items on the phone I'd like to ask Josh about. The first is an app called WeTransfer.' She turned to Josh. 'It's used to transfer large files such as videos, music files, photos…' she lingered over that last word and felt a pang of guilt as Josh flushed.

'As Josh is aware, some private photos on his phone found their way onto another phone. WeTransfer was used to send them. Josh then claimed the recipient blackmailed him into stealing an iPad.'

'I didn't send the photos to anyone,' Josh said, his voice small. 'Why would I? I don't know how they got hold of them.'

'It's not uncommon,' Clare said. 'Young men and women often exchange intimate photos. Perhaps you sent them to a girlfriend, or boyfriend, and they passed it on to your blackmailer?'

His head was shaking violently. 'I only took them for myself,' he said. 'Wish I'd never done it. I didn't send them to anyone.'

'You said there were two items on Josh's phone,' the solicitor said.

'The other was a malware program.'

The solicitor raised an eyebrow. 'What sort of malware?'

Clare hesitated. 'The kind that would allow someone else to control Josh's phone.'

'So, in fact,' the solicitor said, 'it would be possible for whoever installed the malware to have taken control of Josh's phone and sent these photos to the blackmailer, yes?'

'That is one scenario,' Clare admitted.

'And jailbreaking a phone could compromise its security?'

'It could.'

'So the malware could have been installed at the same time as the transfer app, and the photos sent, all without Josh's knowledge?'

'Unless Josh himself jailbroke the phone,' Clare said. 'Perhaps it was his intention all along to share the photos with someone else but unfortunately they fell into the hands of the blackmailer.' She smiled at Josh. 'It's so easy to type in the wrong number.'

Josh shook his head. 'I keep telling you. I don't know how it happened.' He was near to tears now and Clare's heart softened. He really was a victim here. She was sure of that, even if he did send the photos to a friend. 'Josh,' she said, her voice gentler, 'if you did send the photos to someone else you haven't committed a crime. Please don't worry about that. Jailbreaking your phone isn't a crime either. You're not in trouble here. We just want to get to the truth. So I'm going to ask again: did you jailbreak your phone?'

Clare thought there was some inner turmoil going on and she let the silence hang in the air. 'I… er… maybe,' he said, eventually. 'I might have done something like that.'

'How did you do it?'

He avoided her eye. 'Google,' he said. 'You can do lots of cool stuff with Google.'

The solicitor glanced at him. 'Is there something else, Inspector? Or can Josh go now? He's clearly very sorry for this whole business.'

Clare didn't answer this directly. Instead she pushed a sheet of paper across the desk, another phone company printout. She tapped the burner phone number. 'This number,' she said, 'who is it?'

Josh seemed at a loss. 'I don't know.'

'It's the number the photos were sent to.'

He stared at it again. 'Is it one of my contacts? I can't remember all the numbers.'

'No,' Clare said. 'It's not saved as a contact. But it is the same number that sent you messages, instructing you to steal the iPad.'

He sighed. 'Wish I'd never done that.'

Suddenly Clare changed subject. 'How's school?' she asked.

He was watching her carefully, as if trying to work out why she was asking. 'It's okay,' he said eventually.

'You're doing Highers this year, yes?'

He shook his head. 'Repeating some of my Nationals. Didn't get the grades for Higher.'

She smiled. 'I was hopeless at school. No matter how many times I sat maths I still failed.'

His expression was wary but she thought he was unbending. 'Hate maths,' he said.

'What are your subjects?'

'Not maths! I like language stuff. I'm doing French and German, Art, Music, History, PE… and English. We all have to do English. I don't mind, though. I like it.'

'Me too,' Clare said. She asked a few more questions but Josh was either unwilling or unable to tell them any more. She was about to end the interview when Chris sat forward.

'Josh, are you absolutely sure you jailbroke the phone on your own?' he said. 'Or did someone maybe help you do it? Or do it for you, even?'

Josh didn't speak for a moment. He flicked a glance at Chris then away again.

'You don't need to answer this,' the solicitor said.

And then Josh seemed to gather his wits and he met Chris's eye. 'I did it,' he said. 'I jailbroke my phone.'

—

'They've both lied,' Chris said, flicking off the interview room light. 'No question about it.'

'Agreed,' Clare said. 'I don't believe Ethan lost his phone for a day and I don't believe Josh is capable of jailbreaking his phone. He doesn't do any maths or computing.'

'I dunno about that,' Chris said. 'Kids these days are seriously tech-savvy.'

'That jailbreaking, though,' Clare said. 'It sounds difficult.'

'Anything techy's difficult for you, Grandma.'

'Bet I could do a wedding speech, though.'

'Touché.'

'The question is, if Josh didn't jailbreak his phone, who did it for him?'

–

Clare couldn't settle to work after the two interviews and she decided to call it a day. The DCI was at a community outreach event and she stopped off at Spice Palace for a takeaway curry. Benjy greeted her with the earth-clad remains of the basketball, covering her trousers in mud.

'How did you get that inside the house?' she said, picking it up between two fingers and firing it out the front door. He made to follow, clearly thinking it was a game, but came slinking back as she roared at him. She ruffled him behind the ears, conscious she'd spoiled his fun, and went to take his food from the cupboard. He fell on it before she'd stopped pouring it into the bowl and she shook her head. She should have made him wait, really. But she was too damn tired. 'You're such a thug,' she said, unpacking the takeaway bag. 'But I won't tell Al if you don't.' She spooned curry onto a plate and took it through to the sitting room on a tray. She flicked on the TV and channel hopped until she found something mindless and silly. Benjy, having scoffed his food, jumped onto the settee beside her and nestled into her side, clearly hopeful of a few titbits. As she ate, her eyes glued to the TV, enjoying the warmth of the little dog, the cares of the day began slowly to melt away.

Tuesday

Chapter 36

Clare had called a briefing for eight and she was pleased to see the incident room full when she entered, notepad in hand. Tony had sent the usual message to say he was running late and, if she was honest, she was relieved. It was useful having a DCI for warrants and the like but otherwise he wasn't a great deal of help.

'Thanks, everyone,' she said, bringing the briefing to order. 'There's a lot to get through so let's start with a quick recap.' She scanned the room to make sure they were all attending then went on. 'Our murder victim, Cliff Craven, died from suffocation, most likely with a cushion. Male DNA was found on the cushion but it doesn't match any of Cliff's family or regular visitors to the house. So let's keep looking into his background. See if we can turn up anyone else he was in contact with.'

Bill raised a hand. 'If we're looking for a male, I've got Keith Lambert coming in at ten.'

There were a few frowns round the room and Clare hastened to explain. 'As you know, Hazel Sullivan was a frequent visitor to Cliff's house. She told us initially he was helping her with some research but we later learned Cliff was a sex pest who had raped Hazel's mother. Hazel also told us she'd tracked down other victims. Keith Lambert is the son of one such victim. Allegedly,' she added. 'Give me a shout when he comes in,' she said, and Bill nodded.

Max caught her eye. 'The cleaning woman, Alma – no connection to the council.'

Clare acknowledged this and glanced down at her notepad. 'Cliff's son Rory's business is in financial trouble,' she went on. 'He owes the Revenue forty grand and there may be other debts. We've not spoken to Rory about this but I will have to raise it with him.' She gave them a smile. 'I just need to pick the right moment.' There was a ripple of laughter round the room and Clare said, 'Rory thinks some items have gone missing from his father's house. I've spoken to a couple of dealers both of whom have had phone calls from a male asking about selling similar items – possibly an older male. The calls weren't followed up but the dealers have my details if the caller gets in touch again.'

'Could be whoever took the items is lying low until the fuss dies down,' Max said.

'Yep. It wouldn't make sense to try and sell Cliff's valuables while we're hunting his killer.'

Erin raised a hand. 'Do we think the thief is the killer?'

'We haven't enough evidence to say one way or the other,' Clare said. 'So far...'

'What about the Craven kids?' Janey asked. 'Seems to me they're more likely to have taken a few bits from the grandad's house – sell them for some extra cash. They'd have regular access to the house and didn't you say the lad had taken a painting down for his grandad?'

'So he told us,' Clare said.

'They might have got themselves into debt,' Janey went on. 'Maybe they're using – habit's getting out of hand and they need a few extra quid.'

Clare looked round for Chris. 'Anything in their finances?'

He shook his head. 'Both had a generous allowance from Cliff. Money in their bank accounts.'

'There's Cliff's will, though,' Max said.

'Good point. Marcus and Lauren Craven each inherit ten grand from Cliff's estate.'

'Are we definitely ruling them out of involvement in his death?' Erin asked.

'At this stage, I think so,' Clare said. 'It sounds like Cliff was pretty generous to them; and their DNA wasn't on that cushion, remember.'

'They could have worn gloves,' Erin persisted. 'And ten grand – depending on what's going on in their lives, it could be a motive.'

Clare nodded. 'It's a fair point, Erin. I'll bear it in mind.'

Sara raised her hand. 'I've gone through the footage from Retworth's shop around the time we think the items went missing. I've taken stills of their customers. I can add them to the network if it would be useful?'

'Good idea, Sara. Are there many?'

'About forty or so.'

Clare acknowledged this and she went on. 'As well as Cliff's sexual shenanigans it looks like he may have taken a backhander to approve a planning application. The development was called the Banarvale Estate. The committee was advised to reject it at the time but it was approved anyway. The contract was then given to a pretty shoddy builder.'

'Name?' Chris asked.

'Pete Willis. Has a yard on the way to Newburgh.'

Benny rolled his eyes. 'He's shocking. Put a kitchen in for my mate's mum. In the end she gave up trying to get him to put it right and brought in a proper builder. I'm amazed he's still trading.'

'Was he the landowner?' Janey asked.

'No. A woman called Monique Taylor. We think she's the one who gave Cliff and another councillor called Johnny Meadows a backhander.' She looked across to Max. 'Any luck finding Meadows, by the way?'

'Shouldn't be much longer,' he said, and Clare pressed on.

'I'm waiting on a call back from the planning department. Once I have dates I'd like Chris and Max to find who Monique banked with at the time. Might have been a business account so it's worth looking on Companies House first. It'll be archived but let them know it's a murder enquiry.'

'But if this Meadows guy did take a backhander,' Chris said, 'he won't want to admit it.'

Clare nodded. 'We'll cross that bridge when we come to it.'

Benny raised his hand. 'I might be reading this wrong, but I don't see how this Banarvale thing relates to Cliff's murder?'

It was a good point. It was so long ago now. Even if Cliff had taken a backhander, would they be able to prove it? And did it really have anything to do with his murder?

'You're right,' she said to Benny. 'I can't see it either. But it's part of who he is so we can't ignore it.' She looked round at them. 'Keep digging into his background. This wasn't a housebreaking gone wrong. Cliff was targeted. Let's find out why.'

—

Keith Lambert arrived on the dot of ten. He was tall and well built, a suntan evident through his pristine white shirt. He seemed tired and Clare caught him yawning as she led him to an interview room.

'Sorry,' he said. 'I'm just back from Dubai.'

'Holiday?'

'Business. I'm a civil engineer. Been working on a new hotel complex. No expense spared.'

Unlike Banarvale, Clare thought but did not say. 'Were you out there long?'

'Just over a month. Got back yesterday but I'm still catching up on sleep.'

That let him out of Cliff's murder. They'd have to check it of course but he'd come in voluntarily so she couldn't see why he'd lie about it. They exchanged a few more pleasantries then Clare got down to business.

'We're investigating the death of Cliff Craven.'

He raised an eyebrow. 'So I heard. No great loss to mankind.'

'Can I ask why you say that?'

He shrugged. 'I mean it's only what my dad's told me, but the man was a menace.'

'In what way?'

'Women. He wouldn't leave them alone. Only, he reckoned without my dad.'

'Can you tell me what happened?' Clare said.

'Mum worked in the planning department. From what Dad said, Cliff had always been a bit handsy, you know? Patting them on the shoulder, sometimes on the bottom.' He shook his head. 'I reckon he did it to see how they'd react. If they didn't kick off – and no one did back then – he'd ask them to stay late, help him with a project. Made them feel important. Flattered them, I suppose. Waited until the office had emptied then he'd break out the brandy or the whisky, pour them a drink. I'm sure you can guess the rest.'

'I'm sorry to ask,' Clare said, 'but this happened to your mum?'

He nodded. 'Only she managed to get away from him. Fortunately the caretaker heard Mum shout and came to see what was going on and she got away. Thank goodness she had the presence of mind to tell my dad. Next day he marched into the office and told Craven to leave his wife alone or he'd knock his fucking block off.' He laughed. 'I think those were his exact words.'

'And that stopped it?'

'Yeah. Mum was moved to another department but I don't think she minded, to be honest. It got her away from him. I think she was embarrassed, not that she'd any reason to be. He's the one who should have been embarrassed. But that kind never learn, do they?'

Clare studied Keith Lambert, trying to work out his age. Forty-five maybe. Fifty at most. His dad might still be fairly young. 'Do your mum and dad still live in the area?'

He shook his head. 'Dad died five years ago and Mum moved down to the borders, closer to her sister. I'm away a lot so it made sense for her to move.'

Clare noted this down. That let the Lambert men out, then. Keith was in Dubai when Cliff was killed and his father five years dead. She asked Keith to contact her if he remembered anything else and she let him go.

When he'd gone she sat on in the interview room, mulling the case over. They weren't making any progress; and nor were they any further forward in finding who'd hacked into the two lads' phones. Maybe she was losing her touch.

She rose, flicked off the light and headed for her office.

'What news from the front?' A voice behind her. Tony.

'I wish I had some. Fancy a coffee?'

'Always. I'll make it. You're rubbish at coffee.'

They took their drinks into Clare's office and she filled him in on the murder case. 'Sara's done headshots from the second-hand shop,' she said. 'I'll have a look through them later on.'

'What about the two porn kings?'

'Josh and Ethan? I reckon someone helped jailbreak their phones but they won't say who.'

'Scared?'

'Possibly.'

He sat back, drumming his fingers on Clare's desk. 'Thing is, this could be a lot bigger than those two lads. They're only the ones we know about.'

'I know. But I'm not sure what else we can do.'

He thought for a moment. 'Which of the two's the flakiest?'

'As in the most nervous?'

'Aye.'

'Josh, I'd say. He seemed more embarrassed by what he'd done.'

'He the one that took the iPad?'

'He is. What are you thinking?'

'Have you told him he'll get off with a caution?'

'Yes, but I did say we might look into it further.' She stared at him. 'What's in your mind?'

He smiled. 'A honey trap.'

'Oh no,' she said. 'You're not serious?'

'You've nothing to lose and potentially quite a lot to gain.'

'We'd never get authorisation,' she said. 'It's immoral. These are teenage lads. The press would have a field day.'

'It's a lot less immoral than half the stuff the Met get up to in the name of fighting crime. I'm not thinking of using the lad himself. Just his phone.'

'Okay. Tell me.'

Chapter 37

Clare arranged a Zoom call with Tony and Diane from Tech Support. Diane listened, asked a few questions and was silent for a minute. Eventually she spoke. 'And you reckon you can get authorisation for this?'

'You do your end,' Tony said, 'I'll get it authorised.'

'I'd want it in writing,' she said. 'It's my career too. I'm not taking any chances.'

'Leave it with me.'

The call ended and for a moment Clare didn't speak. 'She's not happy about it,' she said eventually.

'She doesn't have to be happy,' he said. 'She just needs to do it. I'll get onto Penny Meakin now. If she gives us the go-ahead you get the lad in. Better have a parent as well.'

'He won't like that,' Clare said. 'I don't think he's told them about the photos. I'll see if Jim can drum up an appropriate adult instead.'

'And a solicitor,' Tony said. 'I'll call Penny now.'

'She'll eat you for breakfast.'

'Nah. I helped bump start her car the other day. She loves me.' He took out his phone to make the call but Clare's phone began to ring and he rose to make his call elsewhere.

'Dave Cross,' the voice said. 'From the planning department.'

'Oh yes,' Clare said. 'Thanks for calling back. Were you able to find anything out?'

'I was. You got a pen?'

Clare snatched up a pen. 'Yes. Go ahead.'

'The application was approved on thirtieth of July 1987. The applicant was a Mrs Monique Taylor. There were a few caveats about flood protection. Otherwise, pretty straightforward. Is that okay? Or do you need to know anything else?'

'When was the application lodged?'

'Hold on…' he was quiet for a moment then said, 'Fifteenth of April. Same year.' Clare noted this down and thanked Dave for the prompt reply. She went in search of Tony and found him in full flow on the phone.

'You got that new battery yet?'

Clare couldn't hear the other end of the conversation, then Tony burst out laughing. She had to hand it to him, really. Anyone who could (if he was to be believed) wrap Penny Meakin round his little finger had to be admired. But would it work this time? Would Penny go for their plan? Like Diane, she wasn't convinced it was a good idea. But it might just work.

'I'll hold you to that,' Tony was saying.

Clare decided she couldn't stomach any more of Tony's charm-fest and she made to leave the room but he waved her back.

'Better go,' he said. 'DI Mackay's cracking the whip here.' There was a silence, then another burst of laughter and he ended the call.

'Well?'

'Told you she'd go for it. Get back on to the code monkeys and tell them we're on. Then get the lad and his minders in. Let's get this set up.'

–

It took Jim a couple of hours to find a duty solicitor and appropriate adult. 'They can't be here until three,' he said. 'Is that okay?'

'Thanks, Jim. I appreciate it.' She stood thinking for a minute. 'Let's get a message to the school. Confidential. Ask Josh to leave at quarter to three. No details and no one else is to be informed. Then I want an unmarked car and a plain-clothes officer waiting outside for him. I don't want Ethan to know what's going on.'

'Sounds a bit cloak and dagger,' Jim said.

'The less you know, the better,' Clare said and she went to find Chris and Max.

In her office she closed the door and told them what was planned. 'You won't be in the interview, though. Tony and I will see Josh, and not a word to the rest of the team. I want this kept as quiet as possible.'

Benny was despatched to collect Josh and they arrived at the station just before three. Josh's face was ashen, his eyes full of worry. 'I'm not sure how much more of this I can stand,' he said to Clare.

She gave him what she hoped was a reassuring smile. 'Don't worry. We'll explain everything shortly.'

Clare was pleased to see Jim had managed to get the same solicitor as on the previous day and she nodded to the young man. 'Thanks for coming in again,' she said and he acknowledged this. She was also relieved the appropriate adult was another man in his late twenties. Hopefully Josh would be more relaxed with the two of them in his corner.

She began with a brief account of Josh's attempted theft of the iPad right up to the interview yesterday when they'd asked him about jailbreaking his phone. 'As far as we're concerned the matter of the iPad is over. We had planned to issue Josh with a formal caution. But DCI McAvettie has proposed an alternative.' She smiled at Josh. 'If you agree to help us with our investigations your record will be wiped. No caution,' she added, in case he hadn't understood.

'This is starting to sound like blackmail,' the solicitor said.

'Not really,' Clare said. 'What we propose doesn't really involve Josh. But we need his consent.'

Josh looked from Clare to Tony. 'I don't understand.'

Tony sat forward. 'It's like this, son. We want to use your phone to try and flush out the person who stole your photos.'

'And how do you propose to do that?' the solicitor asked.

'Before we go any further,' Tony said, 'I want an assurance from Josh – from all three of you – that what we say will go no further than these four walls.' He fixed Josh with a steely gaze. 'If you can't do that, now's the time to tell us.'

The solicitor scraped back his chair. 'I think it's only fair to Josh if I hear what is proposed first. If I deem Josh's participation might be harmful to him I will advise him against it.'

Clare glanced at Tony. 'I think that's fair enough.'

Tony nodded and he rose to open the door. 'If Josh and...'

'Gavin,' the appropriate adult said.

'If Josh and Gavin would step outside for a minute.'

They waited until the pair had left the room then Tony closed the door and resumed his seat. The solicitor looked at them expectantly.

Clare glanced at Tony again then she began. 'As you know from the interview yesterday, Josh's phone was jailbroken, either with or without his knowledge. For whatever reason he isn't keen to tell us who did that. But that doesn't matter. We believe whoever jailbroke his phone also blackmailed him into stealing the iPad.'

'Yes,' the solicitor said, 'you've already said so.'

'What we propose,' Tony said, taking up the thread, 'is to upload what appears to be a pornographic video to Josh's phone.'

'Appears?'

'Yes. Our techy guys will mock something up. It won't be clear but they'll save it with a name that'll make whoever sees it think it's pornographic. They'll add some...' he broke off.

'Metadata,' Clare said, and he nodded.

'Yeah, that. Stuff that'll help the hackers spot it. But when they try to download it to their device – phone or laptop – it'll look like it's buffering.'

'But while it's apparently buffering,' Clare went on, 'it'll be uploading malware to the hacker's device. That'll give us the IP address and the location of that device.'

'And a tracker,' Tony said. 'So we'll find whoever is hacking these kids' phones and blackmailing them.'

The solicitor sat for several minutes, his fingers steepled. 'I'm concerned,' he said at last, 'that the video will have originated from Josh's phone. On the face of it a prosecutor could argue Josh himself sent the video to the hacker using the transfer app.'

Clare shook her head. 'We've logged the date and time Josh's phone was seized. Our tech department did a full download of the content and any video we upload as bait will be date and time stamped.'

Again, the solicitor sat for a few minutes, processing this. 'And Josh gets a clean bill of health?'

'He does,' Tony said.

'Whether this works or not?'

'Absolutely. You have my guarantee.'

Privately Clare thought Tony's guarantees weren't worth having but she'd back the solicitor up if it came to it.

'Then I will advise Josh to do as you suggest,' he said. 'Can we have him back in please?'

Josh's eyes were like saucers when they explained what was proposed. 'So that would be... on my phone?' he said.

'Only for as long as we need it,' Clare said. 'Once we've secured a conviction your phone will be returned to you, the video completely removed.'

'Should Josh's parents be told about this?' Gavin asked, but Josh shook his head vehemently.

'I don't want them to know,' he said. 'They... they wouldn't understand.'

Clare thought he underestimated his parents. 'They were young once too,' she said, but Josh wouldn't have it.

Gavin glanced at the solicitor who gave him a nod. 'It'll be fine,' he said.

'Josh?' Clare said. 'What do you think?'

He shrugged. 'Sounds pretty cool. I'm in.'

–

Diane said as soon as written authorisation came through from Penny Meakin she'd get to work on the video. 'Hopefully have it by tomorrow morning.'

'Thanks, Diane. I really appreciate it.'

'I just hope it works,' and she ended the call.

Clare put down the phone, unable to shake off a feeling of discomfort. She knew Diane wasn't happy and she didn't like it. They'd been friends and colleagues for years but now there was a tension between them. And then she thought of Sophie Bakewell and the tragic end to her life. She thought of Sophie's parents, haunted and broken by their daughter's last desperate act, and her resolve strengthened. It wasn't an ideal solution but if it worked it would be worth it.

She found it hard to settle, her head full of Tony's plan, so she wandered through to the incident room to see what was happening.

'We've found Monique Taylor's bank,' Chris said. 'Max is putting in an access request for her records – 1987 to 1989. Same for Cliff Craven.'

'Any luck finding Johnny Meadows?'

'Not yet,' Chris said. 'But we're on it.'

Clare smiled her thanks and wandered over to where Sara was tapping at a laptop. 'Did you put those stills from Retworth's shop up on the network?'

Sara nodded. 'Want to see them?'

'Go on.' She stretched and yawned while Sara loaded the photos. Already it felt like it had been a long day. The photos began to appear and Sara handed Clare the mouse.

'That's the first. You can set them to play like a slide show.'

She watched as the photos flicked on and off the screen, studying each in turn. None looked familiar and she was starting to think it was a lost cause when one caught her eye. 'Stop,' she said. 'Can you make it go back?'

Sara took the mouse and began flicking back through the images.

'That one.' Clare jabbed the screen. 'I've seen him before, but I can't remember where.' The photo was of an elderly man in a tweed jacket. His hair was receding at the temples and he was clean shaven.

'Do you know him?' she asked Sara, but the PC shook her head.

'You could do a reverse image search?' she said.

Clare yawned again. 'Could you do that please? See if we can place him.'

It took Sara a few minutes to search for the image then the results filled the screen. To Clare's disappointment it showed a series of similar faces but there wasn't another of the same man.

'Never mind,' Sara said. 'We'll find him. If you've seen him before, chances are someone else has too. I'll pass it round the room. Get it out to other stations as well.'

Clare thanked her and went back to her office. It was gone five now and she'd been in the station for almost ten hours. Time to call it a day. She logged off her computer and went out to her car.

It was only when she was lying in bed a few hours later, sleep eluding her, that she realised where she'd seen the man before.

Wednesday

Chapter 38

'You're remembering about Benjy?' the DCI said over breakfast.

Benjy, hearing his name stopped chasing his tail and put his head on the DCI's knee.

Clare stared at him. 'Umm…'

He drained the last of his coffee, nudged Benjy's head off his knee and rose from the table. 'I knew you'd forget. He has the vet's at six. His annual health check? Ring any bells?'

It had completely slipped her mind. 'Oh that,' she said. 'Yes, I was remembering.'

'It's a good job you don't perjure yourself in the witness box,' the DCI said. 'You're a dreadful liar.'

'I was remembering. It's just…'

'You want me to take him? Clare, we went through this. I'm off to Tulliallan for the day. The focus group?'

'Sorry, Al,' she said. 'You know what work's like just now. There's so much going on. Maybe I could ask Moira.'

'She's going to Edinburgh tonight,' he said. 'Remember? She's tickets for a show.'

'Dammit, so she has. She said she'd set off after Benjy's afternoon walk.' She sat contemplating this.

'Want to cancel the appointment?'

She shook her head. 'Don't worry. I'll make sure I'm finished in time.'

He stooped to kiss her. 'See you do. And not just for Benjy. You were talking in your sleep last night. That's a sure sign you're stressed.'

'Oh yeah?'

'Yup.'

'Anything interesting?'

He inclined his head. 'I did hear Tony mentioned once or twice. You carrying a torch for the world's worst DCI?'

She picked up a tea towel and balled it, preparing to fire it at him. 'You're making that up.'

'You'll never know for sure,' he said. 'See you tonight!' And, with that, he went out, slamming the front door behind him.

She sat on for a minute or two, wondering if she had been dreaming about Tony. 'That,' she said to Benjy who was hovering, hoping for a stray bit of toast, 'would be a nightmare.'

—

She drove into work with the car windows down, the sunshade tilted to keep the sun out of her eyes. It was going to be another lovely day. A couple were sitting in their garden, mugs in hand, their faces upturned to the sun. An early breakfast, Clare guessed. Further along a sprinkler was playing on a front lawn. It had been a lovely spell and she hoped the weather would hold for Chris and Sara's wedding, only ten days away.

Sara was in the station kitchen, putting a pair of matching lunchboxes in the fridge.

'Can you do me a favour?' Clare asked.

'Sure. What is it?'

'Can you print out that photo? The one I thought I recognised.'

'Will do. Have you worked out who he is?'

'No,' Clare said. 'But I'm pretty sure I saw him in Strathkinness High Road the day I went to ask Cliff about the stolen items. I'm going to ask Rory Craven if he recognises him.'

'I'm actually coming into town,' Rory said when Clare asked if she could call on him. 'I could look into the station, say about ten?'

'Perfect. See you then.'

Chris ambled into her office as she was ending the call. 'S'up?'

'One of Sara's photos,' she said. 'From Retworth's?'

'Yeah. What about it?'

'I'm pretty sure I saw the man in the photo near Cliff Craven's house the day before his body was found.'

'Any idea who he is?'

'Nope. But Rory Craven's coming in to see me at ten so I'm going to ask him. And,' she went on, 'I'll have a crack at his money troubles as well. It'll be easier to bring it up here than at his home. More formal.'

Chris nodded. 'Want me to sit in?'

'Please.' Clare's phone began to ring and Chris hovered, settling himself down on a chair, waiting to hear if the call was important.

'Raymond,' Clare mouthed as she swiped to take the call. 'Hiya,' she said. 'What can I do for you?'

'It's more what I can do for you,' he said. 'I have some news.'

Clare raised an eyebrow at Chris and switched her phone to speaker. 'Go on.'

'I've run all your DNA tests, as you know, and we don't have a match for the cushion. But I also did some familial checks.'

'And?'

'Hazel Sullivan has a 50 per cent match with Cliff Craven.'

'She's his daughter?'

'Almost certainly.'

Clare glanced at Chris but Raymond was still talking.

'There's more.'

'Not another child?'

'The opposite, actually. Rory Craven is not Cliff's child.'

Clare was silent for a moment. 'You sure?' she said, eventually. 'No mix-up?'

'Definitely. I checked it myself. Hazel and Cliff are first degree relatives but Cliff and Rory are not related.'

Clare put down her phone and stared at Chris.

'You gonna tell him?' Chris said.

She considered this. 'I'm not sure. He has a right to know but the case takes priority and I'm not convinced that family's telling the whole truth.'

'On the other hand…'

'Go on.'

'If you do tell him you'll almost certainly get a reaction. Might be worth it.'

She considered this. 'It's a good point. I think I'll see how the interview goes.' She lifted her phone again. 'Better let the FLO know.'

Paul Henry answered the phone on the first ring.

'Can you be overheard?' Clare asked.

'Nah. Rory's out and the kids are mooching about in their rooms. Not sure what I'm doing here, to be honest.'

'Then pay attention. We've had some news,' and she relayed the conversation with Raymond.

'Jeez,' Paul said, 'I wonder if the old man knew his wife was putting it about.'

'Keep your voice down,' Clare hissed. 'And keep that to yourself. If anyone's going to tell the Cravens, it'll be me.'

'Whatever you say.'

'He's such an arse,' Chris said when she'd finished.

'No argument there.' She checked her watch. 'Any luck with Monique Taylor's bank?'

'Nothing back yet. Hopefully it won't take too long.'

'Okay,' Clare said. 'Can you set up the interview room for Rory please?'

'Suppose. What are you going to do?'

'Inspectory stuff. So scoot and let me get on.'

Rory Craven arrived just before ten. He was more formally dressed than when she'd seen him at his home. Maybe he was going back to work.

'Thanks for coming in,' she said, showing him to the interview room. 'Would you like some tea or coffee?'

He shook his head. 'I'm heading to the office. I only stopped in town to do a couple of things.' He waited until Clare and Chris had sat then said, 'So, what was it you wanted?'

Clare opened a folder and took out the photo of the man she'd seen in Strathkinness High Road. 'Do you recognise this man?'

He took the photo and studied it for a minute, then his face cleared. 'I remember now,' he said. 'That's Johnny Meadows. Dad worked with him at the council. I'm pretty sure he used to visit Dad.'

'You're sure?'

'I think so. It's not a great photo but I'm fairly sure it's him.' He handed it back to Clare. 'Where was it taken?'

She ignored the question. 'Was your dad still in touch with him?'

'Yeah,' he said. 'I think so. Like I said, he visited Dad. Talked over the old days.' His face softened at the memory. 'They were company for each other. I reckon Johnny'll miss Dad.'

'Do you have an address for him?' Clare asked. 'Or a phone number?'

He shook his head. 'Sorry, no. Might be in Dad's phone, I suppose.'

Clare nodded. 'We'll check.'

'Well,' he said, 'if that's all...'

'Actually there is something else,' Clare said. 'Something we wanted to ask you about.'

He looked from one to the other, his eyes narrowing. 'Oh yeah?'

'I understand your company has a sizeable debt.'

He stiffened and for a moment he said nothing. 'Why is that relevant?' he said, at last.

'In a murder enquiry, everything's relevant.'

He put a hand to his chin, rubbing it slowly. 'Let me see if I understand correctly. You're suggesting I benefit by my father's death, yes? Now he's dead my money worries are over?'

'Is that true?' Clare asked.

He met her eye and seemed to be weighing what to say next. 'Would it surprise you to know, Inspector, I haven't the faintest idea what my father's worth?'

'Did he own his house?'

'Yes. And of course it's a substantial property, but there is such a thing as inheritance tax. Then there's the bequests to the kids.'

'He was insured of course,' Clare said smoothly.

He eyed her. 'Done your homework.'

She smiled. 'It's what we do.'

He fell silent for a minute, as though ordering his thoughts. 'Okay,' he said, eventually. 'I do owe the Revenue a bit. Couple of other creditors too. But I'm sorting it. Obviously Dad's money will help but I was on top of things before… well, I was handling it. And, yeah, the insurance policy will come in handy, too. No doubt about it. But if you're asking if I killed him for his money then the answer's a categoric no.' He scraped back his chair and rose. 'And if you want to discuss it any further I'll see you with my solicitor.'

Clare was silent for a moment then she came to a decision. 'There is just one thing more.'

Rory stopped in his tracks and turned back to face her. 'Which is?'

'You might want to sit down.'

He looked pointedly at his watch. 'I do have a business to run.'

Clare nodded at the chair. 'Please.'

He sat back down heavily and met her eye. 'So?'

'I have some further news,' she said. 'News which I think may be difficult for you.'

His jaw tightened. 'About Dad?'

'In a way.' She took a deep breath. 'As you know we took DNA from you all, for elimination purposes. So we knew which profiles we could ignore.'

'And?'

'As part of our investigations we also took DNA from your father; and I'm afraid it appears you and your father – Cliff Craven – are not blood relatives.'

He stared at her, his eyes narrowed. 'What are you talking about?'

'First degree relatives – father and son, siblings – they have a 50 per cent match in their DNA. I'm afraid there was no match between you and your father. I'm so sorry, Rory, but Cliff Craven is not your biological father.'

His lips parted as if he was about to speak but, for a moment, he said nothing. The air in the room hung thick and Clare was suddenly conscious of her own breathing.

'I don't believe you,' he said at last.

She gave a slight nod. 'I understand that. But it's been carefully checked. I'm afraid it is true.' She glanced at Chris again. 'And there is something else I would like to warn you about.'

The expression in his eyes had grown wary, fearful even, as if dreading what was to come. 'Jesus,' he said. 'Go on, then. Let's have it.'

She took a moment to order her thoughts. Strictly speaking, she couldn't tell Rory about Hazel's DNA. Not without her permission. But surely he had the right to know something? She'd never encountered a situation like this before. He was watching her, his eyes narrowed.

'Well?'

She took a deep breath. 'It appears your father has a 50 per cent DNA match with another person. One who is not part of your family,' she added.

Rory opened his mouth to speak then he hesitated, as if processing this. 'What are you talking about? One who isn't part of the family – what do you mean?'

'Your father had another child,' Clare said. 'One I believe he didn't know about.'

He stared and, again, he seemed at a loss. 'Rubbish,' he said, eventually. 'You've made a mistake.'

In spite of his manner, the brusqueness he'd shown since the first day they'd met, Clare's heart went out to him. His father had been murdered, he'd just learned he wasn't actually Cliff's child and now she'd told him someone else was. 'I'm afraid there's no doubt.'

'Who is it?' he said.

'I can't…'

'You can't drop something like this on me and not tell me who it is.'

'I can't tell you without the person concerned giving her permission.' Too late, she saw her mistake.

'Her? So it's a woman?'

'Figure of speech,' Clare said quickly, but he wasn't listening. She could see him turning it over in his mind, working it through.

'It must be… it must be someone you've interviewed – or someone whose DNA's already on the system,' he said. 'Otherwise, how would you know?'

'I really can't…'

And then she saw his face clear and she knew he'd worked it out.

'It's her, isn't it?' he spat. 'That Hazel woman. You're telling me her DNA's a match for my dad's? Or maybe I shouldn't call him that!' He shook his head. 'No, I'm not having it. You've mixed the DNA up. You've mixed mine up with hers. There's no way she's his child and I'm not.'

'I'm afraid that's not possible,' Clare said. 'You see, we can tell someone's sex from their DNA, so we couldn't mistake female DNA for yours.'

He shook his head. 'It is her, though, isn't it?'

Clare spread her hands. 'I really can't say any more. Not without permission from the other person. I only mentioned it because I thought you should know.'

Rory's hand went to his face. 'She's after Dad's money, isn't she? Trying to do me out of my inheritance.'

'We think there may be more to it than that,' Clare said.

'I don't give a damn what you think.' He rose again, kicking the chair back noisily. 'Well she can try but she'll have a fight on her hands. She gets her mitts on Dad's money over my dead body.'

He made for the door and Chris stepped forward to open it. Rory stared at Clare for a long moment then he walked out without a backward glance.

'That went well,' Chris said, closing the door and sitting down on the chair Rory had just vacated. 'Maybe you shouldn't have...'

Clare exhaled audibly. 'No shit, Sherlock. Well, it's done now. I'd better warn Paul Henry.' She reached for her phone then stopped. 'What do you reckon?'

Chris considered this. 'Not sure. I'd say the DNA thing was news to him; and he didn't know about Hazel either.'

'Agreed.'

'The old man dying has got Rory out of a hole, though,' Chris went on. 'And it wasn't a violent murder. Not like some we've dealt with. It would have been over quite quickly. Maybe he wanted to spare him a lingering death.'

Clare nodded. 'And solve his financial problems at a stroke. He wouldn't be the first. All the same, I'm not sure.' She was quiet for a moment. 'Johnny Meadows. Soon as you've tracked him down we'll have him in.'

Chapter 39

'That's your video ready to go,' Diane said. 'Just say the word.'

'Hold on.' Clare rose from her desk. She found Tony in the room he was using as a temporary office. 'Diane's done the video. We okay to go ahead?'

'Yep. Do it.'

'I heard that,' Diane said. 'Uploading it now. Should be done in a minute.'

'And you'll let us know?'

'Soon as it's accessed.'

She went in search of Chris. 'Anything doing?'

'We've found Johnny Meadows.'

'Excellent. Address?'

'Langlands Road,' Chris said. 'Not too far from here. You want him picked up?'

She nodded. 'Yeah. Let's bring him in. I'd like to take his DNA to check against that cushion.'

Chris frowned. 'I can't see the motive, though. One old duffer killing another.'

'Sounds to me like he's the thief,' Max said. 'He was in Retworth's CCTV and both those dealers said the phone calls were from an older man.'

'Send a couple of uniforms round,' Clare said. 'Let's not waste any more time.' She glanced at Max who had turned back to his computer. 'Any luck with the bank?'

'Yes. They rushed it through for me. I'm going through Monique Taylor's account now.' He checked his notepad. 'I've gone from the fifteenth of April when the plans were submitted...'

Clare pulled up a chair and sat looking over his shoulder.

'This looks iffy,' Max said, jabbing the screen with a finger. 'She's withdrawn twenty grand on the thirtieth of April.'

'Check Cliff's account for the following couple of weeks,' Clare said.

Chris moved his chair so he too could see Max's screen.

Max began tapping at the keyboard and a minute later Cliff's account appeared. He scrolled back to 1987, stopping at the end of April. 'Okay, that looks like a salary,' he said, 'then it's mostly debits until… there you go!' He clicked with the mouse and highlighted a transaction on the fourth of May.

'Star Wars Day,' Chris muttered and Clare threw him a look.

'That's only for ten grand,' she said, studying the transaction. 'Scroll on to see if there's another ten later on.'

Max scrolled through the rest of May but there was no sign of another large transaction.

'Does he have another account?' Chris said.

'No. Not that far back. He opened a second one four years later but, as far as I can see, he only had the one account in 1987.' He sat back. 'So where's the other ten grand gone?'

'Johnny Meadows?' Clare said.

Chris nodded. 'I reckon so. She probably had to bribe two of them to be sure of getting it through.'

'Makes sense,' Clare agreed. She took out her phone and began tapping at the keyboard.

Dave Cross could barely hide his dismay at hearing from Clare again. 'I've sent the records back to the archives,' he said. 'Might take a bit of time to get them out again.'

'It is important.'

He sighed heavily. 'Okay. Let me go and look. It might still be waiting to be filed.' He promised to call Clare back as soon as possible and she set her phone down on the desk. 'Might as well wait to see if he calls back.'

Gillian and Robbie appeared in the room, coffees in hand, and Clare called them over.

'Can you pick up a Johnny Meadows, please?' She reeled off the address. 'No details. Just that we'd like him to help us with enquiries.' She glanced at their mugs. 'Finish your coffees but don't leave it too long.' Her phone began to buzz on the desk and she snatched it up.

'Dave Cross,' he said. 'You're in luck. It was sitting in the tray waiting to be archived.'

'Great. Can you tell me who was on the planning committee for that decision please?'

Dave began reading out a list of names. 'Hold on,' Clare said, 'let me write them down.'

'I can email a copy of the names if that's easier.'

'Actually that would be good, but can you read them through anyway please?'

He carried on reading and she stopped him on the fourth name. 'Can you repeat that one? Just to be sure.'

'Johnny Meadows,' he said.

'Perfect. If you could email it, and hopefully I won't need to bother you again.' She put down her phone and relayed the information to Max and Chris.

'I bet that's where the other ten grand went,' Max said, and Chris nodded.

Clare glanced across at Robbie and Gillian. 'Actually, could you go now please? I really want this man picked up.'

They slipped off the desks they were perched on and headed out to pick up a pool car. Twenty minutes later they were back, empty-handed.

Gillian shook her head. 'No one at home.'

'Well,' Robbie said, 'I reckon there was someone in the house. Pretty sure I saw a movement at the upstairs window.'

'You knocked again?' Clare said.

'Yeah. Knocked, shouted through the letterbox. Checked round the back. But if he was in he wasn't for answering.'

Clare sat thinking for a minute. 'Does he have a car?'

'Hold on – I'll find out,' Chris said.

A few minutes later he had the registration of a blue Nissan.

'There was a blue Nissan parked in the street,' Gillian said. 'Might have been his.'

'Right,' Clare said, rising from her seat. 'Get back round there and don't take no for an answer this time. If that car's gone he must have been spooked by seeing you two at the door. Either way, let me know.' Robbie and Gillian headed for the door and Clare turned to Chris. 'I want an alert out for ANPR cameras and get onto other stations in Fife and Tayside as well. If he is on the move I want to know where he's gone. It sounds to me like our Mr Meadows has something to hide.'

The blue Nissan had gone by the time Robbie and Gillian returned to Langlands Road.

'Sorry, boss,' Gillian said. 'Looks like he's legged it.'

'Can't be helped,' Clare said. 'But make sure the other stations in the area know we're after him. He'll turn up. Don't worry.'

She went back to dealing with her Inbox, hoping to make some headway, and she worked on steadily until early afternoon when an alert sounded on her phone. Glancing at the screen she saw a reminder for Benjy's appointment. Could she go home early? And then Chris came into her office without knocking.

'Think we've found Johnny Meadows' car,' he said. 'Leuchars railway station.'

'Checked the station itself?'

'There's a cop from Cupar doing that now. Waiting on him calling back. Apparently there's a blockage further down the line south of Kirkcaldy. A few trains were cancelled so we might be lucky.'

Clare glanced at her phone again. If they did find Johnny Meadows she wanted to be the one to interview him. And then there was the video Diane had put on Josh's phone. There was no way she could go home early, but she couldn't leave Benjy either. Moira would have given him his afternoon walk and he'd be in his usual place at the window looking for one of them returning home.

Chris's phone rang and he swiped to take the call. 'Yep?'

She watched, hearing only one side of the conversation then his face lit up. 'Great work. Can you bring him here?'

She rose from her seat. There was nothing else for it. She'd have to bring Benjy back to the station. 'I need to nip out,' she said. 'Ask Jim to organise a solicitor for Meadows. I'll be back in half an hour. Don't begin the interview without me.'

Benjy, alerted by her car crunching into the drive, was standing on the arm of a chair near the window. She heard his barking above the engine and hastily clicked off her seat belt. She unlocked the front door and struggled past him, staggering as he ran round and round her legs. 'Stop it!' she shouted but he paid no attention. In the kitchen she picked up his bowls and grabbed a box of his food from the cupboard. At this he sat obediently, face upturned, awaiting what he thought was his next meal. Ignoring this she collected a blanket from his basket and a well-worn chew toy. Then she clipped on his lead and led him out to the car.

She arrived at the station as two uniformed officers were accompanying Johnny Meadows in through the front door. She recognised him immediately as the man she'd seen in Strathkinness High Road the day she'd gone to ask Cliff Craven about the thefts. She climbed out of the car and opened the back door to unclip Benjy from his harness. As she did so she wondered about Johnny Meadows. Had he been in the habit of visiting Cliff Craven? Talking over old times on the council? Maybe he'd fallen on hard times and had taken advantage of Cliff's weakened state, helping himself to one or two items around the house. It would explain why he was in Retworth's and possibly why he made phone calls to the two dealers – if it was him. His phone records would confirm that.

She clipped Benjy's lead on again to stop him rushing across the car park and gathered up his bits and pieces. Then she made for the side door. Jim was the first person she met and Benjy disgraced himself by jumping up, leaving pawprints on Jim's otherwise immaculate uniform trousers.

'Benjy!' Clare hissed, but Jim waved this away.

'I take it you're stuck for a dog-sitter,' he said and Clare nodded.

'I'll have to cancel the vet's appointment as well.' Her brow creased. 'I think I saw a possible suspect arriving with a couple of Cupar lads. I'd like to interview him myself.' She paused for a moment. 'I don't suppose…'

'You want me to take charge of the wee dog?'

'Would you, Jim?'

'Course. No problem at all. I'll stick him with Zoe. She loves dogs.'

Clare thanked Jim and went quickly to the incident room where Chris and Max were chatting. 'Come on,' she said to Chris. 'We've an interview to prep for.'

Chapter 40

Johnny Meadows glanced up as Clare and Chris entered then looked away, affecting disinterest. A younger man in a dark suit sat beside him, his solicitor, Clare guessed. He nodded at Clare and picked up his pen as if signalling he meant business.

Johnny was tidily dressed, an olive-coloured hacking jacket over a cream checked shirt. A dark green tie was knotted neatly at the neck and she briefly pictured him with a shotgun and a couple of Labradors. And yet the shirt collar had signs of wear and the jacket wasn't new. Maybe he had fallen on hard times.

His hands dotted with liver spots were clasped in front of him but they were shaking. Was this due to a medical condition or was he simply nervous? If her theory was right he had cause to be.

She took a moment to study his face, assuring herself he was the man she'd seen in Strathkinness High Road the day she'd visited Cliff; then she began the recording, introducing herself and Chris. Johnny acknowledged the standard caution and she went on.

'Two of my officers called at your house this morning. Your car was parked outside but you didn't answer.'

He glanced at his solicitor. 'I was probably in the shower. Sorry,' he added.

Clare nodded at this then looked down at her notes. 'You were at Leuchars railway station this afternoon,' she said. 'With quite a large suitcase.'

'Correct.'

'Were you going away?'

'Obviously.'

'Can I ask where?'

'Hadn't decided. I fancied a change. I threw a few things in a bag and drove to the station. I thought I'd head for Edinburgh and take it from there.'

'Do you often do that?'

The solicitor cleared his throat. 'Can I ask where this is going?'

'Just trying to understand Mr Meadows' sudden departure from home.'

'There's no evidence this was a sudden decision,' the solicitor said and Clare conceded the point.

'I'd like to ask about your time as a councillor,' she said. 'Particularly your involvement with the planning committee.'

He raised an eyebrow. 'That was a very long time ago.'

'1987,' Clare said. 'You were involved with an application for a development which became known as the Banarvale Estate.'

Johnny's eyes widened. 'You can't expect me to recall an application from the 1980s – we dealt with literally hundreds over the years.'

'This was a particularly memorable one,' Clare said. 'The committee was advised to reject it on grounds of flood risk.'

'That happened all the time,' Johnny said. 'And most of the stuff they objected to turned out to be entirely trouble-free.'

'But Banarvale wasn't. Trouble-free,' she added. 'There were complaints about the finish—'

'Oh well,' he said, 'you can't blame the committee for the applicant employing a rogue builder.'

'And there were floods,' Clare persisted. 'In fact the development closed just before the millennium.'

He shrugged. 'Not uncommon. Many businesses fail. That wasn't our concern,' he said. 'We simply assessed the plans and voted for or against.'

Clare took a moment to form the next question. 'Were you ever offered... inducements to pass an application?'

'Bribes? I should say not. I'd hardly be living in a two up, two down if I'd been in the habit of taking backhanders.'

'So you didn't take a bribe to pass the Banarvale application?'

'No I did not.'

'Have you ever met the applicant?'

'Monique?' he said. 'No.'

She saw he'd realised his mistake. 'You have a remarkable memory.'

'Hers was one of those names that sticks,' he said. 'She was in the papers a lot.'

'I see.' Clare held his gaze for a moment then returned to her notes. 'I gather you were friendly with a fellow councillor – a Mr Cliff Craven.'

There was a flicker of something in his eyes. Momentary, but it was there; and then he forced a smile. 'Cliff? Oh yes. We were on the committee together, you know? We had some good times too.' He adjusted his face. 'Terribly sad about Cliff. He'll be sorely missed.'

'Did you see Mr Craven after you both retired from the council?'

He appeared to consider this. 'Now and again, I suppose.'

'When did you last see him?'

He inclined his head and was quiet for a moment. 'I'm not sure I remember.'

'Might you have seen him one week ago today?' Clare persisted. 'Last Wednesday.'

He shook his head. 'You'll have to forgive me, Inspector. I'm afraid I'm getting on a bit. As you noted I can recall details from years ago but recent things? Well, that's more difficult.'

'The day before Cliff's body was discovered,' Clare said, her smile pleasant. 'I'd have thought you'd remember that, given you may have been one of the last people to see him alive.'

'Are you accusing my client?' the solicitor said, his tone sharp.

Clare ignored the question. 'If Mr Meadows did see Mr Craven around the time he died, he may have some information that could help us.'

The solicitor raised an eyebrow but said nothing.

Clare took a moment before continuing. 'Last Wednesday,' she said, 'you were observed parking a dark blue car in Strathkinness High Road and walking towards Cliff Craven's house.'

His eyes narrowed and for a moment he didn't reply. 'Was I?' he said eventually.

'Yes.'

'By whom?'

'Do you deny you were there?'

He spread his hands. 'As I said, my memory isn't what it was. If you say I was there I suppose I must have been.'

'The day before the body was discovered,' Clare repeated.

'Again, if you say so.'

'Let's accept you visited Cliff last Wednesday,' Clare went on. 'One week ago today, yes?'

'All right,' he said. 'Let's accept that.'

She watched him as she formed her next question. 'Think carefully before answering. Did you ever take any items from Cliff Craven's house? Items which did not belong to you?'

'No.'

'You're sure?'

'Quite sure.'

'So if we obtained a warrant to search your house we wouldn't find any items which belonged to Mr Craven?'

He smiled. 'Let me guess. Rory Craven's been complaining.'

Clare glanced at Chris. 'Perhaps you would explain what you mean by that?'

Johnny folded his arms. 'It's like this. Cliff knew he was coming to the end of his days. Bloody rotten disease. His wife was long gone and he said Rory would probably bring in the auctioneers. Sell off the better pieces. *Take anything you like,* he told me. *Help yourself, Johnny. I'd rather you had it than some moneygrabber in an auction house.*'

Clare was impressed at Johnny's ability to think on his feet. 'Then you did take some items from Cliff's house?'

'With his blessing. He was most insistent,' he added.

Clare picked up a pen. 'And the items you took?'

'I was given,' Johnny corrected.

'My apologies,' she said, her tone cool. 'The items you were *given*?'

'Erm, a couple of ornaments, a medal and a painting. Nice pieces,' he added. 'Not particularly valuable but I thought they'd brighten up the house.'

'It wasn't your intention to sell them?'

'No.'

'You didn't, for instance, contact specialist dealers in artworks and medals?'

There was the hint of a smile playing on his lips and she wondered if he had a grudging respect for her. 'I did not,' he answered, finally.

Clare reached into a folder and withdrew a print of the photo from Retworth's CCTV. 'Do you agree this is a photograph of you?'

His eyes narrowed and he drew the photo across the desk, reaching into his breast pocket. He withdrew a pair of wire-rimmed spectacles, unfolded the legs and put them on, spending a few moments adjusting their position. Clare had the impression he was playing for time.

The solicitor leaned forward and studied the photo then he sat back, giving Johnny a slight shake of his head. Clare saw Johnny note this and she watched as he went through the motions of scrutinising the image. Finally he passed it back across the desk.

'Impossible to say.' He removed his specs and folded the legs back into place.

'We have a witness who identified you from that photo,' Clare said.

'As a resident of the town,' the solicitor interrupted, 'I'm sure Mr Meadows visits a good many shops.'

Johnny smiled. 'I like to do my bit. Support local businesses, Retworth's included.'

'Ah yes,' Clare said, smoothly. 'Retworth's.' She let the name hang in the air for a moment. Then she put the photo back in the folder. 'I think we're almost done here.'

The solicitor clicked off his pen and closed his notebook. Johnny straightened in his seat, as though preparing to leave.

'There's just a couple of things more,' she said.

He affected a sigh. 'Go on, then. Let's have it.'

'Could you roll up your trouser legs please?'

Johnny laughed. 'Are you planning to induct me into the masons?'

The solicitor sat forward. 'I think this has gone on long enough. Mr Meadows has been very patient.'

'If you could just do it, Mr Meadows.'

He glanced at his solicitor. 'And the other thing?'

Clare paused for a moment, studying him, watching for a reaction. 'I'd also like your permission to take a DNA sample. For elimination purposes,' she said, 'given you visited Cliff so close to his death.'

The smile vanished as quickly as it had appeared.

'On what grounds?' the solicitor asked.

'We've isolated multiple DNA samples from the house. It's important we identify as many profiles as possible.'

'I don't see the point, really,' Johnny said.

'All the same.'

'And if I refuse?'

Clare smiled. 'Then we'll simply arrest you. That will give us the power to examine your legs and to take your DNA, with or without your consent.'

Chapter 41

'You reckon he did it?' Chris asked as they sat in the kitchen, drinking mugs of coffee. Benjy lapped noisily at his bowl, splashing water in every direction.

Clare nodded. 'He slipped up mentioning Retworth's when I showed him the photo. I particularly didn't mention the shop name. And he remembered Monique Taylor, and that was back in the 1980s.'

'I dunno,' Chris said. 'They do say older folk remember stuff from years back but can't tell you what they had for breakfast.'

'He's as sharp as a tack, that one. His story about Cliff giving him permission to take stuff from his house – I don't believe a word of it. Why would he hawk it round dealers if he was taking it for sentimental value? And besides, Cliff asked Marcus to bring that painting down because he missed seeing it. I don't think he gave Johnny Meadows the painting or anything else. I reckon Meadows had been helping himself for weeks. Most likely he told Cliff he'd make a pot of tea – or something like that – and he took the chance to have a nose around. Cliff nods off and he slips something in his pocket.'

'He'd hardly fit a painting in his pocket.'

'You know what I mean. He could easily have moved that painting into the hall when Cliff was out of the room. If Cliff had noticed he'd probably tell him the cleaning lady must have shifted it. Then he tells Cliff he'll see himself out and picks it up as he leaves.'

'You could have a point,' Chris said. 'Strikes me he's not as well-heeled as Cliff. Whether Cliff gave him the things or he nicked them he probably saw his chance to make a few quid. I bet it was him phoning round the dealers. It's not like Cliff was ever going to find out.'

'Suppose.'

Benjy having finished drinking came across to Clare and sniffed at her trousers. She reached down to rub his neck. 'I reckon he did it,' she said. 'I just hope his DNA's a match for the cushion. Otherwise we'll struggle to prove it.'

'Even with the DNA you could struggle. He could claim he plumped the cushion up when he was sitting down.'

'He could,' Clare conceded. 'But Raymond says the DNA was found either side of the cushion, consistent with it being held in two hands. And we have the photos of his legs. There's clear evidence of bruising. Yellowed now but it's there.'

'That's pretty circumstantial.'

'I know. But we're building a case, Chris. Slowly but surely. I'll get Tony to authorise a warrant to search the house. Bank accounts as well.'

Chris rubbed a hand through his hair. 'I could be missing something but I can't see how that'll help us. So he took a bribe back in the Eighties. That doesn't mean he killed Cliff.'

'Unless...' Clare fell silent.

'Yeah?'

'Cliff...'

'Still yeah?'

'Hazel Sullivan.'

Chris eased himself back in his seat and crossed one leg over the other. 'I'm just gonna sit here until you start making sense.'

She turned to him. 'Think about it, Chris. Hazel wants to know about all the women Cliff worked with so she can find the other abuse victims. But she can't tell him that so she pretends to be writing a history of the council.'

Chris's face began to clear. 'And you're thinking...'

'Cliff tells Johnny about her. Maybe he's flattered a younger woman's interested in his past and he wants to show off. But Johnny—'

'He realises Cliff might blurt something out about Banarvale.'

'Exactly.'

'But wouldn't Johnny just warn Cliff not to mention it?'

Clare shrugged. 'He probably did. But could be Johnny doesn't trust Cliff not to let it slip. Or more likely he doesn't trust Hazel. Let's face it, her story about writing a book's pretty thin. Cliff's flattered by the attention. He doesn't see it. But let's say our Johnny's more suspicious than Cliff.'

'So he thinks Hazel has an ulterior motive?'

'Could be. Maybe he thinks she's a journalist looking into historic cases of corruption in the council. And Johnny, well, he has so much more to lose than Cliff. Even if Banarvale bribes did come to light and we investigated, Cliff wouldn't live long enough to end up in court. He's nothing to lose.'

'Whereas Johnny...'

'He could end up in prison. Unlikely, I know. But he might not know that.' She thought for a minute. 'It's pretty extreme, though, killing Cliff to avoid a scandal.'

'Unless there was more to it,' Chris said. 'Maybe word got out the two of them could be bought. Maybe they were taking backhanders for years.'

Clare rose and went to the sink to rinse her mug. 'You've just earned yourself a job, Sergeant.'

His face fell. 'Why is it always me?'

She smiled. 'Because you do it so beautifully; and it was your idea. I'd hate to steal your thunder.'

He rose and handed her his mug. 'Steal away, Inspector. How far back should I go?'

She thought for a moment. 'Start at 1980 and work forward. Any cash deposits over a thousand.'

He made for the door but Clare's phone began to ring and she forestalled him. 'It's Diane,' she said, swiping to take the call.

'He's taken the bait,' Diane said. 'The phone was accessed about twenty minutes ago and the hacker's currently attempting to download the video.'

'And you built in a tracker?'

'Yep. We should be able to get the IP address and the location pretty soon.'

Clare went to find Tony.

'Told you it would work,' he said, leaning back in his chair and stretching his hands behind his head. 'So where is it?'

'Waiting to hear.'

'Best ready the posse, then.'

'Already done. And could you authorise another warrant?'

He yawned and brought his hands back down. 'That's all I am to you, isn't it? A warrant machine.'

'Your words, not mine.'

She left him to draw up the warrant and was about to go back to her office when Zoe caught her.

'Want me to take this wee fella home when I go?' she said, indicating Benjy.

Clare looked down at the little dog who was sniffing at Zoe's tartan leggings. 'I couldn't ask you...'

'I know. That's why I'm offering.' She bent down and gave Benjy a hand to sniff. He began licking it methodically. 'He's brilliant. I'd love to have him.'

'Zoe, you're a lifesaver. I'll pick him up later – or I'll send Al round.'

She grinned. 'Oh, send him. He's pretty hot!'

Clare laughed. 'I'll do that!' Her phone began to ring. Diane. She clicked to take the call.

'Got the location,' she said. 'Got a pen?'

Clare rushed through to her office and grabbed a pen from her desk. 'Go on.' She began to write down the address, then stopped. 'Say that again?'

Diane repeated the address.

'You're absolutely sure?'

'Yep. The tracker's giving us live information.'

'Is it static?'

'At the moment.'

255

She thanked Diane. Then she went to her office door and shouted for Chris. Max appeared, his expression shifty.

'He's just nipped out.'

Clare shook her head. 'Of all the times. Okay, Max. I need you with me. I just have to make a couple of calls.'

She ran back to her office to find Josh's home number and tapped it into her mobile. It rang out and she was on the point of hanging up when she heard his voice, breathless as if he too had been running.

'Josh, this is very important; and it's urgent too so don't mess me about. I'm going to ask you a question and I want a straight yes or no.'

'Umm, okay…'

'Was the person who jailbroke your phone Marcus Craven?'

There was silence for a moment. When he spoke his voice was small. 'Yes. But you won't—'

'No, we won't mention it. Not at this stage, at least.' She thanked him then she clicked to find another number.

Paul Henry was laughing when he answered the call. 'Yello,' he said. Clare rolled her eyes at his lack of professionalism but now wasn't the time.

'Listen, I want you to keep Marcus there.'

'What here?'

'Yes. Keep him in the house until I get there, yeah?'

'Well I would, but he's not here.'

'Eh? You sure? He's not in the garden?'

'Nope. Went out a while ago. Him and the sister. She's back but he's still out.'

Clare's mind was working overtime. This didn't make sense. The address Diane had given for the tracker was the Cravens' house. And it fitted. Marcus went to the same school as Josh and Ethan. Josh had confirmed Marcus was the jailbreaker. It had to be him. Maybe he'd left the phone in his bedroom. She stood thinking for a minute. The last thing she wanted to do was to warn Marcus off. But she was close now. She could feel it. 'Listen,

Paul, I'm going to dial a number and I want you to listen out. See if it rings in the house. Can you do that, please?'

'Hold on…' She heard a murmur of conversation and a pause then he came back on the phone. 'Okay, Lauren's gone to make a coffee. What is it you want me to do?'

'Listen out for a phone I'm going to ring. It's a burner. I think it might be in the house.'

'Suppose. It's a pretty big house, though.'

'Probably one of the kids' bedrooms,' she said.

'Okay. Hold on…'

She heard him moving through the house. 'Right. Try now,' he said, his voice low. 'I'm outside the kids' rooms.'

She accessed the report of Sophie's death and scrolled down until she found the number for the burner phone. With one eye on the monitor she tapped it into her office phone, checking it before hitting *call*. 'It's ringing,' she said, after a few seconds.

There was silence, then the sound of Paul moving. 'Nothing,' he said. 'If it's here it's on silent.'

'No matter. But if Marcus comes home keep him there, okay?'

'Sure, but what's he done?'

'I'll explain later.' She went to see if Chris had returned.

'He won't be a minute,' Max said.

'We don't have a minute.'

Jim approached, his face full of concern. 'Problem?'

'No time to explain,' she said. 'But can you tell Tony we need another warrant please? I want to search the Cravens' house as well.' Then she nodded at Max. 'You're with me.' And she headed out to the car park, Max trailing in her wake.

Chapter 42

'Marcus Craven,' she said to Max as she threw the car into reverse and backed out of the space. 'He's our porn king.' She headed for Lamond Drive preparing to run the gauntlet of the speed bumps. As she turned into the street her phone began to ring. She fished it out of her pocket and handed it to Max.

'Get that, would you?'

He took the phone and listened for a few seconds. 'Turn the car round,' he said to Clare. 'The tracker's on the move.'

She put her foot to the brake and switched on the siren. 'Direction?'

Max made to repeat this but Diane cut across him. 'I heard. He's heading for Guardbridge. Just passed the Old Course Hotel.'

'Put it on speaker,' Clare said and Max complied.

'Can you stay on the line?' she said to Diane as she executed a three-point turn, causing cars in both directions to screech to a halt.

'No problem. It's moving pretty fast,' she added.

Clare accelerated back along Lamond Drive, making no allowance for the speed bumps. Max reached up to the grab handle. 'Let us know what he does at the roundabout,' he said.

They tore down Largo Road, cars pulling into the side to let them past.

'He's gone right,' Diane said. 'Towards Leuchars.'

'Got it.'

There was a buzzing from Clare's phone.

Max glanced at it. 'Another call.'

'Ignore it.' She accelerated up Bridge Street, her mind on Marcus Craven. Where was he going? He must be in a car, but which car? She thought back to the vehicles parked on the Cravens' drive. The black Audi had to be Rory's. She doubted any insurer would cover a teenager for a car like that. And Rory must have taken it to work anyway. There was the pink VW Beetle but surely that was his sister's…

Her phone buzzed again. Momentarily distracted, she swerved to avoid hitting an elderly man who'd begun pushing a walker on the pedestrian crossing, seemingly unaware of the blues and twos.

'He's gone past the railway station,' Diane said. 'Really moving now.'

'Dundee, then?' Max suggested and Clare gave a nod.

Could Marcus be in a taxi? Maybe told the driver he was late for an appointment. Or someone else's car? Suddenly she realised the impossibility of locating him. They didn't even know what they were chasing. How would they know which car to stop? The tracker was good but, in a line of fast-moving traffic, it wouldn't tell them which car he was in. There was no time to set up a road block and, anyway, he was hardly Public Enemy Number One. She'd never be able to justify the expense to someone like Penny Meakin.

Her phone began to buzz again. 'Jesus!' she said. 'Leave a voicemail.'

Max glanced at her. 'Might be important.'

She clicked her tongue in irritation. 'Go on, then. But make it quick.'

'You okay to hold?' Max asked Diane and he swiped to take the other call without waiting for an answer. Jim's voice came through the phone speaker.

'It's Hazel Sullivan,' they heard him say. 'Her house is on fire.'

'What?' Clare's foot touched the brake as she approached a mini roundabout.

'The brigade's on the way but Chris has gone ahead of them.'

'How bad is it?' Clare asked. She was at the roundabout near Petheram Bridge and she accelerated on and out of town.

'It's well alight.'

'Try her mobile,' Clare said. 'The number'll be on the system.'

'Already done. It's ringing out. And… her car's parked outside.'

Clare swore under her breath. For a moment she didn't know what to do. 'I…' she broke off.

'There's nothing you can do,' Jim said. 'Chris'll be there now. Bill and Janey following. The firies won't be far behind. You carry on after the lad. Best you pick him up.'

Suddenly Clare remembered Cassie, Hazel's dog, and she thought of Cassie's awkward gait as she padded around on arthritic joints. She opened her mouth to tell Jim there was a dog as well. And then she stopped. Hazel was fit and strong. If she was in that house there was every chance she'd manage to get herself out. Maybe help Cassie out as well. And if she wasn't at home, she might have Cassie with her. The last thing Clare wanted was to give Chris another reason to burst his way in.

'Tell Chris he is not to go anywhere near that house,' she said. 'Tell him it's an order.'

Max ended the call and went back to Diane. 'Any update?'

'He's gone through St Mike's. Looks like he's heading for the bridge.'

Clare increased the pressure on the accelerator. Marcus would be far harder to find if he managed to get over the Tay Road Bridge to Dundee. There were half a dozen different ways he could go from there. They had to stop him. She came to a decision.

'Get back onto Jim and get the bridge shut.'

Max asked Diane to stay on the line and he tried Jim again. But there was no reply. 'He's likely dealing with the fire,' he said. 'I'll keep trying.' He went back to Diane. 'Location?'

'Heading north on the A92. He'll be on the bridge in a minute.'

'Dammit,' Clare said. 'We're going to lose him.' She pulled out to pass a lorry, lights flashing, siren blaring, narrowly making it past in time, thanks to an oncoming car pulling up short.

'Erm…' Max began.

'Sorry. That was stupid.' They were in Leuchars now and she turned left at the roundabout, accelerating towards St Mike's crossroads. An image of Chris outside Hazel's burning house came into her mind and suddenly she doubted herself. What the hell was she doing going after this lad? She should be at Hazel Sullivan's, stopping Chris doing something stupid. They'd be at the crossroads in a minute. The road was wider there. She could do a U-turn.

'Wait,' Diane said, 'he's slowing down.'

'Is he on the bridge?' Clare called.

'No. He's gone past the entrance. Looks like…' There was a pause, then Diane came back on the line. 'I think he's gone into the bridge car park.'

They waited, the sound of murmured conversation in the background. Clare killed the siren, hoping to hear what was being said. 'It's slowed right down,' Diane said at last. 'But it's still moving. We reckon he's on foot. My guess is he's heading up onto the bridge.'

Max's face clouded. 'Why would he do that?'

Clare said nothing, her eyes fixed firmly on the road ahead. 'My fault,' she said, after a moment. 'I sent a test call to the burner phone and asked the FLO to listen out for it. Marcus was out at the time but he must have come back and seen the missed call. Probably came up as a withheld number.'

'He's worked out we're onto him,' Max said.

'Yup. And there's only one reason he's making for the bridge.'

'Dammit. He's going to lob the phone into the river.' He glanced at Clare. 'Can we catch him?'

They were approaching the crossroads but Clare's mind went back to the fire at Hazel Sullivan's house. On an impulse, she signalled left and pulled into the car park at St Michael's Inn, just off the crossroads. The blue lights were still flashing and faces appeared at the windows, clearly wondering if there was an emergency. She sat, staring straight ahead, saying nothing, the idling of the car engine the only sound.

'Clare?' Max said eventually, his voice gentle.

'We're going back,' she said, ramming the car into first gear.

'No!' he said. 'Absolutely not,' his voice firmer.

She stared at him, one hand on the gear lever, her foot playing on the accelerator.

'They're dealing with it,' Max said. 'And it's not just Chris. Bill and Janey will be there by now and Jim will have drafted in every spare officer. We're a good fifteen minutes away. By the time we reach Hazel's house the fire brigade will be in charge. They won't let you anywhere near it.' He indicated the road beyond the crossroads. 'We've a job to do. Here,' he added. 'You've a real chance to nail Marcus, get justice for Sophie. So for fuck's sake just drive!'

Clare's eyes widened. Never in all the time she'd worked with Max – super polite Max – had she heard him swear.

'Drive!' he said again, slapping the dashboard. 'Or get out and let me do it.' He unclipped his seat belt, hand on the door.

The moment passed. She was back. 'Buckle up,' she said, checking over her shoulder. 'If he's on foot we might just make it.' She threw Max a smile. 'Sorry.'

He shook his head. 'Tough call.'

A member of hotel staff was approaching the car but Max waved him away. Clare turned on the siren and accelerated out of the car park, the wheels skidding on gravel. 'Can you get me an update from Hazel's house, though?'

'Sure.' Max tugged his seat belt back on and picked up the phone. 'Diane, can you hold?'

Diane had been quiet all the time they'd sat outside St Michael's Inn but she confirmed she'd stay on the line. Max tried Jim again but there was still no reply.

'Try Chris,' Clare said. 'I want to speak to him.'

After what seemed like an eternity he answered. 'It's well alight,' he shouted, over the crackling of the flames.

'Hazel?'

'Can't raise her. Bill's brought a big red key. I'm going to put the front door in. The worst of it's at the back so…'

'Chris, you are to do nothing of the sort,' Clare shouted. 'You could create a draught. Make it worse.'

'I can't stand here and do nothing,' he yelled. 'She could be in there.'

She heard the sound of a siren over the phone. 'I can hear the engines,' she said. 'Stay outside.'

For a few seconds she waited, her knuckles white on the steering wheel as the car raced on, only the sound of the fire audible; and then the call cut off. She thumped the steering wheel. 'Jesus, Chris,' and she flashed a look at Max. 'He's getting married in just over a week.' For a moment Max said nothing. She saw the roundabout up ahead and pressed the brake as they hurtled towards it.

'Chris is sensible,' Max said, at last.

'You don't believe that any more than I do,' she said. 'Oh God, Max. If something happens to him.'

They were on the A92 now. 'Check with Diane,' she said, accelerating past the petrol station towards the bridge roundabout.

'Definitely on the bridge,' Diane's voice said. 'But still moving slowly. He must be on foot.'

The cars in front moved over to the left lane and Clare flew past, braking as the roundabout came into view. She took it at speed and swung the car round and into the bridge car park, braking hard. It was quiet at this time of day, most of the commuters who used it as an unofficial park and ride having picked up their cars. The bridge stood out, tall and majestic, the twin concrete legs looming large as she drove to the far end of the car park. And then she saw it. The pink VW Beetle. Lauren's car. Marcus must have taken it and now he was up on the bridge. She thanked Diane for her help.

They walked quickly to the car. 'Can he even drive?' Max said.

Clare shook her head. 'No idea.' She lifted her gaze and stood for a minute, scanning the bridge; but from so far below they couldn't see the central walkway. 'Come on,' she said. 'Let's get the little scrote.'

Chapter 43

The midsummer sun was still high in the sky out to the west; but as they ran up the sloping walkway clouds were gathering to the north, darkening the sky, a brooding darkness that matched Clare's mood. Some car headlights had come on and it felt to her like a strange in-between time, no longer day but not quite dusk. A steady stream of traffic thundered towards them, the rumbling from lorries making it hard to be heard. A fire engine went screaming past and she wondered if it was heading for St Andrews. Was the fire at Hazel's spreading? She tried to remember how close Hazel's house was to her neighbours. It was windy up here, high above the river, but was it as windy back in St Andrews? If so they could be in real trouble. There were houses in every direction.

And where was Chris now? Had he and Bill put in the front door? A sudden image of a backdraught of flames shooting towards him came into Clare's mind and she gasped as if hit in the chest. Again she wondered what the hell she was doing on this windy bridge when Chris, her sergeant, dammit, her friend, could right now be in a burning building, searching through the choking smoke for Hazel Sullivan.

A cyclist, head down, came speeding towards them, bringing Clare back to the present. She'd made the call and they were on the bridge now. They had to make it count. Her determination to reach Marcus Craven and that burner phone became all consuming. Max ducked behind her to let the cyclist past then she raised a hand and shielded her eyes. 'There,' she said, pointing to a figure walking ahead, too far away to make out.

She handed her phone to Max. 'Check with Diane.'

They walked quickly on as Max dialled.

'Still on the bridge,' Diane said. 'A third of the way along.'

Clare checked the lampposts. She knew there were seventy-five so Marcus must be around number fifty. They were at seventy-one now. 'Come on,' she said to Max. 'Let's catch him up.'

They picked up speed but as they came closer they realised the figure ahead wasn't Marcus.

'That's not him, is it?' Max said.

'Not unless he's suddenly grown long curly hair. That's Lauren.' Clare increased her speed. She could make her out now. Of course it was Lauren. That explained why the phone was at the Cravens' house when Marcus was out. Had it been Lauren all along? Was she the one who'd hacked the boys' phones? As they drew nearer they saw her stop. She was carrying a bag – a laptop bag, Clare realised. They were three or four lampposts away now and Lauren was standing looking across the carriageway, into the sun. They were gaining on her and she glanced back. She saw them and for a minute she stood, watching as they raced towards her.

And then she changed her stance, as though she was about to bowl a cricket ball, the arm holding the laptop bag drawn back. Suddenly the bag was flying through the air. They watched as it cleared the northbound carriageway and, just as it seemed it would clip the outside barrier and fall back to the road, it landed on the top rail where it sat for a few seconds. Lauren, her long hair swirling in the wind, was preparing to climb onto the carriageway. A car approaching saw her, swerved and blasted the horn. They were almost upon her and Clare too prepared to leap the barrier to retrieve the laptop bag. But, as Lauren dropped onto the carriageway, making another car swerve dangerously, the bag wobbled, was caught by a gust of wind and fell from the barrier down to the swirling waters of the River Tay, far below. Clare had caught up with her and put a hand out to grab Lauren's arm. But she dodged Clare and reached into her pocket. The mobile phone was lighter and it soared through the air, clearing the barrier easily.

She stood, looking out at where she'd thrown the phone, her frame silhouetted in the evening sun. Then she turned back, a smile of satisfaction on her face.

Max leaned across and took a grip of Lauren by the shoulder. 'Back over,' he said, indicating the barrier. Another car gave a blast on the horn and Lauren responded, giving the driver the finger. She shook Max's hand off her shoulder and swung herself up and over the barrier, landing both feet squarely on the walkway. He took a firmer grip of her arm and steered her away from the barrier.

'Come on,' Clare said, pointing towards the end of the walkway. 'Let's get down to the car.'

Lauren stood for a minute as though she might argue the point then she gave a shrug, tucked her hair inside her jacket with her free hand and began walking back towards the car park.

By the time they reached the car Clare's phone was ringing. She glanced at the display and her face lit up. 'It's Chris,' she said, clicking to take the call.

'You wanna loosen your grip?' Lauren drawled. 'Getting a bit tight.'

Max ignored her. 'Clare?'

The phone was clamped to her ear and then she heard Chris's voice. Relief swam over her. 'Oh thank God, Chris,' she said. She clicked to unlock the car and opened the back door for Lauren. And in that second the wind dropped and she caught a whiff of something. Faint, but it was there. She moved closer to Lauren and sniffed. And there it was again. Max was waiting for news from Chris but she held up a warning finger. She lowered her voice and nodded towards the back of the car.

'I'm going to fetch a forensic suit for Lauren then I'll call SOCO. And after that,' she said, her jaw tight, 'I'm going to get hold of Paul Henry.'

'You absolutely stink,' Clare said, handing Chris a packet of biscuits. They were standing in the kitchen, the three of them cradling milky coffees.

He helped himself to two of the biscuits. 'So would you if you'd been standing downwind of a towering inferno.' His voice was thick and he cleared his throat.

'It's a bungalow.'

'Same difference.'

'And you went in?'

'Had to. The car was at the door and we couldn't raise her. We didn't know she was at work.'

'You could have phoned.'

He shook his head. 'No time. And besides... we heard the dog.'

Clare shook her head. 'You put the door in to save the dog?'

He shrugged. 'Like you'd have left it.'

She met his eye. 'You could have been killed. If that door to the hall hadn't been a fire door.'

'Yeah. Bit of luck, that. Apparently her dad was a fireman. Insisted she put fire doors on all the rooms. Told her they saved lives. Lucky for the dog its favourite spot was in the hall under that window, or he'd have been a goner.'

'She.'

'Whatever.'

'What happened to her?'

'The dog? Neighbour ran her along to the vet. Pretty sure she'll be okay. The smoke hadn't reached the hall.' He sipped at his coffee, grimacing as it hit his throat.

'They've checked you out?'

He nodded. 'Neighbours called an ambulance, thinking Hazel was in there. Paramedics took me into the van and gave me a good going over.' He coughed and Clare raised an eyebrow.

'Sure they said you're okay?'

'Yeah. Don't fuss. Or maybe make a wee bit of fuss.'

'Hah. I reckon you'll live.'

'What about Hazel?' Max asked.

'Staying with a friend,' Chris said. 'The fire's out now but the firies reckon they'll be there another day at least, until it's cool enough to investigate.'

'But they think it's suspicious?'

'Yup. Started around the back door. Looks like an accelerant was used. Petrol, most likely.'

Clare's expression darkened. 'I'll be taking that up with Lauren Craven, as soon as forensics have finished with her.' She glanced at the door. 'Is he here yet?'

'Paul?' Max rose and made for the door. 'Should be. I'll check.' He went off to see if Paul Henry had arrived, closing the door behind him.

Left alone with Chris, Clare took him in and found she'd a lump in her throat. He could blunder around acting first, thinking later, his tact with witnesses was non-existent and he positively could not be trusted around a pack of Wagon Wheels; but he'd put his life on the line at Hazel's house – gone in there with little thought for his own safety. She opened her mouth to tell him she was proud of him but the lump was too big. She swallowed, took a breath in and out and tried again. 'You're an absolute numpty,' she said, 'but I'm so proud of you.'

To her surprise she saw his eyes become misty. 'Goes with the patch, doesn't it?' Then he reached for the kitchen roll and tore off a couple of sheets. He blew his nose and held the paper away, taking in the sooty snot. 'Yeuch,' he said. 'Is that what's up my nose?'

Clare laughed and slapped him gently on the back. 'Speaking of snotters, I've an apology for an FLO to bollock.'

'Aw, let me watch? Please?'

'Home, you!' she ordered and went in search of Paul Henry. She found him sitting on her desk, playing a game on his phone. 'Off,' she said, indicating the desk. He looked at her for a moment, his expression faintly amused. Then he slid slowly off and turned to face her.

'I'm on the naughty step, then, am I?'

Clare sat down and made a pretence of looking in her drawer for something while she did battle with her temper. The last thing she wanted was to lose it in front of Paul Henry. She took a breath in and out and lifted her face to meet his. 'Take a seat.'

He dragged a chair from the corner of the room and sat down, his body language an attempt at nonchalance. But his eyes betrayed him. Did he know he'd messed up? If not, he was about to find out.

She let him sit for a moment while she chose her words. 'We have Lauren Craven in custody.'

His eyes widened. 'Lauren? What's she done?'

'Well,' Clare said, 'where to start? It's probably a toss-up between *attempting to defeat the ends of justice* and *wilful fire-raising with danger to life.* Take your pick.'

Paul's jaw dropped open. 'No!' he said after a moment. 'Surely not?'

Clare ignored this. 'Let's go back over your conduct in this case, shall we? See how it fits with Lauren's actions?'

He sighed audibly and crossed his arms.

'You no doubt remember I phoned to tell you Rory Craven wasn't Cliff's biological son, yes? And your words, if I recall correctly, were, *I wonder if the old man knew his wife was putting it about.* Let's suppose either Lauren or Marcus overheard that. They were, according to you, *mooching about in their rooms.* But what if they weren't? What if they were out of sight but listening to your end of the call? If they had overheard, it wouldn't take a genius to work out you were talking about Cliff; and as Rory's an only child they'd have sussed it out pretty quickly.'

He shrugged. 'But you told Rory anyway. They'd have found out from him eventually.'

He had a point but Clare wasn't about to concede it. 'It wasn't your news to tell. End of. He might not even have wanted the kids to know. And, the reason Lauren's in custody is she's suspected of setting fire to Hazel Sullivan's house – the woman we now know is Cliff Craven's biological daughter.'

He stared at her. 'She never!'

'She did. And if I find out she did this, not because her father told her about the DNA, but because she overheard you on the phone to me, I promise you will be very, very sorry.'

He said nothing and Clare went on. 'Thankfully Hazel Sullivan was at work so it's only her house that's damaged. But she could have died tonight.'

Paul was quiet for a moment. 'I'd never have told her,' he said. 'And I'm sure she wasn't listening. It must have been her dad.'

'You'd better hope so,' Clare said. 'But that's not all. That burner phone – where was Lauren when I asked you to listen out for it?'

'I told you. She'd gone to the kitchen to make a drink. I asked if she'd do me a coffee. Keep her out of the way. Then I nipped upstairs to listen for the phone.'

'How do you know she didn't follow you?'

'She didn't.'

'You sure?'

There was a hesitation. Brief, but it was there. 'Yeah. Course I am.'

'So, if that burner had been in Lauren's pocket, say on vibrate, and she saw you heading up stairs, ear cocked listening out for something…'

'Look, do you mind telling me what this is about? You're firing all these questions at me and I've no idea what I'm supposed to have done. To be honest, *Inspector*,' he said the word deliberately as though feigning respect for her seniority, 'you've done nothing but pick on me since I came up here. Let's be frank. You don't like me, do you?'

Clare felt herself flush. Was there a grain of truth in what he was saying? She didn't like him. Maybe she hadn't done enough to hide that. 'Okay, Paul,' she said. 'Cards on the table. I don't think you take this job seriously enough. I'm not sure you're cut out to be an FLO.'

He raised an eyebrow. 'We all have to start somewhere.'

'Not at the expense of victims' families,' she shot back.

He leaned forward, his eyes burning into Clare's. 'You want me off the case? Suits me. But I don't think you've been entirely fair.'

Clare opened her mouth to protest but he cut across her.

'See, I'll admit I slipped up. I've no problem with that. We all make mistakes. But you don't like me so, in your book, my mistakes are so much worse than anyone else's. You might not admit it to me but at least be honest with yourself.'

She stared at him, astounded at how outspoken he was. She'd always prided herself on being willing to listen to her officers, no matter what they had to say. But not one of them had ever spoken to her like this. Was that because they were... *afraid* of her? Was Paul Henry really as lazy as she thought? Or was he right about her being unfair to him? He'd certainly hit on an uncomfortable truth about Hazel's DNA.

'Okay,' she said. 'Let's talk some more about Lauren. I think she found out about Hazel being Cliff's daughter and Rory not being his son. I also think she enjoys having money. She was probably looking forward to inheriting from Cliff's estate; and to her dad having more money. Then along comes Hazel Sullivan and suddenly there's a very real danger that she – and who knows how many others – might claim against Cliff's estate. They might not have a valid claim but Lauren wouldn't know that. Suddenly Rory's share isn't looking so healthy. He's bills to pay so the inheritance Lauren was looking forward to is dwindling by the day. She goes along to Hazel's house in the afternoon to have it out with her. Maybe she plans to break in. Mess the house up. Give Hazel a fright. Or maybe she thinks there's an easier way to deal with Hazel. She takes a petrol can from the boot of her car and heads along there – or she finds a can of petrol in Hazel's garden shed. She soaks a rag and lights it from a distance. Then she heads home for a shower; but I phone and ask you to listen out for the burner. Could be her guilty conscience has made her more alert. Who knows? I reckon she realised you were listening for that phone ringing and she knew she had to get rid of it.'

He shrugged. 'Maybe.' His brow creased. 'You've still not told me why the phone's important? What have they been up to, Marcus and Lauren?'

Clare explained the connection to Sophie's death. 'But the lads wouldn't tell us who'd jailbroken their phones. So we set up a fake porn video and put it on Josh's phone in the hope the hacker would take the bait.'

'And it had a tracker?'

She nodded. 'We traced it to the Tay Road Bridge and found Lauren up there. Max and I saw her throw something off the bridge. First what looked like a laptop bag, then a mobile phone. Most likely our burner,' she added. 'So the evidence has gone.'

'Might be backed up to the cloud,' Paul suggested.

'I doubt it. She used a VPN and the porn site's in Romania.'

'You're stuffed, then.' He shoved back his chair. 'So, do you want me to stay on as FLO? I'm not fussed either way, to be honest.'

She regarded him. 'Right now I don't have a choice. I need someone to go back to the Cravens' house and tell them Lauren's been arrested.'

'Fine.' He got to his feet. 'I'll call you later.' And with that he left Clare feeling somehow he'd got the better of her.

Chapter 44

Lauren Craven sat in a white forensic suit, a young woman at her side. Clare thought Lauren seemed smaller, somehow, probably because the suit was far too big for her. Her face was pale, eyes enormous. The self-assured Lauren who had thrown the laptop and phone from the bridge had all but gone, the apprehension she now felt evident. The woman introduced herself as Lauren's solicitor. Max sat down beside Clare and began the recording. Clare repeated the caution she'd delivered to Lauren in the Tay Road Bridge car park. Lauren glanced at her solicitor who gave her a reassuring nod.

'I'd like to ask you about your movements this afternoon,' Clare said.

Lauren eyed her but said nothing.

'I gather you left the house with your brother Marcus around...' she consulted her notepad, 'two fifteen.'

Lauren shrugged but made no reply.

'Is that correct?' Clare repeated.

'Suppose.'

'Where did you go?'

'Town.'

'Shopping?'

'Yeah.'

'Buy anything?'

'Nope.'

'Which shops did you visit?'

Her expression darkened. 'Does it matter?'

'It will help us corroborate your account of your movements. We can check the shop CCTV.'

'Didn't go in any shops,' she said. 'Just looked in the windows.'

'Did you walk into town?'

Lauren stared at Clare as if she was stupid. 'Course not.'

'How did you get there?'

'Drove. Took my car.'

'Ah yes,' Clare said. 'Your car is a VW Beetle convertible, isn't it?'

'Yeah.' There was the faint trace of a smile on Lauren's face. Clearly she loved her car.

'It's pink, yes?'

'Yeah.'

'Where did you park?'

'Dunno. Some space. Harbour, I think.'

'And Marcus was with you?'

'Yeah. But he wanted to go and see mates. So I dropped him in South Street.'

Clare paused for a moment, ensuring she had Lauren's attention, then she continued. 'Think carefully before you answer this next question, please: did you drive to Irvine Crescent?'

'Nope.'

'I have to tell you, Lauren, we have a witness who saw a pink VW convertible in Irvine Crescent parked close to a house owned by Hazel Sullivan.'

Lauren avoided Clare's eye. 'Wasn't mine.'

'I have an officer currently running a check on pink VW Beetle convertibles,' she said. 'I very much doubt there are many in this area.'

Lauren made no reply and Clare went on. 'I believe you were the driver of this car, that you went round the back of Ms Sullivan's house and wilfully set fire to it, endangering her life. When I arrested you this evening there was a strong smell of petrol or a similar accelerant. Our forensic staff will analyse the traces of fuel found on your person and compare that with the fuel used to start the fire. If they match we'll charge you with attempted murder.'

Lauren's eyes widened and she glanced at her solicitor, panic written all over her face. 'But it could have been from the petrol station,' she said, a tremor in her voice.

'Were you at the petrol station today?' Clare asked.

'Can't remember.'

'If you were we'll be able to see you on their CCTV.'

The solicitor sat forward. 'Perhaps there's another explanation for fuel being on Lauren's person. Maybe the last time she filled up she splashed some on her hands. That might have transferred to the car interior.'

Clare smiled. 'It's possible, and we will carry out a thorough examination of the car as well.'

Lauren was looking round wildly. 'But she wasn't even there.'

'Who wasn't?' Clare said quickly and Lauren's face betrayed her. She saw her mistake.

'One of your guys said,' she muttered. 'Said how she wasn't hurt.'

'Which officer was that?'

'Dunno. They all look the same to me.'

Clare watched her carefully. 'I'm fairly confident none of my officers would say any such thing, Lauren. So let's have the truth. You went to Hazel Sullivan's house. But you say you knew she wasn't there?'

There was a silence. A long silence. Lauren's eyes flitted left and right as if she was trying to decide what to say. 'Okay, I went there,' she said eventually. 'But I never set fire to the house.'

'Thank you,' Clare said. 'You went there this afternoon. Was Marcus with you?'

'No!' she said. 'Marcus was nothing to do with it.'

'Okay. So you went alone. Why did you go?'

'I wanted to have it out with her,' she said. 'Dad had told me about the DNA and stuff. That he wasn't Grandad's real son and that Hazel woman was his daughter. I couldn't believe it. He was absolutely gutted. And he was worried he wouldn't get any of Grandad's money. That it would all go to her.' She swallowed and took a sip of water. 'So I went round there to tell her. Tell her to leave us alone. Leave my dad alone. I don't care about the DNA stuff. Grandad loved my dad. And he didn't know anything about that Hazel. I thought it was time someone set her straight.'

She met Clare's eye, her expression mulish. 'Only she wasn't in. But I never set fire to it,' she repeated. 'I wouldn't do that.'

Clare looked at her. 'One of my officers went into that house, believing Ms Sullivan's life was in danger. He put his own life at risk, Lauren.'

Her gaze dropped and she said nothing.

'Okay,' Clare went on. 'We'll revisit this when the forensic results are through. Let's move on to later in the afternoon. You returned home after visiting Irvine Crescent. Is that correct?'

'Yeah.'

'What did you do at home?'

'Dunno. Usual stuff.'

'But you went out again. Can you tell us why?'

She hesitated. 'Fancied a drive.'

'Was it a sudden decision?' Clare wondered if it had been prompted by Paul Henry listening out for the burner phone. But Lauren made no reply.

'Let's agree it was a sudden decision, then,' Clare said.

'Suppose.'

'What prompted you to go to the Tay Road Bridge?'

She was quiet for a moment. Then she flicked a glance at Clare. 'It's nice up there. Great views.'

'While you were up there my colleague and I observed you throwing a bag from the central walkway over the carriageway. This was highly dangerous and could have caused an accident. Why did you do it?'

'Dunno. Just a bag I didn't want.'

'You had a bag you didn't want and you went to the trouble of driving to the bridge and going up onto the walkway to throw it over two lanes of traffic into the river?'

She shrugged. 'Seemed like a good idea.' She flicked a glance at Clare. 'Sorry. Suppose it's litter or something.'

Clare raised an eyebrow at this. 'Then you threw a mobile phone after the bag. That too landed in the river.'

Lauren shook her head. 'Nope. It was a stone. Found it on the beach a while back. It's been in my pocket and I decided to get rid of it.'

Clare sat watching Lauren for a moment but she wouldn't meet Clare's eye. 'Are you involved in pornography?' she said suddenly.

Lauren eyed her. 'Eh?'

'Have you downloaded and shared any images or video files with pornographic content?'

She looked away. 'No.'

'You didn't, for instance, hack into the mobile phones of two pupils at Kinaldy College for the purpose of viewing and sharing images on these phones? Before you answer,' Clare went on, 'I should tell you a young woman – Sophie Bakewell – featured in a video on one of the phones. Sophie took her own life when she learned the video had been uploaded to a pay-per-view website. So I will ask you again. Did you hack into any mobile phones and download media of any sort?'

'No.' Her voice was small and she wouldn't meet Clare's eye.

They tried a few more questions but Lauren seemed to have shrunk further into the huge forensic suit, her answers increasingly monosyllabic. In the end Clare informed Lauren she would be detained for twenty-four hours pending forensic test results. 'It's likely charges will follow,' she said. 'For the sake of Sophie Bakewell's parents I urge you to think carefully about your response to any such charges.'

Chapter 45

It was almost half past eight by the time Clare arrived at Zoe's to pick up Benjy. Zoe opened the door and Benjy barrelled out to meet Clare.

'Come in,' Zoe said, stepping back from the door. 'Want a coffee? Or some food? You look shattered.' She led Clare into a large gaily painted room with a kitchen at one end and a sitting area at the other. Clare looked round and instantly felt more cheerful. The walls were painted a cobalt blue, a large poster of Frida Kahlo over an oak mantelpiece. None of the chairs matched, each one brighter than the next, and a low coffee table was scattered with magazines and cookery books. It was exactly like Zoe: an explosion of colour and fun.

'I like this,' she said, and Zoe smiled back.

'Can't be doing with all that minimalist crap.' She bent and lifted Benjy's food and water bowls slipping them in a carrier bag. Benjy seeing this thought he was going to be fed again and he immediately went to sit at Zoe's feet, his face upturned.

'Sorry Benj,' she said. 'You've had your tea.' She studied Clare. 'What about you? You must be starving.'

Clare waved this away.

'How about a fish finger sandwich, then?' Zoe said. 'Ten minutes, tops.'

Suddenly Clare thought that sounded amazing. Zoe saw her weakening and steered her towards a shocking pink easy chair, a knitted blanket draped over it. 'Have a seat,' she said, 'and I'll bring the food over in a bit.'

Clare sank into the chair and kicked off her shoes. She stretched her feet out, flexing her toes. Benjy, having given up hope of food, padded over and jumped up beside her. Clare made to shoo him down but Zoe told her not to worry. It was an odd reversal of roles, she realised. At work she was Zoe's boss but, here, she was a guest and in Zoe's domain; and yet she felt more relaxed than she had for days. Her eyes wandered round the room and she thought what an unlikely couple Zoe and Max were. He was as neat as a pin, tidy and organised, but somehow the two of them seemed to work.

Zoe chatted on as she cooked the fish fingers and buttered the bread, Clare adding the odd remark; but gradually Zoe's voice faded away as Benjy's breathing became a soothing rhythm, hypnotic in its effect. Suddenly she started, and realised Zoe was shaking her arm. She opened her eyes and took a few seconds to register where she was.

'You were out for the count,' Zoe said. 'Absolutely sound!' She indicated a tray on the coffee table. 'Get that inside you.'

Clare pushed Benjy off her knee and leaned forward to pick up the tray. The bread was white and doughy, the fish fingers crisp and hot, and her mouth watered. Zoe brought through two huge mugs of tea and put one on the tray. Then she curled up on a seat opposite. Benjy sniffed hopefully at the sandwich but when Clare ignored him he went over to Zoe and jumped up to sit on her knee.

'You've made a friend there,' Clare said, and Zoe laughed.

'I'll babysit him anytime you like.'

It took Clare less than five minutes to demolish the sandwich. 'That was wonderful,' she said, and Zoe beamed. 'I'm not sure when I last enjoyed a meal so much.'

'You're just tired,' Zoe said. 'Anything tastes good when someone makes it for you.' She began rubbing Benjy under the chin. 'I can keep this one for you, if you like? Just for tonight. Bring him back in the morning.'

Clare smiled. 'That's so kind, Zoe, but I'll drink this then take him home. Thanks, though. For today. I'm honestly so grateful.'

The house was in darkness when she returned, the DCI not yet home from his day at Tulliallan Police College. For a moment she considered switching lamps on around the room, closing the curtains, making the house more cheerful. Then she looked at the clock. She'd another early start in the morning. So she switched a solitary lamp on in the hall for the DCI, settled Benjy in his bed and began wearily to climb the stairs.

Thursday

Chapter 46

'I had supper at Zoe's,' Clare told the DCI over breakfast.

'Really?' He began buttering a piece of toast. 'How come?'

'Well…'

'Oh, don't tell me…'

'Sorry, Al. I had to cancel the vet appointment. I had a suspect heading in one direction and a suspicious house fire in the other.'

'Surely the fire brigade—'

'It was Hazel Sullivan's house.'

He stared. 'Seriously?'

'Yup. Fortunately she was out otherwise we'd probably have had a second death on our hands.' She rose from her chair and put her mug in the dishwasher. 'When I have a couple of hours to spare I'll explain it all. As it is, I'm struggling to keep up with it myself.' She kissed the top of his head then went to clean her teeth.

To her amazement Tony had arrived before her. 'You gone part-time?' he quipped, smiling at his own joke.

'What's got you out of bed so early?' she asked. 'Don't tell me the latest Mrs Tony's finally had enough?'

'Quite the reverse,' he said. 'Pamela's young lad—'

'Pamela, eh?'

'That is her name. Anyway, her young lad's off to football camp. Bus left at seven so…'

She studied him. 'I can't work out if you're genuinely smitten or if you have an ulterior motive.'

'You of all people should know it can work second time around.' He blushed and she wondered briefly if he might have a heart inside there after all.

'Sometimes it's almost like you're a real boy,' she joked.

'Very funny. Anyway, what's this I hear about you upsetting young Paul?'

'Oh him.'

'Yes him. He thinks you don't like him. Obviously I've told him you're very nice really. But he doesn't see it.'

She shook her head. 'Honestly, Tony. What's the deal with him? Does he try to be an arse or does it come naturally? He's like a younger version of you, only worse.'

'He's okay,' Tony said. 'He just needs to settle down a bit.'

'Well I'd rather he settled somewhere else.'

'You want rid?'

She sighed. It would be so easy to say yes. Get on the phone and find another, a better FLO. But that wasn't ideal for the Craven family. They'd been through enough and there'd be more to come once the forensic report on Lauren came back. She was sure of that. She'd turned a few difficult characters round over the years. Could she do it again with Paul Henry? Maybe it was worth another go.

'Leave it for now,' she said. 'We'll see how it goes. But he'd better bloody well sharpen up his act.'

'I'll tell him not to forget his homework, then,' Tony said. 'So, what's happening today?'

What indeed! 'Hopefully quite a lot,' she said. 'If the warrants are through for the Cravens and Johnny Meadows we'll get started on that. I know Lauren got rid of her laptop last night but I'd like to see what else is kicking round that house. There might be a tablet. Hopefully we can link her with the Romanian porn site.'

They were interrupted by Chris and Sara arriving.

'I told him he should take the day off,' Sara said, 'but he won't have it.'

Chris coughed and cleared his throat. 'I'd rather be here than writing thank-you notes for wedding presents.'

Sara threw him a look. 'We agreed we'd do half each.'

'Yes we did.'

'How's the snot?' Clare asked, suppressing a grin.

'Still black.'

'Yeuch.' Tony rose from his seat. 'That's my cue to leave. I'll be in my broom cupboard if anyone needs me.'

'It'll be a cold day in hell before anyone needs him,' Chris muttered.

'I heard that,' Tony called. He disappeared down the corridor. Clare waited until she heard his door shut then she fixed Chris with her eye.

'Sure you're okay?'

'Right as rain. So, what's first?'

Clare thought for a minute. There were so many loose ends to tie up. 'Let's start with Lauren. Hopefully we'll get the forensics back on her. Raymond knows the clock's ticking. Meantime, can you get onto the bridge authority please? Ask them to check footage from the cameras at the Fife end. They should have picked Lauren up. With luck they'll have captured her lobbing the laptop and phone off the side. Put out a shout for dashcam footage as well.'

'Time?'

Clare took out her phone and checked her calls. 'I tried calling you last night at five forty-five. So say from ten minutes before that.'

'The bridge cameras are okay,' Chris said, 'but I doubt they'll pick up what she threw.'

Clare nodded. 'I know. But we'll nibble away at it. Bit by bit we'll build our case.' She turned to Sara. 'Once the warrants are through I'll need you and a few others going over the Cravens' house. Any computers, tablets, phones – I want the whole lot down to Tech Support.'

Sara went off to organise this and Max appeared at the door.

'Zoe wants a dog,' he said, shaking his head. 'I suppose I've you to thank for that.'

Clare gave him an apologetic smile. 'She really helped me out, Max. I'll have to buy her some flowers.'

'She says she'll have Benjy anytime you like.'

Clare laughed. 'I'm going to check my Inbox and, if there's nothing new, I'd like you to carry on with checking the bank accounts for possible bribes.'

Max looked less than thrilled at this but he went off to make a start. Clare opened her Inbox and saw the warrants she'd requested were through. There was an email from Raymond too.

> Waiting for forensics on your potential fire-raiser but a positive match on the cushion. DNA from Johnny Meadows on both sides, consistent with him gripping the cushion.

'It's enough,' she said, getting to her feet.

Max was in the incident room, waiting for his laptop to warm up. 'I must have the slowest machine in the whole station,' he said.

'Forget that,' Clare told him. 'Bring Johnny Meadows in again.'

'DNA?'

'Yup. Warrant's through as well so take Sara and a couple of other uniforms. I want paperwork, laptops, phones – anything at all.'

She rose and made for her office but Robbie forestalled her. 'Boss. Might be nothing but…'

'Go on?'

'One of Hazel's neighbours from yesterday's come in to sign her statement. She's the one who saw the pink Beetle.'

'She's not retracted it?'

'No. She's sticking to what she said. But she's remembered something else.'

Clare sighed. 'I'd better see her.'

Patricia Egan was sitting to the side of the public enquiry area and rose when Robbie and Clare approached. She was in her late seventies, Clare thought, neatly dressed in grey trousers and a lilac top, and she reminded Clare of a neighbour she'd had when she'd lived in Glasgow. A nice woman, widowed and probably quite lonely. She was always bringing Clare a pot of home-made soup, or a lemon drizzle cake, and Clare always tried to make time to have a cup of tea with her. She smiled at Patricia and introduced herself but her smile wasn't returned.

'Let's find somewhere we can talk,' she said and she led Patricia and Robbie to an interview room. Patricia stood taking in her surroundings, twisting her hands together. Clare indicated one of the chairs and she eased herself down, perching on the edge, her eyes full of concern.

'I'm so sorry about this,' she said. 'It was the shock of Hazel's house. I just forgot.'

'Please,' Clare said, 'don't worry at all. Anything you can tell us will be so helpful.'

Patricia attempted a thin smile in return. 'Yesterday I told one of your officers I saw the pink car parked outside Hazel's house. A young woman – not much more than a girl, really – she got out, tried the doorbell then went round the back. At the time I thought she was maybe doing some work for Hazel. Gardening, or some such thing. Anyway, she was only there a few minutes and she appeared again, got into the car and drove away. I'd been deadheading some roses and I was finished so I went inside to make myself a coffee.' She broke off for a moment then her face cleared. 'That's right. I made a coffee and I took it into the front room to sit down and that's when I saw him.'

They waited and when she didn't go on Clare prompted her. 'Who did you see?'

Patricia gave herself a little shake. 'Sorry. The man. I noticed him you see because of how he was dressed. It was the shirt, really. Tattersall. You don't see many of them these days. But my late husband liked to wear them.' She allowed herself a little smile. 'I think he liked the idea of being a country gent, you see.'

'Tatter…' Clare broke off. 'What kind of shirt was it?'

'Tattersall. The kind you see in country living shops,' Patricia explained. 'This one was cream with a check pattern. More criss-cross, really.'

Something was stirring in Clare's memory. 'Can you remember anything else about him?'

'He'd a kind of country jacket,' Patricia went on. 'A khaki brown colour – olive, maybe.'

Clare nodded. 'Anything else?'

Patricia's brow creased for a moment. 'A tie I think,' she said. 'But I can't be sure. He was across the road, you see.'

'And what was it about this man that made you come in today?' Clare asked.

'Oh, he went round the back of Hazel's house as well,' Patricia said. 'I thought maybe he was an uncle or something. He was too old for a gardener, anyway.'

'Could you see what he was doing round the back of the house?'

She shook her head. 'Not once he went round, no. And I'm not sure how long he was there. I sat down with my coffee and my magazine and I didn't see him after that. So I don't know how long he stayed or even if he went in the house. But I did think it might be worth trying to find him because he could have seen something – about the fire, I mean. He might be able to help you.'

Clare excused herself, leaving Patricia with Robbie, returning a few minutes later with a selection of the CCTV photos from Retworth's shop. She passed the photos across the desk and asked Patricia if any of them looked familiar. She leafed through them, stopping at Johnny Meadows' photo. She was quiet for a moment then she raised her gaze to meet Clare's.

'I'm pretty sure that's him,' she said, and her brow furrowed. 'You have his photo.' She looked from Clare to Robbie. 'Is he… is he dangerous?'

Clare smiled. 'Nothing like that.'

She left Robbie to finish taking Patricia's statement and went to find Chris. He'd requested the CCTV footage from the bridge and was poring over bank statements for Cliff Craven.

'See if Max has left yet,' she said. 'I asked him to bring Johnny Meadows in again so he might be there already. Get over there yourself and take a pile of evidence bags. I want whatever he was wearing yesterday.'

'Ew,' he said. 'Dirty washing?'

'Hope so.'

'Wanna tell me?'

'I think we're wrong with Lauren Craven. I don't think she did set fire to Hazel's house.'

'Surely not Meadows?'

Clare's expression was grim. 'That's what I mean to find out.'

Chapter 47

Raymond confirmed the presence of petrol on the swabs taken from Lauren Craven. 'I guess that's your fire-raiser then.'

'I'm not so sure,' Clare said. 'If I'm right I'll have more for you to look at.'

He let out a groan. 'We're working overtime for you as it is. Please tell me you're nearly done with this case.'

'Hope so.' She pulled a notepad across her desk and was about to begin prepping for Johnny's second interview when Jim appeared at the door.

'Sorry,' he said, 'but I've a young lad out here in a dreadful state. I think you should see him.'

She sighed and rose to follow Jim. Marcus Craven stood in the front office, tapping a hand on his thigh. Then he saw Clare and rushed over. 'I need to tell you,' he said. 'About Lauren. It's not her.'

Clare put up a hand to stop him. 'Let's find somewhere private and we can chat properly.'

He opened his mouth to speak again but Clare forestalled him. 'Please, Marcus. Give me a minute to find one of my colleagues.' Chris and Max were on their way to arrest Johnny Meadows and she put her head round the incident room door. Janey looked up and Clare beckoned her over. 'Can you sit in on an interview please?'

'Course.' She clicked to lock her laptop and followed Clare to the front office.

They led Marcus to the interview room where Robbie had just finished taking Patricia's statement. Clare indicated a seat.

'Perhaps we should wait until we find you a solicitor,' she said, but he shook his head vehemently.

'No,' he said. 'No solicitor. It's very simple. I just need to tell you.'

'Okay, but if I judge you should have legal advice I will pause this.'

She proceeded to set up the recording then, unsure of what Marcus might say, delivered the standard caution. Marcus indicated he understood and Clare began.

'I gather you've come here to give us some information,' she said. 'Is that correct?'

'Yes. I need to tell you,' he repeated.

Clare smiled, hoping to put him at ease. 'Go on then, Marcus. What is it you want to say?'

He took a deep breath in and exhaled slowly as if trying to control his nerves. 'It was me,' he said after a moment. 'The phones, the porn – all of it. It was me.'

Clare studied him. 'Marcus, I really think you should have a solicitor.'

'I said I don't need one! There isn't time for that. You need to listen. You've got Lauren locked up and it's not right. It's not her you want. It's me.' He was becoming agitated and Clare decided to let him speak.

'Go on, then,' she said. 'Explain from the start, if you can.'

He rubbed a hand through his hair, suddenly at a loss, as though he hadn't thought beyond this point. And then he met Clare's eye. 'The phones,' he said. 'I'd jailbroken mine. Got a lot of cool stuff on it you can't normally get.'

'How did you learn to do that?'

'It's pretty easy. Tutorials on YouTube. Plus I do computing at school. That helps. Anyway, I told the lads in my class I'd done it and some of them asked if I'd do it on their phones.' He hesitated. 'Thing is, it takes a bit of time. So they left the phones with me for a couple of hours. And, well, sometimes I had a look round the phones. See what they had on them.' He shot Clare a glance.

'You know teenage lads. They send stuff to their girlfriends. Girls send stuff back. No clothes,' he added. 'And I knew Lauren had an account on this website. Perfectly legal. Pay per view. If you upload stuff – and anyone can do it – you get paid when people watch it. So I said to her I'd seen some stuff on the lads' phones and she said we could make some money from it.'

Clare studied him. 'You both received an allowance from your grandfather, yes?'

His eyes widened at this but he said nothing.

'Don't you?' Clare persisted.

'Suppose.'

'Isn't it enough?'

He shrugged. 'You can always use a bit more. Besides, it wasn't really about the money.'

Janey sat forward. 'So what was it? Why did you do it?'

He appeared to consider this. 'I suppose,' he said at length, 'because I could.'

Janey and Clare exchanged glances and for a moment neither of them spoke.

'You are aware,' Clare said, breaking the silence, 'that sharing intimate content without permission is illegal?'

He shrugged. 'We never thought of that.'

Clare nodded. 'Go on.'

'When I jailbroke the phones I had a look round them before handing them back. Some of them had photos and videos we could use so I installed some extra software. Let me access the phones remotely.'

'How did you learn to do that?' Janey asked.

He hesitated. 'Dark web. But that was all me. None of it was Lauren's doing. She just let me use her login. We split the money,' he added.

'How were you paid?' Clare asked.

His brow creased. 'I'm not exactly sure. Lauren, she has this bank account. Somewhere abroad.' He broke off for a moment. 'Armenia, maybe?'

Clare glanced at Janey. For a pair of youngsters they were frighteningly astute.

'How many videos did you upload to the site?'

'Not sure really. Maybe seven or eight.'

'And the photos?' Clare said, thinking of Josh McNeil.

He shook his head. 'No good for the Romanian site. They only want videos. So...' He broke off again and after a moment Clare prompted him.

'Did you use the photos to blackmail boys whose phones you had jailbroken?'

He nodded, his face scarlet. 'Yes.'

'Names please?'

His eyes were on the floor now, the implications of what he'd done dawning on him. He gave them five names, including Josh McNeil. 'Mostly they gave me money not to share the photos but Josh said he didn't have any. He'd just paid for a course of driving lessons so I said he'd have to get me something else.'

'Whose idea was the iPad?'

'Mine,' he said. 'I didn't actually think he'd do it. I was watching from a café across the road and I saw you guys lift him.' He shook his head again. 'Idiot.'

Clare was tempted to say Josh wasn't the only idiot but she didn't want to interrupt Marcus's confession. 'Was Lauren involved in this?' she said. 'The blackmail?'

'No. That was just me. And that's why you have to let her go. It's not fair. She's done nothing wrong.'

She watched him carefully. He was sitting back in his seat, as if spent. 'Is that everything?'

'Yes,' he said. 'That's it all.'

'And is there anything else you wish to say before I end this interview?'

He met Clare's eye and she saw his lip was quivering. 'Only that I'm sorry. Especially about Sophie.' And with that he began to cry.

'He's been charged under the Abusive Behaviour and Sexual Harm Act,' Clare told Tony. 'The dad's coming to collect him.'

Tony shook his head. 'Weird thing for a young lad to get into. Did he make much from it?'

Clare frowned. 'I'm not sure. To be honest I think it was more about control than money. I think he enjoyed messing with his schoolmates. I doubt money was his prime motive.'

'All the same, the court will take the scale of the operation into account for sentencing. What about that offshore bank account? Any chance of tracking it down?'

'Doubtful. Marcus thought it was in Armenia.'

'No chance, then,' Tony said. 'They're not signatories to the Common Reporting Standards.'

She stared at him. 'How did you know that?'

He tapped his head. 'Brains, Inspector. Anyway, what about the sister? You charging her with fire-raising?'

Clare shook her head. 'I think we may have someone else in the frame for that. But I do need to know why she smelled so strongly of petrol yesterday.'

'Okay,' he said. 'Keep me posted.'

She left him to what appeared to be the same pile of papers he'd apparently been working on for the past week and went in search of Chris and Max.

'Still at Meadows' house,' Jim said. 'Seems he's taken ill and they've called a doctor. They're staying with him while the others go through the house for evidence.'

She thanked Jim and stood thinking for a minute. They were still waiting on the CCTV from the bridge authority and clearly she couldn't interview Johnny Meadows until a doctor had pronounced him fit. She took out her phone and dialled Hazel Sullivan's number. She answered after a few rings, her voice raised slightly. Clare could hear noise in the background and she realised Hazel was out somewhere.

'I'm shopping,' she said. 'Can't get back into the house and I need a change of clothes. Thankfully the insurance will cover it.'

An impulse seized Clare. 'I'd like a chat,' she said. 'Just to keep you updated. I don't suppose you fancy a coffee?'

'I would *love* one,' Hazel said. 'Do you know The Coffee Stop in North Street?'

'Give me twenty minutes.'

–

The café was busy when Clare pushed opened the glass door. It dinged as she stepped inside and a young man looked up from cleaning a table.

'For one?' he said, but Clare had spotted Hazel who'd arrived before her and she indicated she was joining someone. Hazel looked up as she approached and gave Clare a smile. She was dressed in her work uniform, the pink polo shirt baggier than usual. She had dark circles underneath her eyes, but otherwise seemed well.

Clare sat down and the young man approached. 'Just a coffee,' she said. 'Americano.' She glanced at Hazel.

'I've already ordered. Treating myself to an early lunch. I'm due at work in an hour.' She indicated the polo shirt. 'One of the lads at work lent me this. It's enormous but the rest of my uniform's in the house. Or what's left of it.'

'Surely they won't expect you to go in,' Clare said.

'My choice. I'm staying with a friend, across town. But there's only so long you can sit in someone's kitchen flicking through magazines.' Her brow creased. 'Any idea when I'll get back into the house?'

'Not yet. I think they're bringing in an engineer to check the structure. Make sure it's safe.'

Hazel nodded. 'Makes sense. But all my stuff…'

'I know. It must be awful for you.' The coffees arrived and the young man promised to bring Hazel's sandwich in a minute.

Clare added milk to her coffee. 'We thought you were in there,' she said. 'Your car was at the door.'

'Ah. Sorry about that. I walk when I can,' she said. 'I did mean to drive yesterday but it was such a lovely day I changed my mind.'

'And you didn't take Cassie?'

A spasm of pain crossed Hazel's face. 'I could have lost her,' she said, her voice thick. 'It's too far for her to walk and I was only doing a couple of hours anyway so I left her.' She shook her head. 'When I think…'

'Best not to,' Clare said. 'The main thing is you're both safe. How is she?' she added.

Hazel's face cleared. 'Oh she's right as rain, thanks to the fire door. The vet kept her under observation for twenty-four hours but she seems none the worse for it.'

The sandwich arrived and Hazel picked it up and bit into it. She chewed for a minute then said, 'How did it happen? The fire, I mean?'

'It's still under investigation. But we do think it was started deliberately.'

Hazel stared then she put down her sandwich. 'Seriously?'

'Afraid so.'

'But who would do that? I don't understand.'

'I was hoping you might be able to tell me,' Clare said. 'Is there anyone you know who was upset with you? Anything at all?'

Hazel shook her head. 'No! I can't think of anyone.' She shivered. 'What a horrible thought.'

Clare gave her a smile. 'Don't dwell on it. But if anything does come to mind…'

But Hazel seemed not to be listening, as though she was processing what she'd been told. Then she looked intently at Clare. 'Have you arrested someone?'

Clare hesitated.

'You have, haven't you? Who is it? Surely I've a right to know?'

'We did detain someone last night but, since then, further evidence has come to light and we think this person may be innocent.'

294

Hazel's eyes narrowed. 'You're not going to tell me? They've gutted my house, damn near killed my dog and you're not going to tell me?'

'Honestly, Hazel, as soon as I have something definite, you'll be the first to know.'

Clare glanced round at the café. It was busy, the staff flying back and forward between tables. She saw Hazel had almost finished her sandwich and she came to a decision. 'Let me get this,' she said, taking out her purse. 'And then, do you fancy a stroll?'

Hazel looked surprised. 'I mean, if you like.'

Clare went up to the counter and paid the bill then she returned to the table and smiled. 'Ready?'

They strolled up to the end of North Street and crossed over to the gate that led into the grounds of the ruined cathedral. The sun was high in the sky, warming the ancient sandstone.

'There are some seats round the side,' Clare said, and she led Hazel to a line of south-facing benches, their backs against the nave wall. Clare chose the furthest away and they sat, Hazel setting down her shopping bag.

'Why do I have the feeling you've something to say?' she said.

'You're very perceptive. Normally I would be having this kind of conversation with you at your home but obviously that's impossible just now. So I hope you'll forgive me speaking to you here. But I think it's important you know what's happened.'

Worry settled on Hazel's face. 'You're scaring me,' she said. 'What is it?'

'Sorry,' Clare said. 'It's a bit delicate.' She took a breath in and out. 'As you know we took your DNA so we could compare it with any samples found in Cliff Craven's house. This was purely for elimination purposes so that, if we found DNA and knew it was yours, we could disregard it.'

'Yes,' Hazel said. 'I understand that. But I don't see—'

'We also took DNA from the body of Mr Cliff Craven.'

Hazel was silent and Clare thought she could see her working it out.

'I have to tell you there is a 50 per cent match between your DNA and the sample we took from Mr Craven.'

Hazel opened her mouth as if to say something then closed it again.

'A 50 per cent match indicates a first degree relative.'

'So,' Hazel said slowly, 'Cliff Craven…'

'…is your father,' Clare said. 'I can only assume when he assaulted your mother he made her pregnant. With you,' she added.

Hazel turned and stared straight ahead. For a few minutes she didn't speak. 'That man,' she said, at length. 'That horrible, odious man… is my father?'

'Yes. I'm sorry to be the one to break it to you but I thought you had the right to know.'

She was quiet for a moment. 'Do they know?' she said at last. 'The Cravens.'

'They know there was another match. I didn't give them your name but I think Rory Craven's worked it out.'

In spite of the sun Hazel shivered. 'I can't believe it.' She wrapped her arms round herself. 'I feel… oh, I don't know what I feel. I hate to think of his blood running in my veins.'

Clare put a hand on Hazel's arm. 'I'm no expert at these things,' she said, 'but your father – the man you knew as your father – I'm sure he loved and cared for you. Even though they divorced I'm sure both your parents loved you as much as any parents could.'

Hazel was quiet again for a few minutes then she shook her head. 'Even now he's dead, he's still damaging lives.'

She seemed lost in her thoughts but a question had been niggling away in the back of Clare's mind. 'Can I ask about the last time you spoke to Cliff, please?'

Hazel looked at her. 'Surely you don't still think it was me?'

'Oh no,' Clare said. 'It's not that. But I am interested in your last conversation with him. When was it?'

'Monday.'

'Last week?'

'Yes. It was my day off so I went round to see what else he could tell me. To be honest I could see he wasn't well. He told me as much. Said he'd have to remember all his stories before it was too late.'

Clare took a moment to form her next question. 'Did Mr Craven ever speak about planning applications?'

Hazel rolled her eyes. 'He never stopped talking about them. Obviously I was trying to get him to talk about the women who worked for him. But sometimes he'd drift off, boasting about the big developments he'd approved.' She shook her head. 'I could hardly tell him I wasn't interested, given I was pretending to write a book about the history of the council.'

'Did he ever mention receiving... inducements?'

A smile played at the corners of Hazel's mouth. 'Bribes, you mean? Funny you should say that.'

Clare sat forward. 'Oh yes?'

'In all the times I visited him he never mentioned anything like that. Not once. Until that last Monday.' Hazel's brow furrowed and she seemed to be thinking back.

Clare waited.

'I'd asked him about the work that had to be done before a decision was made. I hoped he'd say something about the women who serviced the planning committees. But he started to smile and said sometimes there wasn't as much work as usual. So I asked what he meant and he said he could tell me but it would have to be strictly off the record.'

'And you agreed?'

Hazel nodded. 'I'd no idea what he was going to say and I'd no intention of keeping my word anyway. Not to someone like him. But I said *of course,* that I wouldn't quote him if he explained what he'd meant.'

A young man with a camera slung round his neck wandered languidly past, stopping a little beyond Clare and Hazel. He removed the lens cap and raised the camera to his eyes, firing off a few shots. Hazel watched until he'd moved away then she went on.

'He told me some applications were approved with minimal investigations. So I asked why that would be and he was quiet for a moment. Then he said he was sure I could work it out. So I asked if people gave him money, or gifts, to approve their applications.' She turned to look at Clare. 'He was so blasé about it. *Money, free holidays, expensive wines. Hazel,* he said, *if they want it badly enough they'll pay handsomely.*'

'Did he mention any particular developments?'

Hazel shook her head. 'He might have but, of course, I wasn't writing it all down. Just enough to make it look like I was interested. I did ask if the other councillors had queried any of the applications. *No,* he said. He thought they were a lazy bunch, not given to scrutinising the plans. And besides, he had a councillor friend also on the take. Between the two of them they saw to it that certain applications were approved, and quickly.'

Clare thought back to Hazel's notes. The printout she'd given Clare was all about Cliff's abuse of her mother. She couldn't recall reading about planning applications. 'Did he mention the other councillor's name?'

'Only his first name. He said he'd better not drop him in it. I assured him it wouldn't go any further. Anyway, I wasn't interested in his backhanders.'

Clare's mouth was dry and she ran her tongue round her lips. This felt like an important moment. 'Can you remember that first name?'

Hazel smiled. 'Yes,' she said. 'As soon as I was out of the house I made a note on my phone. I'd no idea if it would prove useful but I thought I ought to.'

Clare waited a moment and when Hazel didn't go on she prompted her. 'The name?'

'Johnny.'

'You're sure?'

'Oh yes.' She fished the phone out of her pocket and tapped at the screen, holding it out for Clare to see. And there it was:

Johnny

Councillor who backed Cliff up on planning applications

Hazel tucked the phone back in her pocket and sat forward, reaching for her shopping bag. 'I have to get to work.'

Clare nodded. 'Hazel, you've been a great help. I'll want to take a proper statement from you but it can wait. You'll need time to process the DNA news but, maybe once you've had a chance, you should think about some counselling.' She smiled. 'It can help.'

Hazel inclined her head. 'Maybe.' She attempted a watery smile. 'Thanks for telling me. Can't have been easy.'

They sat on in silence for a few minutes then Clare said, 'I've been wondering.'

Hazel looked at her but said nothing.

'That introductory offer you mentioned – when I first came to your house.'

'What about it?'

Clare smiled. 'I thought I might book a few sessions.'

Hazel appraised her. 'You look pretty fit to me,' she said. 'But there's always room for improvement. Call the sports centre and ask for me. I'll make sure they squeeze you in.' Then she rose, adjusted her grip on the shopping bag and walked towards the gate.

Chapter 48

As Clare walked back towards the car her phone began to buzz. Max.

'Sorry,' he said, 'but Johnny Meadows is off to hospital. GP's orders. He says he won't take a chance with someone of his age.'

Clare frowned. 'What do you reckon?'

'Chris and I both think he's at it. Soon as we said we wanted to see the clothes he was wearing yesterday he said he wasn't feeling well. Clutched his chest, cracked on he was struggling to breathe, all that malarkey. He should be at the hospital pretty soon.'

'Ninewells?'

'No. Community hospital up the road. He may end up being transferred to Ninewells but they've agreed to give him a check-up.'

'Let's hope he's given a clean bill of health,' Clare said. 'And send a cop to keep an eye on him. After his railway station stunt the other day I don't trust him. Erm, what about his clothes?'

'You were right, there,' Max said. 'They were in the washing machine but not washed yet. And there was a definite whiff of petrol about them.'

'Bagged?'

'And on their way to Raymond who says, by the way, you owe him an enormous bottle of whisky for all the rush jobs he's done lately.'

'Hah. He'll be lucky. Anything else?'

'Desktop PC and his mobile phone,' Max said. 'Sara's on her way down to Tech Support with them now. Diane's out today but her assistant Craig's going to look them over.'

'Perfect,' she said. 'Thanks, Max.' She walked briskly back to the car. Then she took her phone out again and called Jim, asking for Lauren Craven to be brought to the station. Hopefully a night in the cells would have concentrated her mind. It was time to find out what she really was doing round the back of Hazel Sullivan's house.

—

Lauren arrived just before lunchtime. She looked tired and drawn, dark circles beneath her eyes. Although the outsized forensic suit had been swapped for a plain grey tracksuit, she seemed smaller still, as though her night in custody had somehow withered her. Clare thought she probably hadn't slept much and gave her an encouraging smile. If she was right about what had happened at Hazel Sullivan's house Lauren would sleep in her own bed tonight.

She eyed Clare but said nothing until they were in the interview room, the solicitor again at her side.

'Could I have a glass of water please?' she said, her voice small.

Clare smiled. 'Of course.' Janey, who was sitting in on the interview, went to fetch a plastic cup of water, returning as Clare was setting up the recording. Lauren took the cup and muttered her thanks. She drank half of it straight away then put it down, her eyes never leaving Clare's face.

'Am I going to be charged?' she said, eventually.

'We'll get to that.'

'I think Lauren has a right to know why she's being interviewed again,' the solicitor said, and Clare nodded.

'If you'll bear with me while we get started.' She reminded Lauren she was still under caution then she began. 'Lauren, I want to go over your movements yesterday afternoon. You told us you went to Hazel Sullivan's house to reason with her, to ask her to leave your family alone. Yes?'

'Yes.'

'But when I arrested you in the Tay Road Bridge car park I could smell petrol and I detained you overnight, pending further investigations.'

Lauren shrugged. 'Yeah.'

'I have to tell you our forensic investigations confirmed the presence of petrol on the swabs we took from you. And I do not believe your explanation for this is credible.' She glanced at the solicitor. 'It's my view we have sufficient evidence to charge Lauren with wilful fire-raising and possibly attempted murder.'

Lauren's eyes were brimming with tears and she reached for a tissue from a box on the desk.

'However,' Clare went on, 'I would like to give you the opportunity to tell us once again exactly what you were doing round the back of Hazel's house.' She looked intently at Lauren. 'I believe there may be more to this fire than we first thought but I need you to be entirely truthful with us.'

Lauren blew her nose but said nothing.

'To be frank,' Clare went on, 'you have nothing to lose. If you don't give us further information we'll go ahead and charge you anyway. But if there is something…'

The solicitor raised a finger. 'I'd like to confer with Lauren for five minutes, please.'

Outside the room Clare and Janey stood, one eye on the door for the solicitor indicating they were ready to continue.

'You really think she's innocent?' Janey said.

'Not entirely. She definitely had petrol on her hands and traces on her clothes. But I don't think she set fire to that house.'

They chatted on for almost ten minutes then Clare saw the solicitor indicate Lauren was ready to continue.

She restarted the recording and the solicitor cleared her throat.

'Lauren has been through a most distressing time,' she said. 'Since leaving school she's struggled to find her way but she was close to her grandad and losing him in such a dreadful manner has hit her particularly hard.'

Clare thought that might be stretching the truth somewhat but she acknowledged this and the solicitor continued.

'Lauren does have some information she wishes to impart but I am of the opinion her actions were both irrational and out of character, a direct response to the emotional trauma she has experienced.'

Clare turned to Lauren. 'What is it you want to say?'

Lauren cleared her throat. 'I'm really sorry,' she said. 'Sorry for what I did. I'm not proud of it and she didn't deserve it.'

'Maybe we should go back to when you parked your car outside Hazel Sullivan's house yesterday afternoon,' Clare said.

There was a pause then Lauren began to speak again. 'Like I said last night, I went to her house. I was angry and I wanted her to stop upsetting us. I was going to tell her that. I knocked on the door, rang the bell. The dog barked, but no one came. Then I thought maybe she was in the garden so I went round the back of the house. But she wasn't there either. I tried the back door handle in case it was unlocked.'

'Why did you do that?'

The colour rose in Lauren's cheeks. 'I don't know. I'm not sure. I think… I think I just wanted to see where she lived, what she was like. See if there was something I could use against her. Something to make her stay away from us.'

'Okay,' Clare said noting this down. 'Go on.'

'I looked round to see if she'd left a key anywhere. Under a plant pot, that sort of thing. I couldn't see one but she had a shed – bottom of the garden, you know? So I wandered down, thinking maybe she kept a key in there. The shed was unlocked and I went in for a snoop around. That's when I saw it.'

'Saw what?'

'The petrol can.'

Clare tried not to react. They were close now. 'Go on.'

Lauren's head drooped and she wiped at her eyes. 'I thought about setting fire to her house. I really did. And I don't know what came over me – I was just so angry with her. I took the can and went up to the back door. The cap on the can was really tight and the more I struggled with it the angrier I became – angry for all the trouble she'd caused. And then the cap came loose and the petrol sloshed out everywhere. All over her back step and up the back door.' She raised her eyes to meet Clare's. 'But it was like doing that – smelling the petrol – like I suddenly realised what I was doing. I was horrified at myself. I don't know what had come over me.' She shook her head. 'I didn't even have any matches. Nothing like that. Couldn't have set fire to it even if I'd wanted to. So I ran down the garden and put the can back in the shed. Then I got away from the house as fast as I could.'

'You didn't think to hose the petrol away?' Clare said. 'Make it safe?'

She shrugged. 'I thought it would dry up in the sun. Never thought it would catch fire.' She glanced at her solicitor, then back at Clare. 'Is that what happened? Was the sun so hot it set the door on fire?' She picked up the water and drank from it again. 'I never meant it to go on fire. Please believe me. I'd never have done it. I'm so sorry.'

Clare watched her carefully and, for the first time, she felt sure Lauren was speaking the truth. Maybe the fear of being charged with attempted murder had done the trick. She decided to press home her advantage. 'Can we go on to what happened after that please? You returned home, I think?'

'Yeah. I wasn't planning to go out again. I wanted to have a shower, get that smell off me. But I saw this phone Marcus had been using – on the bookcase. He'd been trying to download some video. Said it was taking ages. Must have been a big file. He'd forgotten it when we'd gone out. So I put it in my pocket. Didn't want that Paul guy getting his hands on it. Then I saw he was on the phone. Next thing he's asking me to make him a coffee so I knew something was up. He was prowling round like he was looking for something, or listening, maybe. Then I felt the phone buzz in my pocket and I knew.'

'What did you know?'

Lauren glanced at her solicitor who gave her an encouraging nod. 'I knew you'd found out about Marcus and those videos. So I had to get rid of the phone. And his laptop.'

'And that's why you went to the Tay Road Bridge?' Clare said.

'Yeah. I thought if I threw them in the river you'd never find them.' She shook her head. 'Stupid boy.'

—

'I've charged her with attempting to defeat the ends of justice,' Clare told Chris and Max. 'But I don't think she put a match to the petrol.'

'Pretty dangerous all the same,' Chris said.

'No argument there, but I reckon Johnny Meadows is the real culprit. I'm just not sure why. What did he have to gain from burning Hazel's house down?'

Chris shrugged. 'Beats me.'

'Any news on him?'

'Doc says four hours observation,' Max said. 'He's stable and if there's no change they'll let him home.'

'Fit for interview?'

Max nodded. 'Hopefully. But it might be an idea to do it at his house, rather than here.'

'Agreed,' Clare said. 'We don't want to be accused of putting pressure on him. We play it by the book. Better make sure he has a solicitor as well.'

'What about Marcus?' Chris wanted to know.

'He'll be charged with the sextortion,' Clare said. 'Abusive Behaviour and Sexual Harm Act.'

Chris shook his head. 'I can't help feeling sorry for Rory Craven. What a shit week he's had, having his dad murdered, then he finds out Cliff's not his real dad and now his two kids have criminal records.'

'Don't forget his money troubles,' Clare said.

'That's good point,' Max said. 'Will Rory still inherit Cliff's money? Or could it all go to Hazel?'

Clare sat back considering this. 'I'm no expert, guys. But I'd have thought Rory would still inherit. I'd guess Cliff's name is on his birth certificate and he's brought Rory up believing him to be his own son. But whether Hazel has a partial claim is another matter.'

'She might not want his money,' Max said.

Chris snorted. 'Money's money these days.'

'I'm not so sure,' Clare said. 'Hazel strikes me as a pretty principled woman. She's nothing but contempt for Cliff Craven. It wouldn't surprise me if she didn't want a penny of his money.'

Chapter 49

'Definitely petrol on Johnny Meadows' shirt and jacket,' Raymond said, later that afternoon. 'Traces on his shoes as well but that could easily be explained away if he walked around a petrol station.'

Clare thought back to Lauren's statement, that she'd sloshed petrol around Hazel's back door. Johnny Meadows could easily claim he'd stood in the petrol when he'd knocked on the back door, or peered through the glass to see if anyone was at home. But the shirt and jacket – surely that would be enough.

'If you want to spend the money,' Raymond was saying, 'we can tell you the brand of fuel but it will cost more.'

Clare was intrigued. 'You can do that?'

'Yeah. Simple case of identifying the additives in the fuel. They linger long after the petrol's evaporated. Different brands use different additives. Want us to do it?'

She considered this. 'You say the additives don't evaporate.'

'Not like the petrol. We have the samples here anyway so they can always be analysed later on, if you need that done.'

'Always keen to save a few quid.' She thanked Raymond, and went to find Tony.

'Positive match for petrol on Johnny Meadows' shirt and jacket.'

'You charging him?'

'Not at the moment. He took ill when the lads went round to arrest him.'

'Convenient.'

'Yep. He's under obs at the community hospital. Soon as they let him out we'll get round there.'

'Maybe get a police doc to say he's fit to be interviewed,' Tony suggested.

'Will do.' She turned to leave and almost bumped into Paul Henry, his hand raised as if about to knock. She forced a smile. 'The very person. Spare me a minute?'

He rolled his eyes and followed Clare to her office, his expression defiant. She nodded at a chair.

'Take a pew.'

He eyed her and pulled the chair across, sitting down heavily. 'So,' he said. 'What have I done now?'

'My God, you're prickly. Can you just drop the attitude for a minute so we can talk properly?'

He said nothing but she saw his shoulders relax a little.

'I wanted to say...' she broke off, casting around for the right words, '...I think you maybe have a point. I'm probably a bit set in my ways, Paul. Used to working with the same officers. Then you came along and – I have to be honest here – I found it difficult working with you.'

'You're not kidding,' he muttered.

'And maybe you were the same? Maybe you took an instant dislike to me too. I don't know. But, as you said, everyone has to start somewhere. So I'm putting it down to inexperience.'

'Big of you.'

Clare fought to keep her temper. 'You see, that's exactly what I'm talking about. Here I am trying to meet you halfway and you cannot lose the attitude.'

He had the grace to blush. 'Fair point,' he said. 'So what exactly are you saying?'

She sighed heavily. 'What I'm trying to say is that, yes, we got off to a bad start. Rubbed each other up the wrong way. But I'm willing to start again if you are.' She smiled. 'I'm not saying we'll ever be best mates but I'd like if we could work together without all this crap.'

He inclined his head. 'Makes sense.'

'Good. I've a pretty difficult conversation to have now. Fancy joining me?'

Cars were parked nose-to-tail on Kinnessburn Road when Clare drew up outside the Bakewells' house. She crawled along and saw a tiny space fifty yards ahead.

'Bit tight,' Paul said. 'Want me to have a go?'

Clare indicated to pull in and threw the car into reverse. 'If I mess it up, I buy you a pint. But if I get in it's your round.'

'You're on,' he said.

She turned, one arm round the back of his headrest, and began edging the car backward. Halfway she realised the angle was wrong and she pulled back out again.

'Eighty Shilling,' he said.

'In your dreams.' She checked her mirror and saw another car had appeared and was waiting for her to finish the manoeuvre. She felt her face grow warm then she heard her dad's voice back in the days when he was teaching her to reverse park. *Take your time,* he'd said. *Let them wait.* The angle was right this time and she engaged reverse and began to ease the car back. She saw the kerb in the nearside mirror and pulled the steering wheel down, lining the car up inches away. Then she brought the wheel back round and nosed forward until the car was dead straight.

'Peroni,' she said, taking the key out of the ignition.

'First round to you,' he said. 'So, this is the part where you remind me they've just lost their daughter, to be sympathetic, yadda yadda.'

'Nope,' she said, opening the door and climbing out. 'I trust you.' This wasn't entirely true but she was trying to build bridges here.

They walked through the garden gate which had been left open and Clare stepped forward to ring the doorbell. There was a noise that sounded like a gate scraping against concrete and she moved round the side of the house to see Brian Bakewell. His face was full of concern and Clare hastened to reassure him.

'We're just here to update you on our investigations.'

He nodded and indicated the gate. 'We're sitting in the sun. But we can go in if you like?'

'It's nice to be outside. Can we join you?'

He led them through the gate into a small but rather lovely garden to the rear of the house. Although it was semi-detached the neighbouring gardens were screened by a variety of flowering shrubs, trained along a fence. A border below the fence ran round three sides of the garden, the edges softened by summer flowers spilling over onto a neat lawn. Clare took it in and thought wistfully of the garden at Daisy Cottage. It was in dire need of some attention, despite the DCI's best efforts, and she made a mental note – again – to try and find a gardener.

Laura Bakewell was sitting on a charcoal-grey recliner, her face shaded by a large freestanding garden umbrella. She too looked concerned and she sat up, the recliner clicking into an upright position as she did so. She made to rise but Clare waved her back down.

'We won't stay long,' she said, accepting the chair Brian offered. She glanced at Paul then began to relate the sorry tale of Marcus and the mobile phones. Laura dabbed at her eyes, her emotions raw and evident, but Brian's face was a mask. Clare wondered if he'd shed a tear yet. He seemed so buttoned up.

'We should be able to return Sophie's things quite soon,' she went on. 'Her laptop and phone.'

Laura shook her head. 'She has so much stuff. I've not touched any of it. I can't bear to.'

Clare smiled. 'It's very early days.'

'We thought,' Brian said suddenly, 'we thought it might be nice if we did something. Maybe something so folk would remember her.'

'But we don't know what,' Laura said. She blew her nose and tucked the crumpled hankie in her pocket. Clare sensed Paul sit forward and she turned to throw him a warning glance. But he ignored this.

'Sophie climbed, didn't she?' he said.

The couple nodded. 'She was really talented,' Brian said, his voice wooden, his eyes somewhere across the garden.

'Would you think about some kind of competition?' Paul went on. 'A climbing thing, I mean. You could buy a cup, or a shield. Award it annually.'

Laura and Brian exchanged glances and Clare thought she saw the spark of something in Brian's eyes. A little chink of light in the darkness and she threw Paul an approving glance.

'That way, she'd be remembered every year,' he said.

Laura's eyes filled with tears. 'I'd like that,' she said. 'Brian?'

Clare watched him. He seemed to be struggling with his emotions. As though he couldn't afford to let his guard down for a single second. 'Yes,' he said eventually, his voice thick. 'Let's think about that.' He lifted his gaze and looked at Paul. 'Thanks, son.'

–

'Double or quits,' Paul Henry said as they climbed back into the car. 'You get it out of this space in two cuts and I'll buy you two pints.'

Clare regarded the car in front. It was a different one from when she'd backed into the space. And it was right up against her front bumper. But she felt she'd made some progress with Paul. It would be worth two pints to hang onto that. 'Challenge accepted.'

At that moment a man emerged from another house and jumped into the car behind. Clare watched in the rear-view mirror as he tugged on his seat belt, gunned the engine and pulled away.

'Think I'll just about manage this,' she said, reversing a few feet then drawing out of the space. 'That's two pints you owe me.' She glanced at him. 'Well done in there,' she said. 'That was a good idea.'

'Yeah. I know.'

'You spend far too much time with Tony McAvettie.'

Chapter 50

'He's home,' Chris said. 'Doc says we can interview him but he'd prefer it was done at his house.'

Clare nodded. 'Me too. He's a slippery sucker and I don't want to lose him at this stage. Solicitor?'

'On his way.'

–

The young man Clare remembered as Johnny's solicitor opened the door. He stood on the threshold, as if unwilling to admit them. 'Mr Meadows is not a well man,' he said, his voice low. 'I trust this interview will be neither long nor oppressive.'

Clare smiled. 'Just a few questions.' She indicated the hallway. 'Shall we?'

He stood back and they stepped into the hall. Clare was struck by how dark it was, all doors closed except one to the right which she presumed was where Johnny was holding court. There was a heavy silence about the house and even the solicitor's steps were soft and deliberate, reminding Clare more of an undertaker than a solicitor. Hopefully his client was still alive and kicking.

They entered the sitting room and Clare was immediately taken back to some play her ex-boyfriend Tom had dragged her to. Some miserable angst-ridden evening she'd napped through until he'd nudged her, whispering she was snoring.

The room was half in darkness, a pair of brocade curtains pulled across the window, the only light coming from the gap where they didn't quite meet.

Johnny Meadows lay back in an old leather armchair, his feet resting on a footstool. He was wearing a burgundy dressing gown with piping round the edges, open just enough to expose his turkey neck. A tartan rug was draped over his knees and his hands were crossed on top of this. He was feigning sleep, she was sure of that, and she cleared her throat loudly. His eyelids fluttered and eventually opened.

'Hello again,' she said, her voice raised so he couldn't claim not to hear. 'Detective Inspector Clare Mackay and Detective Sergeant Chris West.'

He eased himself up in his seat, the solicitor fussing about him. Clare looked round the room and saw a small two-seater cottage settee and she nodded at this. Chris took the cue and pulled it across so they could sit opposite Johnny. The solicitor drew a chair up close to his client and looked expectantly at them.

Clare informed Johnny she would be recording the interview then she cautioned him. He glanced at his solicitor who waved this away as if to say *nothing to worry about, here.*

'You recall you were seen in Strathkinness High Road the day we believe your friend Cliff Craven died, yes?'

He inclined his head. 'If you say so.'

'We did agree you visited Cliff that day.'

'As I said, my memory isn't what it is.'

'I'd like to ask if you and Cliff argued? Fell out at all?'

'No,' he said. 'As I recall our conversation was entirely cordial.'

'And yet there were bruises on your legs, consistent with an injury occurring around that time.'

'I believe it's not uncommon for elderly people to bruise easily,' the solicitor said.

Clare ignored this. 'So you didn't fall out with Cliff?'

'Far from it.'

'Then how do you account for your DNA being found on the cushion used to smother Mr Craven?'

He took a moment to answer. 'I was a regular visitor. Probably touched lots of cushions, door handles and so on. My DNA's most likely all over that house.'

She watched him carefully as she formed her next question. 'The pattern of DNA is consistent with someone gripping the cushion tightly by opposite edges, the kind of grip if you were holding it against someone's face.' She smiled. 'Can you explain that please?'

He shook his head. 'Only to repeat what I said. I was a frequent visitor and probably picked the cushion up multiple times. That calico material is a magnet for sweat. I was always telling Cliff to have it cleaned.'

'Which cushion was that?' Clare said.

He saw his mistake. 'Lots of them, I imagine,' he said trying to recover. 'Cliff had lots of cushions.'

'But only one with calico backing,' Clare said. She wasn't entirely sure this was true but the cushion used to smother Cliff had been different from the others in the room. The needlepoint, the calico backing, it had reminded her at the time of one her grandmother had stitched. A family heirloom that now sat in her mother's favourite chair.

'How odd you would think of that exact cushion,' she said.

'It was doubtless a favourite of Mr Craven's,' the solicitor said. 'Prominent position,' he added.

There was the hint of a smile on Johnny's face. He reckoned he'd won that round. She decided to change tack.

'Did Mr Craven tell you about his other visitor? The one who was writing a book about his time in the council?'

He blinked and put a hand to his chin. 'I think he mentioned it.'

'What did you think about that?'

'Not much, to be honest. Most of what we did was pretty routine. Can't imagine anyone wanting to buy a book about it.'

'Were you concerned she might reveal some information to show you in a negative light?' Clare said, her tone pleasant. There was a flicker of something in Johnny's eyes – brief, but it was there; and then he regained his composure.

'What are you implying?' the solicitor asked.

Clare met his gaze. 'I have officers going through the bank accounts of Mr Craven, Mr Meadows and a Mrs Monique Taylor, among others. We believe there may have been some… discrepancies in planning applications.' She turned back to Johnny. 'And if there were, we'll find them.'

He said nothing and she pressed on. 'Where were you yesterday afternoon?'

His eyes narrowed. 'Why are you asking?'

'Just answer the question please.'

'Well I'm not sure I recall. Maybe a bit of shopping. I might have gone for a walk. It was a nice day.'

'Did you walk along Irvine Crescent?'

His eyes widened in what Clare thought was mock surprise. 'I really don't know.'

She watched him for a moment. 'What were you wearing?'

'Really,' the solicitor said. 'Is this necessary?'

'It is,' Clare said. 'So I will ask again. What were you wearing yesterday? And please bear in mind we have a witness who has given us a description.'

Johnny coughed and reached to a small side table for a glass of water. Playing for time. He sipped then set it down, dabbing at his lips. 'What I usually wear. Shirt, trousers, jacket – that sort of thing.'

'And any clothing found in this house would belong to you?'

'I suppose.'

Chris sat forward. 'This morning my colleague DS Evans and I removed items of clothing from your washing machine. These have been tested and our forensic staff have detected petrol. How do you explain that?'

He smiled, a pleasant smile. But Clare thought she saw something in his eyes. *He hadn't expected them to find the clothes.*

'I have a car,' he went on. 'I put petrol in it.'

'Did you do so yesterday?'

'I'm sorry, Sergeant. I can't remember. Perhaps I wore these clothes when I last filled up.'

Chris glanced at Clare and she took over. 'Our witness saw a man fitting your description in Irvine Crescent yesterday afternoon. The witness was able to describe the man's clothing and that description matches with the items my colleagues found in your washing machine today. The clothing contaminated with petrol,' she added. 'We believe this man was you. We also believe you went round the back of a property belonging to Hazel Sullivan, that you realised petrol had been spilled on or around the back door of the property and you set a match to it, causing the house to catch fire.'

'Absolute rubbish,' Johnny said. 'I did no such thing. I didn't even know where this Hazel – whoever she is – lived.'

'What reason would Mr Meadows have for doing this?' the solicitor asked.

Clare took a moment before answering, watching Johnny carefully. 'Cliff Craven was interviewed on several occasions by Hazel Sullivan. He believed she was writing a book about his time at the council. We now know Mr Craven took bribes to approve certain planning applications and he named you, Mr Meadows, as a fellow councillor who also took bribes. As I said, we are currently investigating bank records from your time at the council and I'm confident we will prove you colluded in this malpractice. Mr Craven, as a terminally ill man with a short time left, would have nothing to fear by revealing this. But you, Mr Meadows, you stand to lose everything; and when we prove this – and we will prove it – you'll lose your reputation, your money, perhaps even your liberty.'

Johnny flashed a look at his solicitor who put a warning hand on his arm.

'Ironically,' Clare went on, 'Hazel Sullivan wasn't writing a book about the council.'

Johnny Meadows sat forward, his apparent heart problem forgotten. 'What?'

'No,' Clare smiled. 'Her real reason for interviewing Cliff was to gather names of employees – female employees – who had worked for him. I'm sure you know he was a sex pest, a man who raped and abused the women in his office. Hazel Sullivan's mother was one of his victims. *That* is why she was visiting Cliff. It had nothing to do with the bribes he took.'

Johnny's mouth fell open. He blinked a couple of times and seemed to be struggling for the right words.

'Say nothing,' the solicitor advised. 'Nothing at all.'

'So you see, Mr Meadows,' Clare said, 'it was all for nothing. You smothered Cliff Craven to stop him talking about your time at the council and you set fire to Hazel Sullivan's house to stop her writing about it. But there never was a book and you had nothing to fear. Your secrets would have been quite safe. But now...' She broke off, relishing his expression as the implications of his actions finally dawned on him.

The solicitor glanced at Johnny. 'If I might have a private conversation with Mr Meadows...'

–

Clare phone was buzzing and she nodded to Chris to follow her out to the garden.

'Spoke to Craig,' Max said as she answered the call.

'Oh yes?'

'Johnny Meadows' PC. His internet search history's very interesting. He searched for Hazel Sullivan's address on 192 so he definitely knew where she lived. Lots of searches for Banarvale Estate,' Max went on, 'for Cliff Craven, for himself and, best of all, mercy killing and suffocation. One of the web pages was an account of a woman who was charged with suffocating her husband. He was dying slowly of some horrible disease and she held a pillow over his face.'

Clare punched the air. 'We've got him!' She checked her watch. 'As soon as you've finished at your end get off home. It's been a long week and I think we all deserve an early finish.'

She saw Johnny's solicitor hovering at the front door and she nudged Chris. 'Come on. Let's see what he has to say.'

Chapter 51

Tony stretched back in his chair and yawned widely. 'So?'

Clare sank down opposite. 'We've got him,' she said. 'Soon as we revealed what Cliff had told Hazel, the solicitor asked to speak to him alone. When we resumed the interview Meadows was singing like a canary. Said the bribes were nothing to do with him. It was all Cliff's doing. He said Cliff told him he'd won some money in an illegal betting ring, that his bank would ask questions if he paid too much in at one time so Johnny looked after some of the money for Cliff.'

'I can't see a jury believing that,' Tony said.

'Me neither. Especially when we pull up his bank records.'

'What about the planning applications?'

'He claims he only ever approved those he thought were sound but he couldn't account for Cliff's motives.'

'And the stuff he nicked from Cliff's house?'

'Still saying they were gifts. I don't believe him but we'll have to let that go. He did admit to being at Hazel's house, though. Said Cliff had fed Hazel a pack of lies about the bribes. He even suggested Cliff's mind had been affected by the cancer. So he'd gone round there to tell her the truth – or his version of the truth. There was no answer at the door so he went round the back the back to see if Hazel was in the garden but she wasn't there.'

'And the fire?'

'Still denying it. Claims he was a bit agitated so he smoked a cigarette and tossed the dogend away. Didn't realise there was petrol around the back door.'

'Like hell.'

'Quite. He still denies suffocating Cliff but his internet search history should be enough to convince a jury.'

Tony pushed his chair back and got to his feet. 'If his brief's any use he'll tell him to plead diminished responsibility. Get a couple of doctors to say he's gaga and he'll get off.'

Clare's expression was grim. 'Not if I've anything to do with it.'

'I love it when you're angry,' Tony quipped. 'Anyhoo, I'm off to see a man about a dog.' He headed for the door and turned. 'Good work.' And with that he ambled out, leaving her office door to swing shut.

—

She was about to log off her computer when she heard gales of laughter coming from the incident room. Curiosity took her through and she found the whole room huddled over something on a desk. As she approached, Gillian turned and her face flushed.

'Oh shit,' Gillian said.

Clare pushed through the crowd and saw half a dozen photo prints on the desk. They looked like stills from a porn video with black banners across various body bits. At first she thought there was no more to it than that and then she saw.

Someone had photoshopped her and Chris's heads onto the bodies. The room was deathly silent, all eyes on her. Clare scanned the faces, the smirks and giggles gone. 'Okay,' she said. 'Who's the joker?'

'Honestly, boss, we've no idea,' Gillian said. 'They were here when we came in ten minutes ago.'

'What? On the desk?'

Gillian shook her head. 'Printer. I sent a document to print and went to get it. That's when I found them.'

'Who was here?' she said.

They exchanged glances. 'Think we were all out,' Robbie said.

She studied them then turned and marched out of the room. Jim was tapping away at his computer with his usual two fingers and he looked up as she approached. 'What can I do for you?'

'Was there anyone in the incident room this afternoon?' she said.

He thought for a moment. 'Don't think so. It's been pretty quiet. Mind you, that young lad did ask me which printer to select for the one through there.'

'Young lad?'

'The FLO, lad. Paul Henry.'

—

'It's completely inappropriate,' she told the DCI as she glugged her second glass of red. 'Honestly, I wish you'd stop laughing.'

'But he covered up the naughty bits, didn't he?' He began laughing again.

'That's not the point. It's so bloody sexist.'

'Well it would be if he hadn't given Chris equal billing. Anyway, look on the bright side. You've charged the Craven kids with the porn stuff and I'd say you've a good chance of convicting Meadows with the murder, and the fire-raising. It's not a bad day's work.' He reached for her glass. 'Come on. Let me top you up. Then you can show me your best porn moves!'

Nine Days Later

Chapter 52

'On behalf of my wife and myself...'

The room erupted with cheers and Sara, looking radiant in ivory silk, beamed at her new husband. Chris carried on, sheet of paper in hand, trying not to look at it. Max and Zoe were seated opposite Clare and she watched in amusement as Max mouthed every word of Chris's well-rehearsed speech, like a proud parent. And then it was over. Chris, perspiring visibly, was toasting the bridesmaids then he sat down, relief evident, and kissed his bride on the lips. It took a minute for the whistling and applause to die down then the best man got to his feet.

The speech began with the usual embarrassing anecdotes and Clare let her attention wander. Across the room she caught sight of Chris's cousin Alan and his wife Kim. They'd been victims of a particularly nasty crime the previous year and Kim especially had struggled with the aftermath. It was good to see them enjoying themselves. She hoped they'd managed to put it behind them. As if sensing Clare's eyes on her Kim turned and, after a moment, recognised her. She smiled and gave a small wave and Clare waved back.

'...and the final card's come all the way from Australia,' the best man was saying. 'So sorry we can't be with you...' he read on. Clare's attention was caught by the function room door opening. A waiter was approaching the top table with two cocktails in champagne coupes. She watched, intrigued, wondering if this was something the best man had arranged for Chris and Sara.

'Lastly, in a break with tradition, we have a message for Chris and – sorry Sara – not his lovely bride but another lady in the room.' He indicated the waiter now standing to the side of the top table. 'A friend of the groom's, Tony McAvettie, recently worked with Chris and his boss, Clare, on a difficult case.' He looked across the room. 'Clare's on table seven. Take a bow, Clare.'

Chris's face was like thunder, Clare's like a beacon. What the hell was going on?

'Tony wanted to thank his two officers for all their hard work so he's sent a couple of cocktails for Chris and Clare. I'm sure we're all aware of the dangers our police officers face every day so let's raise our glasses to Chris and Clare.'

The waiter had placed one of the drinks on the top table in front of Chris and was weaving his way through the tables to where Clare sat. She was hoping her fixed smile wasn't betraying her anger. How dare Tony hijack Chris and Sara's special day with this stunt. The glass was placed in front of Clare and she nodded her thanks to the waiter.

'To Chris and Clare,' the best man said. 'Enjoy your pornstar martinis.'

Acknowledgements

I had such fun researching and writing this book but, as usual, I was dependent on a host of friends and family who bore my questions with such patience! Sometimes it's small details that make a book more interesting and my brother Stuart never fails to oblige, this time pointing me towards the work of Glasgow artist, Jamie O'Dea. My son Euan and his partner Rebecca introduced me to the hugely talented climber, Shauna Coxsey who inspired the character of Sophie. Rebecca is also a mine of technical information and never bats an eyelid at my questions, no matter how daft; and, if you ever want to know anything about petrol and other accelerants, Tom and Jim Darbyshire are your go-to guys! Alan Rankin was on hand, as ever, with background information on Police Scotland while fellow author Angela Nurse filled in the blanks on banking and finance. I'm so grateful to you all for so willingly answering my questions. Any errors in these matters are entirely mine.

Team Canelo have, as ever, been incredible. To Thanhmai, Nicola, Kate, Alicia and my editors, Katy Loftus and Deborah Blake, the most enormous thanks for all your help; and to Miranda Ward for her eagle-eyed proofreading and Blacksheep for the stunning cover art, thank you for making this book something I can be so proud of. My agent Elizabeth is a constant source of support and advice and I'm very lucky to have her in my corner. Thank you so much, Elizabeth.

Finally, to all the booksellers, bloggers, reviewers and readers, and to the whole writing community, this book would be nothing without your unending support and friendship. Thank you all for making my dreams come true.

Do you love crime fiction and are always on the lookout for brilliant authors?

Canelo Crime is home to some of the most exciting novels around. Thousands of readers are already enjoying our compulsive stories. Are you ready to find your new favourite writer?

Find out more and sign up to our newsletter at canelocrime.com